Range War Legacy

Patricia Stinson

Published by BookLocker.com, Inc., Bradenton, Florida.

Printed in the United States of America on acid-free paper.

This book is creative fiction based on some historical facts. The characters and situations in this work are fictional; they do not portray and are not intended to portray any actual person.

BookLocker.com, Inc.
2015

First Edition

My sincere gratitude to Pam Knotz,
Marilyn Lueth, and Kat Mursak

Introduction

In April 2001, The Wild West Magazine published an article by David Braly. In the article, he wrote that a young girl, Lorene Lakin, and her parents had witnessed the killing of sheep, the herder and his dogs while on a picnic west of the Maury Mountains. The family knew the identities of the killers but did not tell who they were. Lorene Lakin was 85 when she was interviewed for the Prineville Central Oregonian. She still kept the secret and did not name any murderers. I wondered why. Range War Legacy is fiction based on my wonderings. The names of some of my characters are from that article. Creed Conn was shot twice in the heart, and it was declared a suicide. Shorty Davis disappeared. I fictionalized the accounts of their deaths.

I wrote about President McKinley being assassinated by Leon Czolgosz. This act brought Theodore Roosevelt into the President's Office. Would President McKinley have tried to stop the cattle and sheep war? I don't know. Many Republicans did not want Roosevelt as President, despite the fact he was a Republican, and now he was in the highest office in the land. He did want to stop the killings even though he had two cattle ranches and was not a sheep rancher. I fictionalized his involvement in the ending of the war, but it is based loosely on fact.

In President Roosevelt's administration, Gifford Pinchot helped to get the land from the Department of the Interior, to the Department of Agriculture, so there could be more control of the land from the logging industry. A.S. Ireland was a forest supervisor, and it was his job to settle the grazing dispute. I have used the names of these people of history, but the account is fictionalized.

As you read this book I hope you wonder if you would do what Molly did, what Aaron did, and what Tim and Ruth did in raising their sons.

Now, let's begin the adventure.

Chapter One
Oregon 1905

Grasping his whiskey bottle, the scruffy man yanked on the reins and slid off his horse. He stumbled to a poplar by the trail and leaned his back against the trunk. He then slid down to the ground and pulled the cork from the bottle, taking a swig. Hearing hoof beats, he turned to see a rider approach. He grinned and waved the man over to the tree. "How come you're out this way?" he asked.

"I heard what you said in the bar in town, Creed, and I wanted to hear more."

"I didn't see you."

"You had a pack of men hanging on every word you said about the gunnysackers. I was in the back."

"Yep, I had everyone's attention. And why not? I spoke the truth."

The man dismounted from his large bay and crouched next to Creed. "Yeah, but you've been known to stretch a good yarn. You said you knew who the gunnysackers are, so prove it and tell me their names."

"Oh, I do, all right, but I ain't telling. They're good fellas, and I ain't going to get them into any trouble. No siree. My secret."

"How did you find out who they are, if you aren't one of them?"

"I was in the barn over in Hay Creek, working in a back stall, when ten or eleven men came in and talked about where they were going that night and where they would meet up. They didn't know I was there, and I kept real quiet. Didn't take no chances I might spook them, if you catch my meaning." Creed laughed and shoved his bottle toward his companion. "Have a drink."

The man took the bottle and sipped the booze before handing it back. "I didn't take much, as money is tight, and a whole bottle is dear."

"Don't worry. There's more where this came from." Creed guzzled several gulps.

"Really?"

"Yep. Those gunnysackers are good guys. I think they'll do the right thing by me and help me out when I need money. I just have to get one guy off by himself and let him know I ain't telling anyone what I saw. He'll pass the word around, and they'll all be grateful to Creed." He smiled. His throat uttered a guttural "yeah," he waved the bottle toward his friend. "Here, drink as much as you want."

"Looks like enough for one good drink. I think you should be the one to finish this."

"All right, if you insist." Creed raised the bottle to his lips and gulped down the last swallow. Smiling and sliding sideways farther to the ground, he sputtered, "I think I'm drunk. Yes, siree, I'm drunk."

"I think so, too. Better let me take your gun from your holster, so you don't lie on it."

Creed pulled himself upright against the tree. "You're a good guy, like the gunnysackers. A good guy." Creed closed his eyes and exhaled a foul breath. His head slumped forward.

"I'm a good guy, all right." He pulled Creed's gun from the holster, pointed it at Creed's heart, and squeezed the trigger twice. The roar disappeared into the air as quickly as it had shattered it.

The man took Creed's hands and laid them in his lap. He positioned the gun between them and pointed it toward Creed's chest.

"You're a good guy, too, and I know you'll be keeping your secret." He mounted his horse and headed off down the dirt trail.

Chapter Two
Buffalo, New York

"Mr. President, we are honored you accepted our invitation to attend the Pan-American Exposition."

"Thank you for the opportunity to greet the citizens in Buffalo, New York," said President McKinley as he shook hands with each man in the small welcoming committee. "Shall we begin?"

"Yes, sir. Come this way." The men led the President to the Temple of Music auditorium. "If you will stand here, sir, you can shake hands with the people as they go through the door into the hall. We estimate fifty thousand people have been lining up for the past two hours to meet you."

President McKinley smiled and shook hands as men in suits and ladies in elegant afternoon dresses swirled by. Seeing a young, handsome, dark-haired man with his right hand in a bandage and using his left hand to shake, the President leaned forward with a smile.

Two shots erupted from the bandaged hand. The President staggered backward. The closest men helped him to a chair. He lifted his eyes and saw the crowd become a mob. They grabbed the shooter and began pummeling him. The guards joined the fray. Cursing and swearing added to the din and the confusion.

President McKinley whispered, "Be careful how you tell my wife. She's so frail."

The assassin yelled, "I killed President McKinley because it was my duty. I killed him because he was an enemy of the good people, the working people. I'm proud to be an anarchist!"

* * *

"Sir, sir, please stop. Wait!" Wheezing and huffing to catch his breath, the messenger struggled to speak.

A man with a cleft chin, drooping mustache, and thickset body turned from the rocky climb up Mount Tahawus, in the Adirondack Mountains. His muscles in his jaw clenched as he pinched the bridge of his nose, removed his pince-nez glasses and stared with his good eye at the intruder. "Well, what is it? I'm hoping to get to the top within the hour. That's a challenge I've set for myself."

"Mr. Vice-President Roosevelt," the messenger took a deep breath and exhaled. "I have the grave duty of informing you President McKinley is dying. You are needed in Buffalo, sir." He bent over and placed his hands on his knees, gasping for air.

"I was told the President was recovering from his wounds." Teddy stared at the panting messenger.

"Yes sir, but he has taken a turn for the worse. The doctors are certain he will not live long. A special train is at the depot to take you straight to Buffalo."

"It's a ten-mile walk to the nearest road and then a forty-mile buggy ride. The roads are treacherous after last week's rain. We're in for a wild ride tonight, but we will arrive at the train station by dawn. You have my word on it." Vice- President Roosevelt led the charge down the rugged terrain.

The messenger's eyes widened in surprise and disbelief. Teddy Roosevelt rushed past him at a run, with rocks and pebbles spinning down the path as his feet dislodged them. Taking deep breaths, the messenger stumbled down the steep mountainside, grasping at bush and tree branches as he lurched forward.

Chapter Three

Pigtails flying, the young girl charged through the screen door; it screeched and banged against the wood siding. Before it slammed back into its doorframe, her booted right foot hit the porch floor, and her left boot hit the dirt beyond.

"Molly, don't bang the door! Slow down!" shouted a woman's voice from the kitchen.

"Okay, Ma." The girl raced across the yard to the corral where a man was dismounting his horse.

"Uncle Tim! Uncle Tim!" Molly leapt into her uncle's arms, and he swung her around. "Why'd you come today? I thought you were coming on Saturday to help Pa with the well pump."

"Well, miss, aren't you glad to see me today?" Uncle Tim put Molly down.

"Of course I am, but Aunt Ruth and the boys were to come with you on Saturday."

"They're still coming. I'll help your pa with the pump, and your aunt Ruth is fixing to bring her good biscuits. Your ma will make us her delicious Sunday chicken dinner."

"Yeah, chicken dinner." Molly stared at the ground as she dug her boot heel into the dirt.

"Don't you like your ma's chicken?"

"I love it, but she has to kill the hen. I laugh when I see the chicken running around without its head, but at the same time, I hate it. The bloody neck is wobbling back and forth as its legs keep running until it flops dead in the dirt. It looks funny, and it's not."

"Killing chickens is part of ranch life, child. When the hen no longer lays eggs, it feeds us. I bet you don't like to pluck the feathers. Tell the truth."

Molly saw Uncle Tim's mischievous smile belie his stern face. "No, I like to pluck feathers. Ma douses the dead chickens up and down in hot water, and the feathers come off real easy, except for those darn pinfeathers."

"Molly, your pa and ma don't like the word darn."

"I'm sorry, but those tiny feathers don't want to be plucked."

Uncle Tim laughed. "Pluck them good, Molly. I don't want to bite into your ma's chicken dinner and come up with a mouthful of feathers."

"That would be funny, Uncle Tim," said Molly as they both laughed.

"Maybe for you, but not for me." Uncle Tim handed the reins to Molly. "Water Jumper for me. I'm going to talk to your pa."

"Sure, Uncle Tim." Molly took the reins and guided Jumper to the water trough near the barn. Her fingers tapped against his neck in slow rhythm with their walk. She held her face by his muzzle, and they exchanged breaths. Molly's joyful exuberance, which usually came bursting out, had stilled.

Jumper slurped the water as Molly watched her uncle walk to the ranch house. Pa came out on the porch, but Ma stayed in the kitchen, peering out the screen. Uncle Tim stopped before he got to the porch.

"Hi, Tim. How are Ruth and the boys?" said Ma from indoors.

"Jumper, what's wrong with them?" whispered Molly as she stroked Jumper's neck. "Pa always goes right up to Uncle Tim and stands shoulder-to-shoulder, and Ma, she didn't open the screen door and come out on the porch. She usually comes out to greet folks, especially family." Molly recalled the family stories of Pa and Uncle Tim growing up. They were eleven months apart in age, but they were one in spirit. Each knew the other's thoughts and plans. When one didn't think up an impish trick, the other did. Whatever they planned, they did together. They shared the blame, or they shared the praise.

Molly thought grown-up talk was boring, but today she strained to hear her uncle and father.

Uncle Tim adjusted his Stetson to shield his eyes from the sun. "Fine, thank you, Anna. I thought I'd stop by to see what you decided, Paul."

"I can't do what you want, Tim. I understand your thinking, but your way isn't for me. I won't oppose you none, but don't count me in."

"I won't fault you for your decision, but the others and I feel we have to do something. We can't ignore the situation any longer."

"I agree we can't ignore it, but I can't go along with you on your solution." Paul gazed past the corral at the horizon. He shook his head. "I think it'll make things worse. No good can come from it, I figure."

"Okay, Paul. I won't bring it up again." Tim lowered his head and stared at the ground. Then he straightened up and glanced at his brother. "Long as I'm here, do you want to show me the well pump we're going to fix on Saturday?"

"Sure." Relief sounded in Paul Langster's voice as he put his newspaper down on the porch rocker and walked with his brother to the tool shed.

Molly watched them, noting the space between them. In Molly's ten-year memory, this was the first time her father and uncle were not going to do something together. Molly licked her lips and shivered.

She pressed her nose against Jumper's neck and inhaled his scent. She glanced down at his legs. "Why, Jumper, whatever have you gotten yourself into? Uncle Tim wouldn't like this. He takes good care of you. How did you get dirt on your white stocking?" Molly bent and took a bandana from her pocket as she rubbed Jumper's one white stocking. The black, gooey smudge wouldn't budge. She tied Jumper's reins to the pump handle and fetched a bottle of horse liniment from the barn. She washed off the black smear. "We won't say a word to Uncle Tim. as he works hard to keep you handsome."

"What weren't you going to say to me?"

Molly stood as her uncle approached her. "A secret between Jumper and me." She smiled. "Say, Uncle Tim, do you remember Cassie? Her folks are Jennifer and Hayden Miller. They're friends of Ma and Pa's."

"Yes, I know them. They lived near Prineville before they married and moved across the Cascades. We were all friends."

"Cassie came for a visit last year. She'll be here again for a whole month. She's coming up with her pa's flock when they summer graze. She should arrive this week." Molly saw a hard glint flash in her uncle's eyes and stumbled on. "Some nights, we'll sleep out with the flock. We'll count the stars, tell stories, and have barrels of fun."

Her uncle grabbed her by both shoulders. "You listen to me, Molly. You aren't to sleep out in the pasture. Not once all summer, you hear? You and Cassie sleep right here in your house. Promise me!"

Molly heard the harsh tone in his voice as she peered into her uncle's eyes. Fear stared back at her. She swallowed hard and stepped back. His hands continued to grasp her shoulders.

"But it's safe, Uncle Tim. The sheepherder Voyager, and his sheepdog, Rolf, will be with us. They're good protectors. They won't let the wolves or bears harm us. We did it last year, and we were fine."

"It's not the wolves or bears. Molly, give me your word you won't sleep out in the pasture this year. Not once. Promise!" Tim Langster roughly shook her before he let her go.

"I promise, Uncle Tim." *Why is he angry with me? What did I do wrong?*

She watched Uncle Tim mount Jumper and turn down the road to his ranch. She noted his straight back and the easy way he sat in the saddle, then kicked a stone with her boot. She ran to the corral and called, "Judy!" A pinto trotted up to the fence and stretched out her muzzle. "I wish you could talk and tell me what is going on with my family. We hardly visit back and forth like we used to. We seldom go to town. The mountains, the pastures, and the ranch are the same as they used to be, but the people are different." Molly climbed on the top rail and stroked Judy's neck. "Pa and Uncle Tim have changed. It makes me feel shaky inside. Please, Judy, don't you ever change."

Chapter Four

Three days later, Molly saw her father ride up to the corral and tie off. She threw down the dishtowel and ran out the screen door. It slammed against the house and back into the frame.

"Molly! Don't bang the door."

"Okay, Ma!"

Paul Langster smiled. "Hey, Silly Bug, why don't you saddle up Judy and Buster and ride up to the low meadow? You might meet someone there."

"You mean it? Cassie's here! She's come! Oh, Pa!" Molly spun around, her arms flying in every direction.

"Yep. I talked with her and Voyager. They arrived in the pasture this morning. I could've brought her back down with me, but I thought you might like to ride to the meadow and bring her home. But don't linger. I want you both in the house before nightfall. You hear me?"

"I hear, Pa. I promise. I'll go straight up and back!" Molly yelled as she ran to the barn to saddle the two horses.

Twenty minutes later, Molly, leading Buster, urged Judy to a trot across the pasture to the foothills. She followed a winding path, leading higher and higher into the mountains surrounding her home.

An hour and a half after leaving the ranch, she entered a meadow carpeted with fresh, green spring grass. She reined in on the crest of a hill, savoring for a moment the lush mountains, the green pines against the blue sky and the sheep dotting the pasture. As she took a deep breath, the mountain scent filled her with a sense of security and vitality. Two dogs roved the flock's outer edge. Molly spotted a man and a girl setting up a camp area. She put Judy into a trot toward the camp, but as she neared the flock, she slowed to a walk, as she didn't want to startle the sheep.

"Molly! Molly's come!" A girl Molly's age dropped the blanket she was arranging on the ground and ran toward Molly.

Molly dismounted and also ran to meet her. "Cassie, I've been waiting and waiting for you to come. It feels like forever since last summer."

The two girls jumped up and down between hugs.

"Me, too. I could hardly wait. It feels like it's been ages since we left our ranch to bring the sheep to pasture. Voyager is here, and our sheepdogs, Rolf and his son Jake. We're training Jake to be a great sheepdog like Rolf, and he's learning real fast." Cassie's words tumbled over each other like a gushing waterfall.

A weathered sheepherder extended his arms. "Ah, my friend, Molly. She has come to see us."

"Voyager!" Molly jumped into his arms and kissed him on his whiskered cheek. She smiled when she saw his blue-gray eyes sparkle with laughter as he lifted her above his head.

He removed his corncob pipe from his lips and gave her a kiss on her cheek before he put her down. "Aye, our dear friend Miss Molly, to be sure. Come and join us at our camp. You must meet Jake. This is his baptism of herding sheep on the trail. He's doing a first-rate job, that one. One day he'll be a champion, like his father." Voyager adjusted his crumpled hat on his gray hair. He picked up a staff from the ground and twirled it over his head. The stick sang as it swung through the mountain air.

Two dogs saw the signal and approached at a fast trot.

"Oh, Rolf is more than a champion." Cassie blurted. "I think he's a legend, from the way people talk back home. He knows before we do when a storm's coming. He seems to count the sheep, as he always knows when one has wandered away and needs rescuing. He can track that sheep down quick as a wink, and if that stupid animal got himself into trouble, Rolf comes and fetches you and leads you right to him. Ain't I right, Voyager?" Cassie chattered as she gathered up her bedroll.

"Aye, I'd say you are right, if I was the braggin' kind. I'll leave the braggin' to others, though." Voyager smiled with the pipe stem clenched in his teeth.

Cassie lowered her eyes. Molly knew she was embarrassed. She jumped in quickly, saying, "I want to watch Jake work, but I can't today. Pa says Cassie and I have to be back at the ranch by dark. We've got to leave right away."

"Aye, Miss Molly, you do. Your pa is right. You two get up on them ponies and be on your way. Come back early in the day to meet Jake and to visit with old Voyager. I'll be lookin' forward to it."

"And you can meet the lamb my pa gave me for my own. Her name is Lammie Star," said Cassie as she tied up her bedroll and looked over at Buster. "Do I get to ride Buster like last year?" Her excitement carried in her voice.

"Yep, he's yours for a whole month," replied Molly.

Cassie patted Buster and kissed his muzzle. "I've missed you, Buster. You're a good fellow. I'm going to curry you for hours. See if I don't."

Cassie flung her bedroll behind the saddle, and Voyager tied it tight. As he cupped his hands, she put her left foot in his palms, and he lifted her into the saddle. After helping Molly onto Judy, he took the pipe from his teeth. "You girls go straight home. No dilly-dallying. And you look after Cassie, Miss Molly. Her mama and papa charged me with her care, and I'm giving it over to you and your family. You watch out for her."

Molly saw the serious, sad expression in Voyager's eyes. It made her insides feel both somber and important. She sat taller, saying, "Sure I will, Voyager. I promise."

The girls turned the horses away from camp and started out across the meadow.

* * *

On their ride across the grassland, they stopped briefly to listen to a jay call and to admire the radiant lupines, Indian paintbrush, and the vivid lavender flowers on the shrubby penstemon bush.

"I think our ranch in the Oregon mountains is the most gorgeous place in the world. I don't want to live anyplace else," said Molly.

"Me, neither. Let's make a pact. When we grow up and get married, we'll live in the mountains on ranches close to each other. Our children can become friends as we are, and maybe marry each other, if one of us has a boy and one has a girl." Cassie held out her hand.

"That's a deal." Molly shook Cassie's hand, and they giggled.

The horses stepped forward; then Molly reined Buster back. Cassie halted. "What's up?"

"My ma said when I'm twelve I have to wear a dress, long stockings, and shoes every day, unless I'm helping to clean the barn. Can you imagine? Every day. Not just on Sunday."

"My ma says the same thing. She says boys don't like to spark tomboys, so I have to act and dress like a young lady. If I was going to school in town, I would have to wear dresses now. I'm glad I'm learning school at home," said Cassie.

"Same with me. Imagine, boys not wanting to marry us because we wear jeans. We're the same people, whether we wear jeans or a dress. I don't see the difference."

"Me, neither."

They chatted, giggled and sang, and before they were aware of the time, they were dismounting at the corral and leading the horses into the barn. The sun's edge simmered on the horizon, and the evening shadows filled the yard. The girls unsaddled, cooled the horses, and wiped them down. After putting the horses in the stalls, the two grabbed Cassie's bedroll and headed for the house. They tiptoed onto the porch and stood by the screen door. Trying to hold in their laughter, they listened to the voices inside.

"Paul, the girls should be here by now. You shouldn't have sent Molly to get Cassie. I'm worried."

"You're right, Anna. I'm going to saddle Snooker and go out to find them. I'm likely to meet them on their way home. I'll hurry them along."

"No need to. We're home!" The girls burst out laughing and shouting as they ran into the kitchen. The screen door thumped behind them.

Startled, Paul and Anna jumped up; each grabbed a girl and gave her a hug and then switched girls for hugs.

"You scamps. You two snuck up on us. No more pranks. My, how you've grown, Cassie."

"As much as Molly. See, we're still the same height."

"Yes, you are. That must mean my Molly has grown right here under my nose. Well, you all wash up, because the stew and biscuits are ready, and there's pudding for dessert."

"Dessert, Mama, on a weeknight? We only have dessert on Sundays."

"Tonight is special. We have our second daughter home, don't we?"

"We sure do, for a whole month," Paul said.

Molly beamed. Cassie made the family complete.

* * *

After supper, the girls went up to Molly's attic bedroom. Paul had set up a cot in her room for Cassie, although he knew the two girls would share Molly's bed. Molly had cleaned out a dresser drawer and space in her closet for Cassie's belongings.

Cassie had plenty of room for the few items she'd brought to wear.

She knew she would wear Molly's clothes during her visit, except for the dress shoes in her bedroll and her Sunday dress.

"Ma says when I go back home, I'm to leave my clothes that fit you for you to wear. We won't remember which clothes are whose by month's end anyway, because we'll trade back and forth. Except my boots and shoes. They didn't fit you last year. Ma supposed they wouldn't this year, either."

"I reckon not." Molly tugged her boots off and held her stocking feet next to Cassie's. She sighed. Having short, fat feet made her feel homely. Cassie's feet were long and slender. But that was okay, she decided. Cassie was perfect in every other way, so it stood to reason her feet would be perfect, too.

Molly watched Cassie as she unpacked her bedroll. Nothing broke, fell, or tore when she handled her toiletries. It was the opposite for Molly. She sighed again.

Ma said she was impulsive and didn't take her time. Her favorite expression, besides "Don't bang the screen door," was, "Think before you act." Ma's favorite story was about when Molly was five years old and always falling down or bumping into things. Ma would say to her, "Molly, you don't look where you're going. Slow down, and look in the direction your feet are moving. Watch your feet." Molly remembered how happy she was finally to have the secret to walking without crashing. She watched her feet. She watched them every place she went. Once, while walking in the pasture, from the corner of her eye, she saw her ma as she headed toward the barn. Molly turned her head and said, "Look, Ma, I'm watching my feet, and I'm not falling down." Right as she said it, she walked into a corral post. She fell backward and landed in horse manure. Her ma loved to tell the story, but Molly didn't think it was all that funny.

Cassie knelt on the bed and pointed out the window. "What's that light? It isn't a star."

Molly knelt beside her and looked. "Pa said the light is a lamp Mr. Auldrich puts in his upstairs window. His house is on the big hill next to the church at the end of town. He hopes his missing brother-in-law, Shorty Davis, will find his way home."

The two girls sat on the bed.

"Missing?"

"Yes, he's a cattle rancher, and one day he rode away from the ranch and hasn't been seen since. Some folks say he just took off to live someplace else as he'd said he wanted to travel. But he didn't tell anyone, not even his wife, and he didn't take anything with him. Other folks say he snuck out when it was pitch-dark at night and spread saltpeter on the grass in the meadow to poison sheep. Cows can eat it and not get sick. The sheep ranchers got mad and made sure he wouldn't come back."

"Sounds like a scary ghost story told around a campfire at night." Cassie laughed. "I don't believe anyone hurt him. They would be afraid of getting caught and put in jail. I think he will be found someday. He might have had a heart attack. It happens."

A cool light breeze wafted in through the window. The girls snuggled under the blankets. Together they gazed at the stars.

"My pa and ma nearly didn't let me come."

Molly sucked in her breath, asking, "Why not?"

"They wouldn't say other than they didn't know if it was so safe this year. They thought I should wait until next spring. They said you could come and visit us."

"I liked visiting with your family last winter, but Pa was afraid this year that the passes may close up with snow, and I'd be there until spring. Last year was a mild winter. Ma and Pa took a chance and let me stay for two weeks. They think this winter we'll have tons of snow." Molly felt constricted, so she kicked loose the blankets around her feet. "And in the summer, we can go out with the sheep and the dogs. We can't do much outside in the winter.

"I wish Pa hadn't sold his flock last year. I miss the sheep. But he said we are going to do more cattle and horse ranching. I think it's better you come here. We can have a whole month together and not worry about being snowed in, and we can go out to the pastures." Molly traced with her fingers the Big Dipper on the glass. "Yep, I think you should come here each year. That's the best way."

"Well, Ma and Pa are worried about something, but they won't tell me what. My folks say I should tell them when I'm worried, but they won't tell me when they are worried. Aren't adults funny?"

"My folks are the same way. I guess it's part of being grown up."

"Well, I'm not going to be that way. I'm going to tell my kids everything."

"Me, too." Molly yawned as she snuggled against Cassie.

The girls, deep in sleep, did not see the moon light up the room as it slid across the night sky, nor did they hear a wolf keen in the distance.

Chapter Five

"Hey, Voyager!"

"Hullo, my dear hearts. 'Bout time you came up to the pastureland to see old Voyager and Lammie Star. She missed you, Cassie. She thinks you're her mama. I see you found us okay." The old man turned from watching the sheep and went toward the one pack mule and two riders entering his camp.

"Yes, we didn't have any trouble. Ma and Pa sent up supplies. They said they thought it was best for you to stay with the sheep and not go into town."

"Wise folks you have, Molly. And my sweet Cassie, how are you enjoying your visit?"

"Great. Last night, Ma shared with us her secret recipe for popcorn balls, and she let us help make them. We brought you one. They're the best. I promised I'd never tell anyone the secret to the syrup."

"Thank you, girls, for remembering old Voyager."

They began unloading the pack mule.

"Voyager, why did my folks say you shouldn't go into town?"

"You saw the pasture where you met Cassie a week back?"

"Yes."

"When the flock left the pasture, the land was still suitable for grazing. But other flocks came after me, I bet."

"Yes, there were signs that thousands of sheep have pastured there," Cassie said.

"Each flock tears up the grass a bit more. The sheep will eat right down to the roots, and their sharp hooves tear out the rest. It takes the grass a long time to come back. And sometimes, it doesn't come back. The loss of good pasture in these parts is due to overgrazing. Cattle and horses don't crop the grass down to the roots, and their hooves don't tear it up. It grows back faster. The cattle ranchers want the sheep ranchers to stay on their own land and not use the government range. Their cattle need the grass. Cattlemen get real upset with sheep grazing in the pastures."

"But Voyager, my pa says he doesn't have enough pasture land for his sheep on the range in Willamette Valley. He has to send part of his flock to graze here, or the sheep will starve, and we'll lose the ranch."

"Aye, that's the truth, Cassie, for him and for many other folks in the same predicament. Trouble has been brewing for years, and each year it gets worse as more sheep come in from the other valleys." Voyager scanned the flock; the sheep grazed in bunches, and the dogs patrolled the far side. "The more us outside herders stay out of town, the better it will be. No need to remind folks we're here."

They tethered the animals, and Cassie strode into the flock. She led a lamb with a bright blue ribbon around its neck over to the campsite. "Isn't she adorable? Her name is Lammie Star." Cassie hugged the lamb as she and Molly petted the short curly wool. Its eyes were wide, and it bleated as the girls stroked it.

Molly glanced sideways at Voyager. "Voyager, can I ask another question?"

"You can, my miss."

"It's a personal question, and my pa says it's not polite to ask folks about personal things."

"True, but I'm not folks. Questions don't bother me a hoot."

"I was wondering about your name. Is Voyager your last name or first name?"

Molly saw his eyes twinkle.

"Nay, young one. I'll tell you over cold coffee, providing you want a cup."

The girls laughed as they sat cross-legged on the ground by the cold campsite.

"No, thanks," they answered in unison.

Voyager sat on the ground and poured himself a cup. "My Christian name is Ian Voy. When I was a wee lad, my ma and pa were tenant farmers and sheep tenders in Ireland. Ma was Scottish, and Pa was Irish. Their farm skirted the edge of a big lake. I liked to get in a boat and pretend I was taking sea voyages with pirates. My folks would say, 'He's a voyager, for sure.' And the name stuck." He grinned when the girls giggled. "Oh, I was a fanciful boy. Full of daydreams."

Voyager stirred the fire pit's cold embers with a stick. "My pa got tossed off the farm by the owner. He gave it to a fella who said he'd pay more rent."

"Gosh, that wasn't fair," Cassie said.

"Didn't your pa fight and get justice?" Molly asked.

"Most of life isn't fair, and there's a heap of injustice in this world. Ma and Pa left the farm and roamed around after that, getting along as best they could. I got the notion in me to travel, so off I went to a sheep farm in England. I think I was around thirteen. Later, I went to Australia. I've been traveling now for near forty years and more." Voyager winked at Cassie. "Leastways, until I began working for your folks. Been with them fifteen years. Reckon my wandering days are over."

"Don't you miss your ma and pa?"

"Oh, I sure do. I got back to see them a few times before they passed on to their reward."

"What does that mean?" Cassie asked.

"Means heaven, leastways for me. I know I'll see them again in the Lord's pasture."

"Oh, they were God-fearing folk, like Pastor Weatherby says."

"There I have to disagree with your man of the cloth, but meaning no disrespect." Voyager gazed into his cup as he swirled the coffee. "My folks never feared the Lord. Nope, not a mite. They loved Him and served Him as best they could in their own way, but fear? No, not with fear. No more than the lads there fear me." Voyager pointed to the dogs lying near the sheep. "And my dear ones," he added, nodding toward the flock, "know they have nothing to fear from me or my staff."

Rolf stood and sniffed the air, then trotted around the flock. Jake joined his sire, and they sniffed the ground and stopped to lift their heads and cock their ears. Rolf loped, with Jake following, into the rocky hillock.

Voyager stood and kept his gaze in the direction the dogs had gone. Rolf came back, stood on a rock outcropping, and stared at Voyager. Voyager whirled his staff and pointed it in Rolf's direction. The dog turned and went back among the rocks.

"I've got me a darlin' in trouble. You girls want to come?"

"Sure, but what about the other sheep?"

"They'll graze here. I have to leave the ninety-nine to go after the one, as in the Lord's good book."

Voyager put his staff in his other hand and picked up his rifle. They all followed on Rolf's trail. When Voyager called Rolf's name, the dog barked, and the three followed the sound. They soon came to a rocky area with shallow ruts and ravines. In a depression lay a fat ewe on its back, pawing the air and bleating.

"Aye, just as I thought, 'tis Mattie. She gets herself cast every few days. She doesn't understand she can't lie down and roll into a spot where she'll end up on her back and not be able to touch her feet to the ground." Voyager walked down the rocky depression, grabbed the ewe's feet and rolled her onto her side. He talked softly as he helped her get her feet under her. She bleated till she drowned out Voyager's words. Rolf came down into the rut and began herding Mattie back to the flock. Jake joined in. "The lads will get her back where she belongs."

Jake and Rolf trotted around the whole flock, sniffing the air and ground.

Voyager saw the dogs lie down in their stations. "The lads say, 'It is well.'"

"Time to start for home. We've a long way to go, and we have to keep our promise to Ma and Pa to be home before dark. We've got to be ready for church tomorrow. Where will you go next?"

"I figure by the end of next week I'll take the flock to the pasture between the two mountains, over there." Voyager pointed to jagged rock mountains covered in ponderosa pine eight miles farther north.

"The high field," said Molly.

"If Pa and Ma say it's okay, we'll come to see you," said Cassie. "Take care of Lammie Star for me."

Voyager watched the girls mount and ride away. Their chatter drifted on the mountain air. He picked up Lammie Star. She bleated and pawed the air. "Those two girls are like you, my pretty, young and innocent. I fear there will be tough times ahead. And I fear for my other darlin's." Voyager gazed at the flock, repeating, "Tough times ahead."

Chapter Six

"I like Sundays. Don't you, Cassie?" Molly swung her feet over the wagon back as Pa guided the horses to the field behind the church.

"Especially this Sunday. Warm weather means we don't need to cover up our dresses with a coat. What's the sense of wearing a special dress if you have to keep it covered?" Cassie said as the two girls jumped down from the wagon and walked with the adults to the church steps.

Molly saw her cousin Ned playing with the other children and her cousin Charlie standing near his girlfriend, Mandy.

"You girls go play with the other kids. Your ma and I want to visit with the neighbors. When you see the pastor come, you hightail it in and sit with us," said Pa.

Molly and Cassie ran over to Cally Olson, Sue and Ellen Mae Parker, Jimmy Donners, Delvin Pryon, and Ned Langster, who were playing tag. Molly, glancing back, saw Aunt Ruth and Ma barely greet each other, and Uncle Tim and Pa stood on opposite sides of the gathering.

Cousin Charlie and Mandy Dawes headed to the back of Mr. Auldrich's house and the porch swing he kept there for folks to sit on before and after church.

"Charlie and Ned, come here and join the men," said Uncle Tim. Disappointment crossed Charlie and Mandy's faces.

"Mandy, why don't you join the women? We're planning the box social." Aunt Ruth approached Mandy and drew her into the women's circle. "Tell me how you will decorate your basket. I can tell Charlie, and he will know which one to bid on."

Mandy beamed as she joined the ladies.

Charlie is way older, but Ned is the same age as me. Why should he go over to the men and listen to their talk instead of playing? Molly's stomach felt queasy. She picked up a stick and dragged it behind her as she stepped closer to the men. When she got near enough to hear them talking, she squatted down and drew pictures in the dirt. She didn't notice her dress hem getting dirty.

"I tell you, weather like this is a sign. A sign we are heading for a hot, dry spell. A drought! With the overgrazing from last year and what's happening this year, plus a drought to boot, it will be the end of the grassland!" A cattle rancher, Nutter, waved his fist in the air. "We'll never recover. We've got to do something quick."

"A few warmer-than-usual days does not mean we'll have a drought. Besides, we can't control the weather. If God sends a drought, He sends a drought," said Paul Langster.

"We can't control the weather, but we can control the overgrazing. That's why I say what happened last night to the Nebekers' flock was good riddance. The herder didn't get hurt, and he can go back and tell the others to stay on their range. If they send their sheep over here, it's at their own risk," a cattle rancher said.

"Those sheep getting slaughtered is good news, I say," Nutter's voice chimed in.

"I don't think we can call it good news, but it's certainly serious. We need to find a solution that doesn't mean killing sheep," added Paul Langster.

"Well, no one has found a way in years of talking. All folks have done is talk and talk. Time folks acted. Past due, I say. Things go on as they've been, ain't none of us will be ranching in five years, as there won't be enough grass to sustain a worthwhile cattle herd."

Molly observed Uncle Tim and many of the other men nod in agreement with the rancher.

"I wish we knew who the sheep-killers were. Make my mind rest easier," Nutter said.

"I heard the sheriff rode out to the range and investigated. He's a good man, served us well for ten years, but he can't pull any miracles out of his hat. The herder can't recognize anyone. He dove under his wagon when the shooting began. The horses' hoof prints couldn't be identified, and the bullets he dug out of the dead sheep were forty-fours. Every man in the county owns a forty-four. He ain't going to find out who did it," another voice spoke up from the crowd.

"That sheep man better not identify someone. If he does, that will be the end of him. I hope the sheriff don't find out who they are. They're trying to protect our interests, aren't they? Those outsiders bring in flocks of 1000 to 2000 head. They drive them right through the main street of town and right up to my doorstep at my ranch. Some sheepers burn the grass when they leave. They leave nothing for us cattlemen. No, sir, those sheep-shooters are fighting for us." More heads nodded in agreement with the speaker.

Paul Langster stared at his brother. "Are they fighting for us, or killing for us?" Molly looked up at her father when she heard the anger in his voice. Tears welled up in her eyes.

"Whatever they're doing, they're doing right, and it's for *all* of us," Nutter said.

"You're right," several voices joined in.

"Watch it. Pastor Weatherby is coming."

The men broke up and greeted the pastor as he tethered his horse and entered the church. His congregation followed him. Molly dropped her stick and joined her parents as they sat in a pew. She slid over for Cassie to get in.

Cassie squinted at her; her eyes fell on the tearstain on Molly's face and the dirty hem. She handed Molly her handkerchief and motioned with her hand to wipe her cheek. She smiled encouragement at Molly.

The congregation sang two hymns before the pastor stood behind the pulpit.

"Before I begin my sermon, let us take a few moments and remember the devastating earthquake in San Francisco. Let's bow our heads in silent prayer for the victims."

Men shuffled their feet. Mothers hushed the children and folded their hands. The call of a killdeer, the katydids humming, and a fly buzzing broke the silence.

The pastor began, "I'm using several texts for my sermon today. John 10:11: 'I am the good Shepherd.' John 10:27: 'My sheep hear my voice, and I know them, and they follow me.' 'Love the Lord your God with all your heart and with all your soul and with all your strength and with all your mind, and love your neighbor as yourself,' Luke 10:27, and 'Love ye one another as I have loved you,' John 13:34. Today, our congregation needs to think on these words of our Master. In the past few years, violent acts against sheepherders and sheep ranchers by cattlemen, and against cattle ranchers and cowhands by sheep men, have been increasing. As you've heard, Silas Nebekers' flock was run off a cliff last night. That's not the Lord's work. He's against violen—"

"Hey, you hold on, Pastor." A rancher in the back stood. Everyone turned to stare at him. "Your job is to preach the sermon. It ain't to stick your nose in our business. The outside sheep men come from Willamette Valley, west of here, and from Wallowa County, northeast of here. They pay no local taxes. They don't put any money into the area. Do you think the Lord wants us to lose our ranches because these outsiders come in with their flocks and overgraze until the land is barren? He didn't make this land to be stripped. He spoke of sheep and being a shepherd 'cause that was all they had. I bet back in those Bible days, they didn't have cattle ranches. If they had, I reckon He would have talked about being a cattleman. We got families. Our lives are rooted in this place."

Several cattle ranchers clapped. The sheep ranchers cast angry glances at the speaker.

"These sheep-shooters are taking back what is ours. I don't know who they are, and I ain't one now, because they ain't asked me to join them, but I would in a heartbeat. I say you'd better keep your nose where it belongs if you know what's good for you."

Many people nodded their heads in agreement.

Molly's eyes widened, and her mouth dropped open. *People should not be arguing in church and certainly not with the pastor. Pa and Ma said this was a place of worship and peace.*

Her head jerked to the side to watch her mother when she spoke.

"Nutter, let the Pastor finish. He might have an answer," said Anna Langster.

"I don't have an answer, Anna. I wish I did. But I know what's happening is not the answer. This violence is wrong and has to stop." As he said this, the pastor shook his head and pounded the pulpit.

Molly gasped in surprise when the pastor banged his fist. She wiggled in the pew. She looked at the bench across the aisle just when Uncle Tim stood.

"Pastor, you don't understand. I don't mean disrespect to you or the cloth you wear, but some of us are second- or third-generation ranchers. It's all we know. We run sheep and cattle and horses, but most of us, like my brother Paul and me, sold off the sheep. We could see they were destroying the land, especially once the outsiders brought in their sheep. And it's worse every year. Our cattle and horses need the pastureland, or this place is going to be a ghost town, and the ranches will be history." Tim scanned the congregants. He eyes stopped when they got to Paul and Anna. "We've got to find a way to defend ourselves. Outsiders are attacking us. We've got to save our homes." Tim sat down. Ruth and their two sons, Charlie and Ned, nodded. Many in the congregation applauded.

Molly noticed her ma and pa's folded hands. She glanced up at their faces and saw the tears in their eyes. Cassie was staring down at the floor, biting her lip. Her face was red.

"As you know," the pastor walked from behind the pulpit to the altar front, "the Antelope Wool Growers Association has offered a reward for information leading to the arrest of any sheep-shooters. This may make things more dangerous."

"You're right, Pastor." Another rancher stood. "Those sheep-shooters aren't going to leave any witnesses around so they can claim a reward. The herders and camp-tenders need to stay out of the way, or it'll be dangerous for them." The man laughed. "Yeah, that reward is going to increase the danger a whole bunch more, to my way of thinking." The rancher then sat down.

Jake Allerton, sheep and cattle rancher, stood to speak. "You folks all know me. I think Oregon can be the best sheep and cattle producer in the world. It will be good business for everyone. I think our sheriff Tom Durkson is doing all he can to find out who is doing the killings." He turned to look at the sheriff. "We all know you are doing what you can, Tom, so I ain't faulting you, but I think we should get Governor Chamberlain involved. He could send in the militia."

Angry voices yelled, "No! No!" "Over my dead body!" "The government can't tell us what to do."

The sheriff stood, and the shouts quieted to murmurs. "Folks," Tom Durkson began, and faced Jake Allerton, "and especially you, Jake—thank you for the words of support. I'm doing my best with the information I have. No one can identify the men as they wear gunnysacks over their heads or blacken their faces and tie on bandanas. The horse tracks are not identifiable. Believe me, when I get a good lead, I'll follow up on it. And, if the evidence warrants, the judge here...." Tom looked to where Judge Wimple sat with his wife and son Henry, "...will send the culprits to jail."

The congregation focused on the judge. He nodded soberly; his wife and son smiled. "Now, as to getting our governor involved, I don't think that will work. If he did send the militia in, the Sheep-Shooters Association would just lay low until the governor recalled forces. Then we would be right back where we are now." Tom Durkson ran his fingers through his black hair and the white streak from his forehead to the back of his head. "I honestly don't think Governor Chamberlain will want to risk losing the cattle ranchers' votes in the next election, and the cattle ranchers outnumber the sheep men by a long shot." Tom Durkson sat next to Judge Wimple.

Judge Wimple stood and adjusted his string tie. His black suit hung on his string-bean body frame. He cleared his throat, said, "I agree with Sheriff Durkson," and sat down again quickly.

Nutter shouted from the back pew, "That's right, Tom and Judge. We are all aware of what just happened recently to Idaho's governor, Frank Steunenberg. He got himself blown up by a bomb because he called in troops for a miner's strike in 1899, just six years back. Folks got a long memory about any governor calling in the militia."

"Nutter, we ain't certain that was the reason. The hearing hasn't been held yet," Tom Durkson said.

"Don't need a trial. Everybody knows it." Nutter's face spoke his thoughts plainly: *If you don't know it, you're an idiot.*

The Pastor regarded his congregation. He surveyed the sheep ranchers, the cattle ranchers, and those who had both. He shook his head, and then stepped back behind his pulpit. "I ask all of you to go home and think about what I said today. If anyone wishes to stay after the service and meet with me to search for an answer, please do. May the peace of God go with each of you. Amen."

People didn't wait to talk outside the church. As the pastor finished the benediction, voices erupted. Everyone left, except Paul and Anna Langster and the girls.

"Pastor, do you have any ideas on what we can do?"

"No, Paul, I don't. This problem isn't just local. Sheep-shooters are showing up in several counties. My other congregations are having the same problem, and no one has come up with an answer."

"Why don't we write to Teddy Roosevelt? My dad says he's a smart man and a good President."

"Cassie," said Paul, "he lives in Washington, D.C., clear on the other side of the country. He can't help us."

"Perhaps he can. When you read the copy of the speech he gave to Congress about passing the Pure Food and Meat Inspection Act, you thought that was a good thing. It was part of his Square Deal program," said Anna.

"Presidents are supposed to help, aren't they?" Molly asked.

"Yes, Molly. You and Cassie are right," Pastor Weatherby said. "Mr. Roosevelt did push through Congress the Blue Mountain and Elk Creek Reserves here in Oregon a short time ago. Congress wanted to leave the land for the loggers, but Teddy stopped them. Perhaps he can do something for us. I think you girls have the right idea. Let's each write to him and ask for his help. I can ask my other congregants to write, too."

"Okay, Reverend, we can give it a try." Paul shook the pastor's hand and they walked down the steps of the church. "How is your baby doing?"

"Much better now, since she's gotten over the colic. My oldest is eleven, and he's a big help to his ma and the other four kids when I'm away."

"Good to hear, Pastor. Give your missus our regards," said Paul, and the reverend walked to his horse.

Cassie skipped ahead as the group continued to the wagon. Molly hung back and held her parents' hands. She sensed her ma and pa felt alone and sad.

Chapter Seven

"Tim, come to bed. Pacing back and forth won't help. You're doing what you can."

"But am I doing what is right, Ruth? I'd feel better if Paul would join with us."

"You've explained the situation to your brother many times. You invited him to join the Sheep-Shooters' Association. There's nothing more you can do."

"Yes, I know. And I see no other way out for me than becoming a member of the Sheep-Shooters. I wish Paul could see it that way."

"You know him better than any of us. It's true you two have always done everything together, but on this matter he can't muster up the courage to join. You're the strong one."

"Paul's strong in his own way. I'll not fault him for his decision, but I wish he felt different. He doesn't believe Creed Connelly's death was a suicide. No one does. The inquest was a farce. Everyone knows it was a gunnysacker." Tim continued pacing.

Ruth rolled over in bed to face her husband. "What they know and what can be proved are two different issues. I'm glad Charlie is joining the association with you."

"Yes. He needs to take on a man's responsibilities, and I'll keep a close eye on him. I've made it clear to him that we're only after the sheep. No one will get hurt." Tim walked in his stocking feet and long underwear. His firm, sure voice hid his feelings of doubt. "After the sheep ranchers from Willamette Valley get the message they're not wanted here, they'll quit driving their flocks to our cattle range." Tim ran his fingers through his thick, black hair. "I can't understand why a few local ranchers, like Ben Allen and Newt Williamson, are increasing their flocks. Can you believe Jack Edwards is importing Rambouillet sheep from France and cross-breeding them with his sheep to make a new breed? The Baldwin, he wants to call it. The range will be ruined beyond repair. It won't take many years to lose everything my ma and pa fought hard to build. They worked fifty years to make this ranch for us." Tim paced across the bedroom floor. "I can't let everything they fought for, we've fought for, go because of sheep. I've got to fight back. Why can't Paul agree with me?"

"He can't take a stand like you have. He did what he could last year, when he sold his sheep and switched to cattle and horses. He isn't as strong as you are. Come to bed and sleep, honey. Things always seem worse at night."

"Before I sleep, I am going to pray that God will open Paul's eyes and get him to join with me and the others in fighting the sheep-owners. When he does, I'll feel better. I can't believe God wants the sheep to kill the range. It can't be His plan. The only way to stop the sheep from grazing is to kill them. I believe God is on the Sheep-Shooters' side."

Tim walked down the stairs to the kitchen. He needed a cup of coffee to go with the prayer. Ruth turned over and drifted into sleep.

* * *

"Paul, please come to bed. You're going to wear a hole right through the floor with your pacing. There's nothing more you can do."

"That's the problem, Anna. I feel like I should do something, but I don't know what. Ranchers are expanding their flocks, and more ranchers from other counties are bringing their flocks in. The area can't survive it. Already, massive grassland areas are ruined. Nothing can graze on the pastures. The land is washing away. At the present rate, everything could be gone in five to ten years. We will lose the ranch. Could Tim be right? Do we have to fight back by killing the sheep?"

"You and I both realize the violence may not stop with the sheep. People could wind up killed. Which can't be right, no matter what the reason. The sheep men only want to make a living, the same as us. They're not out to destroy us. We can't try to kill them. There must be a way both groups can work together."

"I agree. But Tim believes differently, and we've always thought alike before. Why can't we join together this time?"

"Perhaps it's because he inherited the larger share of your parents' property, and as the oldest he helped you establish your ranch. Your brother has been a leader in the community ever since your parents passed on. He feels he has a responsibility to the people here. He has always rushed in and taken charge. You're more laid-back. You can't go against your nature. You help folks, but in a quieter way." Anna pushed back the covers and patted Paul's side of the bed. "Come to bed, dear. We wrote letters to President Roosevelt, even the girls wrote. Pastor said he would write his today, and he would talk to others about joining in."

"I hope you're right. But does President Roosevelt care about us out here? Oregon is a long way from Washington D.C. He's a cattleman with two ranches in North Dakota. Would he want to stop the Sheep-Shooters' Association? He might be on their side." Paul sighed. "I'll come to bed after I pray. God must have the answer to this."

Paul sat on the edge of the bed and gazed out the window. Moonlight silhouetted the pine trees on the hillcrest. Chilled air filtered in around the panes. He shivered. "I'm going downstairs to write a letter."

"Another one to Roosevelt?"

"No. This one is going to the *Portland Oregonian* editor. I've got an idea."

"Don't sign it."

"Oh, it will be signed. But I won't use my name."

Chapter Eight

"Hey, listen up! The Sheep-Shooters' Association meeting is called to order. Everyone shut up. I've got something important to say." Tom Durkson slammed the Portland Oregonian newspaper into his hand. He lifted it for all to see and waved it about. "I want to know which of you idiots wrote this letter to the paper."

Calvin stood from his perch on a hay bale. "I don't know who wrote it, but the letter sure was good. It said what I would say if I could write that well." He sat down, nodding his head and smiling at his fellow gunnysackers.

Sheriff Durkson glared at Calvin. "I know you didn't write it, Calvin. The grammar is good. Has everyone read the letter?"

Several men shook their heads.

"Listen." Tom read loudly. "'I'm the corresponding secretary of the Sheep-Shooters' Association, and I want to inform the press and all elected officials to stay out of our business. We have our own governing power in Crook County, namely us, and we want the governor and this newspaper not to meddle in the range question between cattlemen and sheep ranchers. The Association killed between 8,000 and 10,000 sheep this year, and we intend to kill a lot more in the coming year if the wooly-tenders dare use the land we cattlemen have the rights to for grazing. Signed, Corresponding Secretary, Crook County Sheep-Shooters' Association.'"

Many heads nodded in approval, and some men said, "That's right," "That's telling 'em."

Durkson said, "This letter sounds like we're bragging."

"That's right. We should brag. We're proud of what we are doing, aren't we?" Charlie Langster spoke up.

Tim whispered to his son, "Charlie, be quiet and sit down." Tim tugged on Charlie's sleeve, and the boy sat.

"This will incite people against us, even some cattlemen." Tom Durkston eyed Tim Langster, who stared right back at him.

"Let's hope it doesn't rile up the governor, so he thinks he has to take action. No more letters. Spread the news to anyone not here today. No more letters!" Tom slammed the paper onto the barn floor and kicked it into an empty stall.

"The governor had better not get involved."

"He knows where his votes are. He wouldn't dare."

The shooters continued the conversation as they exited the barn.

Chapter Nine

The orchestra's rendition of "Zenobia" floated over the guests' voices as they wandered the room. Waiters mingled, offering silver trays filled with drinks and hors d'oeuvres.

"Good evening, Mr. Vice President. Your wife is making mine envious."

"Why so, Mr. Stanley?" Vice President Charles Fairbanks took a canapé from a silver tray as it passed by him.

"Her dress, sir. Elegant as usual."

"The price is also elegant. Paid more than twenty-five dollars. She feels she needs to dress her best for the Roosevelt parties. Edith believes in being fashionable, and my wife will not be outdone."

"I must say, they do give entertaining parties. Notice the President's cowboy friend talking with the British Ambassador. I heard the President tell him not to shoot at the Ambassador's feet to make him dance as it could cause an international incident. Most amusing, I must say."

The Vice President listened to the orchestra begin playing, "Wait Till the Sun Shines, Nellie." "We may be lucky if that is all that happens tonight."

"What do you mean, sir?"

"Stanley, you're a logging lobbyist, aren't you?"

"Yes." Mr. Stanley eyed Vice President Fairbanks warily.

"Check out Senator John H. Mitchell, from our illustrious state of Oregon, conferring with Prineville's Representative, Mr. Carter. I wish my ears could catch their conversation. I bet they want to get the Oregon forests opened to you loggers."

"I think it would be a good move for the federal lands to be opened for our companies to go in and harvest the timber. It would create jobs."

"Yes, in the short term. Over by the doorway stands Mr. Gifford Pinchot. He's the tall, thin man with the mustache. My wife says the ladies think his eyes are charismatic. I don't. They are the eyes of a fanatic. Roosevelt himself said, 'If I wanted to win something away from Pinchot, I would have to kill him to do it.'"

"Yes, I've met him several times." Stanley turned his back to Pinchot. "We disagree on many issues." The orchestra now played, "Mary's A Grand Old Name." Quentin Roosevelt began running through the partygoers' legs, chasing his brother, Teddy. Mrs. Roosevelt caught both boys and told them to go upstairs to roughhouse. The President smiled at his sons and said, "I will come up and join you for a bit of roughhousing before bed."

Mr. Stanley turned back to the Vice President. "With the President pushing Congress to enact the Federal Food and Drug Act, many people believe we are on our way to socialism and government control. Did you realize what the President and Pinchot were up to when the President distracted Congress with indictments of trust-busting against the Northern Securities Company and Standard Oil?" Mr. Stanley sipped his champagne. "McKinley would not have pushed it. In my opinion, he was a friend of big business."

"Yes, I hear what people say, but I think it's a good piece of legislation. Why do you say he *distracted* Congress?"

"Because Pinchot walked the corridors of Congress pushing, lobbying, and arm-twisting to get the forest land out of the Department of Interior and transferred to the Department of Agriculture. He contends bureaucrats run the Interior, and he says foresters run the Forest Service in Agriculture. He views the trees as a crop. Can you believe such nonsense? No wonder Mitchell and Carter might come to blows with Pinchot. I may even help them."

The Vice President smiled. "Pinchot and the President are of like mind, that's for sure. Together I think they have withdrawn over 235 million acres of timberland from potential sale to loggers. Some Congressmen are wondering when Pinchot will declare the Great Salt Lake as part of his forest service. You take on one of them you take on both of them." The Vice President chuckled. "I wouldn't advise it."

The two men stood in awkward silence. "Excuse me, I see Elihu Root. I'd like to speak to him. As Secretary of War, Elihu and the President have forced this country into foreign affairs." The Vice President's face became serious, and then his eyes lit up in mischief when he saw a man standing by the fireplace. "You might want to go over and talk to Senator Thomas Platt and commiserate with him. He's the man responsible for Teddy being President. And he is not too happy." The Vice President shook hands with Stanley and ambled over to the Secretary of War.

Stanley found another glass of wine and stood next to Senator Platt. "Sir, how are you this evening?"

"As well as can be expected, with Roosevelt in the White House."

"He's a fellow Republican and from your state of New York."

"Yes, and I worked with him when he was governor, but I didn't like his flair for publicity and his unconventional dictates in politics. I helped to maneuver him into the Vice President spot on the McKinley ticket. I figured it was a dead-end job. He couldn't do any harm. Wouldn't you know, an anarchist kills President McKinley, and Roosevelt is in the top party position, doing the things I feared he would. He wins a second term, and here we are with a liberal Republican President and a conservative Republican Congress."

Mr. Stanley raised his glass and smiled somberly at Senator Platt. "As they say, 'the best-laid plans of mice and men....'" The two men sipped wine and glowered at the President as he strolled over to the crowd of ladies surrounding Pinchot.

"Gifford, I want to see you in my office tomorrow at nine," said Teddy Roosevelt.

"Yes, Mr. President."

Roosevelt moved toward the doorway.

"Dear."

"Yes, Edith?" The President stopped by his wife's elbow.

"Alice went upstairs with her younger brothers. Please, remind her to act like a lady, and send her back to the ball."

"Dear, I can be President, or I can control Alice, but I can't do both. Besides, she promised to show me the new jujitsu move she learned today. Excuse me for a minute, ladies, I promised my boys a run upstairs before they go to bed. I'll be back shortly."

* * *

"Mr. President, you wanted to see me?" A lean man with intense eyes entered the President's oval office.

"Yes, Pinchot. Sit down."

"Thank you, Mr. President."

"What's going on in Oregon?"

"Sir?"

"What's going on with the cattlemen and sheep men? These letters, some are from children, telling about the sheep-killing." Teddy Roosevelt picked up a paper stack and threw them down on his desk. He grabbed a newspaper and waved it in the air. "Someone sent me a copy of the...the *Oregonian*. They published a letter written by a person who said he was the 'the Sheep-Shooters' Association's Corresponding Secretary.' He wrote the paper and the state governor, warning them to stay out of their business, namely the 'progressive line of sheep-shooting.' It goes on to brag—brag, mind you—about the killing of thousands sheep in one year and the plan to kill more this coming year." Teddy stood and stomped to the other side of his desk. "Letters from folks indicate people are disappearing. A man named Shorty Davis hasn't been seen for months. Just vanished." The President grasped another letter, saying, "This one tells me a Mr. Creed Connelly was shot two times fatally in the heart. An inquest said it was suicide! This happened right after he claimed he knew some sheep-shooters. Outrageous! Other letters are filled with similar tales." He flapped the letters as his pince-nez slid down the bridge of his nose and dangled by its cord.

"Sir, the conservationist John Muir called sheep 'hooved locusts.' When they over-graze the land, the cattle starve. I can understand the cattlemen's point," Pinchot said.

"I can, too. But the killing has to stop!"

"Mr. President, this is for the local and state governments to solve."

"Pinchot, it's on federal grazing land. This land is in the Blue Mountain Reserve and the Maury Mountain Forest Reserve. You're the chief forester. You have control over the hydro- electric leases and the grazing licenses. We can't let this slaughter continue."

"Do you want me to send in troops? Is that what you're saying?"

"No! That's the last resort. Send an agent to investigate and come up with an answer, one both the cattlemen and the sheep men can live with." Teddy held his pince-nez and tapped it in the palm of his hand. "Get it done, Pinchot."

"I may know just the man who can do it. His name is Ireland. He's a negotiator, and he's smart. I'll make him the forest supervisor of both reserves. He can set up a forestry office in Prineville. I'll get him on it right away."

"Good. See to it I'm kept informed."

"Yes, Mr. President."

Chapter Ten

"Do you think we dare do it, Paul?"

"Nothing has happened for weeks. Folks heard the pastor is getting people to write to President Roosevelt. Besides, nobody would be interested in us. We're just going out for a picnic. The girls want to see Voyager, and we're taking Cassie home in a week."

Paul took the picnic basket and blankets from his wife and put them in the buckboard next to his Winchester. "Come on, girls! Let's get going. Snooker and Buster are champing at the bit."

Molly and Cassie ran from the house. "We've got coffee, sugar, and flour for Voyager and a new ribbon for Lammie Star." Each girl lugged one end of a heavy burlap bag. Paul helped them heave it into the buckboard. The girls climbed on top and sang together, "We're ready. Let's go!"

Anna climbed onto the front seat next to Paul. "We're off to the high meadow."

"The weather is perfect. Just like the day in April on my birthday. Ma, Pa, Uncle Tim, Aunt Ruth, Cousins Charlie and Ned, and I had a picnic. It was glorious! We played leapfrog and guessing games, and we had fried chicken and birthday cake. It was a perfect day. I wish every day could be the same." Molly bounced up and down on the sack. She turned and twisted around to look in all directions. Cassie sat still, watching the grass pop back up from under the wagon as they drove to the foothills.

The songs, "Old MacDonald had a Farm," "Old Dan Tucker"and "Bingo was His Name" rang out across the grassland along with chatter and laughter as the wagon bounced on the rutted path.

Paul Langster held the reins with steady tension as the horses stepped lively. Hours later, he reined them in at the top of a rise. They gazed down the rocky, grassy slope to a meadow with pines and mountains surrounding it. They saw Voyager seated near his flock on the valley's far side. The two dogs, Rolf and Jake, were trotting around the sheep. They took off and chased a ewe and lamb back into the flock at the far end. Another herd grazed at the other end of the field, and its two sheepherders were talking with Voyager. The valley was wide and the grass fresh and green.

"Isn't it the most fabulous sight?" said Molly.

As Paul slapped the reins against the horses' rumps, sharp cracks split the air. Paul pulled back hard on the reins. Pawing the ground, the horses shook their heads.

Five riders wearing rain slickers with gunnysacks over their faces and one rider wearing a bandana covering his face galloped out from behind a rock outcropping. A seventh, short rider sat on his horse at the ridge top. The six riders charged down into the flocks, shooting rifles.

Paul grabbed his rifle, cocked it, and laid it across his lap. "Anna, get the girls down."

Anna had already thrown herself into the back of the buckboard. She pulled the girls down on the wagon bed. Grabbing blankets, she covered their heads. "Girls, stay down and don't look."

Cassie struggled to sit up, but Anna pulled her back down. Molly lifted the blanket edge. She peered through the crack between two wagon sideboards.

Her eyes opened wide, and she stared at the scene below. She wanted to close her eyes but couldn't. The sheep milled about in panic. The dogs raced around the flock trying to hold them together. The three sheep men yelled and ran toward the riders.

Voyager waved his staff in the air. He signaled the dogs to keep the sheep moving away from the masked men.

A young sheepherder picked up his Winchester and fired. The sheep-shooters stiffened and stopped their horses. They stared at the sheep tenders, and in one motion the six horsemen opened fire at the three sheep men. Molly choked on a scream tight in her throat as Voyager staggered toward his flock and fell, reaching out to a fallen ewe. In less than a minute, the three sheep men lay fallen on the ground.

Jake left the sheep and ran toward a horse. A rifle cracked, and he fell, twisted for a moment, and then lay still. Rolf tore through the flock and charged the horses. He gave a leap. More shots rang out. The Langsters heard the dog yelp as it fell to the earth. Rolf lifted his head. Whimpering, he dragged his body toward his son.

The men turned to the sheep and fired as rapidly as they cocked their guns.

Molly quivered with each shot. Paul struggled to control the horses. Anna sobbed as she held the girls down.

The sheep ran in a panic toward the cliffs. One rider blocked the open grassland. The horse had an odd gait as the rider rode back and forth, directing the sheep to the cliffs. They plunged down onto the rocks below. The bleating and the gunfire echoed over and over as the sound bounced off the mountains. Hundreds of sheep lay dead on the rocks below as the riders rode through the field, killing the wounded animals that could not run.

The rider on the odd-gaited horse dismounted and slit the animals' throats with a long butcher knife. Molly saw the blade slice into a lamb with a blue ribbon. The slicker and gunnysack were spotted with blood. Knife and hand red, the rider mounted. After the last rifle had cracked, the echoes stopped, and an ugly silence settled on the pasture.

The short rider on top of the rise slumped in his saddle. He turned his horse and disappeared over the ridge in the direction he had come.

Molly stared at the others. The rider with the bandana over his face was heavyset. His Stetson had blown off his head and hung by the strap around his neck. She stared at the broad white streak in his hair. A tall, thin man rode up to him. His movements were jerky and awkward. The rider following him had the same movements, only a more youthful body. Two other riders stayed close together. One was younger and slightly shorter. Molly knew he was a boy by the natural way he rode. The taller man was in charge. Her eyes stared in disbelief when she looked at his coal-black horse. Despite the one white stocking having been covered with blacking, Molly recognized it.

The rider on the odd-gaited horse joined them, and the six trotted up to the wagon. The man with the white streak aimed his gun at Paul. Anna screamed, "No!" The man on the coal-black horse charged at the man with the white streak and knocked his mount off balance. The rifle muzzle jerked up as the shot cracked. Forcing his horse between the killer and the wagon and shaking his head, he pointed with his Winchester to the ridge.

The shooter hesitated. Molly held her breath as she stared at him through the crack in the boards. Malicious eyes glared at her pa. The killer glowered at the wagon and glanced into Molly's eyes. He blinked, and his eyes softened. He put his hat on, turned his horse, and led the sheep-shooters up the grassy incline. They rode over the hill and disappeared.

The wagon horses jerked their heads against the tight reins. Bloody saliva foamed at the corners of their mouths where the bits cut into them. Paul slowly eased the tension and guided the buckboard down the hill to the pasture. He drove near the three men lying in the grass. Everyone except Cassie jumped out. She sat up and gaped at the slaughter.

Paul checked the two herders with the second flock. "They're dead." He walked over to Voyager, knelt beside him, and raised his head.

Voyager opened his eyes. "Ah, you've come. I'm glad you didn't come earlier. You might have been caught in this. The sheep?"

"Dead."

"My lads, the dogs?"

Paul glanced over at the dogs. Rolf had dragged himself to Jake. He laid his paw on him as if to wake him. They both lay still. "Gone."

"I know they died bravely. We're family. We lived together, and we perished together. Please, bury us out here on the pasture. This was our life. Put Cassie's Lammie Star with us. This...." Voyager's voice ceased as his eyes closed.

Paul stood. "He's left us."

With shaking legs, Cassie climbed down from the buckboard and ran to Voyager. She sobbed as she kissed him. She stumbled over to Jake and Rolf, hugging and petting them. Choking on her sobs, she crawled on her hands and knees over the dead sheep until she came to the lamb with a faded blue ribbon, turned bright red, around its neck. She raised its wobbly head and laid it in her lap. The blood from its slit throat soaked her clothes. "You followed me around like a puppy. You thought I was your momma, didn't you? You depended on me to protect you, and I let you get killed." She rocked the lamb back and forth as she cried.

Anna walked over to Cassie, sat down, and swayed with her as Cassie held the lamb.

Molly's legs collapsed under her, and she sat hard on the ground. She stared at her father. Tears were streaming down his face.

Paul lifted Molly and carried her to the buckboard. "Molly, you know who did this, just as I do."

Molly nodded her head. She kept her eyes on Ma and Cassie.

"These men are from our county, but other men in other counties do this, too. They know us. If we tell who these shooters are, the others we did not see today will come after us. Listen to me. Look at me." Paul turned his daughter's head until she peered straight into his eyes. The deep sadness she beheld in his eyes would never leave him or her.

"Molly, they'll kill us. Your ma, you, and me. Your uncle Tim wouldn't stand for it. He'd go after the men who hurt us, but there are many of them. They would kill Uncle Tim, Aunt Ruth, and the boys. They wouldn't care he if is a sheep-shooter. We can't ever say who the shooters were. Not as long as we live. We can *never* say. Promise me, Molly. Promise."

Molly nodded. "I promise. Not as long as I live will I ever tell." She shuddered. "What about Cassie?"

"She'll be safe. She won't be able to recognize anyone. She doesn't know the people here. Besides, she's in shock. I don't think she took a good look at the men."

Molly stared at Cassie, thinking this wasn't the Cassie she knew. She wasn't the Molly she knew anymore, either. Feelings of betrayal, inadequacy, and guilt shrouded her in a dark blanket.

Chapter Eleven

"Sheriff Durkson."

He stood when he recognized the woman coming in the door. He tipped his hat and walked around his desk, pulling up a chair. "You care to sit, Mrs. Pryon? How are you doing today? Everything okay?"

"Yes, sir. I want to thank you for your talk with Calvin. I don't know what you said, as he won't tell me, but it sure worked, and I wanted you to know how much I appreciate it. But please don't tell him I spoke with you. He's over at the blacksmith's. I came to your office when I knew he wouldn't see me. We're here to get supplies."

"I won't say a word, Maud. I'll be sure to drop by your place one of these days. I need to see him on business, and I'll not tell him we talked." Sheriff Durkson sat on the edge of his desk. "He's treating you all right? No more hitting, broken bones?"

"No, sir. He gets angry, but he goes out to the barn and takes it out on the horse or the milk cow. He doesn't hit me any more. I feel sorry for the poor beasts, but I feel safer. Thank you. Whatever did you say to him?"

"Nothing much. Don't you worry, though. If he starts on you again, you come and tell me. I ain't going to let him get away with it." The sheriff stood. "I hear a commotion going on outside I should check on. You can go out the back door so your husband won't see you leaving my office."

"Thank you, Sheriff. You're a good man." Mrs. Pryon went out the door as the sheriff headed out to the boardwalk in front of his office.

* * *

Buster and Snooker halted. The sight of six feet sticking out from under blankets in the back of the buckboard drew men and women from the stores like magnets.

Molly slid off Buster's back, and Anna lifted Cassie from her lap into Paul's arms. In moments, the people now on the boardwalk surrounded them. The sheriff stood by his office door. The crowd asked questions and pointed at the bodies. The girls clung to Paul and Anna. Cassie's body quivered, her eyes having gone vacant.

"What's going on here, Paul? What happened?" The sheriff asked.

"We took the girls to the high meadow for a picnic. Six riders rode out from the rocks and started shooting and running off the sheep. The young kid there," Paul pointed to one body, "raised a rifle and fired at the men. I couldn't tell who returned his fire, but the three sheep men were killed. The riders continued killing the sheep and dogs. They ran the remaining flock over the cliff. After they left, we put the dead men in the wagon and came here."

A man standing in the crowd shouted out, "Could you see who the riders were? Can you identify anyone?"

Paul scrutinized the people and picked out a tall, thin man near the back. He recognized the voice as Judge Wimple's. The man's clothes hung on him, straight as a stick. His son, Henry, an inch taller and as jerky and awkward as his father, stood behind him. "No, Judge Wimple, they wore dusters and covered their faces. I don't know who any of them were," Paul said above the din.

The judge strode through the crowd and stood next to the sheriff.

"Anna, could you recognize anyone?" asked Durkson.

"No, Tom, I can't." Anna looked him straight in the eyes.

Nutter yelled out, "Paul, you said the young herder fired at the riders first. The shooters only returned fire at the sheep men?"

"That's right. That's what I saw."

"The sheep men were askin' to get killed. They'd be alive if they hadn't fired first, right?"

"Don't know, Nutter," Paul yelled above the murmuring voices.

"What about the horses? Could you recognize a horse?" asked Durkson.

Paul and Anna answered together, "No." Paul added, "They were blacks and bays. No markings I could see."

The sheriff gazed intently at the two girls. "Well, young ones, did you recognize anyone or any horses? What do you have to say about it?"

Cassie wept. She clung to Paul, wrapping her arms around his neck. "They killed my friends. They're murderers. They're mean people. I don't know who they were." Cassie broke down in uncontrollable sobs.

"Molly, what say you?" The sheriff removed his Stetson and wiped his forehead on his shirtsleeve. Molly could see the white streak from his forehead to the back of his head plastered against his deep black hair. He put his hat back on. Only a trace of white showed.

Molly took a deep breath. She leaned against her pa's leg and held tight to her mother's hand. She felt the tension in her mother's body. She felt the muscles in her father's leg quiver. "I don't know those people. I never knew them. They aren't people I ever met." Her voice shook, but she forced it loud enough to carry through the crowd.

"Well, I guess we will get these fellows to the undertakers. I'll try to notify the sheep owners by telegram. Later, I'll lead my men out to the meadow to take a look-see," Durkson summarized.

"Anna and I will take care of Voyager. We'll pick up a coffin and bury him with his two dogs up on the meadow. That's what he wanted."

The sheriff stared at Paul. "Suit yourself. Will you notify the sheep owner?"

"Yes, I'll do so today. Anna and I will send a telegram."

"Good."

The crowd broke up into small groups. "Good riddance," some said. "It's too bad people died, but it served them right," and, "The authorities will handle it," was the consensus.

"Anna, you take the girls to the hotel and sit in the lobby. I'll get the coffin and send a telegram to Cassie's parents. Cassie," Paul said as he handed the girl over to Anna, "I'm going to telegram your pa to meet me at the pass in four days to fetch you home. Tomorrow, we will bury Voyager. I think it would be best for you and your folks if we start to bring you home the next day."

"Yes, I want to go home." Cassie buried her face in Anna's hair and neck.

"Pa, can I walk around for a while? My legs hurt from riding Buster into town without a saddle."

Paul peered into his daughter's eyes.

"I remember my promise."

"Okay. Stay on the main street. Don't go into any store. Walk where I can keep an eye on you. Go into the hotel when you're ready."

"Yes, Pa." Molly went with Cassie and her mother as far as the hotel, and then continued down the street. People tried to stop her to talk, but Molly moved away from them and up the hill to the church steps. There it was quiet. Folks didn't walk this far unless they were going to church.

She sat on the steps and watched the scattered groups milling about the town. She sighed, and shivers twitched her muscles. She saw her father leave the telegraph office and cross the street to the undertaker's building. She noticed Uncle Tim and Cousin Charlie talking with people along the boardwalk. She watched Aunt Ruth and Ned lead their horses down the street. Aunt Ruth's horse turned a hoof out with his odd gait. Molly rubbed her eyes to keep the tears back. Her uncle and aunt didn't try to talk to her pa. Nobody else saw how unusual it was. *Nobody knows the world has changed. It only looks the same.* Molly wrapped her arms around her body and bit her lips to keep them from quivering. She watched the pastor coming up the road toward her.

"May I sit with you, Molly?"

She nodded and moved over to make room for him on the step.

"A fearsome thing you've seen, child. Do you want to talk about it?"

Molly shook her head and stared down at her feet.

"We can sit here together in silence. Sometimes silence helps."

She nodded. Listening to a whippoorwill and a starling's raucous cry, she sighed.

The pastor broke the silence. "Molly, folks are saying the sheepherders were at fault. They're dead because the one fired on the riders. Do you think it's their fault?"

She shook her head. "They were trying to protect their sheep. The sheep depend on them. Like Nutter Barns said in church, you fight to protect what is yours."

After a minute or two, the pastor asked, "What do you think about your pa?"

"What do you mean?"

"Do you think he should have done something?"

Molly wiped her eyes. She tried to tune out a starling's sound and focus on the Steller's jay singing. "No, I don't. He had a rifle in case we met wolves, but he couldn't use it against the sheep-shooters. Not with us there. They would have shot us. We depend on him. He has to protect us."

"I'm glad you see it that way. I didn't want you to think less of your pa."

After a long moment Molly said, "I think the riders were trying to protect their families. I think they're afraid of letting down those who depend on them."

"But having good reasons does not make doing wrong good, does it?" The reverend's eyes questioned Molly. She sighed and leaned against his shoulder. He put his arm around her.

"No. Nothing was good in what happened. Nothing."

They sat in silence for several minutes, with Molly resting against the pastor.

"Molly, can you share with me anything that happened? I want to investigate this on my own. Maybe we can find a way to stop the killing if we know who's doing it. Can you remember anything that might help?"

Molly scanned the street. The funeral parlor door opened, and her pa stepped out. The sheriff, her uncle, her cousin Charlie, the judge, his son Henry and other men were mounting their horses to ride out of town for the high meadow. They could see her sitting on the steps with the pastor.

"I can't tell you anything you didn't hear from Ma and Pa. I'm sorry."

"Don't be, child. In a way, I'm glad you don't know anything. It's better that way for you. Don't you worry. A pastor hears many things. I'll soon learn something from someone.

"I brought my horse into the blacksmith so he could work on his shoes. I think I'll go get Jasper and catch up with the men going out to the meadow. I might learn something up there. Are you okay?"

"I'll walk with you. I'm going to meet Ma and Pa at the hotel."

They held hands as they went together down the street.

* * *

The sheriff stopped his horse beside Paul Langster. He bent down and whispered, "I see your daughter has been talking to the pastor, and they're walking together. What do you think she's been telling him?"

Paul narrowed his eyes as he stared at the lawman. "She hasn't said anything she hasn't already said. I've got her word on it." Paul glared at the others in the group. He stared at his brother, his nephew, at Judge Wimple and his son Henry. "Nobody has any cause to fear what Anna, Molly, or I saw, but if anything happens to any one of us, you'd better fear a coming wrath the likes of which you've never known before."

The sheriff straightened in the saddle. "Oh, I don't reckon your family need have any concerns." Durkson observed Molly and the pastor coming down the street toward them. "I can't say the same for Weatherby." The lawman swung his horse to lead the posse as they cantered down the road.

The ride back to the ranch was long and quiet. Cassie lay exhausted in Anna's lap. Her overalls were stiff with dried blood.

* * *

Before sunrise, the family left the ranch with Voyager and the coffin, heading for the high meadow. The bone-chilling cold penetrated their coats and blankets.

The sun had been up for several hours by the time Paul finished digging a grave on the pine-covered hill. It looked down on the meadow where the dead sheep lay. Paul placed Voyager in the wood box. Anna laid the stiff, cold bodies of Rolf and Jake on Voyager's right and left side. Molly positioned Lammie Star on his chest. Paul put a rope around the casket's head section, and Anna held a line around the foot end. They slid the coffin over the hole and slowly lowered it with the ropes. They threw the rope ends onto the casket's lid. Paul carried Cassie from the wagon where she was huddled and brought her to the graveside.

Molly picked wildflowers and brought them over to Cassie. Cassie's legs trembled as she sat on the ground. She didn't take the flowers. Her eyes were fixed on the dark grave.

Paul shoveled dirt into the hole. The clods pelted the coffin with heartrending thuds. Cassie shuddered. She gazed in a stupor as they placed flowers on the fresh earth.

"In time, the sheep bodies will be covered by dirt and grass, Cassie, and I'll put a marker on Voyager's grave. It will be a pleasant place for them."

"Will the marker have Voyager's name on it and Rolf's and Jake's and Lammie Star's?"

"Yes, it will."

"Good. Can I go home? I want to go home."

"We'll leave at sunup tomorrow. We should be at the place in two days where we will meet your pa."

Cassie took one more glance at the grave before she turned and staggered to the wagon. She lay down in the back on folded blankets. Molly joined her. Cassie sat up. "Molly, I don't want to come back here again to see you. I don't want you to come to see me. And I don't want to write you any letters, and I don't want you to send me any. You're my best friend in the whole world, but I can't think of you anymore." Cassie swallowed hard.

Molly realized more than people and animals had died in that massacre. She hugged Cassie as the tears cascaded down her cheeks. "I understand. But we'll be best friends forever. Nothing's going to change the way we feel. When we're old, like Ma and Pa, we'll have good memories, and we won't think on the bad. In our minds, we'll always be like we were when we rode out on Buster and Judy to visit Voyager, the dogs, and Lammie Star. We'll remember the happy days." Molly didn't believe the words she said. She didn't think Cassie did, either.

Cassie nodded as she lay down on the blankets. The creaking wagon and the horses' hooves hitting the earth made the silence feel more oppressive.

Chapter Twelve

The sheriff reined in his horse by the barn door. He tipped his hat at Mrs. Pryon as she fed the chickens. She nodded in reply and went on scattering seeds. The flock of hens clustered around her as the sheriff dismounted. He heard the shrill cry of pain stabbing the air as he entered the barn.

Calvin's horse was tied up short to a stall door. He waved a halter at the horse and brought it down hard on its flank. The creature moved its hindquarters away and squealed in pain. The rancher charged after the animal, cursing. "You'll stand still and take it, or I'll keep on hitting you until you do, you lazy bag of dung."

The lawman came up behind Calvin and grabbed his hand. "What did I tell you?"

"Durkson, I didn't know you were here. You said I couldn't hit my missus no more, but you didn't say anything concerning this worthless piece of—"

The lawman twisted the cattle man's arm behind him and forced him down on his knees into horse manure. "Well, it goes for him, too, and all your animals. If I hear you've been abusing any animal, I'll come and abuse you worse, same as I said before for Maud and your kids. You go after them, and I may not stop at beating you to a pulp. I may just shoot you. And you know I mean it."

"We go out and kill woolies. Why shouldn't it be okay to teach this critter who's boss?"

"That's different. Sheep are no better than rats. You leave Maud and these animals alone, or I'll make you the victim of a stray bullet. You get it?" Durkson grabbed Calvin's hair and jerked his head back.

"Tom, let go. You'll break my neck."

Durkson let go and shoved the rancher away from him.

Calvin stood. "A man is a king in his castle. Well, this here place is my castle. Don't see why I can't beat sense into my own wife or kids. You have no cause to interfere with what a man does in his own home."

"My old man hit my ma near every day. When I was ten, he hit and kicked her until she couldn't stand up. She crawled to her bed and died. No one tried to stop him. By heaven almighty, I'm going to stop you." Springing forward, the sheriff grabbed Calvin, twisted his arm, and forced him to the floor. He put his knee into Calvin's back and pushed his face into the dung on the wood floor. He ground his head back and forth in the muck.

"I hear. I hear. Let go. You're killing me. Let go!" Calvin sputtered, choked, and spit out manure.

The sheriff released his grip.

"My arm's nearly broke," complained the cattleman as he sat up.

"Be thankful it ain't. Next time, you won't be able to sit up and talk. I came here to tell you about the next association members' ride, but I changed my mind. I don't want to see you there."

"Ain't fair. I can ride and do my part. No reason you shouldn't let me come."

"I'm in charge, and I say who takes part and who don't. If'n I see you acting like a man with your wife and ranch, I'll let you come the next time. 'Til then, I ain't riding with you." Durkson left the barn, tipped his hat to Maud, mounted his horse Jingo, and rode down the road.

Chapter Thirteen

Men from the ranches and the town shuffled their feet and spoke quietly. The women stood in a group, watching their children play in the church front yard as they shared recipes.

"How are you today, Mrs. Pryon?" Tom Durkson tipped his Stetson.

Maud Pryon stepped back and pulled her sunbonnet closer to one side of her face. She turned away as she answered, "Fine, thank you, Sheriff Durkson."

"So I see. Good day to you." Tom Durkson spoke up loudly. "The pastor is late today for service."

"It ain't time yet. Early by my piece," Calvin Pryon said as he snapped his pocket watch closed and put it into a vest pocket. He averted his eyes from the sheriff as he said, "My missus, she is a lummox, that one. She fell yesterday in the kitchen—spilled grease on the floor and slipped."

"It happens. Kitchens can be a hazard, for sure. I reckon I'm going to ride out and hurry the pastor along. This may be a day of rest, but we all got Sunday chores to do. You want to ride with me, Judge? And how about your son, Henry?" the sheriff asked.

"Sure, we'll ride along."

"I'll come with you," Calvin Pryon said.

"No need, Calvin. We'll handle it."

The three men mounted their horses and rode down the road through town. Lanky Henry rode behind his father. Two beanpoles on horseback contrasted with the heavyset sheriff.

"Ain't like the sheriff to be anxious for church services," Nutter said with a laugh.

* * *

An hour later, people were asking each other why the pastor was late and whether the men had found him. No one had answers, and others repeated the same questions a few moments later to the ones who had asked them. The children sat on the church steps, tired from playing tag. Charlie and Mandy sat on the porch swing at Mr. Auldrich's house.

"Hey, look! The sheriff and judge are coming back leading a horse!" Nutter yelled.

Durkson, Judge Wimple, and Henry Wimple reined in their horses at the church hitching rail. The men gathered around the extra horse; the pastor's body was slung across the saddle. The women gathered their children in their arms and retreated a few steps back.

"Sure am sorry, folks. We found the pastor's horse grazing and Weatherby lying in the road. I think Jasper threw the pastor, and he hit his head on a rock, as you can see, and we found a rock with blood on it. A sad accident."

"Are you sure, Sheriff?" Newt Williamson took a few steps over to Jasper and lifted the reverend's head. "With the pastor saying he was going to try to stop the sheep-shooters, we need to be certain of cause of death."

"Can't be nothin' else. There was the horse, with one shoe missing, the pastor on the ground, and blood on the rock. No other tracks, man nor beast, except for ours. Ain't that right, Judge Wimple?"

"That's right. I'll testify to it at an inquest, if need be. Accident, pure and simple."

Molly hung onto her mother's hand. She stared at the three men sitting calmly on their horses. Their cold demeanor sent a wave of shivers through her. She pressed herself against Anna. "Mom, I want to go home." She peered up at her mother's face. Tears streamed down her cheeks. Many women were crying into their handkerchiefs. Men kicked up dust puffs with their boots and cleared their throats.

"Paul, Molly and I want to go home."

Paul glared at his wife and daughter. "We will, right after the funeral." He turned back to Durkson and spoke directly to him. "We're going to attend the funeral. Weatherby was a good man. He didn't deserve this."

"We'll get the undertaker up here with a coffin, and all the men can help dig the grave. The undertaker is good at saying the last words. Okay, men, let's get at it." Durkson and Wimple took the body from its horse and laid it on the church steps.

"Anna, take Molly down to the general store to visit with Mrs. Hasty. I'll send word when we are ready for the burial."

"The boys and I will go with you, Anna." Ruth, Charlie, and Ned joined Anna and Molly.

"Ruth, Charlie can stay here and help. He's fifteen and near a man," Tim Langster dictated.

Charlie smiled and proudly marched up to the men heading toward the cemetery.

Molly moved to the other side of her mother as Aunt Ruth and Ned joined them on their walk down the hill.

* * *

The women gathered at the general store. Mrs. Hasty made coffee in her home behind the store and brought the pot out to serve. They commiserated with each other, shook their heads, and wondered what Mrs. Weatherby and her five children would do now.

"A tragedy, pure and simple. We're the farthest church on his circuit from his home. Otherwise, we could delay the funeral until his family could come," the judge's wife said. She clucked her tongue against her teeth.

"I reckon we can hold another service when she arrives, but it's best to get the poor man buried as soon as possible in this hot weather," Mrs. Hasty agreed. "You're quite right, Mrs. Wimple."

"I have cream for coffee." Mrs. Hasty set down the huge enamel coffee pot and went back into the living quarters to retrieve the cream. She loved the role of hostess, despite the reason today.

Several ladies promised to bring their egg money and any extra money their husbands could spare to church the next Sunday for a collection for the pastor's wife. Many women thought the other churches on the pastor's circuit would do the same. They assured each other the family would be all right, but secretly wondered how the widow would keep her family together.

Young children played in the dusty street. Their voices and laughter eased the tension inside.

Molly sat on the bench outside the store. Ned sat on the other end and glanced her way. He averted his eyes and focused on the boardwalk when she turned her eyes his way. His body curved forward until his head neared his knees. *He looks like an old man for his ten years,* Molly thought. She recalled seeing the small rider on the ridge and how his straight back had crumpled into a slump as he'd watched the melee in the valley. Molly realized Ned had changed and was no longer the boy she once knew.

* * *

The wagon wheels ground the dirt finer as it rolled over the trail. Buster and Judy nodded their heads in rhythm with their gait and flicked their tails to shoo the flies. Paul held the reins loosely, letting the horses take their time in the heat. The family rode in silence for several miles.

Molly sat between her father and mother. Her head hung, and she stared at her hands in her lap. "Pa?"

"Yes, Molly?"

"Maybe we did wrong by not telling. If we told people who the shooters were and they were arrested, maybe the pastor would still be alive. I don't believe his death was an accident." Tears dripped onto her hands as she mumbled the words.

"Who would we tell? The sheriff, the judge, who?"

"I don't know. But somebody. How about the sheriff in the next county?"

"What if he is a sheep-shooter, too?"

"But we can't just say nothing and let innocent people die."

Paul looked at Molly for the first time on their ride home. "We will always do what we can to protect people, but we can never, never tell. It would cause more violence and bloodshed, and in the end wouldn't help anyone. I'd gladly die if I thought that would stop the war, but it won't, will it?"

"No, Pa, no! I promise, I won't tell anyone." Molly grabbed her father's arm and held on tight.

The horses nodded their heads to the slow rhythm of their walk.

Chapter Fourteen

"Hey, Sheriff. What are you up to?" Calvin rode up beside an oak on his southern pasture.

"I came out looking for you, and I noticed this tree. 'Pears it was hit by lightning. Thought I'd pull this branch down before it fell." Tom Durkson lassoed a stout branch and wound the rope around the saddle horn. "Jingo, back. Back."

"You're wrong, Tom. Ain't nothin' wrong with the tree. The branch is fine."

"I've started. I'll finish. This branch is coming down."

"Okay, I'll help." Calvin lassoed the branch and wound the other rope end around his saddle horn as he backed his horse.

Both horses strained to move back, exerting pressure on the ropes and the branch.

The branch split and crashed to the ground. The ropes slackened. The horses, released from the strain, stepped forward.

"We did it. Sure is big. How come you were out here looking for me?"

"I stopped by your place to tell you the Sheep-Shooters' Association meeting is tomorrow night, at the usual place and time."

"I'll be there. I have my gunnysack in my saddlebag. I'll be ready at a moment's notice."

"We haven't ridden against the sheepers for a while to let things quiet down after Pastor had his accident. Now's about time to teach the wooly-tenders we are still in business." The sheriff dismounted and undid the rope wrapped around the branch.

"You know me. I'll ride anytime."

The sheriff coiled his rope. "Yeah, I know you." He mounted Jingo and looked at Calvin. "I talked to Maud. She was walking slow, favoring her side and stomach."

"I ain't hit her or kicked her. If she says I did, she's lying."

"Why would she lie?"

"She wants to get me in trouble. She's been like that since the day we got married."

"She didn't say anything about you hitting or kicking her. In fact, she said everything was fine."

"What did I tell you? I ain't hurt her none."

"Good. See ya tomorrow."

"Sure." Calvin put his horse on the bit and leaned forward, moving away from the sheriff. Without warning, he fell from the saddle and hit the ground hard before he realized he had been shoved. Tom Durkson dismounted. A gun butt slammed down on Calvin's head. He wanted to get up, but his hands and feet wouldn't respond. Confusion and searing pain roared through his brain. A second blow brought deep, unending blackness.

Durkson dragged Calvin's body over to the branch. He wedged the head and chest under the heaviest section. He balanced himself on the limb over the body and pounded one foot up and down to make sure the branch was embedded deeply into the scalp.

"If no one finds you in a day or two, I'll come out and discover your body. No sense in Maud worrying about you any longer than necessary. You got better than you deserved." The sheriff mounted Jingo and headed for town.

Chapter Fifteen

Pushing the bills and papers into a heap, a round-shouldered man picked up his coffee cup. He noticed the brown ring left on the torn tablecloth. "Jennifer, we're going to lose the ranch. We can pay the hired hands for this month, but that's all. I can't pay the mortgage or the store bills. I can't borrow any more. We're finished. I'm a failure."

Jennifer brushed a strand of hair from her forehead and secured it with a pin in the bun at the back of her head. She sat on the kitchen chair across the table. "Hayden, you aren't a failure. This year, 1907, is a bad year here in Willamette County for lots of folks." She reached over and took his hand. "We would have been fine if we hadn't lost the major flock last year in Crook County." She glanced at Cassie, who was ironing in the parlor. She lowered her voice and leaned forward. "I'm worried we're going to lose Cassie, too."

Hayden twisted and peered over his shoulder at his daughter. Pale and thin, she moved the flat iron across the handkerchiefs.

"I know. She won't go to the barn, or to town. She won't go to the pastureland to see the sheep. She didn't even want the lamb I gave her to replace Lammie Star." He sighed and turned back to his wife.

"She has fewer nightmares with her bed moved into our room." Jennifer rubbed her fingers on the cup stain. "But she can't sleep with us forever." She squeezed Hayden's hand. "It isn't your fault. I blame myself. I shouldn't have let her go to the Langsters'. And I blame the Langsters. They should have known better than to take her to the meadow. They should have realized it was dangerous. They may not be responsible for our losing the sheep, but they are responsible for our losing our spirited, joyful child. I don't think I can ever forgive them."

Jennifer withdrew her hand from Hayden's and brushed away tears as they rolled down her cheeks.

"They are on the losing end, too. Their county is filled with violence. I wonder how Molly is doing," Hayden answered.

"I don't care a whit about them. What are we going to do? We've talked before about going to Iowa and working with my brother and his family on their farm. He's a good man, and I'm sure he would welcome us. In time, we might be able to get our own place again," Jennifer said.

Hayden gazed at his daughter. "Might be good for Cassie. Different surroundings, cousins to play with—might help her forget her heartache." The breath pushed out from his lungs. "Write your brother." He stared down at his callused, empty hands. "I wonder if he will think I'm a failure because I can't provide for my family."

Chapter Sixteen

"Quiet down!" Judge Wimple pounded his gavel on the tabletop. "Quiet down, I say."

Fifty men in wooden chairs and another thirty men standing filled the room in the town hall. Voices stilled to whispers as they stared at the judge seated at a table on a low platform. Next to him stood Sheriff Durkson and a man dressed in a wool suit and a boiled shirt with a stiff collar and wide, starched cuffs. His leather shoes, polished to a high gloss, completed the look of an outsider.

"We need to call this meeting to order. All you sheep ranchers and cattle ranchers know why you are here; everyone who wants to be heard will have his chance later."

The audience erupted in shouts.

"We'd better be heard!"

"Washington isn't going to tell us what to do. This is cattle land!"

"My sheep can graze on federal land, and you can't stop them." Fists pounding and angry, loud voices shouting punctuated the air.

The judge rapped the gavel again. When the raucous voices subsided, he spoke. "Mr. Ireland from Washington, D.C., has been sent by President Roosevelt to look into the sheep and cattle problem. Mr. Ireland, you may address the ranchers."

"Thank you, Judge Wimple." Mr. Ireland stepped forward and ignored the protests arising from the throng. "It's true; I've been sent by our President and Mr. Pinchot, the Chief Forester in the Forest Service in the Department of Agriculture. I'm to assess the situation of cattle and sheep grazing on the federal lands in the reserves of Blue Mountain, Elk Creek and Maury Mountain Forest. The President is keenly aware of the killings of sheep, cattle, and men, and he says it has to stop, or he will send in federal troops."

The men seated in chairs stood and joined their voices with the shouts from men at the back of the room.

"No! We won't stand for it!"

"This is a local problem."

"No martial law for us. We have our rights!"

The judge pounded his gavel several times. "Let's hear him out."

"The President does not want to send in troops," Mr. Ireland clarified.

"He'd better not!" Several men yelled as they waved their fists in the air.

"I've toured all the reserved area, read all the back issues of the *Oregonian,* and I've interviewed many of you in this room. I believe we can settle this issue. Look." He picked up a rolled paper from the table and tacked it to the wall behind the platform. "This is a map of the whole area, showing the ranches and the grazing land. I've divided it up into topographic sections. I propose each rancher who has used the land before submit an application and pay a grazing fee. Each preserve will have a limit as to the number of sheep and the number of cattle allowed to graze on it. Separate areas will be designated for cattle and for sheep. A forest ranger will be in charge to make sure the rules are followed. If he finds someone's herd grazing over the allotment, he will cut back on his quota for the next year. He could impose a stipulated penalty for each head. The ranger will send back reports to Pinchot. If the reports indicate the plan is not followed, the Chief Forester can go to the President and ask for troops to enforce, investigate, and bring order."

"No! No!" Voices from the crowd sounded their protests. "You can't come in here and tell us what to do!"

The judge pounded his gavel.

Sheriff Durkson stepped forward and raised his hands to settle the crowd. "Men, listen up."

The room quieted.

Durkson lowered his arms. "We all agree we do not want federal troops."

"You're right, Sheriff. Keep talking."

"We don't want marital law and more investigations. I think we should all study this map and follow the plan."

"No one is telling me a stranger from Washington knows what will work for us," Nutter said.

"I think Mr. Ireland will listen to our suggestions and modify the plan if need be. Right, Ireland?"

"Right. Of course." He scuffed his feet and nodded his head. "I don't think this plan is perfect. We need everyone's input."

"That's more like it."

"We can take a look at it."

"We want our say."

Judge Wimple pounded the gavel again. He sighed in relief. "It's agreed. Everyone will study the map and make recommendations. Mr. Ireland, the sheriff and I'll take your suggestions and modify the plan where needed, and we can meet here again next week. If the plan meets with everyone's approval, it will be put into place." The gavel hit the table again. "The meeting is adjourned."

As ranchers gathered around the map, the sheriff and Judge Wimple stood to the side.

"I'm glad we found a way to keep the troops out. We don't want them nosing into our business," Durkson said.

"You're right. We don't want folks to know about our part in the Association," Wimple agreed, as he wiped his perspiring face and the palms of his shaking hands.

"Say, where is Henry? He should be here."

"He's in love. He is sparking a girl in Willamette County, Sarah Goodshoe."

"She's cattle-minded, I take it, and not a sheep-lover?"

"She lives in town. She's a teacher."

"Henry won't say anything, will he? He won't brag to her or speak out of turn? We don't want people knowing too much." Tom looked the judge in the eyes.

"Don't worry. Henry won't say anything. If Sarah hears something she shouldn't, he'll know and will handle it. You can trust him."

"Trusting him is one thing. A girl I ain't met is something else. You make sure Henry handles any problems that may come up."

The sheriff walked off, leaving the judge with a knot in his stomach. *What do I know about Sarah Goodshoe?*

Chapter Seventeen

Ned twisted and turned in his bed. He glanced over at Charlie's place. The bed was still made. *He must be out working in the barn.* Ned stuck his bare feet out from under the covers, pushing against the bed. He then threw back the covers and sat on the edge. He glanced at his stack of books. Usually, he loved to read, but lately it had been harder and harder to concentrate.

He stared out the window. The night was blacker than a deep hole. He shivered. He was afraid to sleep. The nightmares were worse each time they came stealing into his head. Charlie, his parents, his aunt, uncle, and cousin were all skipping in the pasture until giant sheep and cattle charged in and trampled them over and over again. Their screams were silent. Yet, they were screaming for him to help them, but he couldn't reach them, no matter how hard he strained against the invisible force that suppressed him. He wanted to tell someone about the dreams, but he was more afraid to tell about them than the nightmarish images.

I don't hear Ma or Pa. They must be in the barn, too. I'm going to get a glass of milk.

In his nightshirt and bare feet, Ned walked halfway down the stairs when his mother's voice, though soft, jarred him into stillness. He listened.

"Charlie's doing well in taking hold of his responsibilities. Ever since the shootings, he has realized this is his ranch to defend," Ruth said.

"Maybe so. But I wish he didn't seem to feel so comfortable about it. He likes going to the meetings and taking part in what we have to do," Tim responded.

"Good, I say. It's Ned who is too quiet. Since he saw the one shooting incident in the high meadow, he's avoided discussing anything about it or the sheep-shooters. He buries his head in his books. Someday, he will have this ranch with Charlie, and he needs to do his part."

"Ruth, he is still too young. I'm not sure he should have been there that day. He needs to grow up. He's just turned eleven. If we still need the association in four years, he can join us then. Let's give him more time," Tim said.

"That's where you are wrong. I agree he is too young to take part, but he should still watch, like he did in the high meadow. He needs to get used to such things and not crawl into his books. When he is fifteen, he can join us in the work we must do."

Ned didn't wait to hear his father's answer. He turned quietly and went back to bed. He shivered and drew the quilt over his head. He stifled the oncoming sobs in his pillow.

Chapter Eighteen

"Charlie, grab the toolbox. Ned, help your ma place the food at the tables Mrs. Pryon has set up in the yard, and then join us. We have a lot of work ahead to rebuild Nutter's barn. At least the sheep men who set it ablaze let the animals out."

"Yes, Pa. Are Uncle Paul and Aunt Anna coming?" Ned asked.

"Yes, they are bringing more tools and a ladder. But you can't play with Molly. You need to help us repair Mrs. Pryon's barn. Besides, Molly will be busy with the women."

Tim jumped down from the wagon and helped Ruth down. "You didn't bring a book to read, did you?"

"No, Pa." Ned hung his head. "I left them all at home, like Ma said."

"Good. You've been spending too much time with your nose in a book when you should be doing the work of menfolk."

"Yes, Pa." Ned picked up a large pan of maple-flavored cornbread and marched to the tables.

Charlie carried the tools to the barn and greeted the other ranchers gathered near it.

Ruth followed Ned and visited with the women as Tim tied the horses in the shade and proceeded to the barn.

Paul, Anna, and Molly arrived in their wagon. Paul pulled the end of a long wooden ladder from his wagon. Tim ran up and helped him carry it to the barn. Molly and Anna walked over to the women by the tables. Molly raced up to Ned.

"Hi, Ned. It'll be your birthday soon. Bet you'll be asking for some books?"

"No. Pa and Ma want me to do more ranch chores." Ned trudged to the barn.

Staring at her cousin, Molly sighed. *He never wants to talk with me. He's a black cloud of sadness.* Molly bit her lower lip.

Judge Wimple and Sheriff Durkson drove up in a wagon loaded with planks. The men unloaded the wood, and soon the noises of hammering, sawing, and men shouting to each other filled the air.

Nutter was the first rancher to stop working and look down the road. Then all the men stopped and stood silently. The women also grew quiet and stared at the rider.

The rider, in a forest ranger's uniform, stopped his horse and removed his Stetson. "Howdy, folks. Thought I would swing by and see if you need any help."

Tom Durkson walked up to the ranger, smiling. "Thanks for the offer, Ranger Luken. But we wouldn't want the sheep ranchers to think you're prejudiced for the cattle ranchers, so it's best you move on." Tom Durkson patted the horse's neck.

"Thanks for the advice, Sheriff, but I'm not worried. I helped a sheep rancher last week rebuild his brush corral after someone tore it down."

"Well, if you do find out it was deliberate, be sure to tell me. I'll arrest him; you can count on it."

"I'm sure of that." Ranger Becker stared directly into the sheriff's eyes.

"We all know you have a lot of work to do. The new quotas and fees will be set next week. I'm sure you need to assess what will be fair." The sheriff stared back at the ranger.

"My work will be completed by the meeting time of all the ranchers."

"We got it handled here, Ranger. Right kind of you to offer, though. We'll see you at the meeting." The sheriff stepped back, still smiling.

Becker also smiled, backed his mount a few steps, turned, and rode back down the street. The hooves kicked up puffs of dust. The women chattered nervously as they returned to their work. The men began hammering and sawing. Signals passed by nods and gestures amongst the Sheep-Shooters' Association members for the next meeting.

* * *

Horses grazed and rested in the shade, still saddled or harnessed to wagons. Men sat on hay bales, crates, and the edge of the hayloft. Tim, Charlie, and Ned sat on hay bales at the back. Tom Durkson and Judge Wimple stood on the buckboard bed.

"Men, listen up. I suspect someone here is responsible for the sheep rancher's corral being busted, which our esteemed forest ranger mentioned. That's okay. Things like barn burnings, sheep killings, and corrals busted are fine so long as no one is caught red-handed. The Judge and I can cover up most evidence, but we can't help you out if you are caught in the act."

The men coughed and shuffled their feet. Some voiced their opinions, saying, "Yeah, that's right, don't get caught."

"We know the risks."

"The main thing is no killing. If there is any killing, especially of the forest ranger, the federal troops will come here for sure. Harassing is fine, but no killings. You all hear me?" Tom scanned the assembly with an even, cold gaze.

"Tom, Judge, we are all doing our bit by letting the ranger and his wife know they aren't wanted. No one socializes with them. Even the townsfolk and sheep folks don't dare to be friendly with them."

"Except for Paul Langster and his family. I've seen them visit with the ranger and his missus."

Everyone focused on Tim Langster. "He is trying to reassure the government that the violence is over, and we are following the quotas. He won't ever betray us."

The men sighed in relief and nodded their heads in agreement.

"I want to remind everyone," the Judge announced, "that next week each rancher will be given the quota of cattle he can graze and told in which section of land. Be sure to pay the fee per head, so the sheep ranchers have nothing to complain about. Of course, if some cattle stray over into the sheep land, no one can fault the rancher unless the ranger finds out. Remember, he can raise your price the next year or ban your grazing rights. Disregarding quotes doesn't go through my court, so don't get caught." Judge Wimple smiled, enjoying the attention of the men's eyes on him and their ears attuned to his words. His chest swelled.

"That's it, men. If we need to meet again, I'll send out the word." Tom jumped down from the buckboard.

The sheep-shooters milled about before ambling their way to the horses and wagons.

Tom Durkson strolled over to the Langsters as they mounted their horses. "This boy sure has grown in the last three years, since he first joined that day in the high meadow." Tom put his hand on Ned's horse and patted Ned's knee. "You can be proud of both of your boys, there, Tim. You and Ruth are doing a fine job."

"Thanks, Tom. You can count on us to be at the next meeting, when it's called." Tim, Charlie, and Ned neck reined their horses to take the road in single file.

Charlie rode up next to his father. "Pa, do you think we will be riding again as gunnysackers soon?"

"Never know, son. We could get the word at any time."

Ned closed his eyes and bit his lower lip as he let his horse go off bit to follow those ahead of him.

* * *

"Charlie, go up and wake your brother. It's time for breakfast, and he hasn't started his chores yet." Tim put his coffee cup down on the table next to his plate of bacon, eggs, hash browns, and toast.

"He's not upstairs, Pa. He was up before me." Charlie sat down at the kitchen table.

"Is he out in the barn?"

"Nope. I was just out there. His horse is in its stall, but he ain't." Charlie reached for the plate piled high with eggs sunny-side up.

"Then where is he?" Ruth asked.

"Don't know." Charlie shoved a piece of toast in his mouth.

Tim rose up from the table. "Well, he has to be here somewhere." He went to the porch and yelled, "Ned! Ned, where are you?"

The chickens squawked, a horse nickered, birds chirped, but Ned's voice was not heard.

Ruth stepped out onto the porch. "Where can he be?"

"Charlie, get out here and help us find your brother." Tim walked to the barn while Ruth ran to the tool shed.

Moments later, Ruth returned to the porch where Charlie was holding his breakfast plate and wolfing down his food.

"Don't worry, Ma. Ned's just hiding someplace reading one of his books."

Tim jogged out of the barn with a paper in his hand. "He's gone. He left this note under the flap of his saddle cantle."

Ruth stared at it, trembling. *Pa and Ma, I must leave. I can't stand it here any longer. Don't worry about me. Your son, Ned. P.S. I do love you.* The paper shook violently in Ruth's hands as she read it over and over. It almost ripped before Tim took it from her.

"He's too young to be on his own. He's only fourteen. We have to find him. We must."

"Don't worry, Ruth. I'll go into town and check to see if anyone has seen him. Charlie, you go to the neighbors west of us. Ruth, you go to Paul's place. He must have left during the night, but he didn't take his horse, so he can't be far. We'll find him. He can't be far. I'm sure of it." Tim kept saying the words not only to reassure Ruth, but also him, as they went to the barn to saddle up.

Charlie put his plate on the porch after taking a bite of his second piece of toast.

Chapter Nineteen

"Charlie, what's taking you so long? Finish breakfast and hitch up the wagon. Your pa's train is due in this afternoon. We need to get started for the station."

"I want to finish reading the newspaper. This stuff about Mexico is interesting. Did you read it?"

"The paper is a month old. I read it, but I didn't see anything on Mexico. I'm not interested."

"Ma, this is important. A guy by the name of Francisco Madero wants to overthrow the government run by Porfirio Diaz, its president. Madero said the last election was a fraud, and he should have won."

"What do I care?"

"The German Kaiser awarded President Diaz his country's highest decoration. Teddy Roosevelt said Diaz is 'the greatest statesman now living,' and Andrew Carnegie said Diaz has 'wisdom and courage.' It's all here in the article."

"Who cares? We're in Oregon, which is a long way from Mexico."

"A revolution by this Madero might put American business interests in the silver mines, railroads, and oil at risk. It would hurt the United States."

"It might hurt the wealthy, but not us. Get the wagon hitched."

* * *

Tim Langster slumped in the passenger seat. He gazed at the buildings of San Francisco slide by as the train left the depot. He scratched at his dirty whiskers. The last of his money had bought the train ticket he clutched in his hand with the letter from Ned with the San Francisco postmark.

Dear Ma and Pa,

I'm sorry I left without saying goodbye. I can't explain why I had to leave. I don't know the reasons in a way to explain them. Please, don't worry about me. I'm doing fine. I do love you, but I can't come home. Love, Ned.

For two months, Tim had used every penny he could to buy newspaper ads in the San Francisco papers giving Ned's description and asking for information. He'd tramped to every police station, hospital, and morgue, looking for anyone who might have seen his son. He'd walked the city streets, inquiring at every store and shop that might hire a fourteen-year-old boy. He'd searched the waterfront, showing every dock worker Ned's picture. He'd stumbled over rubble left from the earthquake. He'd stalked the poor sections of town that teemed with homeless people. No one had information about Ned. He only ate to keep himself alive. His dirty clothes hung on his frame. He'd seen so many broken lives, so much crime and pain that he felt lost and spent. *I don't know what to do next. I'm afraid Ned is gone for good, likely dead. How am I going to tell Ruth?*

* * *

Ruth and Charlie stepped down from the wagon and tied the horse to the hitching post at the train depot. The station was deserted except for the ticket agent inside the building. Ruth walked over to the outside bench facing the tracks and sat down. Folding her hands in her lap, she rested her back against the wall and smiled. "Charlie, we're early. Why don't you find Mandy? I'll meet your father, and we will find you."

Charlie beamed. "I'll be at her house." He started off, and then turned to say, "Ma, Pa will find Ned next time."

Ruth smiled again at her son. "I know. Go find Mandy. I'll wait here." She watched Charlie jog down the dirt street into the main section of town. She sighed heavily and trembled.

"Ruth, I thought I saw you and Charlie. I was in the general store when you drove by. Are you waiting for Tim?" Anna asked as she stepped up on the boardwalk.

Ruth slid over on the bench. "Yes. Tim wrote in his last letter he would return today on the noon train."

"Did he find Ned?"

"No. Anna, I can't understand it. Ned got up in the middle of the night and took off on foot with one change of clothes and whatever money he had in his money can. He left a little scrap of paper saying, 'I'm sorry, but I have to go away. I love you.' He's fourteen. It doesn't make sense. Why did he have to leave?"

"I don't know, Ruth. I wish I had an answer for you."

"We've searched and searched for him. Weeks after he left, we got one letter saying he's fine and not to worry. Worry! We have been beside ourselves with fear and worry. Tim has been gone two months and hasn't found a trace of Ned. How could he do this to us?" Ruth clenched her fingers into fists and pounded her knees. She bent her head as her shoulders shook, and burst into sobs beyond her control.

Anna put her arm around her. The two women sat and rocked silently back and forth.

"Hey, Ma, guess what I did." Charlie jogged up to the women with a grin and laughing eyes. "Hello, Aunt Anna."

"Hello, Charlie. You seem happy." Anna pulled her arm away from Ruth.

Ruth sat up and dried her tears with a handkerchief. She looked at Charlie's beaming face, stood and smiled. "Charlie, you proposed to Mandy. I know you did. It's what I've wanted for years. And she must have said yes, by the grin on your face. I'm so, so happy." Ruth embraced Charlie and kissed his cheek.

"No, Ma. I didn't talk to her. She's working at the hotel and was busy. I went to the post office and then to the telegraph office." Charlie straightened his shoulders. "I'm going to fight in the Mexican Revolution. I wired the Mexican army and said I want to join in its fight to stop Madero's, revolution, and I got a telegram back within minutes saying I was to report in Mexico City. I'm going to Mexico to save the American interests."

Anna sucked in a breath and held it for a moment.

Ruth stepped back. Her hand flew to her face as her eyes opened in terror. "Our country isn't at war with Mexico."

"This is a revolution for constitutional government, and we need to protect our gold and oil interests. I have to protect what is ours, Ma. Plus, its history, and I want to be a part of it," Charlie announced.

Ruth saw the spark in his eyes as the color drained from her face. She sank down on the bench. "You could be killed."

Charlie laughed. "Don't worry. I'm a crack shot. I'll get them before they get me."

"This is a different kind of war."

Charlie sat next to his mother. "Ma, I'm going to be fine, and Ned will return home someday. I bet he ran off because he wants to see the world, like I do. Don't worry. I'll marry Mandy as soon as I come back. I bet the war will be over in a year. Pa's coming home now. You won't need me at the ranch." Charlie put his arm around his mother and cradled her head on his shoulder.

Ruth bit her lower lip and sobbed.

They heard the train whistle in the distance, wailing across the valley.

Chapter Twenty

Lying flat on his belly, Charlie dug his elbows into the dirt. He closed one eye and peered down the rifle's sight. Taking a deep breath and holding it, he waited. Sporadic clouds drifted across the full moon. Moonlight broke forth, casting shadows, accentuating the trees and huts in the rocky valley and illuminating the open areas in mellow light.

Crack! A figure caught in the light crumpled to the ground. Dogs barked; men yelled; a woman screamed.

"Gotcha." Charlie breathed, elated.

Fellow rebel Zapatistas on horses and mules dashed down the steep incline to the dark village.

"They know we're attacking. Hurry, Charlie, we can't give them time to arm themselves."

"I'm with you, Chet." Charlie swung onto his horse and trotted to the body in the dirt. He dismounted, turned the man over onto his back, and tore at his clothing, pulling off his gun belt and three ammunition bandoliers as he rifled the pockets. He pulled out three pesos and a matted, red bandana. "Dirty peon," Charlie muttered. A glint caught his eye as the moon drove away the clouds and darkness. "Holding out on me, eh?" He pulled a roping cuff from each arm. Silver pesos decorated the inside cuff edge near the leather fringe. "That's more like it." Charlie slipped them onto his wrists.

"Hey, Charlie, what did you get?" a whisper came from the depths of the shadow cast by an adobe hut.

"A gun and ammo is all." Charlie twisted the cuffs so the silver discs would not show.

"The army rode to the town square to loot the *hacienda*. Let's you and me take the outlying places. We might not find as much, but we can keep it. What they don't know we found is ours." Chet moved to a house doorway. Flattened tin served as walls and roof. He pushed the door in. He heard whimpers toward the back wall. He struck a match. The flame leapt up and exposed one room with a dirt floor. An unlit lamp on a plank table, a three-legged cot anchored to the wall, and a shelf containing odd-shaped pots and metal dishes furnished the hut. Chet lit the lantern and peered under the bed. He pulled a young Mexican girl out from her hiding place. "Charlie, look what I found. My turn to have her. I stood guard when you had the last one. This one is mine. Stand watch by the door."

"Hurry it up. We won't find much loot in here. We need to search the wealthier homes before the others get everything. She's thirteen or fourteen. She can't put up much of a fight. Don't take long." Charlie turned and closed the door. He leaned against the frame and listened to the shooting, yelling, and sounds of smashing destruction coming from the village center. The girl's crying and begging in the hut competed with the sounds of looting until her voice weakened and evaporated in the steamy night.

Moonlight illuminated Chet's face when he stepped out and joined Charlie. "She was a fresh one. I like it when they're new."

"Remember, my turn next time. Come on. We need to catch up with the army before they grab everything." Charlie and Chet led their horses into the town square.

Chapter Twenty-one

"Hey, Charlie. Charlie Langster, is that you? Haven't seen you for a month." Chet Smith finished pouring coffee into an enamel cup. He stood and walked away from the cook fire in the *hacienda's* backyard. He nodded at the scraggly, bearded man who dumped his bedroll by a back patio wall and came toward him.

"Yeah, Chet. I brought what I took from the last raid in to be divided up. The *hacienda* is getting full. The selling price will bring more ammo and decent food. Any java left? What's cooking in the pot?" Charlie slung his rifle over his shoulder and picked up a cup that had been tossed in the dirt by the fire.

"*Gallina* and *arroz*."

"I'll pass." Charlie poured the steaming liquid into the cup.

"Meet my two friends. This here is Guy Hicker, and the other is Frank Messer. Fellas, this here is Charlie Langster. We rode together last month on a raid."

Charlie nodded at the two men, turned, and went to sit in the shade cast by the veranda. He tilted his Stetson behind his head and leaned against a post, unbuttoning the top three buttons on his shirt.

Chet joined him. "I've been riding with the Zapatista, hitting villages west of Mexico City. Pickings are poor. Most towns had already been hit and burned, and the mules, horses and donkeys confiscated by other Zapatistas. Not much left."

"Same here. My band hit several towns, but the villagers have died from starvation or typhus. The silver mine and cattle ranch owners' *haciendas* are abandoned. The rich fled to the U.S., taking what they could carry with them. We found a few silver tea services, spoons, and fancy furniture. I'm betting the pickings in the entire country are poor. I'm thinking of heading back to Oregon. My folks have a cattle ranch. Life is better there." Charlie lifted the cup and took a sip. His hand shook, and the coffee sloshed out onto two open sores on his other hand. The open wounds were red and runny with pus. He wiped them on his dirt-encrusted pants.

"You got a ranch? Why did you ever come to Mexico? This is an improvement over what I had, but not for you." Chet noticed Charlie's hands, his flushed face, and the rash on his lower neck down to the chest area not covered by his shirt.

"I came when Madero called for a revolution against Diaz's government. I thought it would be exciting. I fought on Diaz's side until he ran off to live in Paris, and Madero took over. He didn't pay much to join his army. Pancho Villa and Zapata decided to oppose Madero and take the land from the rich owners. I joined the Zapatista to get what I could. Good in the first months, but now the villages are picked clean." Charlie put his cup down in the dirt. He rubbed his forehead. "I've got a headache, and I'm cold. I'm going to lie down."

Chet watched Charlie stagger to his bedroll, open it, and flop down. Chet rejoined his friends. "Fellas, how would you like to go to Oregon? Ol' Charlie has a cattle ranch. Likely, we could hire on."

The two men glanced at each other. They shrugged their shoulders. "Suits us. Not much left around here. Is Langster going?"

Chet stared at the prostrate figure. "I reckon he ain't leaving Mexico. Two, three days more, and he'll be out of his head. We'll dump him in the typhus quarantine hospital. Won't be long after that and his misery will be over, and we can head to Oregon to let his family know he succumbed to typhus in the noble cause for justice for the Mexican people."

Guy spat on the ground. "Hospital! It's a dirty shanty. I can smell the stench thirty feet from the place. No one comes out alive, that's for sure. Maybe we should try to take care of him ourselves. He might have a chance that way. And if he is grateful, he'll see that we get jobs on his ranch."

"And get typhus ourselves? Not me. We'll take him to the shack, and I'll burn his extra clothes and blankets, but we can sell his saddle, horse, and rifle in the States. I'll take his leather roping cuffs with the silver pesos." Chet smiled and refilled his cup. "I saw him take those cuffs in a raid, and he lied about it. So, it serves him right to lose them if he weren't willing to share one with me."

Chapter Twenty-two

Ned stood at the open door of the boxcar. The landscape moved past his feet at the edge of the floor. Slower and slower, the train wheels turned as the engineer pulled back on the throttle, and the engine reached the top of the incline leading into the railroad yard.

Ned picked out a spot ahead and to the side and stared at it. As he neared the mark, he crouched. When the grass, gravel, and packed earth were just ahead, he leapt, pushing his legs against the flooring to send his body away from the tracks and onto the little patch of green.

Hitting the earth and rolling once, he sat up and looked around to see if he had been observed. He stood and brushed off his worn jeans, shirt, and ragged jacket. Blowing on his hands to warm them in the cold air, he set out toward the nearest road.

Twenty minutes later, he walked down the main street of Duluth, Minnesota. His hands jammed into his pockets, he looked in the store windows for a "help wanted" sign. He spotted a bookstore and stared in the window at rows and rows of books. There wasn't a "help wanted" sign, but he lingered in front of the window, wishing he had money to spend.

A little bell rang as a man opened the door and stepped out to the sidewalk. "Hey, kid, do you want to make five dollars?"

"Yes, sir."

"Do you know where DuPont Street is, up on the hill?"

"Ah, sure I do." *I can find it for five dollars.*

"My name is Charles Burt. I own this bookshop. A customer ordered books he wants today. I need someone to deliver them."

"I can do that, Mr. Burt."

"Kid, these are valuable." Charles Burt eyed the boy's tattered clothes. "I'll pay you the five after if you come back and I call the house, and the butler tells me they arrived. If you don't come back, and the books aren't delivered, I'll call the police on you."

"Sir, I'm not a thief."

"I'll have to take a chance with you, I guess. I can't leave my shop, and I don't want to lose a good customer. What's your name, kid?"

The question took Ned by surprise. No one had asked his name for months. He glanced into the shop window. A stack of Dickens books caught his eye. "Twain, sir. Oliver Twain."

"Well, Oliver, I'll take a chance on you, and if it turns out okay, I'll hire you for odd jobs and as a sweeper. Deal?" Charles held out his hand.

Ned took his hand, and they shook on the deal.

Chapter Twenty-three

"Mr. Luken, Aaron Luken, you're just the man I want to see. Come into my office."

"Yes, sir, Mr. Houston." Shuffling papers to put them into his left hand, Aaron shook the Secretary of Agriculture's hand and followed him past a row of clerks and secretaries into a small, wood-paneled room.

"Sit down, Luken." Houston sat in his desk chair. "What job are you working on?"

"I've finished this report," Aaron indicated the papers in his hands, "on the Hudson River. It took three years, but I think the problems are in hand now."

"Good. I want to talk to you concerning a new assignment, and it's not an easy one. We have had several forest service agents in Oregon managing the forests and grasslands. The inhabitants are not friendly, neither are they open to the quotas the agents set for cattle and sheep grazing. Everyone I've sent has wanted to transfer in two or three years. I can't blame them. It's a stressful job, but I need a forester who can stay there for the long term. One who is patient, a listener and not a talker. One who keeps his temper and tries to find solutions by working with folks and not imposing his ideas on them. Also, a person who is not intimidated easily and doesn't mind working in the field. Have you had much experience in living off the land and not seeing another soul for days?"

"No, sir, but I knew that was a possibility when I joined the agency. Truth is I enjoy being on my own, away from folks. I've been waiting for a chance like this."

"You're not married, are you? One reason the forest agents want a transfer is their wives get fed up with the people. They're shunned by most folks."

"No, sir, I'm not married. It's obvious I'm not a handsome catch fit for a pretty young woman." Aaron smiled.

The Secretary hesitated and looked away. "Ahem, right. You're the man. Read the back files to find out what you're getting into. Bad things have happened there. File a report every month. I want to keep on top of the situation. Let me know if you need help."

The Secretary shook hands with Aaron and watched him leave. He sat down and stared at the door. *I've heard the snide remarks and jokes concerning his appearance. He's had it tough all his life, I'll warrant. I hope I haven't made his life worse.*

* * *

"Miss Molly, hold up a minute. I'd like to talk with you."

Molly turned and waited. Delvin Pryon shook hands with Pastor Gilbertson and worked his way through the crowd exiting the church.

Paul and Anna stopped next to Molly. Anna smiled and winked at Paul. "We'll wait at the wagon, Molly. Take your time."

Molly smiled at her parents and turned back to greet Delvin.

"How are you and your folks, Molly?" asked Delvin. He removed his hat.

"We're well, and you and your mother?" Molly glanced at Mrs. Pryon, who was visiting with friends.

"Fine. Ma enjoys owning the boardinghouse. She likes cooking and visiting with the people there. I'm learning blacksmithing and machine repair. I think automobiles are the future. I can fix the Model T Fords as well as shoe the horses. Repairing machines will make a tidy business."

"Do you miss the ranch?"

"I do like cattle ranching, and I could go back to it in a heartbeat. I'm looking for a good ranch to manage." He faced the wagons and people mingling in the pasture behind the church.

Molly saw his eyes drift toward her parents and wondered if he pictured their ranch.

"It was good that the judge and the sheriff bought your parents' ranch after your father died," she said.

"Yes, it was. Ma does like town life better than ranch living. I was able to get to school regular, too, all the way through tenth grade." He turned his head. "I see the new forester coming down the church steps."

"I wouldn't say he is new. He has worked in the Cascade valleys for two years now. He's been to our place for supper every month."

"I hear he goes to the sheep ranchers and visits with them," Delvin said.

"I don't think he wants to show partiality. He is fair-minded."

"A fella from Pittsburgh can't know what cattle ranching is about. Setting quotas on the cattle ranchers determined by a government city guy ain't right, and he looks a fool to boot. He should make the sheep ranchers pack up and leave."

Molly noted the contempt in his voice. "He didn't set up the system. Washington did. He's doing a difficult job as best he can, I'm sure." Molly felt a tight uneasiness growing within her. "My parents are waiting. Why did you stop me?"

Delvin spun his Stetson in his hands. "I wanted to ask if you and your folks were coming to the church social. I'd like to bid on your picnic basket, and we could visit." Delvin glanced down at his boot toe as he dragged it in the dirt. "You're the prettiest girl I've ever seen, and the sweetest." He fumbled with his hat.

Molly's eyes twinkled. "Cally Olson and Sue and Ellen Mae Parker are fine young ladies. Mandy Clayton is still single and would be a fine catch."

"Aw, they don't hold a candle to you."

Molly watched the blush creep over his face. "Thank you for asking, Delvin. It's sweet, but Ma and I plan to have one basket, and Pa will bid on it. I'm sorry."

Delvin's face turned crimson. "Another time." He stumbled back, turned, and walked away.

Molly went over to the wagon and climbed onto the seat in the back.

"What did Delvin want, dear?"

"To talk. Nothing special."

"Brad Simons has ridden from his folks' place to visit several times, and Delvin wants to talk with you when we are in town. And the new fella, Chet Smith, has stopped by the ranch many times. I think the young men are buzzing like bees around you."

Molly heard the teasing in her mother's voice. "I wish they wouldn't."

"Why not?" Paul interjected. "They are substantial men. They would be good husbands, and you're twenty-five. Most girls are married by this time." He jiggled the reins. Snooker trotted for a few steps, and then went back into a steady walk. "Your ma and I would like to see you settled, and we would like grandchildren. You'll inherit the ranch one day. You'll need help to run it and keep it."

Hearing the sternness in her father's voice, Molly closed her eyes. Her shoulders trembled as a heavy feeling settled on her. "The local boys don't interest me. Never have."

"Chet Smith is new to the area. He's got a job on the old Durkson ranch. It sure helped when he mentioned he fought with your cousin Charlie in the Mexican Revolution and even brought word of Charlie's death from typhus. He said he thought more people died from the disease than from the fighting. It's a shame," Anna said. "He seems nice enough; perhaps a bit rough, but very polite. And his two friends, Guy Hicker and Frank Messer, are a bit quieter but seem respectable. And they were all friends of Charlie's."

Molly rubbed each gloved finger. *But those men are tied to killings, whether here or in Mexico.* She took a deep breath and opened her eyes. *I know Ma and Pa worry what will happen to me when they are gone. Most women my age are married and have children, but I can't follow the pattern set out for me. I love the ranch, but the thought of living in the same way as others is exhausting. I lost too much in the high meadow.*

They rode in silence until they reached the ranch.

"Molly, help me fix supper. Your pa and I invited the forest agent to sup with us. He said he had questions concerning the watershed in the lower valley. Go get Jenny. She isn't laying eggs. We'll have her for dinner. Change into your old clothes. You can put your Sunday clothes back on before dinner." Anna climbed down from the wagon seat and headed for the house.

Molly glared at the bloody tree stump with the protruding ax. A feather from the previous dead hen stood straight, cemented by blood in a gash in the wood. Molly stepped down from the wagon. "Yes, Ma."

Chapter Twenty-four

"Thank you, Mrs. Langster, for another excellent dinner. I can't thank you folks enough for the help you have given me these past two years." Aaron Luken put down his coffee cup.

"My pleasure, Aaron. We enjoy your company. And call me Anna."

"Yes, Aaron. Anna and I want to offer all the help we can. You're doing an important job. I hope you don't get called up for service, now that our country is in this world war with Germany. You're doing a good job here." Paul reached out his hand to Aaron.

Shaking hands, Aaron said, "No fear there. I'm exempt. Thank you again, folks. I'd better go out and saddle Sparrow. It's a long ride back to town."

"I'll come out to the barn and bed down the stock." Molly got up from the table.

"Good night, folks." Aaron took his hat from the stand and held the door open for Molly.

In the barn, she lit a kerosene lantern. "I'll tend to the stock while you saddle up." She pitched fresh hay into a stall.

Aaron led Sparrow from a stall and tied him to a post. He put on the bridle and then smoothed on a saddle blanket. Lifting the saddle, he placed it behind the withers, then reached under the horse and grabbed the cinch. Standing up, he lifted the stirrup leather and fidgeted with the cinch buckle. "Molly, will you marry me?" He froze as he waited for her reply.

Molly straightened up. She stared at the dark shadows on the wall. "Why do you want to marry me?"

"I want to make a life here and do my job. I need to marry a local woman to get people to recognize I'm here for the long haul, not like the previous foresters. Such a marriage would help me with acceptance. I've talked with your parents and visited in your home. They're good people, and so are you. Everyone I've met in the Cascades has a high regard for you and your parents—sheep men and cattle men alike."

Molly turned and looked at Aaron's face in the flickering lantern light. She saw his thin arms and bony hands make jerky movements as he fiddled with the bridle and cinch.

She walked up to him, taking the cinch from his hand. "Yes, I'll marry you."

"I should tell you I might not be able to give you children." He tugged on the saddle in embarrassment. "I had scarlet fever as a boy. My facial features were affected. My mouth will always be crooked. I developed a twitch, which flares up at times. Lost my hair, even the eyelashes, and most of it never grew back, as you can tell. Folks said I might not be able to father children."

"When I was a little girl, my friend Cassie and I had definite plans about our children growing up and perhaps marrying, but that won't happen now. I guess if we don't, we don't," Molly stated.

"We would need to live in town. I don't want people to think I'm taking sides with the cattle ranchers by living out here. Are you still interested?"

"I am. You can pick the day. I want it to be held in the church in town, with my ma and pa there. I'll wear my Sunday dress."

"Why are you agreeing to this? We haven't courted." Aaron stepped back from his horse as Molly finished tightening the cinch.

She heard the tension mixed with wonderment in his voice. "I want to marry an outsider. All the marriageable men here are connected in some way to the bad days. They have a cousin, an uncle, a father involved in the war. You're doing your best to keep the peace between the two sides. You're fair, honest, and committed." Molly pulled the stirrup down and patted the horse's neck. "I love the ranch, but I'm ready to put it behind me."

Aaron took a step forward. "I'm bone-thin, bald, and twitchy. Can you put up with my looks?"

Molly turned from the horse to face Aaron. She smiled. "I see the good looks on the inside, and besides, you will have to put up with my short, fat feet."

Aaron burst out into a robust laugh. "I'll talk to the pastor after service this Sunday. We will have the ceremony after service the following Sunday."

Molly went to the barn door and picked up the lantern. "Okay."

Aaron led Sparrow out of the barn and mounted. He rode up to the top of the dirt drive leading to the road, stopped and gazed back. He watched Molly carry the lantern to the ranch house and extinguish the light. Her silhouette seemed to open the screen and front door as a flood of light came out onto the porch and captured her form. She stepped in and closed the doors. The light in the parlor shone out the window. He turned Sparrow toward town.

* * *

Molly entered the kitchen. "Aaron proposed, and I accepted."

"What?" Paul and Anna spoke at once. They stared at Molly and then at each other.

"What do you mean, dear?" Anna sat down on the kitchen chair, clutching a dishtowel.

"We're planning to get married right after church service, a week from this Sunday."

"Molly, you can't be serious. He hasn't courted you. He never said anything to us. How could this happen?" Paul set the

107

dirty dishes down by the washbasin in the sink. He stared at his daughter.

"It happened, that's all." Molly sat down. "We might not be able to have children as he was sick as a boy. I hope you don't mind if I don't give you grandchildren."

"Molly, why would you agree to such an idea? This is astounding. You don't know him well. You haven't dated. Your pa and I courted for two years before we married. We were certain we were right for each other. How can you say yes to a marriage with Aaron?"

"Ma, I can't explain it. We haven't gone out for Sunday walks after church, pie socials, barn raisings, picnics, and such. I think the main reason is he has no ties to the sheep-shooters. I've listened to what he's said when he's come here for dinners to talk about his job. I've watched the way he treats people. He is kind, considerate, intelligent, and committed. I feel safe. What more could I want?"

"Don't you want children?"

"I did at one time. When I was a child, I assumed I would have them. But now I don't think I need to have any to be happy in a marriage with Aaron. He'll make a good husband, and if he doesn't become a father, he doesn't. I hope you can accept this."

Paul glared at his daughter. "Molly, you need more time to think this through. It doesn't make sense to marry someone you don't know well. You've got to consider the future here at the ranch. Do you love him?" Paul picked up a spoon from the table and threw it into the sink. They heard a glass break.

"I don't know. Maybe. Anyway, I've made up my mind, and I promised Aaron. I will move into town right after we are married. This is what I want, and I hope you can agree to it."

Sounds of crickets accentuated the silence in the kitchen. Paul sighed as he walked over to Molly and hugged her. "I guess we have to accept it, as I see you have made up your mind."

Anna hugged Molly and dried the tears on her face with her apron. "We should let your aunt and uncle know as soon as possible. They will want to be at the wedding."

"You can invite them if you want. I don't care. I'll do the dishes, and you two can go out on the porch swing and contemplate your new son-in-law." Molly took the dishtowel from her mother and shooed them toward the kitchen door.

"Molly, have you thought about how people will react toward you when you marry an outsider, and a forest service man to boot? Many folks don't accept him."

"I don't care. He likely will have more trouble than I will, because he is marrying a cattle rancher's daughter. People might fear he will favor putting more cattle on the range. That's why it's important for me to move into town with him. I'll come out for visits, of course, and you two can visit us in town. My moving away had to happen someday." Molly busied herself with the dishes to hide the tears dropping into the dishwater.

Paul and Anna opened the screen door and closed it softly behind them. Molly listened to the porch swing squeak as they sat in the night. She listened as Anna sobbed in Paul's arms.

"I thought she would marry Delvin Pryon. He has stopped by several times. I know it was to see Molly. He's learning a good trade at the blacksmith's. They could have a fine life together. He knows ranching, too. He could help Molly run this place when we are gone. I never considered Aaron Luken," Anna said.

Paul's voice choked as he comforted her, saying, "It's for the best. Everything will turn out okay. She has made up her mind. We can't tell her how to live her life."

Chapter Twenty-five

"Hey, Sheriff! What brings you up here? Life too quiet in town?" The cowhand said this with a low chuckle as Durkson rode up.

He reined in his horse and threw a leg over the saddle horn to sit with ease. A strong wind gust blew his Stetson off; the hat hung by the leather string around his neck. "Still got plenty to do in town, Guy. I'm working on Judge Wimple's re-election. But I wanted to check on the mixing of my new herd with the main band. I can run this larger herd, since Judge Wimple and I bought the widow Pryon's ranch years ago and split it between us. How's the new herd mixing in with the main bunch?"

"They're fine. Not used to the wind blowing through the high pasture canyons, but they'll settle into it in a week or two."

"Yeah, helps to mix the cattle from the older herd with the new. The allotment for the sheep got lowered way down from what the beginning quotas were, which has helped us cattlemen have a chance to increase our herds. The Washington fella, Ireland, got the numbers to a level for us to make a living." The sheriff sighed and wiped his forehead with a bandana. He continued talking as another cowhand, Chet Smith, rode up. "That new forester Luken seems okay, but he favors the sheep men too much, as I see it. He shouldn't allow sheep anywhere in the Prineville area."

"He will come around to our way of thinking. He married a cattle rancher's daughter, which shows he has some sense. Sure don't understand why a good-lookin' gal like her got hitched to such an ugly dude," Chet said as he fiddled with his roping cuffs, making the silver pesos glint in the sunlight.

The sheriff's buckskin shifted his hindquarters and bumped against Guy's horse. The horses pawed the ground and tossed their heads. Guy backed away his bay and rubbed its neck.

"Easy, Jingo. I hear the sheep, too," Durkson said as he patted his horse and shifted his leg back over the saddle.

"Ain't sheep, Sheriff. It's the wind. Takes animals time to get used to the strong gusts that come roaring down from the mountains. I rode up the canyon a half-hour ago. There ain't any sheep. The quota doesn't allow them up there this time of the year." Guy's horse lowered its head and stood quietly next to Chet's.

"Jingo and I know sheep when we hear it. A huge flock, I tell ya. Someone is breaking the quota. If you can't hear them, you're deaf."

Jingo suddenly pranced in a circle. Durkson put his foot into the stirrup, leaned forward, and set his heels straight downward. Jingo's leg muscles quivered, and he snorted as the sheriff got him on the bit.

Guy tightened up the reins. "Hey! The herd. Something's spooking them. Watch out. They're goin' ta run!"

The cattle bellowed and tossed their heads. As they milled about, another wind gust blew across the tall grass. The lead steer ran. The herd bolted. Thundering and bellowing, with the wind blowing the echoes across the land, they ran and collided in a wild mêlée across the pasture.

The cowhands stationed around the herd, with Chet, Guy, and Sheriff Durkson, galloped forward. They yelled and whistled, but their voices were lost in the thundering hooves and bellows. Waving their hats in the air, they edged their mounts to the outside of the seething mass. Shoved and gored by the cattle as they bumped against them, the racing horses fought the bits and tossed their heads in panic.

"Turn the herd! Turn the herd! They're heading for the cliffs. I can't lose them. Stop them!" Durkson yelled. The wind picked up his voice and blew away the sound. He rode Jingo closer into the cattle. The horse galloped, struggling to keep his feet under him without being shoved off balance by the steers. The sheriff threw his weight to the side near the cattle as he waved his hat close to their heads. Hit by a cow's flank and horns, Jingo shied over in the opposite direction. Durkson grabbed the saddle horn with his free hand and felt his leg slip under the horse's belly. Eye level to the cattle hooves, he lost hold of the horn and, screaming in terror, fell under the thundering herd.

Jingo raced on with the cattle, rider-less. Veering away from the terror, he stopped in an outcropping of rocks. With heaving sides, sucking in air, he trembled and tossed his head.

The cowhands turned the lead steer before it reached the precipice, and the herd turned. Within moments, the stampede was over. The cattle milled in a circle. Dust choked the air.

Guy galloped over to Jingo. Grabbing his reins, he led him back to a ragged mass on the ground. He grimaced as he squinted at twisted, disjointed flesh, protruding bones, and blood. The head was no longer recognizable. The white streak prominent in his hair was red and plastered to the skull.

Jingo snorted, tossed his head, and pulled back on the reins. Guy fought to control him.

Chet reined up. "Man, I've never seen anyone trampled."

"Hold Jingo." Guy dismounted and threw a blanket over the body. Turning aside, he vomited. "You see any other parts put your blanket over 'em. I'm going to town to get the undertaker. He can touch this stuff and put it into a coffin. I sure can't." He mounted and rode off before Chet could object.

Frank Messer trotted up. "The herd's settled. That the boss?" He nodded toward the blanket.

"Yep, what's left," said Chet. "I wonder why he heard sheep bleating. Ain't any up here. Sure is strange."

* * *

"Aaron, please, listen to me," Molly said.

"I make enough money. We cover our expenses. I don't want my wife working. I've been raised to believe the husband supports his family. The woman's place is in the home."

"It's one room in Mrs. Pryon's boarding house. How is it a home? I have nothing to do all day except help Mrs. Pryon with the meals for cheaper rent. Mr. Hasty wants me to work in the store until his wife is better."

"Most people with heart problems don't go back to work. The job could become permanent."

"I can buy things we need at cost, and he'll pay me a small salary besides. We can save what I make, and we can buy Mr. Auldrich's house on the hill by the church. With him gone it's for sale."

"We don't need a big house."

"You could use the sitting room as an office, and we could let out the extra bedroom to another forester when you get the help you requested. We would have the barn on the property, and you wouldn't need to pay the livery expenses for your horse. And there would be room for a cow for our milk and butter. Plus, I could maintain the cemetery and the church for our tithe, like Mr. Auldrich did." Molly stood before her husband with her hands on her hips. "Aaron, I want to do this."

"What would we do with the house after you inherit your folks' ranch? They're in good health, but one day you will own their place and your uncle's, providing Ned isn't found."

Molly turned and sat down on the unmade bed. She fiddled with the pillowcase. "Is that why you married me? To get the ranch?"

"No, of course not. I never wanted to be a rancher. People already think I'm biased by marrying a cattleman's daughter. I would have to quit my job as a forest ranger to manage it. Or I would have to transfer to another area."

"I don't want the ranch. Once, I couldn't imagine living anyplace else." She sighed. "Would you be disappointed if I didn't keep the ranch?" Molly's hands shook.

Aaron sat next to her. "Would you sell the property? Your parents might not like the idea."

Molly scanned Aaron's face. "Would you mind," Molly lowered her eyes and now fiddled with the bedspread fringe, "if I donated it to the park reserves? The forest service could oversee the place. It would mean more grazing land for the local ranches." Her voice trailed off to a whisper.

"Whoo-ee. You sure you want to give up a fortune?"

"Yes." Molly tried to read Aaron's face. "Would you mind?"

"Let's not make a decision until we need to." Aaron stood. "But we still don't need a house. This is fine."

"Fine? Look at it. Papers heaped on the chiffonier and nightstand. Crates of books and papers stacked against the wall. The only chair in the room is buried under junk, so you can't even tell it's a chair. You have to sit on the bed with a book as a desktop to sign papers." Despite her efforts, tears pooled in her eyes. "I can't stand this mess. I need to get away from it and do something, something that will help people."

Molly watched Aaron study the place. She was sure he was seeing the clutter for the first time from her perspective. He stood and went toward the door. "I could use the office space." He opened the door and stepped out. "I'm going to buy a newspaper to read. I want to find out what President Wilson says about the war. I sure hope he gets that League of Nations started, so this will be the first and last world war. I'll be out on the range for six or seven days. Do what you want about the job."

Molly thought Aaron's voice sounded hard. "I'll start working at the store today." She stood and smiled. "Aaron, please be careful. I feel harsh feelings are right below the surface with the quotas you put in place last month to raise the sheep allotment. And we don't know how the new sheriff feels about the cattle and sheep problem."

"The idea of quotas has been in place for years, since Teddy Roosevelt's time. People are used to it. You're a worrier. I'll be fine." He started down the hallway.

Molly ran to him and put her arms around his neck. "I may be a worrier, but I know these people better than you do. The quota numbers change with the year and the spring grass growth. Several cattlemen encourage their hands to harass the sheep ranchers. The sheep men aren't blameless, either. Tensions could escalate. Please, be careful."

"Okay, my worrier." He kissed her on the cheek.

Molly saw the smile in his eyes. She stepped back into the room and watched from the window as he went down the street to the livery barn while dodging two Model T Ford cars, where drivers honked at each other in greeting. When she couldn't see him anymore, she finished making the bed. She sat down and gazed out the window. *Maybe I should tell now. There are still sheep corrals destroyed, barns burned, cattle poisoned, and sheep killed. No people, thankfully. But who would I tell? Aaron? What would he think of me for keeping such a secret for so long? The new sheriff? Does he stand for justice, or has he taken sides? Am I responsible for the hurt people experience because I've kept my promise? Am I guilty? Lord, I don't know what to do, but please take care of Aaron. These arrogant people have robbed me of so much. Please, don't let them make me a widow."* She brushed her hand across the quilt on Aaron's side and smoothed out the last wrinkle.

* * *

Judge Wimple sat at his kitchen table. The newspaper in his hands quivered. He read the headlines, "Jason Gray Elected as Crook County Judge." He sighed as he read further, "Jason Gray ran on a platform of bringing justice to Crook County and being impartial in cases between sheep men and cattlemen. He also promised to work with the new sheriff, Bradden, to bring justice to any unsolved cases if they gathered enough evidence. Many supporters backing Judge Wimple changed their vote to Judge Gray after Tom Durkson's tragic death. Sheriff Durkson was a leading county citizen and influential in local politics. He was Judge Wimple's most staunch supporter. After eighteen years in office, Judge Wimple lost the election to Jason Gray in an historic landslide."

The judge put down the two-week-old paper. He couldn't muster enough energy to go out to buy another. He ran his thin fingers through his hair and rubbed his sunken eyes. When the sheriff had died, he'd sensed everything was over; everything he'd worked so hard for was slipping away. Sleep had become a stranger to him. He pushed his chair back from the table, pulled off his glasses, and laid them on the newspaper. With that, he stood and looked in the mirror by the door. A gaunt, gray face stared back at him. He shook his head and then picked up a family picture. His voice broke the empty silence in the room as he talked out loud. "I'm glad you went to visit your sister in Idaho, Elsbith. Better you're not here. Henry will look after you." The judge sighed. "Everything could come out about my role in the Sheep-Shooters massacre without Tom's influence. I can't face it. When I lost Tom, I lost my political clout. No one thinks I'm important. Folks probably would turn their backs on me." He stared at his image in the mirror. "I can't run a cattle ranch. Tom ran my herd with his. I don't know about anything but being a judge." He put down the picture and with his finger traced his wife's face. He smiled at his son's image, and a tear formed in his eye. "Henry, you'll run the ranch. You learn fast, and you worked with Tom at his place. You might end up with his share of the business, too. No one is likely to connect you to the Sheep-Shooters. I was afraid the girl you were dating was nosing around too much, but she's gone. You saw to that." He turned and looked at the house he had allowed to become dirty and unkempt. "Elsbith, you were proud of this house. The finest in the county. Sorry, dear. I haven't got the energy to look after it. I haven't been able to feed the horse for three days. I'm sorry about a lot of things."

Plodding out the back door, he went into the barn and led his horse out into a pasture. Reentering the barn, he took a rope and threw it up toward the rafters. It missed and fell to the floor. He coiled it and crouched. Jumping up, he heaved the loose end upward. It went over the rafter's main beam and hung halfway down. He dragged and piled two crates under the dangling rope. His hands fumbled as he tied the stiff, coiled end to a barn stall post. He then climbed up the boxes, made a noose, slipped it over his head and, without hesitation, kicked. The crates crashed to the floor. The birds in the rafters fluttered and flew out in a panic. The rope jerked and tightened. The hemp squeezed and pinched his neck. His eyes bulging, his feet kicking, and his hands clawing, he fought frantically for something, anything, to support his body. Wheezing filled the silence in the barn. Minutes later, his long, thin frame went limp. The wheezing stopped, but a stench filled the barn as the body lost control and defecated, and urine puddled on the floor.

Chapter Twenty-six

Aaron's skeletal frame sat straight in the saddle. He focused on the black smoke billowing in the distance. He tapped his heels against his horse's sides and slapped the reins. Sparrow stepped forward, bunching its muscles to run. Aaron noticed three riders lope toward him. With one hand he jerked short the bay's reins, and his other hand rested on his rifle in its scabbed. The horse stopped.

The men halted next to Aaron. The shortest man took off his Stetson and using a bandana, wiped his forehead. The silver pesos embedded in his worn leather roping cuffs on his arm glinted in the sunlight.

"Chet, Guy, Frank, your boss, Henry Wimple, doesn't have cattle in this area, does he?"

"You know he don't, Luken. Wimple thought there might be some strays in this area. He said to get them out before you found them and got steamed," Chet said.

"You don't need to worry on a few strays. But large herds do need to be kept in their places. Have you been over to Simons's sheep corrals? Appears there's a fire over there?"

"Fire? We ain't seen any fire." The three cowboys turned in their saddles and peered back in the direction from which they had ridden. "By golly, you're right. Plenty of black smoke. Funny, we didn't see it. Must have happened after we left," Chet said.

"I suggest we ride back and check on it. We can offer help."

"Why sure, Luken. We want to help," Frank said.

The men turned their horses, and the four rode toward the smoke blackening the horizon. The three men kept their horses at an easy lope as Aaron urged his horse on to a gallop. He reached the fire several minutes before the other three.

"Chuck, what caused this?" Aaron had dismounted before Sparrow stopped. Running to the blazing sheep corral, he joined Chuck grasping burning brush piled against the fence.

Chuck Simons, black smoke smudges covering his face and clothes, yanked the flaming brambles away from the corral.

"I know who caused it. Cattlemen! I can't prove it—I rode up after it was going good. I got most of the sheep out at the other end, where the fire wasn't as bad. Not all, though. I lost twenty head, I figure." The two men pulled and tore at the burning wood and brush piled against the fence. Aaron dropped a charred board and sucked in his breath.

"You hurt?" Simons asked.

"Not bad."

Chet, Guy, and Frank trotted up. They sat on their horses, gazing at the blaze.

"Do you men know anything about this?" Aaron asked. He turned to face the riders as he put his burned hand behind his back.

"Nope. Sure don't. Likely lightning struck it."

"Lightning! There's not a cloud in the sky," Chuck said.

"I think it was man-made lightning," Aaron said, staring at the three cowboys.

"Well, strange things happen on the range. Life is uncertain out here." The men stared down at Aaron and Chuck. "No use trying to save the corral; too far gone. Might get burned yourself," Chet said.

"Yeah, we can't do anything here. Let's go," Guy said. The three turned their horses and trotted off.

"They're right. We can't save the corral," Chuck said as he stepped back from the fire. "I'm going to help my boy, Brad, see to the sheep we saved."

"I'm sorry, Simons. I'll report this to the sheriff, and I'll tell him I saw those three riding in the area." Aaron stared at the disappearing cowhands. "Might be he can find out who did this. Glad it's not like the old days. With proof, we can get a conviction now."

Chuck Simons surveyed the remnants of his hard work lying in charred disarray on the ground and the smoldering sheep bodies. The smell was sickening. Sparrow pranced and pawed.

"Yeah, better than the old days. You and me, we'd be dead with bullet holes in us, and an inquest would label it an accident or a double suicide."

Aaron snorted. "You're right. Take care."

"We'll keep an eye peeled for any strays that might bring those three back here."

"Good idea." Aaron mounted Sparrow and put him into a lope.

"You keep an eye peeled, too," Chuck Simons shouted at Aaron's back.

* * *

Aaron, studying his blistered hand, headed home. Each jarring hoof beat added to the throbbing. He held his hand up and away from his body to lessen the pain. He dreaded the next four hours before he would reach Prineville.

Hearing hoof beats behind him, he halted Sparrow and wheeled to face the approaching riders. Chet still led the pack. Aaron moved his hand closer to his gun butt, but he knew he wouldn't be able to pull the gun from its holster. He couldn't close his fingers.

"Hold up, Mr. Forest Service man. We're thinking you insinuated we set the fire. We don't like that kind of talk. We figured we'd better give you more time to think it over before you get to town. We decided you should walk the rest of the way, so you might think better of your intentions. Hand over your gun." Chet and his friends pulled their pistols from their holsters. The men surrounded Aaron. Chet grinned and reached out his hand to take Aaron's gun.

Sitting for a moment and scrutinizing the riders, he knew the men could see his injured hand. Breathing in slowly, he dismounted. "You fellows should reconsider this idea." He handed the reins and his gun to Chet. Aaron's left hand brushed against the roping cuff on Chet's arm. A silver peso mounted in the cuff came off and fell into Aaron's palm. The moment he felt it, he closed his fist, pulled his arm back, and cradled his right hand in his left, hiding the peso.

"It ain't us who needs to rethink. You'll find your horse tied up near town. Have a good walk."

The men rode off, leading Sparrow.

Aaron moved his arm away from his side and held it up. He pocketed the peso and began the long trek to town.

Chapter Twenty-seven

Tim put down the empty coffee cup and pushed away his breakfast plate with eggs and half a piece of toast. He stared at the cup.

"What are you doing today?" Ruth glanced at her husband and the food he'd left on the plate. *Why doesn't he enjoy my cooking anymore? Doesn't matter what I make. He barely eats enough to keep meat on his bones.*

"After the chores, I'm going to work on the barn roof."

"Let the ranch hands do it. You're getting too old for that work."

"I'm not asking anyone to do what I can do. This is my ranch, and I fought for it. Don't you forget it." He banged his fist on the table, and the cup tipped over.

"I'm not likely to. I fought right along with you. Don't you forget it!"

"I know!" he yelled. "I know," he whispered.

"You didn't sleep well last night. Why don't we talk about your nightmares? They'll go away if you talk about them."

"You've been saying that for years, and my answer is always the same. No! I'm not going to speak of them. Leave me be."

"You can't be worried about secrets from the past being told. When Creed Connelly's body was found, the cattlemen on the jury ruled it a suicide. Folks are on our side." Ruth poured coffee into Tim's cup. "We haven't had any trouble around here for years, not since 1906 when Teddy Roosevelt sent his men from the Forest Service. Why, we've even got a forest ranger in the family, with Molly's marriage. She's a smart one; she is. Cattlemen don't need to worry about quotas or people finding out what they shouldn't." Ruth put down the coffee pot. "He's been doing a fair enough job."

"And who do we have to thank for the Forest Service being in charge? My brother Paul and his family. They got people organized to bring in the government, looking into things and coming up with that land management deal. I think he was the one who wrote the letter to the *Oregonian* pretending to be the Sheep-Shooters' Association's Corresponding Secretary. That's what stopped the killings."

"Can't be. He wasn't an Association member."

"No, but likely the writer wasn't, either. The way he bragged on the killings and how more would be killed in the future got the people on the other side of the Cascades all fired up."

"Yeah, but would those good people come together and force the government to get involved, if it weren't for the sheep-shooters? It was the killings that brought the situation to a head and put the wheels in motion. Killing sheep and a few herders was a good move."

He stared at his wife. "I wish you didn't believe what you said, but you do, don't you?"

"I do, and it sure doesn't keep me awake at night."

He sighed. "You lose plenty of sleep. I hear you pacing the floor."

"Not because of any wooly-back killing. I want my boy back." Ruth's voice showed her tension. "It's not right he's buried in Mexico." Ruth pumped water into the basin and threw in the cast-iron skillet.

"He isn't coming back. Thousands of typhus victims are buried in Mexico. They can't ship the bodies home."

"He should have stayed and married that sweet Mandy. He fought for this ranch. America wasn't in the war when he went to Mexico to fight those heathens. They live in filth, and that's why he got sick. Typhus is from the fleas on rats. He ought to be buried here."

"Yes, he fought for this ranch and liked the fighting and killing so much he headed to Mexico to join an army the moment he could. He didn't believe in their cause. I shouldn't have pushed him into the Association. I'll regret what I did to him and Ned to my dying day."

"Ned will be back. I know it. He's going to wake up to what's right and come back to this ranch and us."

"He ran away from us and the ranch. His spirit left us the day he sat on his horse on the rise and saw the killing. His body hung around, just pretending to be here."

"What did you say? Don't mumble." Ruth pumped more water into the basin.

"I said he left when he was fourteen, before Charlie left for the army. He probably doesn't know Charlie is dead."

"He sent us that one letter. Which reminds me to add three-cent stamps to the shopping list."

"Could hardly call it a letter. No return address."

"Shows he loves us."

"That was years ago. I'm not waiting around for him to come and fix the barn roof. I'm going out to do it." He rose from the table. "I want to get the chores done so I can listen to President Franklin Roosevelt on the radio tonight."

"Fine, but be careful. Remember, you're not as young as you once were."

He looked at his wife and noticed the dirty gray hair, the sagging breasts under her worn housedress, and the deep lines in her face. The love he'd once felt for her was gone. It had left along with her kindness and compassion. He sighed as he realized her love for him was gone, too. He knew she stayed with him because he was all she had. Neither one had shown a sign of affection for the other in years. His eyes watered. *I'm homesick for the way you were years ago. I'm lonely for my brother and his family. I seldom see them, and when I do, I can't think of anything to say. We're strangers to each other and to ourselves. I'm homesick for the way I was.* He bit his lip and swallowed hard. *I once lived in fear of losing everything; now I've lost everything in spite of my fears. My family died in the meadow with those herders and their sheep and dogs.*

He went over to Ruth and kissed her on the top of her head. His throat felt tight. "I'll be in for lunch." He went out the screen door and let it fall back in the frame with a bang.

Chapter Twenty-eight

Anna led Snooker out the barn doors, wearing overalls and Paul's jacket as protection from the sharp wind. Gathering the reins, she stood staring at the dark house silhouetted against the moonlit sky. A sigh shuddered through her as she mounted and sat deep in the saddle.

The horse moved forward, gathering speed into a gentle lope as it went down the drive to a dirt road and onto a path cutting across fields.

She slowed the horse to a walk. She ignored the tears seeping from her eyes and staining the saddle. The sky turned from night black to gray with shades of pink as she walked her mount up a dirt drive along corral rails to a dark house. She dismounted and tied Snooker to a rail post. Two horses in the corral tossed their heads in greeting.

Anna approached the door and pounded. She waited and knocked again. The ranch house remained dark. Several yards to the side a bunkhouse loomed, dark and shuttered.

She went to the barn. A faint light shone through the cracks in the barn wall. Opening the door set in the double barn door, she entered, shivering from the cold and sadness.

"Ruth, it's Anna."

A gray-haired woman turned and muttered, "Do you hear them?"

"Hear what?"

"The blasted sheep. They hid woolies in here. They thought I wouldn't find them. But I know they're here. I'll get them." Ruth waved a long butcher knife in the air.

"There aren't any animals in here, except for a few chickens and birds in the rafters."

"I hear woolies. I'll get them. I'll slit their bleating throats."
She moved grain bags and scummy water buckets. "Come and
help me move these bales. They're behind them."

"No, the sheep are gone. No one put sheep in your barn."

"Yes, they did, I tell ya!"

"Who are they, Ruth?"

"They! They. The sheep-lovers."

Anna closed her eyes and took a deep breath. "Come. Put
down the knife, and sit with me on the bales. I have news to tell
you. Sad news."

"What news? Who are you? What do you want of me?" She
brushed her hair back from her unwashed face.

"Come and sit with me, please."

"I'll sit only for a minute. My men will want breakfast. We
got work to do today. Bloody work, but it needs to be done."

Anna sat on a hay bale and patted it to indicate where Ruth
should sit. Ruth inched forward. She sat and laid the knife
across her lap. Anna smelled the stench of Ruth's soiled body
and clothes. The odor mingled with the rotting manure and hay.

"Ruth, it's me. It's Anna, your sister-in-law."

"I know who you are. You married Tim's spineless brother
Paul."

Anna gasped. Her fists doubled. "How dare you? Paul had
more courage than anyone I know."

"No, he didn't. He wouldn't ride with the Association.
Charlie and I did. We had to support Tim when Paul wouldn't.
It helped Charlie learn how to be a man and defend what was
his. We knew Ned was too young, but I insisted he watch. I
wanted him to see what he had to do when it came his time. We
fought as a family. Likely, if you and Paul had boys, you would
have done the same. Paul would have developed a spine. You
had a girl. Men need boys." Ruth grabbed the knife handle.

"Shh. They're bleating again. I'd better get Tim and the boys out here to help us."

Anna took a deep breath and swallowed hard. "Don't you remember? Tim died when he fell off the barn roof more than a year ago. Your boys are gone, too."

"You're crazy. My men are asleep in the house, right where they should be."

"Ruth, listen to me. I'm Anna, and I came to tell you Paul died early this morning. He had a second stroke yesterday. He will be buried tomorrow in the church cemetery near Tim. I thought you should know."

"Don't you bury him next to my Tim! My place is next to Tim."

"Don't worry, Ruth, your place is assured." Anna stared at Ruth. She glanced down at the butcher knife laid across her sister-in-law's knees. She closed her eyes for a moment. Tears filled to the brim and spilled out. "Will we see you at the service?"

Ruth stood. "Here, help me move these bales. I hear them calling to me. They want to warm my cold knife blade with their blood."

Anna shook her head. She walked outside and, mounting her horse, rode toward her empty home.

Chapter Twenty-nine

The postmaster withdrew the mail from his box. One envelope caught his eye as he sorted the letters for the ranchers in Willamette County. Taking the mail to his desk, he sat down and, ignoring the official business mail, pulled out the envelope with the woman's handwriting. The letter was addressed to Postmaster of Willamette County, Oregon, with a return address of Prineville, Oregon.

He opened it and skimmed through the neat, one-page contents. Closing the letter and putting it back into its envelope, he got up and slid it into his shirt pocket. "Good excuse to get out into the sunshine."

He walked across the street to the cigar store. The bell above the shop door jingled. "Hey, Bert. Is your ma at home?"

"Yeah, Ed." A man in his fifties stood behind the counter helping his customer. "Go back through the side door, through the living area, and out the back. Ma is knitting out on the back porch, enjoying the sun." He made change as he talked. "I heard you joined the army. When do you leave for basic training?"

"Next week. I'm trying to get the office in shipshape order for the new postmaster. Heard it will be a woman. With Japan's attack on Pearl Harbor, the ladies are filling in for the men."

"Great. Her face will be prettier than yours, I'll warrant. Seriously, though, I wish you the best."

"Me, too."

The elderly customer smiled.

"Thanks." Ed made his way through the house behind the cigar store. He stepped onto the porch. "Mrs. Stather, may I sit and talk with you?"

"Of course. Old folks like me enjoy youngsters taking time to talk with us. What can I do you for?"

"I got a letter from Mrs. Langster in Prineville. Do you know her?"

The old lady stopped rocking and dropped her knitting in her lap. "Langster, Langster." Her face lit up with a smile. "Sure enough do. There were two Mrs. Langsters. Never met either one, but heard about them. Heard good things—well, mostly."

"This one wants to know where the Millers are. They had a ranch here in Willamette County. I've been here seven years, and I haven't heard of them."

"Hayden and Jennifer Miller. Why, sure, I remember them. Don't reckon I remember their girl's name, though. They lost their sheep to the shooters and moved to Iowa. Heard tell they took up dairy farming."

"Do you know where in Iowa?"

The woman picked up her knitting and adjusted her glasses, saying, "No. They kept in touch with the Burtons, but they moved, too; a long time back, but I don't know where. Don't think they knew where they were going. Times were tough back then. I remember Sally Goodshoe kept in touch for a few years with the Millers." The needles clacked, and the yarn unrolled from the ball. "Talk was Sally kept the Millers informed on the Sheep-Shooters whenever she learned anything. But that was gossip. How could she learn about those doings? She died. Drowned in the river while out on a picnic with her boyfriend, Henry Wimple. His father was a judge at one time, if I remember right. A few folks gossiped it might not have been an accident, that maybe she learned too much about the Sheep-Shooters, but there weren't any proof. Gossip is all. Folks do love to gossip. Even I've been known to make up a few stories."

"Would anyone else in town know where the Millers went?"

Putting the needles again onto her lap, she focused on the horizon. "No, don't think so. I'm the oldest hereabouts. You can ask around, but I think it will be a waste of time." She picked up her knitting and counted stitches.

Chapter Thirty

"No, Ma, I won't go." Molly smeared the soap bar against the trousers and rubbed them against the scrub-board. She doused Aaron's jeans in the washtub and slammed them against the board. Gripping the overalls with both hands, she rubbed the denim up and down. Water splashed out of the tub onto her dress. She wrung the pants with her hands and rubbed more Castile bar soap on them, then straightened her back and brushed her hair off her face.

"Molly, don't take your anger out on the clothes. You'll wear yourself out. You have to go to your Aunt Ruth's funeral. You owe her respect. She was family." Anna rinsed a petticoat in cold water and wrung it out. Tossing it into a clothes basket, she reached for a dress.

"Owe her! We haven't been close for years. She and Uncle Tim destroyed my respect. I owe her nothing. She didn't even come to my wedding."

"You didn't invite your aunt and uncle. I did. They thought it was best they didn't come."

"They didn't come because they blamed Pa for not joining the Sheep-Shooters." Molly attacked the scrub-board with the dirty jeans.

"You went to Tim's funeral."

"I went for Pa, not for Uncle Tim's sake. Aunt Ruth hardly said a word to us. She refused Pa when he said he'd help her run the ranch. She said she could run it fine without his 'blessed help.' Did she run her ranch? She got so ornery her cowhands quit. The place fell apart. And did she come to visit Pa after his first stroke? No, not once. Did she come to his funeral? Despite your riding out to her ranch and personally telling her Pa died? No!" Molly sloshed the trousers in the wash water, and then twisted them until the soapy water stopped trickling back into the tub. She tossed them in the rinse tub, stood up straight, and stretched her back.

"I told you; I found her in the barn slashing the air with her knife like she was killing sheep. I don't think she fully understood what I said to her. Once, I was as close to Ruth as you were with Cassie Miller. We went to school together. We were both baptized and married in the church next door. We were best friends, and we married brothers." Anna's memories brought a warm smile to her face. But her smile faded, and her voice trembled. "She bled to death alone in the barn, the butcher knife in her stomach. A horrible way to die. I'm glad I had visited once every week since your pa's passing, or no one would have known she was dead. She had good days where she thought clearly, and she had days when she was in a different world. Honey, please reconsider. You and Aaron are wonderful to me. You invited me to live here in your house these past five months since your father's passing. It's been a blessing. I hate to ask you to do anything you don't want to do, but please, reconsider. Let go of the past, and come with me." She scooped up the jeans.

Molly grabbed the legs and twisted the pants to wring out the water as Anna held the waistband.

"No, Ma. I'm sorry. I can't. I'm not changing my mind. Let's drop the subject. You mentioned Cassie. I saw the mail on the parlor table."

"You saw the letter from the Willamette postmaster?" Anna shook the jeans and threw them in the clothes basket.

"I didn't read it since it was addressed to you. Did you write him concerning Cassie?" Molly asked.

"I wrote asking where the family had moved to. They lost the ranch many years ago, and they moved to Iowa. The postmaster didn't have any forwarding addresses. You can read the letter." Anna picked up the basket and headed for the clothesline.

"No use. It was Cassie's decision. She couldn't let the past go." Molly was glad her mother was out at the line and didn't hear her and the anger in her tone. *I know I haven't, either, but Lord, it's so hard. Should I break my word to Pa now that he is gone and tell our secret? I don't even discuss it with Ma, and she knows the truth. We avoid it, bury it. Are we responsible for the lack of healing? Are we guilty, too?* She put the scrub-board and soap bar on a shelf, and then tipped the heavy tub. The water gushed over the ground, making a muddy, soapy puddle. She turned the container upright. Using an old coffee pot, she dipped water from the rinse tub and poured it on the nearby flowers. After wiping the galvanized tubs dry, she hung each on its hook by the back door. *Aaron and I should get an electric wringer washer. Laundry is getting to be too hard on Ma.* Molly rolled down her dress sleeves; changing her mind, she turned them back up. *I'm going to clean the kitchen floor. I need hard work, or I'll keep snapping at Ma. She doesn't understand the feelings churning inside me when I think of Aunt Ruth.* She blinked to force the tears away.

* * *

Anna followed the pastor and the pallbearers as they carried the pine casket containing Ruth's body from the church to the cemetery. Five older congregation members followed Anna.

The men set the coffin on two ropes laid on the ground next to the grave. Each man took a rope end, and they lowered the box into the hole next to the grave marked, "Tim Langster 1869-1937," on a simple stone.

Pastor Scott led the gathering in a prayer. "'For as in Adam all die, so also in Christ shall all be made alive.' Amen."

As he spoke his last words, Anna threw a flower into the grave. She stared at the box containing both dear and sad memories. She bit her lip, stifled a sob, and glanced up as Molly and Aaron walked through the churchyard gate and threw a flower onto the coffin. Molly turned to her mother. Weeping, they embraced.

* * *

"Hello, Mr. Twain. How are you today?" The man at the newsstand reached toward the back rack of papers and picked up the *Oregonian.* "And the family? Those boys of yours must be getting ready to graduate."

Oliver Twain handed the money to the newsstand man. "We're all doing fine, thank you. My eldest will graduate from college this year, and my other boy will graduate next year."

"That bookstore of yours must be doing well, to put your boys through school. That's great."

"Yes, it is."

The newsman handed Mr. Twain his change. "You know you could have been ordering this paper all these years yourself. You don't need to go through me, although I don't mind the business."

"It works out best for me this way. Good day."

"And to you, Mr. Twain."

Oliver strolled over to a park bench and sat down. He turned each newspaper page, scanning the words. He read a notice stating that Molly Langster Luken was starting a public library and needed donations of new and used books. He turned to the next page. His eyes stopped at an obituary.

"Mrs. Ruth Langster was buried next to her husband Tim Langster in the Prineville Cemetery. Mrs. Langster succumbed to an accident suffered in her barn. A marker indicating their son Charlie died in the Mexican War is erected in the next plot.

The ranch will go to the Langsters' niece Molly Langster Luken, the wife of the Forest Ranger, Aaron Luken. Ruth and Tim Langster's youngest son, Ned, disappeared when he was fourteen and has not been heard from since."

Oliver sat gazing blankly at the article and then stared off into space. Several minutes later, he got up and walked back to the magazine stand. "Say, Burt. You can cancel the subscription to the paper. I won't need it anymore."

"How come?"

"Just lost interest in Oregon, I guess. I'll spend more time reading about what is happening here in Duluth."

The man nodded as Oliver strolled back to his bookstore. He would clip out this article and put it with the one on Charlie's passing, and his dad's. *Now, the past is closed. I never need to return there. This is truly my life now.* Oliver Twain unlocked his bookstore and stepped in confidently. He smiled. *I feel stronger and lighter, younger.* His smile faded. Tears formed in his eyes. *Ma, Pa, and Charlie are....* Tears rolled down his face. *Gone. I loved them, and yet for a few moments I felt happiness, a sense of freedom in knowing they would never find me. I shouldn't feel this way. Why couldn't things be different? How could I have made it different? Ma, Pa, Charlie, I love you.* The bookstore did not open. A slumped figured sat in a back corner in the dark and wept silently.

Chapter Thirty-one

"Molly, I need white cotton cloth. Ten yards, please."

Molly turned from the shelves to the counter where Cally Pryon stood. "Why so much?" Molly asked as she walked to open shelves near a long cutting table containing sewing supplies.

"For my daughter-in-law, Mary. She's dressing my three grandbabies in the grayest, dingiest diapers you've ever seen. Doesn't the girl know to use bleach? Honestly! She tries a saint's patience. I know she married my Tom for his good looks—after all, he takes after Delvin—but you certainly can't be faulted for marrying Aaron for his good looks. Goodness, no! Goodness, no!"

"Aaron is handsome to me, Cally," said Molly as she measured the cloth from the bolt. *Cally has never had tact. She and Delvin think the sun rises and sets on their boy, Tom. I wonder if she knows I turned Delvin down when he wanted to court me.*

"Dear, I'm not being critical, but he's skin and bones, and he hardly has any hair!"

"His kindness, consideration and patience are the qualities I find most attractive." Molly forced a smile as she wrapped the cloth in brown paper and tied string around the package.

"Well, Tom is certainly kind and considerate, and he must have patience to put up with a wife who doesn't bleach his children's diapers."

"He is all those things, Cally." Molly bit her lip to keep from bringing up the past. "But you should be glad he married Mary. You have three adorable grandchildren, and baby Charlie is as cute as can be. It's a full-time job to be a mother and wife and keep the diapers washed. I see her clothesline is filled every day. And yesterday, after she hung the diapers on the line, the train came through, and the wind blew soot and ashes right to her place. She spent the day trying to pick out the cinders from the cotton fuzz. She was in tears when I stopped in to say hello. I helped her for several hours, but it was an impossible task to get those black specks out. Bleach can't make a difference on those diapers." Molly handed the parcel to Cally Pryon.

"She never said a word. I'm going to take her this cloth so she can cut and hem up new ones."

"I'm sure Mary would appreciate it. And if you made the diapers, I bet you could do it better and in half the time, with your experience and your new Singer treadle sewing machine."

Cally straightened, and her eyes opened wide. "I suppose you're right. I certainly would do a better job than she would. I'll take one spool of white cotton thread, too."

Molly unwrapped the bundle and added the thread. "One dollar and fifty cents, please."

Cally opened her coin purse and counted out the money. "Thank you, dear. Always nice to talk with you."

"Thank you."

"Molly." A voice came from a back room.

"Yes, Mr. Hasty."

"You can leave. I'm locking up early. The missus and I are going to the picture show. It's featuring *A Tale of Two Cities*. We missed it when it first came out. Supposed to be great."

"Fine. I'll walk out with Cally Pryon. Good day."

Molly put on her hat, and the two women went out the door and onto the boardwalk.

"How are you doing, Molly, with your dear mother gone? Breast cancer is nasty business."

"I'm doing okay, Cally. Thank you for asking." Molly peered into the sun as her eyes filled.

"Good to hear."

They parted, one to make diapers and the other to head toward to a two-story house next to the church. A Studebaker followed by a Ford shifted gears as they sped up the road. Molly walked up the hill and opened the gate to a picket fence. "This needs painting." She glanced up, adding, "So does the house." Going up the worn, wooden porch steps, she sat down on a rocker. She undid the hat pin and removed her hat, shaking her hair; gray strands lay in her dark curls. She loosened her shoes and pulled them off. *I think Aaron is glad we bought this house from Mr. Auldrich's family, although he never will say so.* Wiggling her toes and stretching her arches, she studied the town's main street. It had changed from her childhood days. Automobiles chugged and roared, mixed with the horses, mules, and wagons on the road. Some walks were cement instead of board, and one parking meter stood by the mayor's office. Many faces had changed as well.

She saw Aaron riding Sparrow down the main street. He stopped and dismounted at the sheriff's office. She watched until he came out and led his horse toward the house. She couldn't stop the disappointment she felt when she saw he was alone. She knew in her head Cassie wasn't coming, but there had been a seed of hope tucked away in a corner of her heart. Early spring, every year, she felt the same hope and the same disappointment.

Aaron walked up the back road and put Sparrow in the barn. He came around to the front, sat on the porch floor, and rested his back against Molly's legs. She massaged his neck and shoulders.

She peered at his hands. "It's been years since you injured your hand, and the scars are just as noticeable today as they were then. I don't understand how you stood the pain after you spilled a pot of hot coffee on it so far from town—and had to walk all the way home, too, since Sparrow ran off."

Aaron glanced at his hands. The dark red-brown cast to the shriveled and puckered skin of one hand contrasted with his other tan hand.

Molly watched him turn his head to the right and shrug. She knew this was his gesture when he was keeping secrets from her.

He shifted his legs and laid his hand on his lap. "It feels fine. Just stiff at times." He changed the subject. "I managed to check on several areas to make sure the sheep men and cattlemen were following the quotas. One sheep corral was torn down, likely by a cattleman—no other damage, though. It can be rebuilt in a few days. I reported it to the sheriff. The south area is wrapped up, settled. Five days is a long time to be out in the field, sleeping on the ground." He yawned.

Molly smiled. Her city-bred husband had learned to live and enjoy life in Oregon, but still it was not natural for him. Years of working in the county as a forester hadn't quite removed his city culture.

Aaron shifted his weight on the porch wood planks. "Henry Wimple is trying to run more cattle on the range than are allowed. I had to speak to Chet Smith and his pals Frank Messer and Guy Hicker. I told them if they continue to do that I'll lower their boss's allotment next year. If he continues, he could lose his application rights to government range for a year."

"Aaron, be careful. Henry has the old Durkson ranch. They don't take kindly to an outsider telling them what to do. And folks around here still think of you as an outsider. They can be good at making accidents happen." Molly stared out at the cemetery and glanced at Pastor Weatherby's grave.

"Don't fear, my worrywart, I'm careful. Besides, the ranchers don't want the government to get more involved and send in troops. They listen, reluctantly." He stretched and yawned again.

"Aaron, thank you for allowing Mom to stay here with us the last five years after Pa died. I'm grateful." Molly reached down and put her arms around him.

"Honey, I'm glad she was with us. She added to our happiness. And I didn't worry about you, being alone here when I was in the field. I felt as close to her as I did to my own mother."

"I miss her, deeply. Are you too tired to go to the ranch for the weekend? We haven't been there since she's been gone. I know the park system and forest service are responsible for the land since I deeded the property over to them, but I feel I should check on the house. I'd like to retrieve my parents' belongings."

"You get a crate and pack up some food. I'll hitch Sparrow to a wagon." Aaron got up and went down the porch steps, following the path to the barn.

Molly shook her head. Aaron never said more words than were necessary, and he never wasted time. *When he was new to the forest service and would come out to the ranch for dinner, he'd talk with Pa on what needed to be done but hardly say two or three words to me.* Molly sighed. She knew her parents told him what happened in the pasture, but they never said who did the killings. Her folks were sure Aaron guessed they knew the men's identities, yet he never asked them who the shooters were. *He never asked me what I knew. Should I tell him? They are all gone, but maybe it would help in some way. There are still men burning barns and corrals and poisoning animals. My promise was to Pa, and he is gone. I don't know. I just can't seem to let go of my promise.*

* * *

The sun slipped below the horizon when they unhitched the horse and led him into the barn. "The power is turned off. It took years to get electricity out to the ranch, and now we don't need it." Molly lit a lantern and carried it and the box of food into the ranch house. The room felt cold and forlorn. Dust billowed out under the crate when she placed it on the kitchen table. She missed the clean, checked tablecloth her mother had always spread on the wooden surface. A deep loneliness gathered within her. She tightened the ties on her coat.

Aaron followed with wood for the stove. She primed the pump as he lit the fire. She lit another kerosene lamp. Gazing up the staircase to the darkness on the landing, she shuddered. "Would you mind if we sleep on the floor in front of the fireplace in the sitting room? We could bring the blankets down from the beds and hang them by the fire to air out the dampness and mustiness."

"I'll get them." Aaron went up the stairs with a lamp and returned with blankets and a quilt.

"Mom's quilt! She made it before she was married. I had forgotten it. I want to be sure we take it home with us." She stroked the quilt as she took it from Aaron.

After eating, they lay in front of the glowing fire. Within minutes, Aaron was asleep. Molly lay in his arms, with her head on his chest. She tugged a quilt corner to cushion her head from his bony frame. Mixed with the old house sounds as it creaked and groaned in the night air, a wolf's keen floated up to the moon. Tears formed in her eyes and spilled onto the quilt. The house had never been the same since that day in the meadow.

* * *

Molly squinted at the sun coming up over the mountain as she pumped water into the coffee pot. The sun made her eyes water momentarily. She could hear Aaron close the barn door. She focused instinctively on the sound and was disappointed to see Aaron walking toward the house and not her pa. She scanned the corral when she heard Sparrow whinny. Judy and

Buster were both gone. They had lived out their lives on the ranch, and each had succumbed to time before Molly had married; still, she expected to see them waiting in the corral for a carrot from two young girls. Molly set the pot on the stove and turned with a jerk to face the door. *Cassie's footsteps on the porch.* When Aaron opened the door, she choked up and turned back to the stove.

"What's wrong?"

"Nothing. Would you mind if we go up to the high meadow this morning? I want to visit it. I haven't been there since I was a girl."

"Sure. We can take food with us."

"No, I don't feel like a picnic," Molly snapped. She then softened her tone. "Let's eat when we come back."

"Okay." Aaron turned and walked out to hitch Sparrow to the wagon. Molly wondered what her husband was thinking as he went out to get the horse five minutes after putting it in the corral. He hadn't asked why she didn't want to have a picnic. Molly shook her head at the quiet understanding her husband had for her.

* * *

The sky's deep blue and the brightness of the sun hurt their eyes. The killdeer and the Steller's jay sang in the spring grass. The wheels creaked, and the hooves clopped on the dry earth.

At midday, they topped a hill. Molly gasped when she saw a lone rider on the ridge to the west. A second later, the rider disappeared below the ridgeline. She realized it was not the boy she had seen there years before, a boy whose shoulders had collapsed as he'd taken in the horror before him, a boy who'd turned his horse and ridden away.

They made their way down the mountainside. The valley was empty, but cattle signs were visible. Molly took the reins and guided Sparrow to a tree.

As she sat in the wagon, her gaze drifted over the grassy field. Blood and death lay in the meadow. She picked out the spot where Lammie Star had fallen and where the two dogs had come to rest. She spotted the places where each sheepherder had gone down. Broken, old sheep skulls were still visible throughout the pasture.

Aaron hobbled Sparrow, and Molly climbed out. She made her way over to a pine tree. Bending down, she pulled the weeds and grass until she could see the stones encircling a grave.

Aaron came over and noticed a crooked marker leaning to the side in the ground. He pulled it out and, taking his jack knife, carved the names in deeper. He put the marker back into its place. Molly filled her skirt with lupines and wild blue flag iris and laid them like a carpet over the site.

An ache shot through her as she realized the hope tucked away in her heart had fled. Cassie would not return to this side of the mountains. The events governing their lives at that time were over; the results, final. She fell to her knees and sobbed. Aaron knelt beside her and rocked her in his embrace. She wept until there was not a tear left in her body. She shuddered until she was spent.

"Aaron, let's go home."

Aaron lifted her in his arms and carried her to the wagon. They drove to the ranch house in silence. Molly closed and locked the wooden front door, placing the key on a hook in the wall. The hinges on the screen door squeaked, but she didn't let the door bang. She closed it softly and held her fingers against the worn wood for a moment. She climbed onto the wagon seat. Laying her mother's quilt in her lap, she put her hands around

Aaron's arm as he held the reins. *Dear Lord, please don't let anything happen to Aaron. Don't let what I most fear come upon me. He's all I have.*

Chapter Thirty-two

A man in dark clothing stepped out from a building's night shadow cast by the moon. He swung the rifle cradled in his arms to a firing position. "Who is it?"

"Aaron Luken. I came by to check out your shearing shed, Newt."

"Wait until I light the lantern." The man backed into the darkness. A minute later, the lamp glow defeated the blackness and cast a circle of comfort. "Step forward into the light, so I can be sure it's you, Aaron."

Aaron approached Newt and extended his hand. "I'm glad you're guarding your property."

Newt shook Aaron's hand. "Yeah, the gunnysackers aren't riding like they used to against us sheep ranchers, but there's always a chance a hothead or two might be around. I don't want any trouble with my new sheds. The shearing season is starting, and the first flock of three thousand will be coming tomorrow."

"You run a nice operation here. The holding pen is ready, I see, with straw laid down to absorb the moisture. And you've added a new roof over the enclosure, too." The men stepped to the shed door.

"Don't want the sheep to get wet if it rains. Shearing wet wool slows everything down. No profit. Time and wool are the moneymakers. Sheep will be arriving at dawn, and the shearers will start at seven-thirty and work till dark." Newt pointed to the sidewall where pegs held shirts and boots. "I had the men hang their equipment in here so I could inspect it and be sure everything was ready. The leather patches in the shirt armholes are mended. The men hold the sheep, and the back legs are up in the armpits. The leather protects the men, and the sheep won't get their legs broken caught in a hole. I patched every boot, too. The leather soles are needed as the floor gets greasy from the lanolin, and the boot laces need the tongue on the outside, so they don't get in the way of the shears." Newt's pride spoke in his voice.

Aaron looked about the shearing shed with interest. When he talked with either the sheep men or the cattlemen, he wanted them to know he listened and understood their viewpoint. "I see you have a larger wool table."

"This one has larger spaces between the boards," Newt said. "When the shearer throws the wool on the table, the rouster picks out the main chaff, dirt, and short wool, and lets that fall between the cracks. I hire the shearers' children to work under the table, to sort out the debris, save the short wool, and sweep up the chaff so as not to contaminate the next batch." Newt squatted under the table. He duck-walked his way to the other side and stood up. Continuing over to a beam supporting long burlap bags hanging by sharp hooks, he opened an empty bag and said, "Other kids will climb into the sack where the wool is packed and jump up and down to force in as much fleece as it will hold." Newt left the bag and pointed with his rifle to a trap door in the floor. "It takes three minutes, and then the sheep is on his way down the chute to the outside pen. I get a percentage of the wool each rancher sells, and he doesn't have the expense of building his own shed, maintaining it and hiring shearers."

"You sound real proud of your setup here, Newt."

"Yeah, I am. It's a labor done with love."

"You're smart to keep an eye on it. Cattlemen are adjusting to having quotas and sheep grazing, but there is still resentment among some. I can help you stand watch if you like."

"No, I'll get one of my herders to do it. Come into the ranch house and bunk down. We can listen to FDR's radio address on the Germans bombing Great Britain. The Brits have held out for over fifty days. I don't understand how they can stay the course much longer. I'm beat, and I bet you are, too."

"I wouldn't mind coming in. I haven't slept in a real bed for a week."

Newt went to the bunkhouse and rousted his boss herder, Roho, out of bed to stand guard. Newt and Aaron shuffled into the house. Within moments, electric lights replaced the kerosene light. The radio's static and whistle-tuning sounds interrupted the quiet night. Roho eased his way into the moonlight shadows, his rifle cradled in his arms.

* * *

A rifle crack split the air. The sound stabbed Aaron and Newt awake and propelled them onto their feet. Cries of "Fire! Fire!" spurred their bodies into motion. Running in their stocking feet they tore out into the yard. Flames leaped in the black sky. Heat blushed their skin. Men in long underwear and women in nightshirts poured out of the shearers' tents. Mothers grabbed their children as they burst from the tent doors into the spark-filled air.

The women ran to the water troughs and pumps to fill buckets. The older children carried buckets of water to the men while the younger ones doused blankets in water. Men grabbed pails and wet blankets and ran to the burning corrals and sheds. The fire's roar and the cracking of the falling timbers almost drowned out the voices of the shouting men, yelling women and screaming children. The wind spun the sparks high into the blackness and hurled them down on the tents, main house, and bunkhouse roofs.

Embers blown by the wind had the barn roof in flames. Aaron and Newt sprinted in and untied the mules and horses. The panicked animals screamed in terror as they jostled and rammed into each other in their struggle to get out. Aaron, kicked by a mule, stumbled and fell on the dirt floor. Dazed, he lay in the stall. *What's wrong with me? What happened? I can't seem to get up.*

Newt darted between the jostling animals. A timber from the roof crashed, sending sparks and flames across the floor. Newt jumped over the burning beam to reach Aaron. He pulled on Aaron's arms and raised him onto his feet. They stumbled through the falling sparks and blistering heat. Both fell on the ground outside the door. Forcing themselves up, they raced to the water trough as the barn roof collapsed behind them.

The tents and the itinerant sheep shearers' belongings became baby bonfires near the conflagration of the barn, corral, and shed. Men rushed in close to the fire, threw buckets of water, and beat flames with wet blankets while dry, hot smoke filled their throats and lungs. Coughing and gasping, Newt dropped the blanket he flailed at the blaze and said, "It's no use. Stand back. It's gone. It's all gone." He fell to his knees as his lungs fought for clean air.

The struggling men and women froze. Their voices fell silent as their eyes stared in disbelief and hopelessness. The little ones cried, and the fire's roar spent itself into a loud crackle.

The women were the first to move. They splashed water onto their children's faces, hands, and feet to cool the rosy skin.

Newt stood and stared at the shearers and their families whose faces were smeared in smoke and ashes. "I'll send some of my ranch hands into town come morning with wagons. Make a list of what you folks lost, and I'll replace it."

"Where's the guard you posted, Newt?" Aaron asked.

"Roho! Where is Roho?" Newt yelled. He stared at the charred barn's remnants and shook his head. "I hope he's not there."

Men scattered. Some walked as close to the fire area as the glowing embers allowed, while others fanned out across the pasture.

Moments later, the cries of "Here! He's over here!" brought everyone to a slight dip in the grass. Aaron squatted near Roho, who was lying on the ground with his wrists bloody from the rope that bound them. His head was uncovered, and patches of his scalp had been torn loose and hung in fragments. Blood congealed from a deep gash behind his ear.

Aaron raised Roho's head. "Roho, do you know who did this?"

Dazed, he opened his eyes and gazed into Aaron's. "The one called Chet and his friends." He closed his eyes as he lost consciousness.

"Did anyone else see them? We need more witnesses, or else it's Chet's word against Roho's." Aaron stood and faced the gathering.

"Likely not. We were all asleep. I only had Roho on guard. Come on, fellas; let's get him to a wagon. John, you drive the buckboard to town and bring him to the doctor." Newt and Aaron followed the men as they carried the ranch hand. They watched the wagon until it was out of sight.

"Newt, let's walk around the fire area and see if we can find any evidence to back up Roho's claim. You start that way, and I'll circle this way. Examine everything, small or big. We'll each continue the circle to make sure neither one of us misses anything." Aaron moved slowly, inspecting everything closely, turning over glowing embers, charred posts, burning leather. He watched Newt start from the same spot going in the opposite direction. Minute after minute, they searched through the debris. They met halfway around and continued forward, each checking the smoking ashes the other had prodded.

"Aaron, come here. I've found something."

Aaron hurried to Newt's position on the shearing shed's far side.

"Look," Newt said as he held up a small, round, metal disc, shiny in the moonlight.

"It's a silver peso. Where have I seen that before?" Aaron asked.

"Chet Smith wears roping cuffs with pesos as decorations. He fought in the Mexican Revolution and picked them up there. He's the only one I've ever seen with them. This proves he was here," Newt said.

"You're right. I missed it when I checked this area. I'm glad you found the peso. With Judge Gray, we might get a conviction of attempted murder and arson."

* * *

Cattle ranchers, sheep ranchers, and the townsfolk—men, women and children—gathered at the boardinghouse. The warm spring air, thick with humidity, seemed to get thicker as the nervous and excited people waited for the door to open.

Mrs. Pryon stepped out and raised her voice above the din: "The dining room and connecting parlor are ready for the trial. There are only chairs for Judge Gray, the sheriff, and the three defendants. Everyone else has to stand. The witnesses are to stand near the front, and the onlookers need to get behind them. Once the room is filled, the rest of you will have to stand outside the windows and this door to catch what you can. Please, enter in an orderly fashion."

Mrs. Pryon stepped aside. The crowd thronged the makeshift courtroom, pushing and shoving through the door.

Aaron Luken, Newt Williamson, and Roho, using a cane and with a large bandage plastered onto his head, stood near the front by the judge's table.

Molly squeezed into a back corner. All she could see was a man's back in front of her, but the crowd was too thick for her to make her way closer to the front. She strained to hear the proceedings. Within moments, she was gasping for air as she was pressed against the wall.

Judge Jason Gray banged his gavel. The crowd fell silent.

"We are here to try Chet Smith, Guy Hicker, and Frank Messer for arson at Newt Williamson's shearing sheds and for the attempted murder of Roho Alvarado. How do the defendants plead?"

The three men stood and answered in one voice, "Not guilty."

Shouts came from the crowd, "Yeah, that's right."

"They're guilty as sin."

"Hang them!"

"They ain't done nothin' wrong."

"They're good boys."

"Order! The spectators are to be quiet, or the room will be cleared." The judge gave the crowd time to settle down. "As it is deemed impossible to find an unbiased jury, this trial will be determined by the judge's ruling. The defendants' rights will be upheld by me, as an attorney could not be found willing to risk his life defending the men. Also, no one wanted to be the prosecuting attorney, which duty I will also undertake. I will conduct the trial on a fair basis. All the witnesses and defendants will take the oath to testify truthfully."

The trial began. The crowd listened intently to every word. People climbed into the window space and blocked the air movement. The room became stifling within minutes.

A half-hour into the trial, Roho was called to testify.

"You were on guard duty at Newt Williamson's ranch when his sheds burned down?"

"Yes, sir."

"Did you see who set the fire?"

"Yes, I was standing in the shadows and heard a noise coming from the pasture. I went to the side of the building and saw Señor Hicker pouring kerosene on the building walls. Señor Smith lit a match and threw it onto the soaked wood, and then they both ran to their horses, which were held by Señor Messer. I saw them clearly in the firelight. They also saw me. Señor Chet threw his rope around me, jerked me off my feet, and dragged me across the ground. I held onto my rifle and fired off two shots. He dropped the rope, and all three rode like lightning was shooting up their tails."

Chet, Frank, and Guy shouted, "Liar! We weren't there. We were on the range with the cattle."

"We will hear from you shortly!" Judge Gray banged his gavel. "Newt Williamson, let's hear from you. You are under oath. What leads you to think Chet Smith and the other defendants burned your shearing sheds?"

"Aaron Luken and I walked around the burned huts, and in the ashes that were once the side of the shed where Roho said the fire started, I found the silver peso you have on your desk. You can see by the hole punched into it that it was used as a decoration, and everyone in this room recognizes it's from Chet Smith's roping cuffs, which we have seen plenty of times. He likes to show them off."

Judge Gray picked up the peso from the table and the roping cuffs next to it. He placed the peso in the indentation where a decoration was missing. "It is a perfect fit. What do you say about this, Mr. Smith?"

"I lost that peso a long time ago. Aaron Luken found it somehow and planted it at the fire to blame me and my friends. Luken don't like us much."

"Newt, who found this peso? Remember, you are under oath to tell the truth."

"It was me, Judge. Aaron didn't see it. I saw it and picked it up."

"Now, before I make a ruling, I want to inform the spectators that the sheriff has my orders to arrest any man, woman, or child who starts a fight or threatens anyone. An immediate fine of fifty dollars will be levied with possible jail time. Even you kids. You understand?"

"That not fair. You can't arrest kids!" voices shouted. The judge gave everyone time to yell, and then he rapped his gavel. "The peso ties Chet Smith to the fire, and the testimony ties the three defendants to the assault. I have decided the evidence is sufficient to prove the three men are guilty, and I sentence each to fifteen years in the Oregon State Prison." The judge pounded his gavel and concluded, "The court is closed," but few heard him as the uproar from both sides drowned out even the defendants' cries of, "We ain't guilty!"

* * *

Molly pulled back on the reins. The horse stopped, and she got down from the wagon seat. As she tied the reins to the hitching post, a woman and her young daughter came out onto the porch.

"Good day, Molly. I see you brought us more books to trade. My Caroline loves *Eight Cousins*. She read it to me twice now. She sure would like to trade it for a new story."

"Sure thing, Mavis. I've got a new issue of *Harper's Weekly* for you, a mystery book for your husband, and for you, Miss Caroline, I have *Rose in Bloom*." Molly exchanged books with Mavis and Caroline. The girl sat on the porch step and began reading the first page.

"Say thank you to Mrs. Luken, Caroline."

"Thank you," Caroline responded without taking her eyes from the book.

"Molly, sit and visit. I made lemonade and have it ready, as I knew you would be by today."

"Thank you, Mavis. I'll do that." Molly stepped up to the porch and sat in a wicker chair.

"Roger and me, and many other sheep ranchers, sure are glad your husband stood up in court with Mr. Williamson and got that Chet Smith and his friends convicted. I hope the cattlemen won't hold it against him."

"I hope so, too. Most cattle ranchers today have grown up with the notion of quotas. I take my rolling library to cattle ranches and haven't heard anything negative, but then, everybody knows I'm Aaron's wife and wouldn't dare say anything in front of me, I suspect. I was at Henry Wimple's last week, and no one seemed to bear a grudge. A few even said those three men were bad apples, and they were glad to see them off the ranch for good. Chet Smith later told the judge that Henry Wimple put them up to burning the shearing shed, but Henry denied it, and there wasn't any proof. The judge thinks the men were trying to get someone else blamed to reduce their sentences."

"Wimple never has been involved in the range war, from what I know. Likely, those three acted on their own. That kind likes to stir up violence, even if there is no need for it." Mavis took a sip of lemonade.

Molly remembered the two lanky riders in the high meadow, one older and gone now and one younger. "I sure hope so. I always feel trouble is just below the surface, but that could be due to the worries I get at times. At least those three won't be killing anymore. And with them going to prison, folks on both sides will know they can't get away with breaking the law."

"Amen to that, Molly."

"I'd better start back, so I get home before it's dark. I have to get ready for tomorrow. That's when I open up the first floor of my house to the town to exchange books. Every inch—except the kitchen and Aaron's office—is filled with secondhand books and magazines. It's all organized, but I'm the only one who thinks so." Molly laughed as she put down her glass. "I'll see you again in about three weeks. Take care."

"You too, dear. Having books to read reminds us there are people and places outside of Crook County. Thanks for not forgetting about us"

Chapter Thirty-three

Aaron reined in Sparrow. "Better rest a bit, fellow. The snow is deeper than I thought. It feels colder, too, with the wind picking up." Aaron removed his gloves and blew on his hands. "Good thing we stayed at the old Tim Langster place last night. Sure saved us when that storm blew in. I'm glad it quit so we could head for town. Six more hours and we'll be home. Molly will be relieved to see us." Aaron put his gloves on and took up his reins again. "I know it's tough going for you, old fellow, but a warm barn is waiting for you."

Sparrow plowed through drifts up to his knees.

Aaron stiffened when he saw a man urging his horse through the drifts to catch up with him. He recognized the rider, even from a distance. *Thought I'd seen the last of him.* Aaron reined in Sparrow. "Might as well rest a bit, old boy. We'll let him come to us."

"Well, if it ain't the forest service representative. Ain't seen you for years, but I've been thinking about you. Often." The rider reined his horse in about ten feet from Aaron.

"Chet, I'd heard you got out of jail. What are you doing back here?"

"I'm working on a ranch in Deschutes County. Only place I could land a job, thanks to you."

"You were lucky we couldn't prove the arson case for the Chuck Simons' sheep corral years back, when you took my horse and made me walk to town. You got careless in the last burning. Fifteen years isn't much, as I see it." Aaron removed his gloves and blew on his hands. He moved one hand closer to his gun.

"Keep your hand away from your pistol. I got me a friend over there with a Winchester pointed right at you." Chet waved toward a stand of trees.

"Just one friend? Thought you had two snakes coiled under your thumb. Which one is it?"

"I ain't saying, but one died in prison. Got knifed for not sharing his food with a friend. Now, tell me something. I wondered every day how that peso of mine got found at the fire. I lost it a long time before that night. I'll bet you know how it got there."

"How could I?"

"Remember when I wanted you to rethink the situation and not lead the authorities in our direction, and left you without a horse? It didn't work. The law started watching me. But I bet it will work this time. Get off your horse. You're going to walk, like before. It will be part of your payback for sticking your nose in my life. I ain't a horse thief, so I'll turn your horse loose near town."

Aaron glanced over to the ponderosa pines. He saw a figure crouched behind a tree with a rifle pointed in his direction.

"Okay, guess you didn't learn anything the last time, either." Aaron dismounted. The snow came up to his knees.

"You ain't got any proof to say we were out here. Your word against mine and my friend there will say I was miles away from here. Give me your gun and holster. Don't want you shooting at me as I ride away." Chet hung Aaron's gun and holster on his saddle horn and gathered Sparrow's reins as he urged his horse through the drifts. "Don't feel bad. The sheepherder who testified against us is going to get worse than a long, cold walk. I won't kill you since you're a Fed, and I don't want the government after me, but he ain't. People can still disappear mysterious-like around here. Enjoy your trip." Chet rode to the trees. A man stood and mounted his horse. They laughed as their animals labored forward in the snow.

Aaron heard the laughter as it cackled back in the crisp air. He stepped in the horse tracks. "Molly, I guess you're right. I'm getting too old for this. My hands were too numb to manage my gun. It's going to be a long walk home. Keep the lamp lit in the upstairs window for me. I'm going to need it."

He plowed through the frigid mounds, hoping the exertion would keep him warm. Soon, his feet were numb, and he couldn't feel them. He kept his eyes on the tracks he followed. A hard windblast hit his back. Exhausted, he stopped and studied the sky. Black clouds came roiling in from the mountains. The wind blew steady and strong. His heart beat faster.

"Wouldn't you know, another storm coming in, and fast. Looks like a doozy. I can't make it to town, and my supplies are in the saddlebags. I've got to find a windbreak." He pivoted around to survey the area. Rolling white drifts surrounded him for miles. "Hate to think this, but the only shelter anywhere near is back where I came from. The stand of trees will block the wind. I can make a snow cave and warm it with my body heat. I'd better turn back." He exhaled and blew on his hands. He followed his tracks, stumbling repeatedly in the soft powder. He couldn't feel his feet, legs, or hands. The wind picked up speed and blew into his face. He couldn't tell whether new flakes were falling from the dark clouds, or the wind was picking up the snow on the ground. "I'm in a whiteout." He felt the wind blow the breath out of his body. He tried breathing through his muffler. The earth gave way beneath him. He fell in the deep snow and lay in needle-piercing white. He squinted to shield his eyes from the stinging pellets. The wind stopped for a moment. He struggled up and headed for the pines.

The wind began again. He lost sight of the shelter and stumbled in the direction he hoped was right. His head hit something hard, and it knocked him down. He felt around with his hands. *The trees! I made it. I made it.* The three trees formed a tight circle. He crawled in and leaned his back against the bark. *At least I'm out of the wind. I can breathe without the air being ripped from me. Warmer, too.*

His frozen jeans wouldn't bend until he pounded on them to break the ice. He forced his legs to bend at the knees and brought them to his chest. He dropped his head down to his knees, struggling to keep his eyes open. "Can't go to sleep. I won't wake up, and I promised Molly I'd come home. Never broke a promise. Got to stay awake." He rocked back and forth. His rocking gradually slowed and stopped.

"Molly, what are you doing here? You're all hazy and fuzzy-looking. Must be this snow swirling around me. You should've stayed home. You're too old to be out here. You said I was too old, and you're right. But, honey, I got tired of sitting around doing the office work and wanted to get out and make a difference. You told me I had to retire sometime. Didn't want to think so, though. But I finally figured this would be my last year. Yeah, you won't say it, but you told me so. You go on home where it's warm, and I'll come soon. I'm just a bit tired right now.

"Wait, before you go, remember how I proposed to you? Fool question. Of course you do. Women remember those things, but so do the men. I was a young jack from the East, a brand-new forest service agent. Your folks were the first to accept me, since I was an outsider. They invited me out to your ranch five or six times for dinner and talk. They filled me in on the people in the area, those who were trustworthy and those I should watch. The night I asked you to marry me, I guess I should have kissed you or at least shaken your hand, but it didn't occur to me, and you didn't say anything about it. I don't think I loved you back then, just admired you and your folks. When I asked you to marry me, it popped out. Don't know where it came from. Hadn't thought of marriage till that moment, but honey, I'm sure glad I did. Bet you got a lamp shining in the upstairs window right now to guide me home. You've been doing that every night for the last forty years when I was out in the field. You go on home now and stay warm."

Aaron raised his head. His eyelashes froze and his eyes were sealed shut. He rubbed the ice off his lashes and peered into the air. A white, swirling mass confronted him. He tried to move his legs, but they wouldn't respond. *At least I feel warmer.* His eyes closed, and his head sank forward onto his knees.

"Ma and Pa, what are you doing here? I haven't seen you for over fifty years. And Anna and Paul Langster. Do you know my parents? Imagine that! And these other folks, I haven't seen them for years. Did you come out to find me? Sparrow, how did you get here? And you brought green grass. How did you do that? The grass is like it's jeweled. I've got to take my boots and socks off. I want to dance in it barefoot. Wait until Molly sees this."

* * *

"Hey, boss, see there, by the lakeshore? The horse looks like it was in the lake. It's in bad shape. There's another one farther up the shoreline."

"Somebody's in trouble, Jess. You go get the horses and take them back to the ranch. Try to save them. They must have walked onto the lake and fallen into open water during the storm. Brad and I will search for the riders."

"Okay, Mr. Simons." Jess rode to the two riderless horses shaking on the snow-and-ice-packed edge of the lake. He took the reins without difficulty, as the animals were too exhausted to run. "Boss, there are tracks of another horse. They are heading for town."

"I hope the poor critter makes it. If you see it on the way to the ranch, take it there with those two."

Jess led the two horses slowly to the sheep ranch.

Chuck Simons and his son Brad rode along the side of Silver Lake.

"Hey, Pa, over there by the brush, hung up in the open water. Do you see them?"

"Sure do. Two men. They likely rode off the shoreline and broke through the thin ice. They got as far as that brush, but the water was too cold, and they couldn't pull themselves out. It's a miracle the horses were able to find a way to shore and climb out. This ice is stable in places and weak in others. We'll walk the horses out as far as we dare."

Ice creaked as they inched their horses over the frozen water. Near the open area, the ice turned from gray to blue-gray. They halted the horses. Brad and Chuck each lassoed a body and tied the rope to a saddle horn. They backed their animals one step at a time. The hooves slipped and skidded, but the animals stayed upright. The bodies were dragged through the open water and onto the solid ice.

Brad turned a body over. "Hey, Pa, isn't this the fellow you thought set our sheep corral on fire years ago?"

"Yeah, that's him, Chet Smith. And this fellow is his friend Frank. I don't remember his last name. Well, we'd better get these bodies to the sheriff. We'll each take one and bring them to town. We saw the tracks of three horses but only found two bodies. Likely the other man is under the ice someplace."

Chuck and Brad Simons struggled to get the two stiff bodies hoisted over their saddles and tied on securely so they would not slide off. The men sat on their horses behind the saddle.

Just as they started forward, the sun was sending its last rays of light and feeble warmth across the snow. The Douglas fir trees hung heavy with white, fluffy powder. At the wood's brush line, a wolf stepped out, lifted its head, and let out a long keen. Chuck and Brad stopped and watched the predator amble back into the snowy trees. In a moment, it was lost from sight.

"Wow, that howl sent shivers up my spine. That was coldest sound I've ever heard." Chuck Simons urged his horse forward.

* * *

"Sorry, Molly. We've been out looking for Aaron for over a week now. We can't find any trace of him. We are certain he is buried under the snow. He won't be found until next spring. We had good hopes for a while, but we don't, now." Sheriff Bradden circled with his fingers the brim of the Stetson he held in his hand. "That last storm wiped out all tracks. We found signs he was at the old Tim Langster place, but he must've been trapped in the next storm and separated from Sparrow. When we found the horse on the edge of town, we thought we would find Aaron. But Sparrow must have traveled a fair piece. Sorry, we couldn't save him. What with his age and being out there so long, he couldn't fight the pneumonia. We had to put him down."

Molly stood from her rocking chair in the living room. She straightened her mother's quilt, which hung over the back, to gain time before she spoke.

"Thank you, Sheriff Bradden. I'm very grateful to you and to all the men who have been looking for Aaron. I know how dangerous it is to be out in the mountains in the winter. Please, tell them not to risk their lives any further. I've had a week to get used to the idea. I grew up in these mountains, and I knew in my heart he was gone when his horse came home without him. Neither man nor beast can make it through a blizzard. I will write to the Forest Service and notify them he is missing. I'm sure they will send someone out to replace him; they may have already as Aaron was going to retire." Molly's hand shook slightly as she offered it to the sheriff. "I'm thankful Aaron didn't die due to the cattle and sheep wars. His death was natural, not violent."

He took her hand and held it for a moment before stammering, "I'm so, so sorry. We'll all miss him."

"Thank you. I will see you out and then go upstairs and put a light in the window, in case there is anyone out in the night who needs help getting home."

The sheriff left. Molly closed the door behind him. She walked to the staircase and reached for the worn banister. She sobbed softly as she climbed each step, one at a time. *Thank you, Lord, he didn't die because of my keeping the secret. Thank you that I am not to blame.*

Chapter Thirty-four

Molly put a can of tomato soup in a brown grocery bag stamped with "Hasty's Grocery and Emporium."

"Molly, how long have you been working at the store?" A woman in her thirties wearing a dress, nylons, and low, high-heeled shoes stood at the counter.

"I started with the original Mr. and Mrs. Hasty, Tate and Fern, and then I worked for their son, Tate Jr., and his wife, and now for Tate Jr.'s daughter, Hazel, and her husband, John. I work two days a week, and that's enough. It seems with more modern conveniences, like this cash register, the printed receipts, and the refrigeration unit at the back of the store, the busier I get." Molly slid a box of Wheaties between the other items in the bag "The bill comes to six dollars and eighty-five cents, Emma."

"Molly, Mom says Wheaties are 'the breakfast of champions.' I'm going to be a champion when I grow up." The boy stood on tiptoes and held the edge of the counter. His smile showed an empty place where a tooth should have been.

"What happened, Emmett?" Molly put her finger under the boy's chin and smiled.

Emma Pryon rolled her eyes. "What doesn't happen with him? He decided he was Superman. He used a sheet as a cape, climbed a tree, and tried to fly down. The dentist said he'll be fine when his permanent teeth grow in."

Two carts pushed by two middle-aged women came up to the counter. "Molly, we are meeting at your house next week for the mission society's quilting bee, aren't we?

"Right, Flora. Seven o'clock on the first Wednesday of the month, as usual."

The bell over the door rang, and a slight, dark-eyed woman entered. She saw the women at the counter and lowered her eyes. She took a shopping cart and rolled it to the back aisle.

"She's the wife of the new Forest Service Ranger," Flora said. "They are not our sort of folks, both being outsiders, and she is Vietnamese, to boot. I guess she's one of those war brides you hear about. Her husband served as a Marine over there. Why he couldn't find a sweet girl of his own kind here in the good ol' United States of America, I'm sure I don't know. And I say we shouldn't be in this war. I'll bet she's a communist."

"Flora, they wouldn't let a serviceman marry a communist," Flora's companion said. "And you should lower your voice. She might hear you."

"Mommy, what's a communist?' Emmett piped up.

"Shush, Emmett. Not so loud. Come on, we're going home." Emma picked up her grocery bag and grabbed the boy's hand.

"Mommy, what's a communist?" Emmett asked louder.

Emma opened the door and pulled her son out to the sidewalk. Flora and her friend paid for their groceries and left after glancing at the new customer coming toward the counter.

"Hello. You are Mrs. Stinson, aren't you?" Molly asked as she lifted items from the cart.

"Yes, thank you. My first name is Ai, spelled A-I not E-Y-E." She smiled and bowed her head in greeting. "I am Confucianist, not communist."

"Don't worry about them. After people get to know you, they will be friendlier."

"It's hard to get to know people when they avoid me. I have been in Prineville for three months, and no one visits or greets me. My husband says few people talk to him except for his work." Ai's hands trembled as she took out her coin purse.

Molly reached across the counter and held Ai's hands in hers. "It is always difficult to become accepted. Give us time. Why don't you come to the quilting circle next Wednesday? It's at my house. Would it bother you if the quilts go to the Lutheran Mission Society?"

"No, Confucianism is respectful of all peoples and all religions. But, I do not know this quilting."

"Are you busy tonight?"

"No."

Molly walked Ai to the sidewalk and pointed to the house next to the church, on the hilltop at the end of the street. "Come to my house about seven, and I will show you the basic stitches you will use next week at the ladies' meeting. It won't be long, and you will know lots of people. You might even like some of them...perhaps."

* * *

Ai stepped up into the pickup truck. "Thank you, Mrs. Luken, for showing me the quilt stitches last night. I practiced them this morning. And thank you for inviting me to go with you today. It's so lonely when Stan is working."

"Call me Molly. Everyone does. And don't thank me yet. This old truck is going to shake and rattle our bones. We'll have to go over a few rough roads to get to some of the ranches. I should thank you for the company. Before my husband died, I began to deliver library books in a wagon. Now I use this Ford truck." Molly started the vehicle and drove it down the driveway and onto the main street.

"The people you take the library books to must be very happy to see you." Ai sat on the passenger seat and kept her eyes on her folded hands.

"I dare say not as much as years ago. Everyone has radios now, and some folks have television, but the reception is poor in these mountains. I think the children especially like to see the books I bring. And the ladies do like the magazines. Helps them keep up with the new trends." Molly shifted gears, and the truck barreled forward.

Ai looked at Molly. "Speaking of children, I…I'm going to have my first. You are the first person I have told, except for Stan, of course."

"Wonderful! You must be thrilled." Molly smiled and turned to Ai. She saw the tense muscles in her face. "What's the matter? Are you afraid?"

"In my country, the wife lives with the husband's parents and grandparents, except when she has her first child. She goes home to her parents and grandparents until the child is born and both are well and able to return to the husband's family, where the daughter-in-law resumes her duties to the household. I live amongst Stan's people, though it is not exactly his family, but I cannot return to my people, as they are on the other side of the world." Ai wet her lips and stared down at her lap. "I do not tell Stan, but I am lonely and scared. Life is very different here."

The truck hit large ruts in the dirt-and-gravel one-lane road. It lurched up and rammed them down. Molly tightened her grip on the steering wheel, and Ai instinctively grabbed the dashboard with both hands. Molly shifted to low gear as they ascended a steep hill. At the top, she shifted again, and the truck tore down the hill like on a roller coaster plunge. At the bottom, the road leveled off. Ai released her hold on the dashboard and rubbed her white knuckles. Molly eased her grip on the wheel and again smiled at Ai. "Just a couple more spots like that and we'll reach the first cattle ranch. After that, we'll head for two sheep ranches and another cattle ranch. This old truck gets a workout." Molly took one hand off the wheel and patted Ai's clenched hands. "I don't know much about your customs, and at seventy-four, I'm too old to step in for your mother, but I could be an adopted grandmother. You could come to my place when it is time for the little one to arrive, if that would be all right?"

A smile warmed Ai's face. "It would be wonderful. The child will be born next spring, in the Year of the Snake."

"I'm very sorry."

"Oh, no, the snake year is a good year to be born. The child will be diplomatic, have great wisdom, and possess a strong will and personality. If it is a boy, we will call him Kim, which means golden one, and if it is a girl she will be An, which is peace."

"And I will be a great-grandmother to Kim or An." The two laughed and seized a piece of framework as the truck careened in and out of the ruts.

"As your new grandmother, I'm going to forbid you to come on my trips to the ranches in the future, so you don't lose the precious one. You can help me at the house, though. My collection of lending books has taken over. You could help me bring some order to it."

"I would be most pleased to be of assistance, dear grandmother." Ai smiled.

"You can start tomorrow if you wish. I just got a huge box of books donated by an anonymous donor. The crate says Duluth, Minnesota, but that is the only address. I get books about twice a year from that donor. Without them, our library would be skimpy indeed."

Both women grasped a piece of the truck's frame as they hit a deep rut and bounced up so hard their heads hit the roof. The truck rolled down the road with gales of laughter and giggles tinkling in the air.

Chapter Thirty-five

A young man in a suit parked his car by the curb and walked up a broken flagstone sidewalk to the front porch. The peeling paint spoke of hard times. The wood steps sagged and groaned under his feet. He removed his hat as he approached an elderly lady sleeping in a rocking chair.

"Ma'am. Mrs. Luken?"

The gray-haired woman jerked awake and stared at the man. "Yes, what do you want?"

"I'd like to speak with you." The man sat down in an old wicker chair with a musty seat cushion. "I'm a reporter for the *Portland Oregonian*. My paper would like to do a story on you."

"Me? Why me, for heaven's sake? I ain't anybody."

"You are Molly Langster Luken, aren't you? And you turned one hundred last week?"

"Yes, the whole town had a big shindig, and now your paper doesn't think I'm going to live one more day? They figure they'd better get a story from me before I turn up my toes, right?"

"No, ma'am." The reporter shuffled his feet. His editor's words rang in his memory: "Get a story from the old lady before she croaks."

Molly laughed and slapped the man on his knee. "Well, your paper is right. Not likely I'll be around much longer. Been here too long, as I see it. But the good Lord hasn't asked for my opinion." Molly laughed again. "You have to excuse me, mister. The older I get, the more ornery I get. What do you want to know?"

"You're the oldest resident in Crook County, and you were born here, right?"

"Yep, you got that right. Born and lived here my entire life. Never left. I'm third-generation. I married an outsider, a bureaucrat, but he eventually fit in. He's buried along with my other family right out there in the churchyard cemetery. Same church where I was baptized, confirmed, and married." Molly gestured with her hand toward the graveyard. "I lived through World War I and II, the Korean War, the Vietnam War, and I hear they're fixin' to have another war. I don't think I want to hang around for it. I'm mighty tired of wars."

"Yes, ma'am. I've been searching the newspaper's back issues. You were a girl during the range war, weren't you?" The reporter cleared his throat. He couldn't find many people who would talk about it. People acted as if it had never happened.

"I was ten when I became aware of it, young fella. It was brewing before, but I didn't pay it no mind until the tenth spring, right after my birthday." Molly rocked back and forth several times.

The reporter smiled in relief; he might not go back to his editor empty-handed. "The papers said you were an eyewitness to the massacres in the range called the high meadow."

"Massacres? They call it massacres? Not back in my day. There sure was death and misery. Not all of it seen, neither. There was death on the inside, too, where it can't be seen. People stopped being the way they were and became different. At times better, at times not."

"How and when did the range war stop?"

"The pastor, Pastor Weatherby, he and other folks wanted to stop the killing, including my ma and pa. They wrote letters to Washington, to Teddy Roosevelt himself. Took a long time, but Roosevelt sent men from the Forest Service. One fella, Mr. Ireland, drew up a plan for ranchers to share the public land in a way it wouldn't be too crowded and over-grazed. Things got better, and years later I married a forester who managed the whole affair. My family all lived to see the program work and the killing stop."

"I couldn't find records of anyone being arrested for the killings up in the high meadow."

"No one was."

"There wasn't any justice?"

Molly laughed and slapped her knee. "Justice? Haven't you ever seen the statue of justice? It's wearing a blindfold. I reckon there have been more than a million crimes committed around this weary, old world that Lady Justice ain't seen." Molly rocked back and forth. Her face saddened. "No justice by men's reckoning, but I figure God took whatever He required."

"Reports in the paper hinted there were witnesses who could identify the shooters."

"Were there? My, my," Molly said as she rocked. Her eyes twinkled.

"Would you tell me who the killers were? They're dead, surely, and couldn't hurt you." The reporter studied Molly's twinkling eyes. "You do know, don't you?"

"Maybe I do, or maybe I don't." Molly sat back and laughed. "What good would it do if I do know and tell you? Their children or grandchildren might be living nearby and could be damaged by it. I personally knew one of the herders killed—Voyager was his name. He lived a simple, quiet life and never hurt anyone. He wouldn't want anyone to be hurt today. As I said, the Lord gets His justice in His own time, His own way."

"This Voyager, he was a sheepherder for the Millers, wasn't he? Do you remember them?"

"Remember! Cassie Sue Miller was my best friend. Still is, too, though I ain't seen her in ninety years." Molly sat back and chuckled.

"According to my research...." the reporter thumbed through a small spiral notebook. "The Millers continued ranching for a year after losing a thousand head in the high meadow. They lost the ranch to the bank and for back taxes. The family moved to Iowa to take up dairy farming. They were both in their sixties when they died."

"I was angry at their daughter Cassie for a long time when she wouldn't stay in touch, but I came to understand it was best for her. It was her way of moving on. Do you know where Cassie is? Where she lives?" Molly sat forward and focused on the notebook in the reporter's hands.

The young man flipped through pages. "She married, had three children. She and her husband owned a candy and pastry store in Minneapolis, Minnesota," he said as his lips parted in a wide smile.

"What? Why are you smiling?"

"The most popular items they sold were popcorn balls in the fall and winter. They shipped them to markets in the Midwest and Canada. Cassie Livy—that was her married name—was interviewed for the local newspaper's taste section and was asked why the popcorn balls were so popular. She said...." He flipped a page. "'They are not too dry and not too sticky. It is an old family recipe I promised never to reveal.'" He studied Molly's expression. "She evidently kept her word and never told anyone. Her granddaughter owns the candy store and quit making the popcorn balls, as she couldn't find the recipe. Popcorn balls! Imagine, your shop becoming a success over such a little thing like popcorn balls. What folks will come up with to make a buck." The reporter stopped smiling. "Cassie died five years ago."

"She did well. She promised my mother she'd never share the recipe. Sounds like she was happy. I'm glad for her." Molly seemed to cherish the memory as she rocked slowly in her chair. "Do you have her granddaughter's address? I want to send her the recipe for my ma's popcorn balls."

"Sure." The reporter wrote an address on a paper in his notebook, tore out the page and handed it to Molly.

Molly stared at the name and smiled. "Cassie Sue Mattson. She'll do well if she takes after her namesake."

"Your husband was a forester for over forty years, wasn't he?"

"Sure was. Did an excellent job. Most cattle and sheep violence ended then as people knew he was fair."

"He testified a few times in court cases where men were convicted of assault and arson, didn't he?"

"Yes, he did when he had to. People respected him for it. He got caught in a blizzard out east of town. He was found the next spring. We buried him in the church cemetery with the family. I still keep a lamp lit in the upstairs room. Folks think I'm daft and that I do it to help Aaron find his way home, but he's home. I do it for the poor souls lost out in the meadows to find their way. Besides, it's easier to do now with the house wired for electricity. I've got a switch at the bottom of the stairs, so I don't need to go up and down with these old knees." Molly continued to rock back and forth, scrutinizing her thin hands and the blue veins that made paths under the skin.

"Tell me more about your life. You started the book mobile in an old wagon?"

She smiled. "Yes, and taught my adopted granddaughter, Ai Stinson, to drive, and we did it together for years. She took over when I was ninety-eight and couldn't manage the climbing in and out. Our little library grew. Twice a year, a big crate of real good books would arrive, shipped in from Duluth, Minnesota. No return address. We got them for years, but they stopped coming several years back. Maybe Cassie had something to do with it, her being in Minneapolis and all. Now, we have a regular library and Ai is head librarian. She and her husband have been a real blessing to our town. They have lived here the longest of all the forest service agents. I helped my great-grandson Kim go to medical school, and now he is our doctor. He's a smart man. Born in the Year of the Snake. Bet you didn't know that."

"Tell me more about your early years and the cattle and sheep wars. The readers would be interested."

It was apparent that she was closing up as she began to draw back into herself. Memories seemed to tug at her. "Nope. I'm weary. Nothing left to say. The Dear Lord is preparing a place for me in heaven, and when He has it ready, He'll tell me to come home. I've been waiting for the call a long, long time."

The reporter smiled at that. *Maybe if we talk about the Lord I'll get her back to the cattle and sheep wars.* "What do you think your place in heaven will be like?"

Obvious relief washed over Molly's face as the topic moved on to a happier time ahead. "The Lord hasn't asked for my advice, and I'm not going to give Him none without His asking, but supposing He was to ask, I'd tell him I want my heavenly home to be the high meadow as it was on my tenth-birthday picnic, with my Uncle Tim, Aunt Ruth, Cousins Charlie and Ned, Ma and Pa there, but I also want Voyager, Rolf, Jake—those are two sheep dogs—Lammie Star—Cassie's pet lamb, Buster, Judy, Sparrow and Cassie there too, like they were, and my dear Aaron." Molly quit rocking. "What are you going to call this article you're writing?"

The reporter thought for a minute. "I think I will call it 'Talking to History.'"

Molly laughed. "Balderdash! Reporters are like politicians. Say what you want. Go now. I'm getting tired, and I got a letter to write to Cassie's granddaughter."

* * *

Molly sat down at her kitchen table with a bottle of ink, a pen, and paper.

Dear Cassie Sue,

You don't know me, and I hope it's all right for me to address you informally. You see, I knew your grandmother, Cassie Sue Miller. She was my best friend in the whole world, and I think she still is even if she is gone. I doubt she ever talked about me, as we made an agreement, and I bet she stuck to it. We had good reasons to make the deal—at least we thought so back then.

I bet she kept her word on another thing. She promised my mother never to tell the popcorn ball recipe secret. I am enclosing the method for you to use as you wish. It doesn't need to be kept a secret anymore. With time and practice, you will make the best popcorn balls in the country, maybe farther.

I'm not going to sign this letter or include my address. It's part of our agreement, and I likely won't be here by the time a letter from you can get here. When I leave this place, all the agreements and all the secrets are done.

I wish you the very best, granddaughter of my dear, sweet friend.

Molly put down the pen, blotted the letter, folded it, and stuffed it in its envelope. Taking another sheet, she wrote out the recipe. She also put it in the envelope and addressed it. She placed a twenty-two-cent stamp on it as she took a deep breath and smiled.

* * *

An elderly woman opened the front door and peered around the corner to the kitchen as she stepped into the hallway. She saw Molly's back as she sat at the table. "Molly, it's me, Emma Pryon. I'm returning the sugar I borrowed from you yesterday. Dear, you shouldn't leave the door open like this. You know, the world has changed. It isn't as safe as it was when you were a girl." Emma walked past the table and put the sugar on the counter as she said, "Did you hear the wolf last night? It wailed something fierce. Gave me the creeps. I thought all the wolves were hunted out of the state. Say, you didn't light the lamp upstairs last night. Did you forget?" She turned and walked to the table. "Dear, are you asleep?"

The woman laid her hand on Molly's shoulder. Molly's head and shoulders slumped down onto the kitchen table. Emma sat in a chair, put her hands on Molly's cold ones, and rubbed them. Tears welled up in her eyes and spilled down her cheeks.

"Why, Molly, you died on us." She touched Molly's gray hair. "I'm gonna miss you for sure. You're one gentle soul. You have a soft smile on your face. It appears the Lord took you peaceful. I'll go fetch Doctor Kim. He'll come right away. I bet his mother Ai will come, too. They sure are a blessing to our community. I'm going to tell Charlie. He and our boy Emmett will be right sorry to hear you are gone from us. The stories Charlie tells of you and his mother when he was a boy growing up are precious. That one of cinders caught in the diapers is a hoot. I tell him he should write them down. He won't, though. He's not much good with pen and paper." Emma took a handkerchief from her apron pocket and wiped her eyes.

She saw an envelope with a stamp on it, addressed and sealed. "I'll mail this for you. I didn't know you knew any folks in Minneapolis. You never spent a day outside Crook County. You led such a peaceful, uneventful life. The only important thing that happened around here was when the cattlemen and sheep men had their troubles, but you were too young to be affected by that." The woman took the envelope and walked out the screen door. It fell back with a loud bang.

CPSIA information can be obtained
at www.ICGtesting.com
Printed in the USA
FFOW01n1109081215
19232FF

The
Voltage
Regulator
Handbook

Compiled by

John D. Spencer
Dale E. Pippenger

TEXAS INSTRUMENTS
INCORPORATED
P.O. Box 5012   Dallas, Texas 75222

LCC4350
75001-107-NS

IMPORTANT NOTICES

Texas Instruments reserves the right to make changes at any time in order to improve design and to supply the best product possible.

TI cannot assume any responsibility for any circuits shown or represent that they are free from patent infringement.

ISBN 0—89512—101—8
Library of Congress No. 77—87869

Table of Contents

Table of Contents (Continued)

Regulator Alphanumeric Index

INTRODUCTION

Voltage regulation is a basic function in the majority of today's electronic systems yet it often takes a back seat in system development. With continual advancement of semiconductor technology and the advent of the microprocessor, electronics are finding their way into an increasingly broadening field of specialized applications. Too often, a design finds itself stalled in the development of a power supply to complete the total system. This problem is being eased with the development of a new generation of monolithic integrated circuit regulators and discrete components which offer design simplification, improved reliability, and a reduction in system cost and size.

This handbook has been written to encompass the total power supply design and aid the engineer in the selection of regulator integrated circuits and associated components. In addition to basic power supply design theory, related topics such as external pass transistor considerations, input filter designs, voltage rectification techniques, and mounting and heat-sinking techniques are discussed. Complete data sheet information on all components and mechanical hardware are included.

Part 1

1
Voltage Regulators

1.1 BASIC REGULATOR

The purpose of every voltage regulator is to convert a given dc or ac input voltage into a specific stable dc output voltage and maintain that voltage over a wide range of load conditions. To accomplish this, the typical voltage regulator (Figure 1.1) consists of:

1) A reference element that provides a known stable level, (V_{REF}).

2) A sampling element to sample output voltage level.

3) A comparator element for comparing the output voltage sample to the reference and creating an error signal.

4) A control element to provide translation of the input voltage to the desired output level over varying load conditions as indicated by the error signal.

Even though regulation methods vary among the three basic regulators: (1) series, (2) shunt, (3) switching, these four basic functions exist in all regulator circuits.

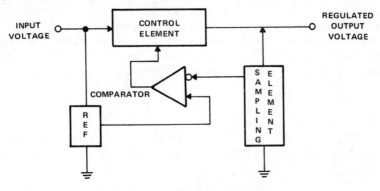

Figure 1.1. Basic Regulator Block Diagram

1.1.1 Reference Element

The reference element forms the foundation of all voltage regulators since output voltage is either equal to or a multiple of the reference. Variations in the reference voltage will be interpreted as output voltage errors by the comparator and cause the output voltage to change accordingly. For good regulation, the reference must be stable for all variations in supply voltages and junction temperatures. Various techniques commonly used in integrated circuit regulators are discussed in detail in the text outlining error considerations.

1.1.2 Sampling Element

The sampling element monitors output voltage and translates it into a level equal to the reference voltage for a desired output voltage. Variations in the output voltage then cause the feedback voltage to change to some value greater than or less than the reference voltage. This delta voltage is the error voltage that directs the regulator to respond appropriately to correct for the output voltage change experienced.

1.1.3 Comparator Element

The comparator element of an integrated circuit voltage regulator not only monitors the feedback voltage for comparison with the reference, but also provides gain for the detected error level. For this reason, the comparator element is also referred to as the error amplifier. The output of the comparator element, the amplified error signal, is then translated by the control circuit to return the output to a prescribed level.

1.1.4 Control Element

All of the previous elements discussed remain virtually unaltered regardless of the type of regulator of which they form a part. The control element varies widely depending on the type of regulator being designed. It is the control that determines the classification of the voltage regulator: series, shunt, or switching. Figure 1.2 shows representations of the basic control element configurations, each of which is discussed in detail. The control element contributes an insignificant amount of error to the regulator's performance since the sense element monitors the output voltage beyond the control element and compensates for its error contributions. The control element reflects directly on the regulator's performance characteristics in that it affects such parameters as minimum input-to-output voltage differential, circuit efficiency, and power dissipation.

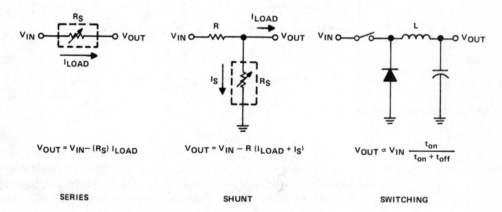

$$V_{OUT} = V_{IN} - (R_S)\, I_{LOAD} \qquad V_{OUT} = V_{IN} - R\, (I_{LOAD} + I_S) \qquad V_{OUT} \propto V_{IN} \frac{t_{on}}{t_{on} + t_{off}}$$

SERIES   SHUNT   SWITCHING

Figure 1.2. Control Element Configurations

1.2 REGULATOR CLASSIFICATIONS

1.2.1 Series Regulator

The series regulator derives its name from the control element it uses. The output voltage is regulated by modulating a series element, usually a transistor, that acts as a variable resistor. Changes in input voltage result in a change in the equivalent resistance of the series element. The product of this resistance and the load current create a changing differential voltage that compensates for a changing input voltage. The basic series regulator is illustrated in Figure 1.3.

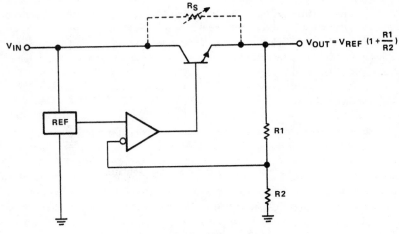

Figure 1.3. Basic Series Regulator

$$V_{OUT} = V_{IN} - V_{DIFF}$$

$$V_{DIFF} = I_{LOAD} R_S$$

$$V_{OUT} = V_{IN} - I_{LOAD} R_S$$

For a changing input voltage:

$$\Delta R_S = \frac{\Delta V_{IN}}{I_{LOAD}}$$

For a changing load current:

$$\Delta R_S = -\frac{\Delta I_{LOAD} R_S}{I_{LOAD} + \Delta I_{LOAD}}$$

Series regulators provide a simple inexpensive way to obtain a source of regulated voltage. In high-current applications, however, the voltage drop maintained across the pass element results in a substantial power loss.

1.2.2 Shunt Regulator

The shunt regulator employs a shunt element that varies its shunt current requirement to account for varying input voltages or changing load conditions. The basic shunt regulator is shown in Figure 1.4.

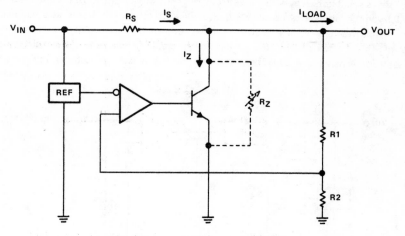

Figure 1.4. Basic Shunt Regulator

$$V_{OUT} = V_{IN} - I_S R_S$$

$$I_S = I_{LOAD} + I_Z$$

$$V_{OUT} = V_{IN} - R_S (I_{LOAD} + I_Z)$$

For a changing load current

$$\Delta I_Z = -\Delta I_{LOAD}$$

For a changing input voltage

$$\Delta I_Z = \frac{\Delta V_{IN}}{R}$$

$$\Delta I_Z = \frac{V_{OUT}}{\Delta R_Z}$$

Even though it is usually less efficient, a shunt regulator may prove to be the best choice for a specific application. The shunt regulator is less sensitive to input voltage transients, it does not reflect load current transients back to the source, and it is inherently short-circuit proof.

1.2.3 Switching Regulator

The switching regulator employs an active switch as its control element, which is used to chop the input voltage at a varying duty cycle[1] based on the regulator's load requirements. See Figure 1.5.

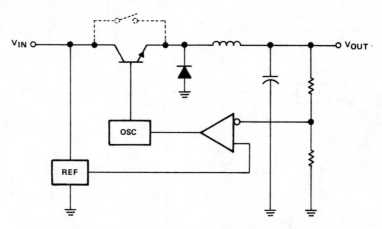

Figure 1.5. Basic Switching Regulator (Step-Down Configuration)

A filter, usually an LC filter, is then used to average the voltage seen at its input and deliver that voltage to the output load. Since the pass transistor is either on (saturated) or off, the power lost in the control element is minimal. For this reason the switching regulator becomes particularly attractive for applications involving large input-to-output differential voltages or high load-current requirements. In the past, switching voltage regulators were discrete designs but recent advancements in integrated circuit technology have resulted in several monolithic switching regulator circuits that contain all of the necessary elements to design step-up, step-down, or inverting voltage converters or mainframe power supplies.

---

1. The duty cycle may be varied by:
   a. maintaining a constant on-time, varying the frequency
   b. maintaining a constant off-time, varying the frequency
   c. maintaining a constant frequency, varying the on/off times.

The performance of these techniques, their advantages, and disadvantages are discussed in Section 3.

2
Major Error Contributors

The ideal voltage regulator maintains a constant output voltage over varying input voltage, load, and temperature conditions. Realistically, however, these influences affect the regulator's output voltage. In addition, the regulator's internal inaccuracies affect the overall circuit performance. This section discusses the major contributors, their effects, and possible solutions to the problems they create.

2.1 REFERENCE

There are several techniques employed in integrated circuit voltage regulators. Each provides its particular level of performance and problems. The optimum reference depends on the regulator's requirements.

2.1.1 Zener Diode Reference

The zener diode reference, as shown in Figure 2.1, is the simplest technique. The zener voltage itself, V_Z, forms the reference voltage, V_{REF}. This technique is satisfactory for stable supply voltage applications but becomes unstable in unregulated supply voltage applications. The instability results from a changing zener current, I_Z, as the supply voltage varies. The changing zener current precipitates a change in the value of V_Z, the reference voltage. The zener reference model is shown in Figure 2.2.

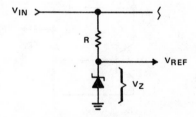

Figure 2.1. Basic Zener Reference

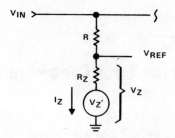

Figure 2.2. Zener Reference Model

$$V_{REF} = V_Z$$

$$V_Z = V_Z' + I_Z R_Z$$

$$I_Z = \frac{V_{IN} - V_Z'}{R + R_Z}$$

$$V_{REF} = V_Z' + R_Z \left(\frac{V_{IN} - V_Z'}{R + R_Z} \right)$$

V_{REF} is a function of V_{IN}.

2.1.2 Constant-Current Zener Reference

The zener reference can be refined by the addition of a constant-current source as its supply. Driving the zener diode with a constant current minimizes the effect of zener impedance on the overall stability of the zener reference. An example of this technique is shown in Figure 2.3. The reference voltage of this configuration is relatively independent of changes in supply voltage.

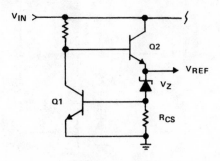

Figure 2.3. Constant-Current Zener Reference

8

$$V_{REF} = V_Z + V_{BE(Q1)}$$

$$I_Z = \frac{V_{BE(Q1)}}{R_{CS}}$$

V_{REF} is independent of V_{IN}.

In addition to superior supply voltage rejection, the circuit shown in Figure 2.3 yields improved temperature stability. The reference voltage V_{REF} is the sum of the zener voltage V_Z and the base-emitter voltage of Q1 $V_{BE(Q1)}$. A low temperature coefficient can be achieved by balancing the positive temperature coefficient of the zener with the negative temperature coefficient of the base-emitter junction of Q1. The only drawback of the constant-current zener reference is that it requires a supply voltage of 9 volts or more.

2.1.3 Band-Gap Reference

Another popular reference is the band-gap reference, which is developed from the highly predictable emitter-base voltage of integrated transistors. Basically, the reference voltage is derived from the energy-band-gap voltage of the semiconductor material, ($V_{go(silicon)}$ = 1.204 V). The basic band-gap configuration is shown in Figure 2.4. The reference voltage V_{REF} in this case is:

$$V_{REF} = V_{BE(Q3)} + I_2 R2$$

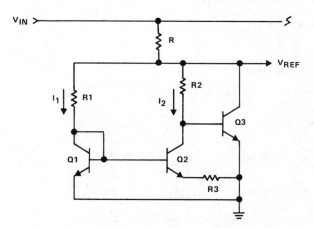

Figure 2.4. Band-Gap Reference

The resistor values of R1 and R2 are selected such that the current through transistors Q1 and Q2 are significantly different ($I_1 = 10 \, I_2$). The difference in current through transistors Q1 and Q2 results in a difference in their respective base-emitter voltages. This voltage differential ($V_{BE\,(Q1)} - V_{BE\,(Q2)}$) will appear across R3. With sufficiently high-gain transistors, the current I_2 passes through R3. I_2 is therefore equal to: $\dfrac{V_{BE(Q1)} - V_{BE(Q2)}}{R3}$

$$\therefore V_{REF} = V_{BE(Q3)} + (V_{BE(Q1)} - V_{BE(Q2)}) \frac{R2}{R3}$$

Analyzing the effect of temperature on V_{REF}: it can be shown that the difference in emitter-base voltage between two similar transistors operated at different currents is:

$$V_{BE(Q1)} - V_{BE(Q2)} = \frac{KT}{q} \ln \frac{I_1}{I_2}$$

where

K = Boltzmann's constant

T = absolute temperature

q = change of an electron

I = current

The base-emitter voltage of Q3 can also be expressed as

$$V_{BE(Q3)} = V_{go} \left(1 - \frac{T}{T_0}\right) + V_{BEO}\left(\frac{T}{T_0}\right)$$

where

V_{go} = band-gap potential

V_{BEO} = emitter-base voltage at T_0

V_{REF} can then be expressed as:

$$V_{REF} = V_{go} \left(1 - \frac{T}{T_0}\right) + V_{BEO}\left(\frac{T}{T_0}\right) + \frac{R2}{R3} \frac{KT}{q} \ln \frac{I_1}{I_2}$$

Differentiating with respect to temperature yields

$$\frac{dV_{REF}}{dt} = -\frac{V_{go}}{T_0} + \frac{V_{BEO}}{T_0} + \frac{R2}{R3} \frac{K}{q} \ln \frac{I_1}{I_2}$$

If R2, R3, and I_1 are appropriately selected such that

$$\frac{R2}{R3} \ln \frac{I_1}{I_2} = \left(V_{go} - V_{BEO(Q3)} \right) C$$

where

$$C = \frac{q}{KT_0}$$

and

$$V_{go} = 1.22 \text{ V}$$

The resulting

$$\frac{dV_{REF}}{dt} = 0$$

The reference is temperature-compensated.

The band-gap voltage reference is particularly advantageous for low-voltage applications ($V_{REF} = 1.2$ V) and yields a reference level that is stable with supply and temperature variations.

2.2 SAMPLING ELEMENT

The sampling element employed on most integrated circuit voltage regulators is an R1/R2 resistor divider network (Figure 2.5) determined by the output-voltage to reference-voltage ratio.

$$\frac{V_{OUT}}{V_{REF}} = 1 + \frac{R1}{R2}$$

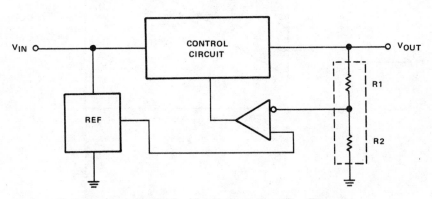

Figure 2.5. R1/R2 Ladder Network Sampling Element

11

Since the feedback voltage is determined by ratio and not absolute value, proportional variations in R1 and R2 have no effect on the accuracy of the integrated circuit voltage regulator. With proper attention given to the layout of these resistors in an integrated circuit, their contribution to the error of the voltage regulator will be minimal. The initial accuracy is the only parameter affected.

2.3 COMPARATOR

Provided a stable reference and an accurate output sampling element exist, the comparator then becomes the primary factor determining the voltage regulator's performance. Typical amplifier performance parameters such as offset, common-mode and supply rejection ratios, output impedance, and the temperature coefficient affect the accuracy and regulation of the voltage regulator over variations in supply, load, and ambient temperature conditions.

2.3.1 Offset

Offset voltage is viewed by the comparator as an error signal, as illustrated in Figure 2.6, and will cause the output to respond accordingly.

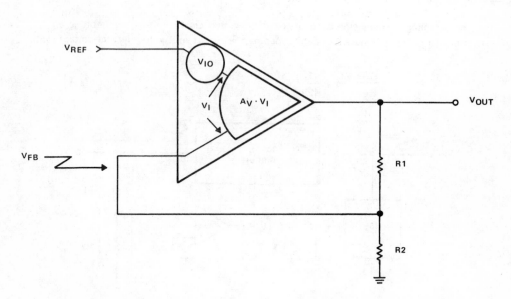

Figure 2.6. Comparator Model Showing Input Offset Voltage Effect

$$V_{OUT} = A_V V_I$$

$$V_I = V_{REF} - V_{IO} - V_{FB}$$

$$V_{FB} = V_{OUT} \left[\frac{R2}{R1 + R2} \right]$$

$$V_{OUT} = \frac{V_{REF} - V_{IO}}{\dfrac{1}{A_V} + \left[\dfrac{R2}{R1 + R2} \right]}$$

If A_V is sufficiently large

$$V_{OUT} = (V_{REF} - V_{IO}) \left(1 + \frac{R1}{R2} \right)$$

V_{IO} represents an initial error in the output of the integrated circuit voltage regulator. The simplest method of compensating for this error is to adjust the output voltage sampling element R1/R2.

Offset Change with Temperature — The technique discussed above compensates for the comparator's offset voltage and yields an accurate regulator, but only at a specific temperature. As experienced in most amplifiers, the offset voltage varies with temperature proportional to the initial offset level. Trimming the feedback circuit as outlined for the externally adjustable regulator does not reduce the actual offset but merely counteracts it. When subjected to a different ambient temperature, the offset voltage changes and thus error is again introduced in the voltage regulator. Nulling the comparator for input offset improves on this problem as the offset voltage is corrected instead of compensated for. Monolithic integrated circuit regulators employ state-of-the-art technology to trim the integrated circuit amplifiers during the manufacturing process to all but eliminate offset. With minimal offset voltage, minimum drift will be experienced with temperature variations.

2.3.2 Supply Voltage Variations

The comparator's power supply and common-mode rejection ratios are the primary contributors to regulator error introduced by an unregulated input voltage. In an ideal amplifier, the output voltage is a function of the differential input voltage only. Realistically, the common-mode voltage of the input influences the output voltage also. The common-mode voltage is the average input voltage, referenced from the amplifier's virtual ground, as shown in Figure 2.7.

$$\text{Virtual Ground} = \frac{V_{CC+} + V_{CC-}}{2}$$

$$V_{IN(AV)} = \frac{V_S + V_{OUT}\left[\dfrac{R2}{R1+R2}\right]}{2}$$

$$V_{CM} = \frac{1}{2}\left[V_S + V_{OUT}\left(\frac{R2}{R1+R2}\right) - \left(V_{CC+} + V_{CC-}\right)\right]$$

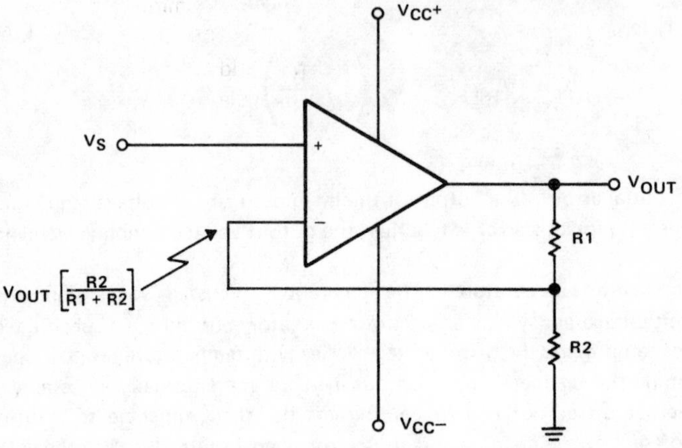

Figure 2.7. Comparator Model Showing Common-Mode Voltage

From this relation it can be seen that unequal variations in either supply rail will result in a change in the common-mode voltage.

The common-mode voltage rejection ratio (CMRR) is the ratio of the amplifier's differential voltage amplification to the common-mode voltage amplification.

$$CMRR = \frac{A_V}{A_{VCM}}$$

$$A_{VCM} = \frac{A_V}{CMRR}$$

That portion of output voltage contributed by the equivalent common-mode input voltage is:

$$V_{OUT} = V_{CM}\, A_{VCM} = \frac{A_V\, V_{CM}}{CMRR}$$

The equivalent error introduced then is:

$$\text{COMMON-MODE ERROR} = \frac{V_{CM}}{CMRR}$$

The common-mode error represents an offset voltage to the amplifier. Neglecting the actual offset voltage, the output voltage then becomes:

$$V_{OUT} = \left(V_{REF} + \frac{V_{CM}}{CMRR} \right) \left(1 + \frac{R1}{R2} \right)$$

The utilization of constant-current sources in most modern integrated circuits, however, yields a high power-supply rejection ratio, of such magnitude that the common-mode voltage effect on V_{OUT} can usually be neglected. Preregulation of the input voltage is another popular technique employed to minimize supply voltage variation effects. In addition to improving the effects of common-mode voltage, preregulation contributes to overall regulator performance.

3
Regulator Design Considerations

Various types of integrated circuit voltage regulators are available, each having its own particular characteristics and advantages in various applications. Which type used depends primarily on the designer's needs and trade-offs in performance and cost.

3.1 POSITIVE VERSUS NEGATIVE REGULATORS

As a rule, this division in voltage regulators is self-explanatory; a positive regulator is used to regulate a positive voltage while a negative regulator is used to regulate a negative voltage. What is positive and what is negative may vary, depending on the ground reference.

Figure 3.1 shows the conventional positive and negative voltage regulator applications employing a continuous and common ground. For systems operating on a single supply, the positive and negative regulators may be interchanged by floating the ground reference to the load or input. This approach to design is recommended only where the ground isolation serves as an advantage to the overall systems performance.

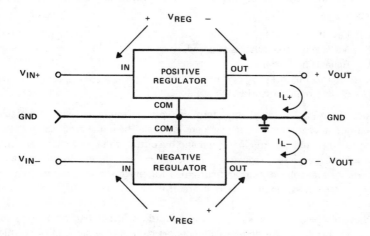

Figure 3.1. Conventional Positive/Negative Regulator

Figures 3.2 and 3.3 show a positive regulator in a negative configuration and a negative regulator in a positive configuration, respectively.

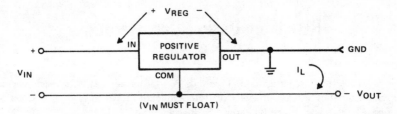

Figure 3.2. Positive Regulator in Negative Configuration (V_{IN} Must Float)

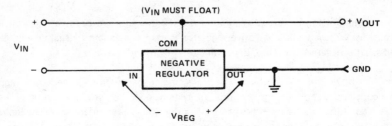

Figure 3.3. Negative Regulator in Positive Configuration (V_{IN} Must Float)

3.2 FIXED VERSUS ADJUSTABLE REGULATORS

A proliferation of fixed three-terminal voltage regulators offered in various current ranges are currently available from most major integrated circuit manufacturers. These regulators offer the designer a simple, inexpensive method to establish a regulated voltage source. Their particular advantages are:

1. Ease of use
2. No external components required
3. Reliable performance
4. Internal thermal protection
5. Short-circuit protection

But life is not all roses. The fixed three-terminal voltage regulators cannot be precisely adjusted since their output voltage sampling elements are internal. The initial accuracy of these devices may vary as much as ±5% from the nominal value and the output voltages available are limited. Current limits are based on the voltage regulator's applicable current range and are not adjustable. (See selection charts for available voltages and currents.) Extended range operation (increasing I_{LOAD}) is cumbersome and requires complex external circuitry.

The adjustable regulator caters to these applications, depending on the complexity of the adjustable voltage regulator. All adjustable regulators require external feedback, which allows the designer a precise and infinite voltage selection.

In addition, the output sense may be referred to a remote point. This allows the designer not only to extend the range of the regulator with minimal external circuitry, but also to compensate for losses in a distributed load or external pass element components. Additional features found on many adjustable voltage regulators are adjustable short-circuit current limiting, access to the voltage reference element, and shutdown circuitry.

3.3   DUAL-TRACKING REGULATORS

The tracking regulator (Figure 3.4) provides regulation for two rails, usually one positive and one negative. The dual-tracking feature assures a balanced supply system by monitoring both voltage rails. If either of the voltage rails droops or goes out of regulation, the tracking regulator will cause the associated voltage rail to vary proportionally. (A 10% sag in the positive rail will result in a 10% sag in the negative rail.) These regulators are, for the most part, restricted to those applications where balanced supplies offer a defined performance improvement such as in linear systems.

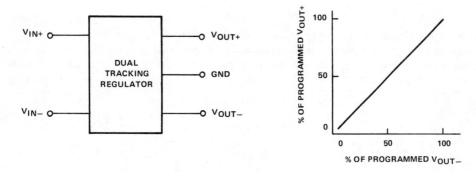

Figure 3.4. Dual Tracking Regulator

3.4   SERIES REGULATORS

The series regulator is well suited for medium current applications with nominal voltage differential requirements. Modulation of a series pass control element to maintain a well regulated prescribed output voltage is a straightforward design technique. Safe-operating-area protection circuits such as overvoltage, fold-back current limiting, and short-circuit protection are easily adapted. The primary drawback of the series regulator is its consumption of power. The series regulator (Figure 3.5) will consume power according to the load, proportional to the differential-voltage to output-voltage ratio. This becomes considerable with increasing load or differential voltage requirements. This power represents a loss to the system, and limits the amount of power deliverable to the load since the power dissipation of the series regulator is limited.

$$P_{REG} = V_{IN} I_{IN} - V_{OUT} I_{LOAD}$$

$$I_{IN} = I_{REG} + I_{LOAD}$$

19

Since $I_{LOAD} \gg I_{REG}$

$$I_{IN} \approx I_{LOAD}$$

$$\therefore P_{REG} \approx I_{LOAD} (V_{IN} - V_{OUT})$$

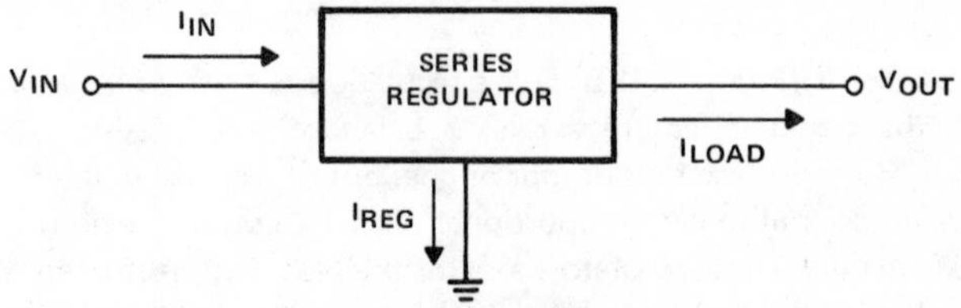

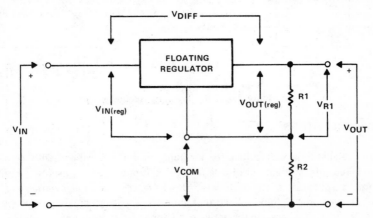

Figure 3.5. Series Regulator

3.5 FLOATING REGULATOR

The floating regulator (Figure 3.6) is a variation of the series regulator. The output voltage is maintained constant by varying the input-to-output voltage differential for a varying input voltage. The floating regulator's differential voltage is modulated such that its output voltage, referred to its common terminal $[V_{OUT(reg)}]$, is equal to its internal reference (V_{REF}). The voltage developed across the output to common terminal is equal to the voltage developed across R1 (V_{R1}).

Figure 3.6. Floating Regulator

$$V_{OUT(reg)} = V_{REF} = V_{R1}$$

$$V_{R1} = V_{OUT}\left(\frac{R1}{R1 + R2}\right)$$

$$V_{OUT} = V_{REF}\left(1 + \frac{R2}{R1}\right)$$

20

The common-terminal voltage is:

$$V_{COM} = V_{OUT} - V_{R1} = V_{OUT} - V_{REF}$$

The input voltage seen by the floating regulator is:

$$V_{IN(reg)} = V_{IN} - V_{COM}$$

$$V_{IN(reg)} = V_{IN} - V_{OUT} + V_{REF}$$

$$V_{IN(reg)} = V_{DIFF} + V_{REF}$$

Since V_{REF} is fixed, the only limitation on the input voltage is the allowable differential voltage. This makes the floating regulator especially suited for high-voltage applications ($V_{IN} > 40$ V).

Practical values of output voltage are limited to practical ratios of output-to-reference voltages.

$$\frac{R2}{R1} = \frac{V_{OUT}}{V_{REF}} - 1$$

The floating regulator exhibits power consumption characteristics similar to that of the series regulator from which it is derived, but unlike the series regulator, it can also serve as a current regulator as shown in Figure 3.7.

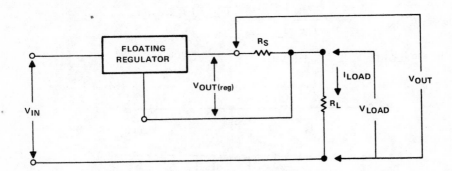

Figure 3.7. Floating Regulator as a Constant-Current Regulator

$$V_{OUT} = V_{REF} \left(1 + \frac{R_L}{R_S} \right)$$

$$V_{OUT} = V_{LOAD} + V_{OUT(reg)}$$

$$V_{OUT(reg)} = V_{REF}$$

$$\therefore V_{LOAD} = V_{REF}\left(1 + \frac{R_L}{R_S}\right) - V_{REF}$$

$$V_{LOAD} = V_{REF}\left(\frac{R_L}{R_S}\right)$$

$$I_{LOAD} = \frac{V_{LOAD}}{R_L}$$

$$I_{LOAD} = \frac{V_{REF}}{R_S}$$

The load current (I_{LOAD}) is independent of R_L.

3.6   SHUNT REGULATOR

The shunt regulator, shown in Figure 3.8, is the simplest of all regulators. It employs a fixed resistor as its series pass element. Changes in input voltage or load current requirements are compensated by modulating the current shunted to ground through the regulator.

For changes in V_{IN}: $\Delta I_Z = \dfrac{\Delta V_{IN}}{R_S}$

For changes in I_{LOAD}: $\Delta I_Z = -\Delta I_{LOAD}$

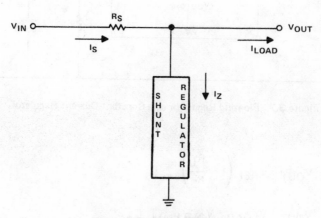

Figure 3.8. Shunt Regulator

The inherent short-circuit-proof feature of the shunt regulator makes it particularly attractive for some applications. The output voltage will be maintained until the load current required is equal to the current through the series element (see Figure 3.9).

$$I_{LOAD} = I_S \ (I_Z = 0)$$

Since the shunt regulator cannot source current, additional current required by the load will result in a depreciation of the output voltage to zero.

$$V_{OUT} = V_{IN} - I_{LOAD} \ R_S$$

The short-circuit current of the shunt regulator then becomes:

$$V_{OUT} = 0 \ V$$

$$I_{SC} = \frac{V_{IN}}{R_S}$$

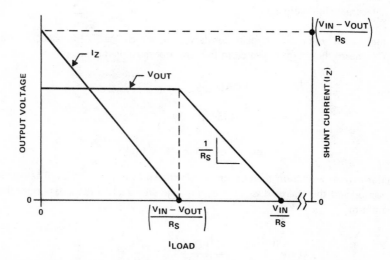

Figure 3.9. Output Voltage vs Load Current vs Shunt Current of a Shunt Regulator

3.7 SWITCHING REGULATOR

The switching regulator lends itself primarily to the higher power applications or those applications where power supply and system efficiency are of the utmost concern. Unlike the series regulator, the switching regulator operates its control element in an on or off mode. Switching regulator control element modes are shown in Figure 3.10. In this manner, the control element

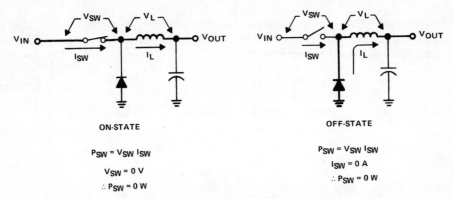

Figure 3.10. Switching Voltage Regulator Modes

is subjected to a high current at a very low voltage or a high differential voltage at a very low current; in either case the power dissipation in the control element is minimal. Changes in the load or input voltage are compensated for by varying the on-off ratio (duty cycle) of the switch, without increasing the internal power dissipated in the switching regulator. Operation of the switching regulator is illustrated in Figure 3.11.

For the output voltage to remain constant, the net charge in the capacitor must remain constant. This means the charge delivered to the capacitor must be dissipated in the load.

$$I_C = I_L - I_{LOAD}$$

$$I_C = -I_{LOAD} \text{ for } I_L = 0$$

$$I_C = I_{L(pk)} - I_{LOAD} \text{ for } I_L = I_{L(pk)}$$

The capacitor current waveform then becomes that shown in Figure 3.11(b). The charge delivered to the capacitor and the charge dissipated by the load are equal to the areas under the capacitor current waveform.

$$\Delta Q + = \frac{1}{2} \frac{(I_{L(pk)} - I_{LOAD})^2}{I_{L(pk)}} \, t \left(\frac{V_{IN}}{V_C}\right)$$

$$\Delta Q - = I_{LOAD} \left[T - \frac{1}{2}t\left(\frac{V_{IN}}{V_C}\right) - \frac{1}{2}t\left(\frac{I_{L(pk)} - I_{LOAD}}{I_{L(pk)}}\right)\left(\frac{V_{IN}}{V_C}\right) \right]$$

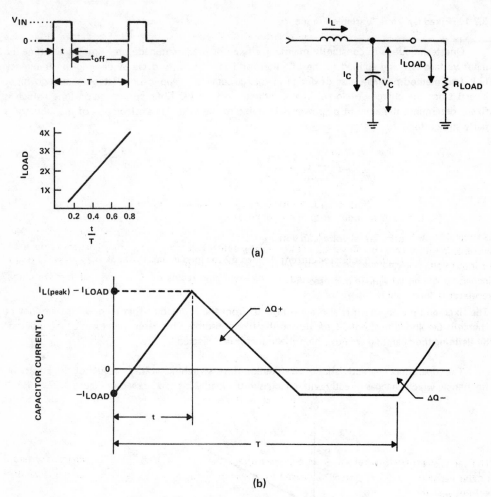

Figure 3.11. Variation of Pulse Width versus Load

By setting $\Delta Q+$ equal to $\Delta Q-$, the relation of I_{LOAD} and I_L for $\Delta Q = 0$ can be determined;

$$I_{LOAD} = \frac{1}{2} I_{L(pk)} \left(\frac{V_{IN}}{V_C}\right)\left(\frac{t}{T}\right)$$

As this demonstrates, the duty cycle $\frac{t}{T}$ can be altered to compensate for input-voltage changes or load variations.

The duty cycle $\frac{t}{T}$ can be altered a number of different ways.

3.7.1 Fixed On-Time, Variable Frequency

One technique is to constantly maintain a fixed or predetermined "on" time (t, the time the input voltage is being applied to the LC filter) and vary the duty cycle by varying the frequency ($\frac{1}{T}$). This method provides ease of design in voltage conversion applications (step-up, step-down, or invert) since the charge developed in the inductor of the LC filter during the on-time (which is fixed) determines the amount of power deliverable to the load. Thus calculation of the inductor is fairly straightforward.

$$L = \frac{V}{I} t$$

where:

L = value of inductance in microhenrys

V = differential voltage in volts

I = required inductor current defined by the load in amps

t = on-time in microseconds

The fixed-on-time approach is also advantageous from the standpoint that a consistent amount of charge is developed in the inductor during the fixed on-time. This eases the design of the inductor by defining the operating area to which the inductor is subjected.

The operating characteristic of a fixed-on-time switching voltage regulator is a varying frequency, which changes directly with changes in the load. This can be seen in Figure 3.12.

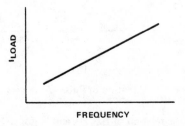

Figure 3.12. Frequency versus Load Current for Fixed On-Time SVR

3.7.2 Fixed Off-Time, Variable Frequency

In the fixed-off-time switching voltage regulator, the average dc voltage is varied by changing the on-time (t) of the switch while maintaining a fixed off-time (t_{off}). The fixed-off-time switching voltage regulator behaves opposite that of the fixed-on-time regulators in that as the load current increases, the on-time is made to increase, thus decreasing the operating frequency; this can be seen in Figure 3.13. This approach provides for the design of a switching voltage regulator that will

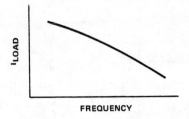

Figure 3.13. Frequency versus Load Current for Fixed Off-Time SVR

operate at a well-defined minimum frequency under full-load conditions. The fixed-off-time approach also allows a dc current to be established in the inductor under increased load conditions, thus reducing the ripple current while maintaining the same average current. The maximum current experienced in the inductor under transient load conditions is not as well defined as that above. Thus additional precaution should be taken to ensure the saturation characteristics of the inductor are not exceeded.

3.7.3 Fixed Frequency, Variable Duty Cycle

The fixed-frequency switching regulator varies the duty cycle of the pulse train to change the average power. The fixed-frequency concept is particularly advantageous for systems employing transformer-coupled output stages. The fixed-frequency aspect enables efficient design of the associated magnetics. Taking advantage of its compatibility in transformer-coupled circuits and the advantages of the transformer in single and multiple voltage-conversion applications, the fixed-frequency switching voltage regulator is used extensively in mainframe power supply control circuits. As with the fixed-off-time switching regulator, in single-ended applications the fixed-frequency regulator will establish a dc current through the inductor for increased load conditions to maintain the required current transferred with minimal ripple current. The single-ended and transformer-coupled circuit configurations are shown in Figure 3.14.

27

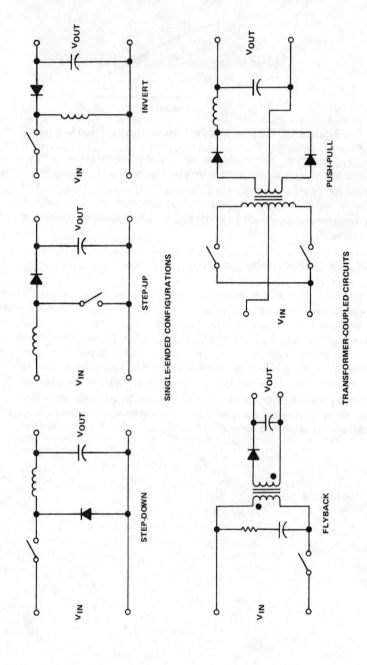

Figure 3.14. Switching Voltage Regulator Configurations

4
Regulator Safe Operating Area

Safe operating area is a term used to define the various supply voltage, input and output voltage, and load current ranges for which the device is designed to operate. Whether or not exceeding these limits will result in a catastrophic failure or merely render the device inoperative, depends on the device and its performance characteristics. Integrated circuit voltage regulators with internal current, thermal, and short-circuit protection circuits, for example, will merely shut down. External components, such as external pass transistors, may respond catastrophically.

4.1 REGULATOR SAFE OPERATING AREA

Although particular design equations depend on the type of integrated circuit voltage regulator and its application, there are several boundaries that apply to all regulator circuits for safe, reliable performance. A typical regulator specification is shown in Figure 4.1.

4.1.1 Input Voltage

The limits on the input voltage are derived from three considerations:

V_I max   The absolute maximum rated input voltage as referenced to the regulator's ground. This is a safe operating area (SOA) destruct limit.

V_{DIFF} min   The minimum differential voltage input-to-output, below which the regulator ceases to function properly. This is a functional limit.

V_{DIFF} max   The maximum differential input voltage input-to-output. Usually, the regulator's power dissipation is exceeded prior to the V_{DIFF} max limit. This is an SOA limit that can be limited by P_D max.

4.1.2 Load Current

I_{LOAD} max   The maximum load current deliverable from the integrated circuit regulator. If internal current limiting is not provided, external protection should be provided. This is a functional limit that may be further limited by P_D max.

absolute maximum ratings over operating free-air temperature range (unless otherwise noted)

	LM105	LM205	LM305A	LM305 LM376	UNIT
Input voltage (see Note 1)	50	50	50	40	V
Input-to-output voltage differential	40	40	40	40	V
Continuous total dissipation at (or below) 25°C free-air temperature (see Note 2)	800	800	800	800	mW
Operating free-air temperature range	−55 to 125	−25 to 85	0 to 70	0 to 70	°C
Storage temperature range	−65 to 150	−65 to 150	−65 to 150	−65 to 150	°C
Lead temperature 1/16 inch from case for 60 seconds: JG or L package	300		300	300	°C
Lead temperature 1/16 inch from case for 10 seconds: P package		260	260	260	°C

NOTES: 1. Voltage values, except input-to-output voltage differential, are with respect to network ground terminal.
2. For operation above 25°C free-air temperature, refer to Dissipation Derating Curves, Figures I, II, and IV, page 90. This rating for the L package requires a heat sink that provides a thermal resistance from case to free-air, $R_{\theta CA}$, of not more than 105° C/W.

recommended operating conditions

	LM105		LM205		LM305A		LM305		LM376		UNIT
	MIN	MAX	MIN	MAX	MIN	MAX	MIN	MAX	MIN	MAX	
Input voltage, V_I	8.5	50	8.5	50	8.5	50	8.5	40	9	40	V
Output voltage, V_O	4.5	40	4.5	40	4.5	40	4.5	30	5	37	V
Input-to-output voltage differential, $V_I - V_O$	3	30	3	30	3	30	3	30	3	30	V
Output current, I_O	0	12	0	12	0	45	0	12	0	25	mA
Operating free-air temperature, T_A	−55	125	−25	85	0	70	0	70	0	70	°C

Figure 4.1. Typical Regulator Specification

4.1.3 Power Dissipation

P_D max — The maximum power that can be dissipated within the regulator. Power dissipation is the product of the input-to-output differential voltage and the load current, and is normally specified at or below a given case temperature. This rating is usually based on a $150°C$ junction temperature limit. The power rating is an SOA limit unless the integrated circuit regulator provides an internal thermal protection.

4.1.4 Output Voltage of an Adjustable-Voltage Regulator

V_O min — The minimum output voltage a regulator is capable of regulating. This is usually a factor of the regulator's internal reference and is a functional limit.

V_O max — The maximum output voltage a regulator is capable of regulating. This is largely dependent on the input voltage (V_O max $\leqslant V_I - V_{DIFF}$ min). As with the minimum differential voltage limit, the maximum output voltage is a functional limit.

4.2 EXTERNAL PASS TRANSISTOR

For applications requiring additional load current, integrated circuit voltage regulators may be boosted with the addition of an external pass transistor. When employed, the external pass transistor, in addition to the voltage regulator, must be protected against operation beyond its safe operating area. Operation outside the safe operating area is catastrophic to most discrete transistors.

I_C max — The maximum current the transistor is capable of sustaining. I_C max now becomes the max load current the regulator circuit is capable of delivering to the load. Associated with I_C max is a collector-emitter voltage, V_{CE}. If this voltage is greater than the input-to-output differential voltage of the regulator application, the I_C max will have to be derated. This will then become a functional limit instead of a catastrophic limit. I_C max is related to power dissipation and junction or case temperature. I_C max must again be derated if the thermal or power ratings at which it is specified are exceeded. The resulting derated I_C max should continue to be considered as a catastrophic limit. Actual I_C max limits and derating information will appear on the individual transistor specification.

V_{CE} max — The maximum collector-emitter voltage that can be applied to the transistor in the off-state. Exceeding this limit will result in breaking down the collector-emitter junction of the pass transistor. This is not catastrophic if current limiting is provided. If current limiting is not provided, it will destroy the transistor.

P_D max   The maximum power that can be dissipated in the device. This is usually specified at a specific junction or case temperature. If the transistor is operated at higher temperatures, the maximum power must be derated in accordance with the operating rules specified in the transistor's applicable specification. Prolonged operation above the transistor's maximum power rating will result in degradation or destruction of the transistor.

4.3   SAFE OPERATING PROTECTION CIRCUITS

Proper selection of the integrated circuit voltage regulators and external components will allow a reliable design wherein all devices operate well within their respective safe operating areas. If the system design is such that under normal conditions the devices operate to within 80% of their capabilities, fault conditions, such as a short-circuit or excessive load, may cause some components in the regulator circuit to exceed their safe operating area operation. For this purpose as well as protection for the load, certain protection circuits should be considered.

4.3.1   Reverse Bias Protection

This condition may occur when a voltage regulator becomes reverse biased, for example, if the input supply was "crowbarred" to protect either the supply itself or additional circuitry. The filter capacitor at the output of the regulator circuit will maintain the regulator's output voltage and the regulator circuit will be reverse biased. If the regulated voltage is large enough (> 7 V), the regulator circuit may be damaged. To protect against this, a simple diode can be employed as shown in Figure 4.2.

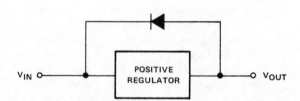

Figure 4.2. Reverse Bias Protection

4.3.2   Current Limiting Techniques

The type of current limiting scheme employed depends primarily on the safe operating area of the applicable pass element. The three basic techniques are series resistor, constant current, and fold-back current limiting.

Series Resistor — This is the simplest method for short-circuit protection. The short-circuit current is determined by the current-limiting resistor R_{CL}, as shown in Figure 4.3.

$$V_{OUT} = V_{OUT(reg)} - I_{LOAD} R_{CL}$$

A short-circuit condition occurs when $V_{OUT} = 0$, thus:

$$I_{SC} = I_{LOAD} @ (V_{OUT} = 0) = \frac{V_{OUT(reg)}}{R_{CL}}$$

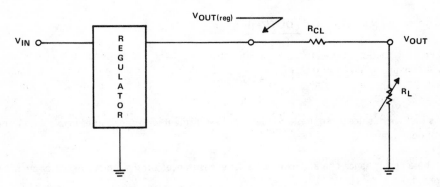

Figure 4.3. Series Resistance Current Limiter

The primary drawback of this technique is error introduced by the voltage dropped across R_{CL} under varying load conditions.

$$I_{LOAD} = \frac{V_{OUT}}{R_L}$$

$$V_{OUT} = \frac{V_{OUT(reg)}}{1 + \frac{R_{CL}}{R_L}}$$

$$\% \, ERROR = \frac{V_{OUT(reg)} - V_{OUT}}{V_{OUT(reg)}}$$

$$\% \, ERROR = \frac{R_{CL}}{R_L + R_{CL}}$$

Maintaining R_{CL} at a level of an order of magnitude less than the nominal load impedance minimizes this effect.

$$R_{CL} = \frac{1}{10} R_L \qquad \% \, ERROR = 9.1\%$$

This also yields a short-circuit current an order of magnitude greater than the normal operating load current.

$$I_{LOAD(nom)} = \frac{V_{OUT(reg)}}{R_{CL} + R_{L(nom)}}$$

$$I_{SC} = \frac{V_{OUT(reg)}}{R_{CL}}$$

$$I_{SC} = 11 \cdot I_{LOAD(nom)}$$

This is inefficient since it requires a regulator or pass element with capabilities in excess (11X) of its normal operation.

These performance characteristics of a series resistance current limited regulator are shown in Figure 4.4.

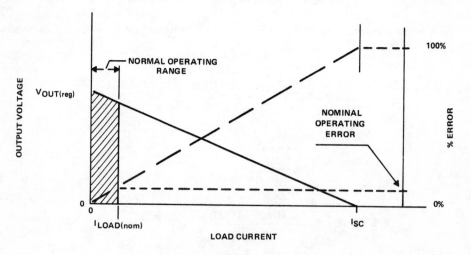

Figure 4.4. Performance Characteristics
of a Series Resistance Current-Limited Regulator

Constant-Current Limiting — Constant-current limiting is the most popular current-limiting technique in low-power, low-current regulator circuits. The basic configuration is shown in Figure 4.5. Implementation of this method requires access to the control element and remote voltage sense capabilities. Sensing the output voltage beyond the current limit, the circuit allows the regulator to compensate for voltage changes across R_{CL} for varying load conditions.

34

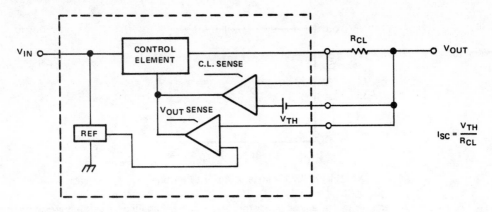

Figure 4.5. Constant Current Limit Configuration

$$I_{SC} = \frac{V_{TH}}{R_{CL}}$$

If an external pass transistor is used, its base current may be starved to accomplish constant-current limiting, as shown in Figure 4.6. Current limiting takes effect as the voltage drop across R_{CL} approaches the potential required to turn "on" the transistor Q1. As Q1 is biased on, the current supplying the base of Q2 is diverted, turning "off" Q2, thus decreasing the drive current to Q3, the regulator's pass transistor. If access to the internal control element is available, it should be used. This provides for the reduction of the current through the regulator's control element (Q2) as well as the pass element (Q3). The performance characteristics of a constant-current-limited regulator are as shown in Figure 4.7.

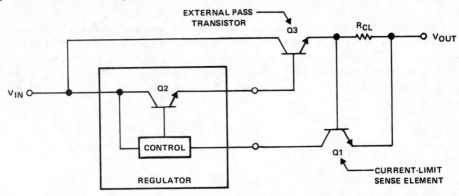

**Figure 4.6. Constant-Current Limiting for
External Pass Transistor Applications**

It should be noted that short-circuit conditions are the worst conditions imposed on the pass transistor since it has to survive not only the short-circuit current but it has to withstand the full input voltage across its collector-emitter junction simultaneously.

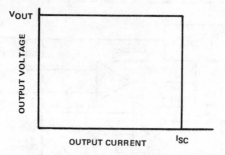

Figure 4.7. Constant-Current Limiting

This normally requires use of a pass transistor whose power handling capabilities are an order of magnitude greater than required for normal operation, i.e.:

$$V_{IN} = 20 \text{ V} \qquad V_{OUT} = 12 \text{ V} \qquad I_{OUT} = 700 \text{ mA}$$

$$\text{NOMINAL } P_D = (20 \text{ V} - 12 \text{ V}) \cdot 0.7 \text{ A} = 5.6 \text{ W}$$

For $I_{SC} = 1 \text{ A}$ (150% I_{OUT}):

$$\text{SHORT-CIRCUIT } P_D = 20 \text{ V} \cdot 1 \text{ A} = 20 \text{ W}$$

Fold-Back Current Limiting — Fold-back current limiting is used primarily for high-current applications where the normal operation requirements of the regulator dictate the use of an external power transistor. The principle of fold-back current limiting provides limiting at a predetermined current I_K at which feedback reduces the available load current as the load continues to increase (R_L decreasing) or the output voltage decays. The voltage-current relation is illustrated in Figure 4.8.

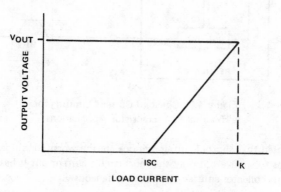

Figure 4.8. Fold-Back Current Limiting

The fold-back current-limiting circuit of Figure 4.9 behaves similarly to the constant-current limit circuit shown in Figure 4.6. In the configuration shown in Figure 4.9, the potential developed across the current limit sense resistor R_{CL} must not only develop the base-emitter voltage required to turn on Q1, but it must develop sufficient potential to overcome the voltage across resistor R1.

$$V_{BE(Q1)} = R_{CL}\, I_{LOAD} - \frac{V_{OUT} + R_{CL}\, I_{LOAD}}{R1 + R2}\, R1$$

$$\therefore\ I_K = \frac{V_{BE(Q1)}\,(R1 + R2) + V_{OUT}\, R1}{R_{CL}\, R2}$$

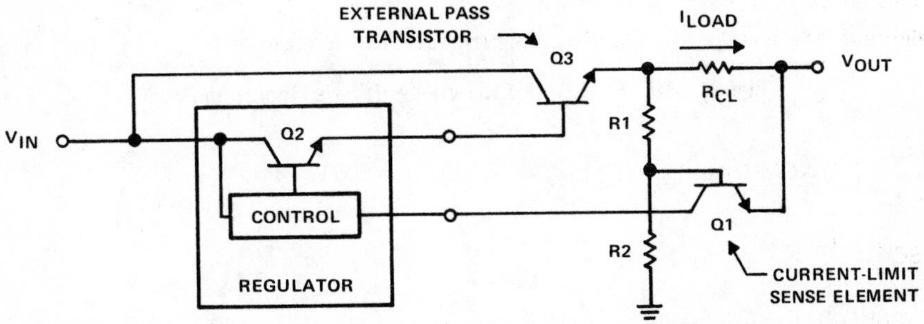

Figure 4.9. Fold-Back Current Limit Configuration

As the load current requirement increases, the output voltage (V_{OUT}) decays. The decreasing output voltage results in a proportional decrease in voltage across R1. Thus, less current through R_{CL} is required to develop sufficient potential to maintain the forward-biased condition of Q1. This can be seen in the above expression for I_K. As V_{OUT} decreases, I_K decreases. Under short-circuit conditions ($V_{OUT} = 0$ V) I_K becomes

$$I_{SC} = I_K\ @(V_{OUT} = 0\ V) = \frac{V_{BE(Q1)}}{R_{CL}} \left[1 + \frac{R1}{R2} \right]$$

The approach shown in Figure 4.10 allows a more efficient design because the collector current of the pass transistor is less during short-circuit condition than it is during normal operation. This means that during short-circuit conditions when the voltage across the collector-emitter junction of the pass transistor is maximum, the collector current is reduced. This more closely fits the typical performance characteristics of the transistor and allows more efficient design matching of the characteristics for the pass transistor to that of the regulator.

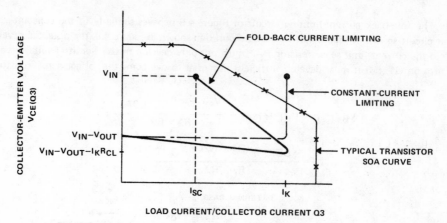

Figure 4.10. Fold-Back Current Limit Safe Operating Area

5
Thermal Considerations

5.1 THERMAL EQUATION

One of the primary limitations on the performance of any regulator is its rated power dissipation. The maximum power dissipation of a semiconductor is determined by the maximum junction temperature at which the device will operate and the device's ability to dissipate heat generated internally. A device's capability to expel the heat generated internally is defined by its thermal resistance; that is, its temperature rise per unit of heat transfer or power dissipated, expressed in units of Celsius degrees per watt. Knowing the rating of a particular device (allowable junction temperature) and the device's thermal resistance, the maximum power of that device may be calculated for a particular application or the required heat-sink thermal resistance can be determined for a desired power dissipation.

The basic relation for heat transfer or power dissipation may be expressed as:

$$P_D = \frac{\Delta T}{\Sigma R_\theta}$$

where:

P_D = power dissipated in the semiconductor devices in watts

ΔT = temperature difference created

ΣR_θ = sum of the thermal resistances of the media across which ΔT exists

For various semiconductor applications, the above expression may be written as follows:

$$P_D = \frac{T_J - T_A}{R_{\theta JC} + R_{\theta CS} + R_{\theta SA}}$$

$$P_D = \frac{T_J - T_A}{R_{\theta JA}}$$

where:

T_J = junction temperature of the semiconductor device in degrees Celsius

T_A = ambient temperature in degrees Celsius

$R_{\theta JC}$ = junction-to-case thermal resistance of the device (°C/W)

$R_{\theta CS}$ = case-to-surface thermal resistance of the mounting technique (°C/W)

$R_{\theta SA}$ = surface-to-ambient thermal resistance of the heat sink or media to which the semiconductor is mounted (°C/W)

$R_{\theta JA}$ = junction-to-ambient thermal resistance of the device (°C/W)

Figure 5.1 illustrates the various paths of heat flow, temperatures, and thermal resistances.

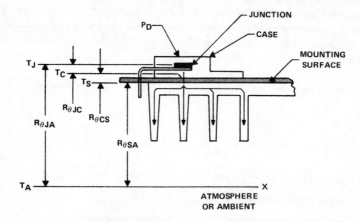

Figure 5.1. Semiconductor Thermal Model

The common practice is to represent the system with a network of series resistances as shown in Figure 5.2.

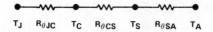

Figure 5.2. Resistor Network Representation of Figure 5.1

In short, the temperature at any point can be determined knowing the temperature at a given point, the power being dissipated, and the thermal resistance of the path of heat flow from the known location to the point of interest. If the path of heat flow travels through several media, the net thermal resistance is the sum of their thermal resistances.

From Figure 5.2, thermal resistance from junction-to-ambient is:

$$R_{\theta JA} = R_{\theta JC} + R_{\theta CS} + R_{\theta SA}$$

The use of the thermal equation is best illustrated through the use of examples.

5.1.1 Example 1: ($P_D$max)

Determine the maximum allowable power dissipation of a semiconductor device:

Given:
$$T_J \text{ max} = 150°C \quad \text{(typical limit)}$$
$$T_A = 70°C$$
$$R_{\theta JA} = 62.5°C/W \quad \text{(TO-220AB package)}$$

Calculating P_D max:

$$P_D = \frac{T_J - T_A}{R_{\theta JA}}$$

$$P_D = \frac{150°C - 70°C}{62.5°C/W}$$

$$P_D \leqslant 1.28 \text{ watts}$$

5.1.2 Example 2: ($T_A$max)

Determine the maximum allowable ambient temperature of a device:

Given:
$$P_D \text{ (device)} = 750 \text{ mW}$$
$$T_J \text{ max} = 150°C$$
$$R_{\theta JA} = 79°C/W \text{ (TO-202AB package)}$$

Calculating T_A max:

$$P_D = \frac{T_J - T_A}{R_{\theta JA}}$$

$$T_A = T_J - R_{\theta JA} P_D$$

$$T_A = 150°C - 79°C/W \times 750 \times 10^{-3} \text{ W}$$

$$T_A \leqslant 90.75°C$$

5.1.3   Example 3: $(R_{\theta JA}\text{max})$

Determine whether or not a heat sink is required.

Given: P_D (device) = 1.25 W

T_J max = 150°C

T_A = 65°C

$R_{\theta JA}$ = 108°C/W   (TO-116, N package)

Calculating $R_{\theta JA}$ max:

$$P_D = \frac{T_J - T_A}{R_{\theta JA}}$$

$$R_{\theta JA} \text{ max} = \frac{T_J - T_A}{P_D}$$

$$R_{\theta JA} \text{ max} = \frac{150°C - 65°C}{1.25 \text{ W}}$$

$$R_{\theta JA} \text{ max} = 68°C/W$$

$$R_{\theta JA} \text{ (device)} = 108°C/W$$

therefore a heat sink is required.

5.1.4   Example 4: $(R_{\theta CA}\text{max of Required Heat Sink})$

From Example 3, determine the thermal resistance of the required heat sink and mounting technique.

Given: $R_{\theta JC}$ (device) = 44°C/W   (TO-116, N package)

Calculating $R_{\theta CA}$:

From Example 3, $R_{\theta JA}$ max = 68°C/W with heat sink:

$$R_{\theta JA} \text{ (system)} = R_{\theta JC} \text{ (device)} + R_{\theta CS} \text{ (mount)} + R_{\theta SA} \text{ (sink)}$$

$$R_{\theta CS} \text{ (mount)} + R_{\theta SA} \text{ (sink)} = R_{\theta CA} \text{ (mount and sink)}$$

$$R_{\theta CA} = R_{\theta JA} \text{ (system)} - R_{\theta JC} \text{ (device)}$$

$$R_{\theta CA} = 68°C/W - 44°C/W$$

$$R_{\theta CA} \text{ max} = 24°C/W$$

The Thermalloy 6007 heat sink for dual-in-line packages exhibits an $R_{\theta CA}$ of 20°C/W.

Tables 5.1 through 5.7 list the thermal resistances of the popular semiconductor packages, their mounting techniques, and commercially available heat sinks. Sources for obtaining these techniques and heat sinks are listed below.

Sources:

Thermalloy, Incorporated
Dallas, Texas
(214)-238-6821

IERC
Burbank, California
(213)-849-2481

Staver
Bayshore, New York
(516)-666-8000

Wakefield Engineering Ind.
Wakefield, Massachusetts
(617)-245-5900

Table 5.1. $R_{\theta JA}$ and $R_{\theta JC}$ — Thermal Resistances of Mounting Packages

JEDEC No.	TO-220AB	TO-202AB	TO-39	TO-226AA	TO-116	TO-116			Unit
TI Designator	KC	KD	L	LP	J	N	JG	P	
$R_{\theta JA}$	62.5	79	210	160	122	108	151	125	°C/W
$R_{\theta JC}$	4	10	15	35	60	44	58	45	°C/W

Table 5.2. $R_{\theta CS}$ — Thermal Resistance of Mounting Techniques

Package	Bare	With Thermal Grease	With Anodized Washer 0.020" Thk	With Mica Film 0.003" Thk	Unit
TO-220AB (KC)	3	1	1.2	1.8	°C/W

*Most other package heat sinks account for mounting technique.

Table 5.3. Available Heat Sinks For TO-3 Packages

$R_{\theta SA}$ Range °C/W	IERC	Staver	Thermalloy	Wakefield
<0.5			6560, 6590, 6660, 6690	
0.5 to 1.0			6159, 6423, 6441, 6443, 6450, 6470	
1.0 to 3.0	E2 1/2" Extrusion		6006, 6123, 6129, 6157, 6169, 6401, 6403, 6421, 6427, 6442, 6463, 6500	641
3.0 to 5.0	E1, E3 1/2" Extrusion HP1 Series HP3 Series	V3-5-2	6004, 6005, 6016, 6053, 6054, 6176, 6141	621, 623 600 Series
5.0 to 7.0	UP Series	V3-7-224 V3-3-2	6002, 6003, 6015, 6052 6060, 6061	690, 390, 680 Series
7.0 to 10	LA Series	V3-3, V1-3 V3-5, V1-5 V3-7-96	6001, 6013, 6014, 6051	672
10 to 13	UP3 Series		6103, 6104, 6105	380 Series

Table 5.4. Available Heat Sinks For TO-226 and TO-92 Packages

Thermalloy	$R_{\theta CA}$ °C/W	Staver	$R_{\theta CA}$ °C/W	IERC	$R_{\theta CA}$ °C/W
2220	75	F2-7	72	RU Single	150
2224	92	F1-70	72	RU Double	180
		F1-8	72	RUR Single	130
				RUR Double	160

Table 5.5. Available Heat Sinks For TO-39 Packages

$R_{\theta CA}$ °C/W	IERC	Staver	Thermalloy
10 to 20	LP Series		1101, 1103, 1130, 1131 1132, 1117, 1116, 1121
20 to 40		F5-5C F5-5B	2227, 1136, 2212-5, 2228 2215, 2262, 2263, 1134
40 to 60	TXBF2-032-036B Thermal Link Series	F5-5A F6-5L F5-5D	2205, 2207/PR11, 2209-4A 2210, 2225, 2230-5, 2211 2226, 2260, 1129,
> 60	TXBF-032-025B TXBC-032-025B	F1-5	1115, 2257

Table 5.6. Available Heat Sinks For TO-220 Packages

$R_{\theta}SA$ Range °C/W	IERC	Staver	Thermalloy
3.0 to 5.0	HP1, HP3 Series	V3-5-2 T-79	6072/6071
5.0 to 8.0	UP Series	V3-3-2 V3-7-224	6072
8.0 to 13	LA Series UP3 Series	V3-5 V3-7-96 V3-3 V4-3-192 V5-1	6034 6032 6030
13 to 20	LB Series PSD1 PB1 Series	V4-3-128	6065, 6070/6071, 6070, 6106, 6038* 3069*, 6025, 6107
20 to 30	PB2 Series PA1 PSB2 PA2	F8-3-220*	6073 6045*
> 30	PSC2-26* PA27CB/PVC-1B*		

*Denotes Clip Mounted Heat Sink. (Thermal Ratings for These Devices are $R_{\theta CA}$).

Table 5.7. Available Heat Sinks For TO-202 Packages

$R_{\theta}SA$ Range °C/W	IERC	Staver	Thermalloy
< 10	LA Series HP1, HP3 Series UP Series		6034
10 to 15	LB Series UP3 PSD1	V4-3-192	6063
15 to 20 20 to 30	PB1 Series PA1, PA2, PB2 Series	V4-3-128 V6-2 F8-3-202*	6046* 6047*
30 to 40	PSC2* PA17CB/PVC-1B*	F7-1* F7-2* F7-3*	

*Denotes Clip Mounted Heat Sink. (Thermal Ratings for These Sinks Are $R_{\theta CA}$)

5.2 HEAT-SINK DESIGN

A wide variety of heat sinks is available commercially offering thermal resistances as low as 1°C/W. For a particular application, the use of a custom heat sink may be preferable. Such factors as convenience, cost, size, or weight determine which approach to take.

In designing a custom heat sink, first consider the three modes of heat transfer: (1) conduction, (2) radiation, and (3) convection. Figure 5.3 describes pictorially the heat flow paths from the junction of a typical semiconductor.

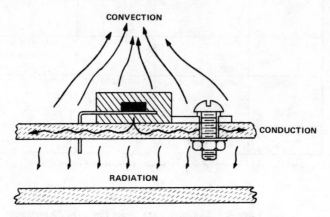

Figure 5.3. Heat Flow Paths of Semiconductor Cooling

5.2.1 Conduction

The basic law of heat conduction in the steady state is:

$$Q = \frac{KA \, \Delta T}{L}$$

where:

Q = rate of heat flow

K = thermal conductivity of the material

A = cross-sectional area

ΔT = temperature difference

L = length of the heat flow path

46

Where conduction is the only mode of heat transfer, the following rules should be observed:

1. Use materials that exhibit the highest thermal conductivity that is consistent with structural and economic requirements.

2. Utilize an optimum cross-sectional area.

3. Maintain T_2 (where $\Delta T = T_1 - T_2$) at as low a value as possible.

4. Keep the thermal path (L) as short as possible.

For quick solution of thermal conductivity problems, the nomograph in Figure 5.4 is a helpful aid.

Example — Using the example nomograph in Figure 5.4, solve $Q = \dfrac{KA\,\Delta T}{L}$ for ΔT.

$Q = 10\ W$

$L = 0.25\ in$

$K = 100\ Btu/hr \cdot ft \cdot {}^\circ F$

$A = 2\ in^2$

$\Delta T = ?$

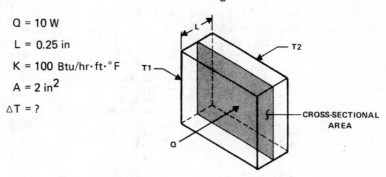

1. Plot the power in watts on the graduated scale Q (e.g., 10 W).

2. Plot the thickness of the heat sink on the L scale (e.g., 0.25 in).

3. Project a line between point 1 and point 2 to establish point 3 at the intersection of the projected line and reference line 1.

4. Plot the thermal conductivity on scale K (e.g., 100 Btu/hr · ft · °F).

5. Project a line between point 3 and point 4 to establish a point 5 at the intersection of the projected line and reference line 2.

6. Plot the cross-sectional area on the A scale (e.g., 2 in²).

7. Determine the thermal gradient (ΔT) by projecting a line from point 5 through point 6 and intersecting the ΔT scale. This intersection indicates the ΔT of the system.

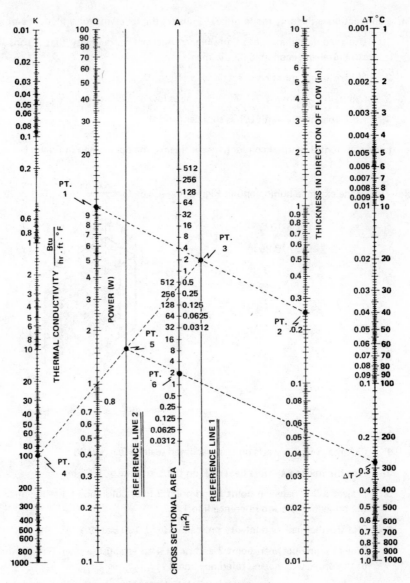

NOTES: 1. Nomograph incorporates conversion of units as indicated.
2. To determine ΔT, first use numbers for A and ΔT on the left side of the respective scales.
If a ΔT > 1 is indicated (off ΔT scale), use A scale on the right side of the A scale and read ΔT
on the right side of the ΔT scale.
3. Multiplication by 10 may be used for the Q, L, K, and A scales.

Q or L X 10 increases ΔT by 10.
K or A X 10 decreases ΔT by 10.

Figure 5.4. Nomograph A — Conductivity of Materials

As seen in Figure 5.4, the ΔT of the example is:

$$\Delta T = 0.285°C$$

Note the ΔT calculated is the temperature gradient from one surface of the plate to the other surface of the plate. To apply this for a device whose thermal gradient from its junction to its case is known requires knowledge of the interface between the package and the heat-sink surface ($R_{\theta CS}$).

$$R_{\theta JA} = R_{\theta JC} + R_{\theta CS} + R_{\theta SA}$$

The interface ($R_{\theta CS}$) is the prime thermal barrier. Failure to move the maximum amount of heat across this barrier can be detrimental, even to the best thermal design. The thermal resistance across this or any other interface is a function of the cross-sectional area, surface finishes, surface flatness, contact pressure of the surfaces, and thermal conductivity of any fillers, if used. To minimize this effect:

1) Maintain surfaces as flat and smooth as possible.

2) Maximize surface contact areas.

3) Use thermal contact fluids, where practical.

4) Torque mounting bolts or screws to manufacturer's recommended values, where applicable.

The graph shown in Figure 5.5 illustrates the effect pressure and various surface finishes have on the contact thermal impedance.

5.2.2 Convection Radiation

The contact of any fluid with a hotter surface reduces the density of the fluid and causes it to rise. Circulation caused by this phenomenon is known as free or natural convection. The amount of energy radiated by a body is dependent upon its temperature, emissivity, and total surface area. Heat transfer by these two means is not as easily expressed as that previously discussed for conductive cooling, and is often done empirically. A reasonably accurate first-order approximation can be calculated using the following approach.

The basic conditions for convection-cooled heat sinks are:

1. Use a heat sink that affords maximum surface area for a given volume.

2. Use a material finish whose emissive properties are as large as the structural, economical, and electrical limitations will allow.

3. Use heat-sink material with as high a thermal conductivity as system requirements allow.

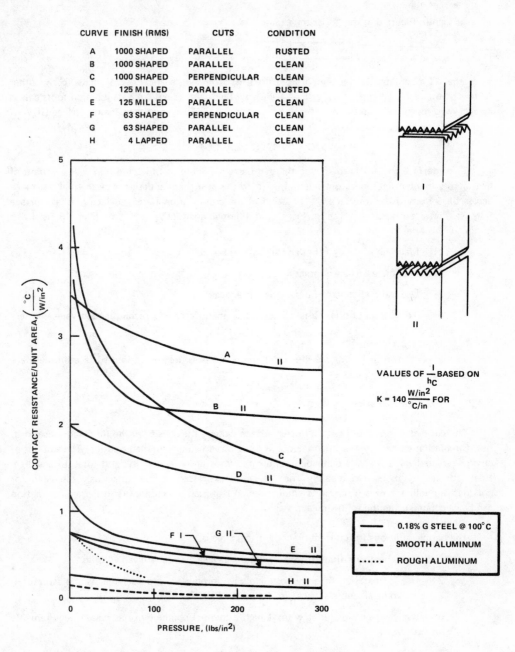

CURVE	FINISH (RMS)	CUTS	CONDITION
A	1000 SHAPED	PARALLEL	RUSTED
B	1000 SHAPED	PARALLEL	CLEAN
C	1000 SHAPED	PERPENDICULAR	CLEAN
D	125 MILLED	PARALLEL	RUSTED
E	125 MILLED	PARALLEL	CLEAN
F	63 SHAPED	PERPENDICULAR	CLEAN
G	63 SHAPED	PARALLEL	CLEAN
H	4 LAPPED	PARALLEL	CLEAN

VALUES OF $\frac{1}{h_C}$ BASED ON

$K = 140 \frac{W/in^2}{{}^\circ C/in}$ FOR

0.18% G STEEL @ 100°C

SMOOTH ALUMINUM

ROUGH ALUMINUM

Figure 5.5. Contact Thermal Impedance as a Function of Contact Pressure
(From Guidelines to Semiconductor Thermal Management, *Joseph P. Laffin*, IERC)

50

4.   In natural convection, mount heat sinks such that maximum length of extrusions (fins) are in the vertical plane.

5.   Mount lowest power or highest thermally sensitive devices on lowest location of heat sinks common to other power devices. (Heat rises.)

6.   Provide proper ventilation such that natural convection currents are not restricted.

7.   Ensure location of the heat sink is such that it radiates thermal energy, not absorbs it from other bodies.

The basic purpose of designing a heat sink is to produce a heat sink that exhibits a thermal resistance ($R_{\theta SA}$) required for the application.

$$R_{\theta SA} = \frac{1}{A \eta \, (F_C h_C + \epsilon \, H_r)} \quad (^\circ C/W)$$

where:

A = surface area of heat sink

η = effectiveness of heat sink

F_C = convective correction factor

h_C = convection heat transfer coefficient

ϵ = emissivity

H_r = normalized radiation heat transfer coefficient

The tables and graphs shown in the following text are used to determine the various unknowns above and finally the thermal resistance of the heat-sink design itself. The use of these tables can best be demonstrated through an example.

Given:

P_D = 2.5 W

Package = TO-220
($R_{\theta JC}$ = 4°C/W)

T_J max = 150°C

T_A = 70°C

Heat sink:

Size: 2" × 2" × 1/8"

Material: Anodized Al

Mounting: Bare ($R_{\theta CS}$ = 3°C/W)

Position: Horizontal on PC board surface

Calculate required $R_{\theta SA}$ of heat sink

$$P_D = \frac{T_J - T_A}{R_{\theta JC} + R_{\theta CS} + R_{\theta SA}}$$

$$R_{\theta SA} = \frac{T_J - T_A}{P_D} - R_{\theta JC} - R_{\theta CS}$$

$$R_{\theta SA} = \frac{80°C}{2.5\ W} - 4°C/W - 3°C/W$$

$$R_{\theta SA} = 25\ °C/W$$

Determine Significant Dimension L From Table 5.8

$$L = \frac{2 \times 2}{2 + 2}$$

$$\boxed{L = 1''}$$

Table 5.8. Significant Dimension L for Convection Thermal Resistance

Surface	Significant Dimension L	
	Position	L (inch)
Rectangular Plane	Vertical	Height (2 ft max)
	Horizontal	$\dfrac{Length \times Width}{Length + Width}$
Circular Plane	Vertical	$\dfrac{\pi}{Diameter}$

Find the Convective Heat Transfer Coefficient from Figure 5.6

$$T_S = T_J - (R_{\theta JC} + R_{\theta CS})\,P_D$$

$$T_S = 150°C - (4°C/W + 3°C/W)\ 2.5\ W$$

$$T_S = 150°C - 17.5°C$$

$$T_S = 132.5°C$$

$$T_S - T_A = 62.5°C$$

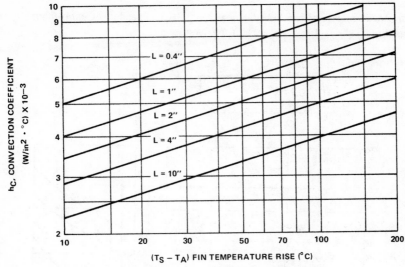

Figure 5.6. Convection Coefficient h_C

From Figure 5.6:

$$h_C = 6.25 \times 10^{-3} \; \frac{W}{in^2 \, {}^{\circ}C}$$

Like the significant dimension L, the convective correction factor F_C is dependent upon the shape and mounting plane of the heat sink.

Determine F_C from Table 5.9

$$F_C = 0.9$$

Table 5.9. Corrective Factor for Convection Thermal Resistance

Position	Vertical Plane	Horizontal Plane	
		Both Surfaces Exposed	Top Only Exposed
F_C	1.0	1.35	0.9

53

The normalized radiation heat transfer coefficient (H_r) is dependent upon thermal gradient across the heat sink ($T_S - T_A$) and the ambient temperature.

Determine H_r from Figure 5.7

$$H_r = 0.77 \times 10^{-2} \, \frac{W}{in^2 \, °C}$$

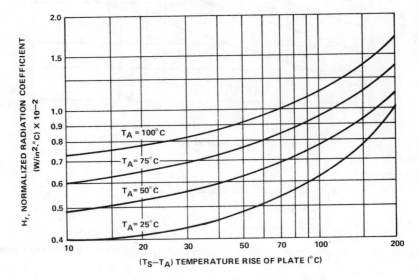

Figure 5.7. Normalized Heat Transfer Coefficient H_r

The emissivity is determined by the heat-sink surface and is the ratio of emissive power of a given body to the ideal "black-body" equivalent of the surface.

Determine Emissivity (ϵ) from Table 5.10

The heat-sink material being anodized aluminum:

$$\epsilon = 0.8$$

Table 5.10. Emissivities for Common Surfaces

Finish	ϵ
Aluminum - Anodized	0.7 - 0.9
Aluminum - Polished	0.15
Aluminum - With Alodine	0.05
Copper - Polished	0.07
Copper - Oxidized	0.7
Iron - Snow-White Enamel	0.9
Iron - Snow-White Varnish	0.9
Iron - Black Shiny Lacquer	0.875
Tinned Iron-Black Shiny Shellac	0.821
Black-Matte Shellac	0.91
Black Lacquer	0.8 -0.95
Flat-Black Lacquer	0.96-0.98
White Lacquer	0.80-0.95
Oil Paint (All colors)	0.92-0.96
Insulube 448	0.91

Find Heat-sink Efficiency η from Nomograph B.

1. Calculate h_T

$$h_T = F_c h_c + \epsilon H_r$$

$$h_T = (0.9 \times 6.25 + 0.8 \times 7.7) \times 10^{-3} \quad \left(\frac{W}{in^2 \,^\circ C}\right)$$

$$h_T = 1.17 \times 10^{-2} \quad \left(\frac{W}{in^2 \,^\circ C}\right)$$

Locate h_T on the nomograph in Figure 5.9.

2. Plot the fin thickness of the heat sink.

3. Draw a line from point 1 through point 2, extending through the scale $\propto$. The intersection of this line and the scale $\propto$, determined $\propto 1$.

4. Determine factor D for the heat sink, using Figure 5.8.

$$D = \sqrt{\frac{2 \times 2}{\pi}}$$

$$\boxed{D = 1.13}$$

5. Project a line from point 4 through point 3 and intersect the η scale. The intersection of this line and the scale determines the value of η.

From Figure 5.9:

$$\boxed{\eta > 94\%}$$

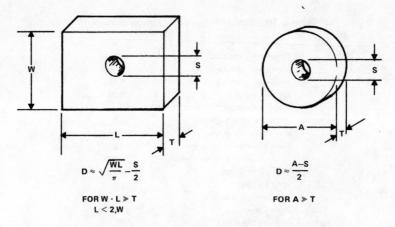

$$D \approx \sqrt{\frac{WL}{\pi}} - \frac{S}{2}$$

FOR W · L ≫ T
L < 2,W

$$D \approx \frac{A-S}{2}$$

FOR A ≫ T

Figure 5.8. Determining "D" for Use with Figure 5.10

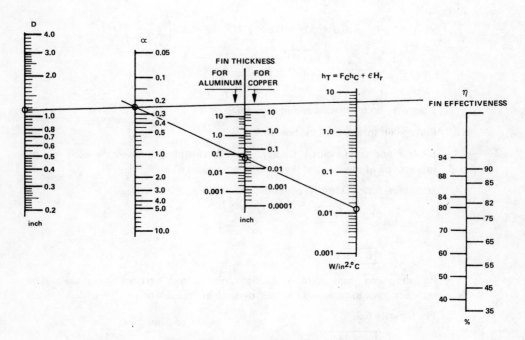

Figure 5.9. Nomograph B — Fin Effectiveness

6. Calculate $R_{\theta SA}$: (consider $\eta = 1$)

$$R_{\theta SA} = \frac{1}{A\,\eta\,(F_C h_C + \epsilon H_r)} \quad \left(\frac{^{\circ}C}{W}\right)$$

$$R_{\theta SA} = \frac{1}{(2'' \times 2'')\,(1.0)\left(1.17 \times 10^{-2}\,\dfrac{W}{in^2\,{}^{\circ}C}\right)}$$

$$R_{\theta SA} = \frac{1}{4.7 \times 10^{-2}\,\dfrac{W}{^{\circ}C}}$$

$$\boxed{R_{\theta SA} = 21.3^{\circ}C/W}$$

Comparing the required thermal resistance to the designed heat sink:

$R_{\theta SA}$ (design) = 21.3°C/W

$R_{\theta SA}$ (required) = 25°C/W

This is satisfactory.

6
Layout Guidelines

As implied in the previous sections, the layout and component orientation play an important, but often overlooked, role in the overall performance of the regulator. The importance of this role depends upon such things as the amount of power being regulated, the type of regulator, the overall regulator circuit complexity, and the environment in which the regulator resides. The general layout rules, remote voltage sensing, and component layout guide lines are discussed in the following text.

6.1 GENERAL

Most integrated circuit regulators employ wide-band transistors in their construction to optimize their response. These devices must be compensated to ensure stable closed-loop operation. Their compensation can be upset easily by external stray capacitance and line inductance of an improper layout. For this reason, circuit lead lengths should be held to a minimum. Lead lengths associated with external compensation or pass transistor elements are of primary concern. These components especially, should be located as close as possible to the regulator control circuit.

6.2 CURRENT PATHS

In addition to a regulator's susceptibility to spurious oscillation, the layout of the regulator also affects the accuracy and performance of the circuit.

6.2.1 Input Ground Loop

Improper placement of the input capacitor can induce unwanted ripple on the output voltage. Care should be taken to ensure that currents flowing in the input circuit are not experienced by the ground line common with the load return line. This results in an error voltage developed by the peak currents of the filter capacitor flowing through the line resistance of the load return line. See Figure 6.1 for an illustration of this effect.

6.2.2 Output Ground Loop

Similar to the problem discussed on the input, excessive lead length in the ground return line of the output results in additional error. If the ground line of the load circuit is located such that it experiences the current flowing in the load, error equivalent to the load current times the line resistance ($R2' + R3'$) will be introduced to the output voltage.

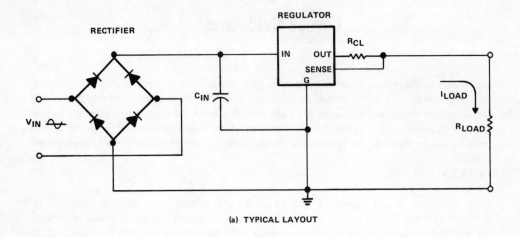

(a) TYPICAL LAYOUT

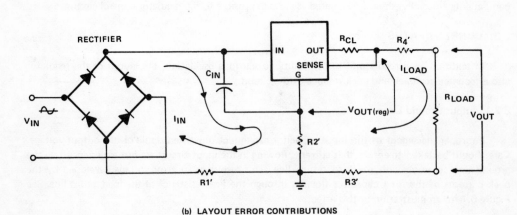

(b) LAYOUT ERROR CONTRIBUTIONS

Figure 6.1. Circuit Layout Showing Error Contributions

6.2.3 Remote Voltage Sense

The voltage regulator should be located as close as practical to the load if the output voltage sense circuitry is internal to the regulator's control device. Excessive lead length will result in an error voltage developed across the distributed line resistance (R4′) as it experiences the current being delivered to the load (I_{LOAD}).

$$V_{OUT} = V_{OUT\ (reg)} - (R2' + R3' + R4')\ I_{LOAD} + R2'\ I_{IN}$$

$$ERROR = I_{LOAD}\ (R2' + R3' + R4') - I_{IN}\ R2'$$

If the voltage sense is available externally, the effect of the line resistance can be minimized. By referring the low-current external voltage sense imput to the load, losses in the output line (R4′ X I_{LOAD}) are compensated for. Since the current in the sense line is very small, error introduced by its line resistance is negligible.

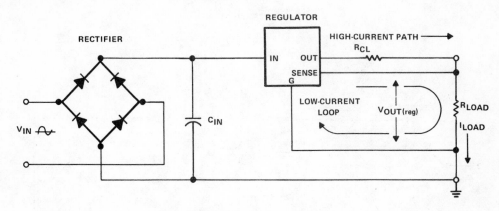

Figure 6.2. Proper Regulator Layout

6.3 THERMAL PROFILE

All semiconductor devices are affected by temperature; therefore, care should be taken in the placement of these devices such that their thermal properties are not additive. This is especially important where external pass transistors or reference elements are concerned.

7
Input Filter Design

Where the power origin is an ac source, the transformer, rectifier, and input filter design are as important as the regulator design itself so far as total system performance is concerned. This section presents input supply and filter design information sufficient to design a basic capacitor-rectifier input supply.

7.1 TRANSFORMER/RECTIFIER CONFIGURATION

The input supply consists of three basic sections: (1) input transformer, (2) rectifier, and (3) filter as shown in Figure 7.1.

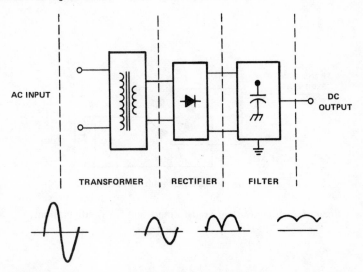

Figure 7.1. Input Supply

The first two sections, the transformer and the rectifier, are partially dependent upon each other as one's structure depends on that of the other. The most common transformer configurations and their associated rectifier circuits are illustrated in Figure 7.2.

The particular configuration used depends on the application. The half-wave circuit [Figure 7.2(a)] is used in low-current applications, since the single rectifier diode experiences the total load current and the conversion efficiency is less than 50%. The full-wave configurations

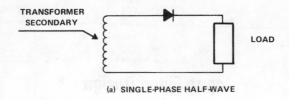

(a) SINGLE-PHASE HALF-WAVE

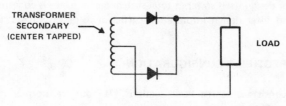

(b) SINGLE-PHASE CENTER-TAPPED FULL-WAVE

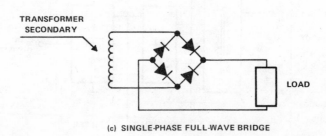

(c) SINGLE-PHASE FULL-WAVE BRIDGE

Figure 7.2. Input Supply Transformer/Rectifier Configurations

[Figures 7.2(b) and 7.2(c)] are used for higher current applications with the center-tapped version [Figure 7.2(b)] restricted primarily to low-voltage applications. The characteristic output voltage waveforms of these configurations are illustrated in Figure 7.3.

Before the design of the input supply and its associated filter can be initiated, the voltage, current, and ripple requirements of its load must be fully defined. The load, as far as the input supply is concerned, is the regulator control circuit. Therefore, the input requirements of the regulator itself become the governing conditions.

64

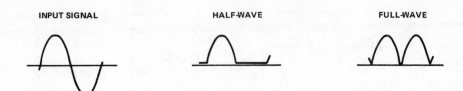

INPUT SIGNAL   HALF-WAVE   FULL-WAVE

Figure 7.3. Rectifier Output-Voltage Waveforms

Input Supply	Regulator Control Circuit

$$I_{OUT}\ max\ =\quad I_{IN} + I_{CC\ (reg)} \approx I_{OUT}$$

$$I_{OUT}\ min\ =\quad I_{CC\ (reg)}$$

$$V_{OUT}\ max\ <\quad MAX\ V_{IN}$$

$$V_{OUT}\ min\ \geqslant\quad V_{IN}\ min > V_{OUT} + V_{DIFF}\ min$$

$$r_f \leqslant\quad \frac{V_{in}}{V_{IN}} = \frac{V_{out} \cdot RR}{V_{IN}}$$

Because the input requirements of the regulator control circuit govern the input supply and filter design, it is easiest to work backwards from the load to the transformer primary.

7.2   CAPACITOR INPUT FILTER

The most practical approach to a capacitor-input filter design remains the graphical approach presented by Schade in 1943. The curves shown in Figures 7.4 through 7.7 contain all of the design information required for full-wave and half-wave rectified circuits.

Figures 7.4 and 7.5 show the relation of dc output voltage developed (V_C) to the applied peak input voltage ($V_{(PK)}$) as a function of ωCR_L for half-wave and full-wave rectified signals respectively. For a full-wave rectified application, the voltage reduction is less than 10% for $\omega CR_L > 10$ and $R_S/R_L < 0.5\%$. As illustrated, the voltage reduction decreases as ωCR_L increases or the R_S/R_L ratio decreases. Minimizing the reduction rate, contrary to initial impressions, may prove to be detrimental to the optimum circuit design. Further reduction requires a reduction in the series to load resistance ratio (R_S/R_L) for any given ωCR_L. This will result in a higher peak-to-average current ratio through the rectifier diodes. (See Figure 7.6.) In addition and probably of more concern, this increases the surge current experienced by the rectifier diodes during turn-on of the supply. Realize the surge current is limited only by the series resistance R_S:

$$I_{SURGE} = \frac{V_{SEC\ (PK)}}{R_S}$$

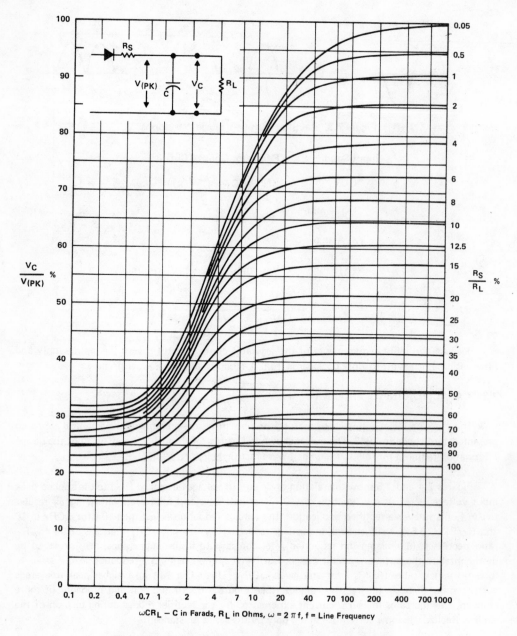

Figure 7.4. Relation of Applied Alternating Peak Voltage
to Direct Output Voltage in Half-Wave Capacitor-Input Circuits
(From O. H. Schade, Proc. IRE, Vol. 31, p. 343, 1943)

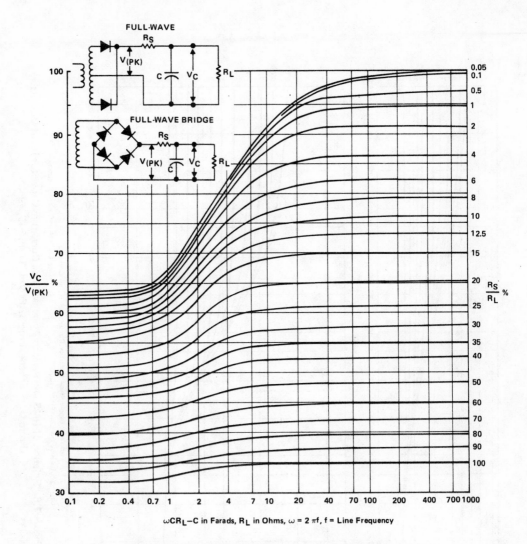

Figure 7.5. Relation of Applied Alternating Peak Voltage
to Direct Output Voltage in Full-Wave Capacitor-Input Circuits
(From O. H. Schade, Proc. IRE, Vol. 31, p. 344, 1943)

67

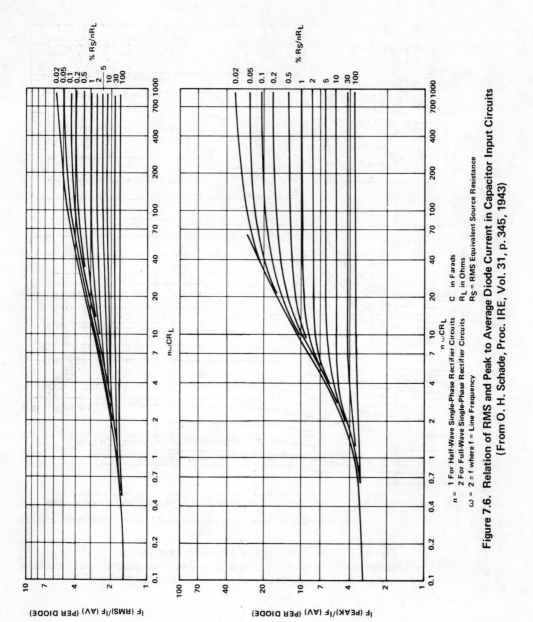

Figure 7.6. Relation of RMS and Peak to Average Diode Current in Capacitor Input Circuits
(From O. H. Schade, Proc. IRE, Vol. 31, p. 345, 1943)

n = 1 For Half-Wave Single-Phase Rectifier Circuits   C in Farads
    2 For Full-Wave Single-Phase Rectifier Circuits R_L in Ohms
ω = 2πf where f = Line Frequency R_S = RMS Equivalent Source Resistance

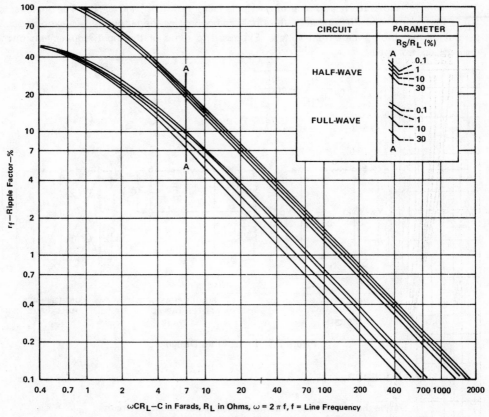

Figure 7.7. Root-Mean-Square Ripple Voltage for Capacitor-Input Circuits
(From O. H. Schade, Proc. IRE, Vol. 31, p. 346, 1943)

In order to control the surge current, additional resistance is often required in series with each rectifier. It is evident that a compromise must be made between the voltage reduction and the rectifier current ratings.

The maximum instantaneous surge current is $V_{(PK)}/R_S$. The time constant (τ) of capacitor C is:

$$\tau \cong R_S C$$

As a rule of thumb, the surge current will not damage the rectifier diode if

$$I_{SURGE} < I_{F(SURGE)} \text{ max and } \tau < 8.3 \text{ ms}$$

Figure 7.7 shows the relationship of the ripple factor r_f, ωCR_L, and R_S/R_L. The ripple factor (r_f) is the ratio of the RMS value of the ripple component of the output voltage expressed as a percent of the absolute dc output voltage. Expressed in terms of the input requirements of the regulator control circuit:

$$r_f = \frac{V_{in}}{V_{IN}} \times 100\%$$

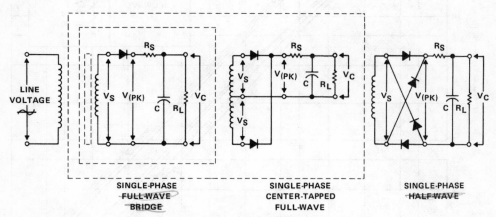

SINGLE-PHASE
~~FULL-WAVE~~
~~BRIDGE~~

SINGLE-PHASE
CENTER-TAPPED
FULL-WAVE

SINGLE-PHASE
~~HALF-WAVE~~

Figure 7.8. Input Filter Design

7.3   DESIGN PROCEDURE

1. Define the known requirements of the regulator control circuit.

    $$V_C = V_{IN} \text{ (reg)}$$

    $$r_f = \frac{V_{in}}{V_{IN}}$$

    $$I_{OUT} = I_{LOAD} \text{ (reg)}$$

    f = frequency of line voltage

2. Determine V_C. The choice of V_C may be random or it may be influenced by the regulator control circuits recommended V_{IN}. The first approximation of the acceptance range of V_C is defined by:

    V_C max ⩽ The maximum input voltage of the regulator
    control circuit minus the peak ripple voltage
    of the filter network.

V_C min ≥ The minimum input voltage of the regulator
control circuit plus the peak ripple voltage
of the filter network.

If a particular value of V_C within the defined range is not prevalent, choose a value
for V_C midway between the limits.

3. Set $V_{(PK)}$ at or near the V_C(max) limit allowing for input line variations.

4. Calculate the acceptable ripple factor (r_f).

$$r_f = \frac{V_{in}}{V_{IN}}$$

where:

V_{IN} = The dc input voltage of the regulator control circuit.

V_{in} = The RMS value of the ripple component of the input
voltage allowed on the input of the regulator control
circuit.

$$V_{in} = \frac{V_{in\ (p-p)}}{2\sqrt{2}}$$

$V_{in\ (p-p)}$ = The peak-to-peak value of the ripple component of
the input voltage.

$$V_{in\ (p-p)} = V_{out\ (p-p)} \cdot RR$$

$V_{out\ (p-p)}$ = The peak-to-peak value of the ripple component of
the output voltage.

RR = The ripple rejection factor of the regulator control circuit.

$$\therefore \quad r_f = \frac{V_{out\ (p-p)} \cdot RR}{V_{IN} \cdot 2\sqrt{2}}$$

5. Calculate the voltage reduction of the filter circuit.

$$\text{Voltage Reduction} = \frac{V_{IN}}{V_{(PK)}}$$

6. From Figure 7.7, determine the range of ωCR_L for R_S/R_L equal to 0.1% to 30%.

7. From Figure 7.4 or 7.5, as applicable, narrow the range of R_S/R_L for the voltage reduction value calculated above.

8. With the tightened range of R_S/R_L, refer again to Figure 7.7 to further define the acceptable range of ωCR_L.

    Several iterations reviewing Figures 7.4 or 7.5, and 7.7 may be necessary to define an exact solution for R_S/R_L and ωCR_L that satisfies the graphs of Figures 7.4, 7.5, and 7.7.

9. Once ωCR_L and R_S/R_L have been determined, calculate R_L:

$$R_L = \frac{V_{IN\ (reg)}}{I_{LOAD\ (reg)}}$$

10. Calculate ω:

$$\omega = 2\pi f$$

11. Determine C:

$$C = \frac{\omega CR_L}{\omega R_L}$$

12. Find the allowable series resistance.

$$R_S = \frac{R_S}{R_L} \cdot R_L$$

13. Determine the peak and RMS forward current to be experienced by the rectifier diodes from Figure 7.6.

    where:

$$I_{F\ (AV)} = I_{LOAD\ (reg)} \text{ (for half-wave circuits)}$$

$$I_{F\ (AV)} = \frac{1}{2} I_{LOAD\ (reg)} \text{ (for full-wave circuits)}$$

14. Determine the surge current required to be sustained by rectifier diodes.

$$I_{SURGE} = \frac{V_{(PK)}}{R_S}$$

15. Determine the peak inverse voltage of the rectifier circuit.

$$PIV = V_{(PK)} \text{ for the bridge rectifier circuit}$$

$$PIV = 2 V_{(PK)} \text{ for all other rectifier circuits}$$

16. Verify that the voltage reduction of the filter ($V_{(PK)}$) and the ripple voltage under worst-case conditions result in an output voltage (V_C) that is satisfactory with the operating input voltage range of the regulator control circuit.

$$[V_{(PK)} + \Delta V_{LINE}] \, K_F + V_{in\,(pk)} \leqslant V_{IN} \text{ max (regulator)}$$

$$[V_{(PK)} - \Delta V_{LINE}] \, K_F - V_{in\,(pk)} \geqslant V_{IN} \text{ min (regulator)}$$

where:

$$\Delta V_{LINE} = \text{variation in } V_{(PK)} \text{ caused by line voltage variation}$$

$$K_F = \text{voltage reduction of the filter section expressed in \%}$$

$$V_{in\,(pk)} = \text{peak value of the ripple component of the input voltage}$$

17. Calculate the required secondary voltage (RMS) of the transformer:

$$V_{SEC\,(RMS)} = \frac{V_{(PK)} + V_{RECT}}{\sqrt{2}}$$

where:

$$V_{RECT} = 2 V_{F\,(rectifier)} \text{ for full-wave bridge circuit } (\approx 2 \text{ V})$$

$$V_{RECT} = 1 V_{F\,(rectifier)} \text{ for other circuits } (\approx 1 \text{ V})$$

18. Find the resistance of the secondary:

   - R_S is the total resistance of the transformer secondary and any additional external resistance in the input supply circuit.

19. The secondary RMS current is:

   - Half-wave and full-wave circuit $\equiv I_{F(RMS)}$*
   - Full-wave bridge circuit $\equiv \sqrt{2} \, I_{F(RMS)}$*

20. Determine the transformer's VA rating.

   - Half-wave circuit $\equiv V_{SEC(RMS)} I_{F(RMS)}$*
   - Full-wave circuit $\equiv 2 V_{SEC(RMS)} I_{F(RMS)}$*
   - Full-wave bridge circuit $\equiv \sqrt{2} V_{SEC(RMS)} I_{F(RMS)}$*

*$I_{F(RMS)}$ is the RMS forward current of the rectifier found in step 13.

Example

Given: uA7805C is the regulator circuit

$$I_{LOAD} = 1 \text{ amp}$$

$$V_{OUT(ripple)} \leqslant 3 \text{ mV (p-p)}$$

$$f_{LINE} = 60 \text{ Hz}$$

From: uA7805C specifications

$$V_{IN} \text{ min} = 7 \text{ V}$$

$$V_{IN} \text{ max} = 25 \text{ V}$$

$$\text{Ripple Rejection} = 62 \text{ dB} \approx 1000$$

Choose full-wave bridge rectifier circuit

- $V_{in \, (p-p)} \approx 3 \text{ mV} \cdot 1000 = 3 \text{ V}$

  $V_{in \, (pk)} \approx 1.5 \text{ V}$

  $\boxed{V_{in} \approx 1.1 \text{ V}}$

- $V_{IN} \text{ min} + V_{in \, (pk)} < V_C < V_{IN} \text{ max} - V_{in \, (pk)}$

  $7 \text{ V} + 1.5 \text{ V} < V_C < 25 \text{ V} - 1.5 \text{ V}$

  $8.5 \text{ V} < V_C < 23.5 \text{ V}$

  $\boxed{\text{set } V_C = 16 \text{ V}}$

  $\boxed{\text{set } V_{(PK)} = 20 \text{ V}}$ (23.5 − 10% line variation)

- $r_f = \dfrac{1.1 \text{ V}}{16 \text{ V}} \times 100\%$

  $\boxed{r_f = 6.25\%}$

- $\text{Voltage Reduction} = \dfrac{16 \text{ V}}{20 \text{ V}} \times 100\%$

  $\boxed{\text{Voltage Reduction} = 80\%}$

- from Figure 7.7:

$$7.3 < \omega CR_L < 25 \text{ for } 0.1\% < R_S/R_L < 30\%$$

- from Figure 7.5:

$$5\% < R_S/R_L < 7\% \text{ for } \frac{V_C}{V_{(PK)}} = 80\%$$

referring back to Figure 7.7

$$\boxed{\text{for } R_S/R_L = 6\%} \quad \boxed{\omega CR_L = 9.3}$$

- $R_L = \dfrac{16 \text{ V}}{1 \text{ A}}$

$$\boxed{R_L = 16 \ \Omega}$$

- $\omega = 2\pi (60)$

$$\boxed{\omega = 377 \ \frac{\text{rad}}{\text{s}}}$$

- $C = \dfrac{9.3}{16 \times 377}$

$$\boxed{C = 1500 \mu F}$$

- $R_S = (6\%)(16 \ \Omega)$

$$\boxed{R_S = 0.96 \ \Omega}$$

- $I_{F\ (AV)} = \left(\dfrac{1}{2}\right)(1A) = 0.5 \text{ A}$

from Figure 7.6:

$$I_{F\ (RMS)}/I_{F\ (AV)} = 2.1$$

$$\boxed{I_{F\ (RMS)} = 1.05 \text{ A}}$$

$$I_{F\ (PK)}/I_{F\ (AV)} = 6$$

$$\boxed{I_{F\ (PK)} = 3 \text{ A}}$$

- $I_{SURGE} = \dfrac{20 \text{ V}}{0.96 \ \Omega}$

$$\boxed{I_{SURGE} = 20.8 \text{ A}}$$

- PIV = 2 (20 V)

$$\boxed{PIV = 40\ V}$$

- $(20\ V + 2\ V)\ (0.80) + 1.5\ V \leqslant 25\ V$

$$19.5\ V < 25\ V$$

  $(20\ V - 2\ V)\ (0.80) - 1.5\ V \geqslant 8\ V$

$$12.9\ V > 8\ V$$

- $V_S = \dfrac{20\ V + 2\ V}{\sqrt{2}}$

$$\boxed{V_S = 15.6\ V}$$

- $R_{SECONDARY} < R_S + 2\ R_{S\ (rect)} + R_{S\ (cap)}$

- $I_{SEC\ (PK)} = \sqrt{2}\ (1.05\ A)$

$$\boxed{I_{SEC\ (PK)} = 1.48\ A}$$

- VA rating = (15.6 V) (1.05 A) $\sqrt{2}$

$$\boxed{VA\ rating = 23.2\ VA}$$

Part 2

Part 2

SERIES REGULATORS

Input Regulation

The change in output voltage, often expressed as a percentage of output voltage, for a change in input voltage from one level to another level.
NOTE: Sometimes this characteristic is normalized with respect to the input voltage change.

Ripple Rejection

The ratio of the peak-to-peak input ripple voltage to the peak-to-peak output ripple voltage.
NOTE: This is the reciprocal of ripple sensitivity.

Ripple Sensitivity

The ratio of the peak-to-peak output ripple voltage, sometimes expressed as a percentage of output voltage, to the peak-to-peak input ripple voltage.
NOTE: This is the reciprocal of ripple rejection.

Output Regulation

The change in output voltage, often expressed as a percentage of output voltage, for a change in load current from one level to another level.

Output Resistance

The output resistance under small-signal conditions.

Temperature Coefficient of Output Voltage (α_{VO})

The ratio of the change in output voltage, usually expressed as a percentage of output voltage, to the change in temperature. This is the average value for the total temperature change.

$$\alpha_{VO} = \pm \left[\frac{V_O \text{ at } T_2 - V_O \text{ at } T_1}{V_O \text{ at } 25^\circ C} \right] \frac{100\%}{T_2 - T_1}$$

Output Voltage Change with Temperature

The percentage change in the output voltage for a change in temperature. This is the net change over the total temperature range.

Output Voltage Long-Term Drift

The change in output voltage over a long period of time.

Output Noise Voltage

The rms output noise voltage, sometimes expressed as a percentage of the dc output voltage, with constant load and no input ripple.

Current-Limit Sense Voltage

The current-sense voltage at which current limiting occurs.

TEXAS INSTRUMENTS
INCORPORATED
POST OFFICE BOX 5012 · DALLAS, TEXAS 75222

GLOSSARY
VOLTAGE-REGULATOR TERMS AND DEFINITIONS

Current-Sense Voltage

The voltage that is a function of the load current and is normally used for control of the current-limiting circuitry.

Dropout Voltage

The low input-to-output differential voltage at which the circuit ceases to regulate against further reductions in input voltage.

Feedback Sense Voltage

The voltage that is a function of the output voltage and is used for feedback control of the regulator.

Reference Voltage

The voltage that is compared with the feedback sense voltage to control the regulator.

Bias Current

The difference between input and output currents.
NOTE: This is sometimes referred to as quiescent current.

Standby Current

The input current drawn by the regulator with no output load and no reference voltage load.

Short-Circuit Output Current

The output current of the regulator with the output shorted to ground.

Peak Output Current

The maximum output current that can be obtained from the regulator due to limiting circuitry within the regulator.

SHUNT REGULATORS

NOTE: These terms and symbols are based on JEDEC and IEC standards for voltage regulator diodes.

Shunt Regulator

A device having a voltage-current characteristic similar to that of a voltage-regulator diode; normally biased to operate in a region of low differential resistance (corresponding to the breakdown region of a regulator diode) to develop across its terminals an essentially constant voltage throughout a specified current range.

Anode

The electrode to which the regulator current flows within the regulator when it is biased for regulation.

Cathode

The electrode from which the regulator current flows within the regulator when it is biased for regulation.

Reference Input Voltage (V_{ref}) (of an adjustable shunt regulator)

The voltage at the reference input terminal with respect to the anode terminal.

Temperature Coefficient of Reference Voltage (αV_{ref})

The ratio of the change in reference voltage to the change in temperature. This is the average value for the total temperature change.

To obtain a value in ppm/°C:

$$\alpha V_{ref} = \left[\frac{V_{ref} \text{ at } T_2 - V_{ref} \text{ at } T_1}{V_{ref} \text{ at } 25°C} \right] \frac{10^6}{T_2 - T_1}$$

Regulator Voltage (V_Z)

The dc voltage across the regulator.

Regulator Current (I_Z)

The dc current through the regulator when it is biased for regulation.

Regulator Current near Lower Knee of Regulation Range (I_{ZK})

The regulator current near the lower limit of the region within which regulation occurs; this corresponds to the breakdown knee of a regulator diode.

Regulator Current at Maximum Limit of Regulation Range (I_{ZM})

The regulator current above which the differential resistance of the regulator significantly increases.

Differential Regulator Resistance (r_z)

The quotient of a change in voltage across the regulator and the corresponding change in current through the regulator when it is biased for regulation.

Noice Voltage (V_{nz})

The rms noise voltage with the regulator biased for regulation and with no input ripple.

REGULATOR SELECTION GUIDE

VARIABLE-VOLTAGE SERIES REGULATORS

SERIES	OUTPUT VOLTAGE V	INPUT VOLTAGE V	INPUT-TO-OUTPUT VOLTAGE V	OUTPUT CURRENT A	PACKAGES‡	PAGE
LM105	4.5 to 40	8.5 to 50	3 to 30	0.012	JG,L,P	91
uA723	2 to 37	9.5 to 40	3 to 38	0.150	J,L,N,U	143
LM117	Floating	Floating	3 to 40	0.5 and 1.5♦	KC,KD,LA	99
LM376	5 to 37	9 to 40	3 to 30	0.025	JG,L,P	91
LM104	−0.015 to −40	−8 to −50	−0.5 to −50	0.020	J,L,N	87

‡ Not every device type is available in each package shown for the series. See individual data sheets for specific information.

♦ The 1.5-A rating applies only to the LM217 and the LM317 in the KC package.

ADJUSTABLE SHUNT REGULATOR

SERIES	OUTPUT VOLTAGE V	TEMPERATURE COEFFICIENT OF OUTPUT VOLTAGE ppm/°C	MAXIMUM CURRENT mA	PACKAGES	PAGE
TL430	2.7 to 30	200 MAX	100	JG,LP	125
TL431*	2.7 to 30	100 MAX	100	JG,LP	129

*Future product to be announced.

SWITCHING-REGULATOR CONTROL CIRCUITS WITH UNCOMMITTED OUTPUTS

SERIES	DESCRIPTION	OUTPUT MODE	MAXIMUM OUTPUT CURRENT mA	PACKAGES‡	PAGE
TL497A	Fixed "on" time, variable frequency	Single-ended	500	J,N	137
SG1524	Variable duty cycle, fixed frequency	Push-pull	100	J,N	113
TL494*	Variable duty cycle, fixed frequency	Push-pull	200	J,N	135

‡Not every device type is available in each package shown for the series. See individual data sheets for specific information.

FIXED-VOLTAGE SERIES REGULATORS

SERIES	OUTPUT VOLTAGE – V														
	2.6	5	5.2	6	6.2	8	8.5	9	10	12	15	18	20	22	24
LM109		+													
LM340		+		+		+			+	+	+	+			+
TL7805AC		+													
uA7800		+		+		+	+		+	+	+	+		+	+
uA78L00	+	+			+			+	+	+	+				
uA78M00		+		+		+				+	+		+	+	+
uA7900		–	–	–		–				–	–	–		–	–
uA79M00		–		–		–				–	–		–		–

SERIES	OUTPUT VOLTAGE TOLERANCE	INPUT-TO-OUTPUT MINIMUM VOLTAGE	MAXIMUM OUTPUT CURRENT	INPUT VOLTAGE RANGE[†]	PACKAGES[‡]	PAGE
	±%	V	A	V		
LM109	8	2	0.5	7 to 25	LA	95
LM340	5 and 10	2	1 and 1.5[§]	7 to 38	KC	105
TL7805AC	3	2	1.5	7 to 25	KC	141
uA7800	5	2 to 3	1.5	7 to 38	KC	149
uA78L00	5 and 10	2 to 2.5	0.1	4.75 to 30	JG,LP	157
uA78M00	5	2 to 3	0.5	7 to 38	KC,KD,LA	163
uA7900	5	–2 to –3	–1.5	–7 to –38	KC	173
uA79M00	5	–2 to –3	–0.5	–7 to –38	KC,KD,LA	179

[†] Individual devices in each series offer a selection of input voltage limits within the range shown.

[‡] Not every device type is available in each package shown for the series. See individual data sheets for specific information.

[§] Some of these devices with higher output voltages (i.e., ≥18 V) must be limited to 1 A maximum.

TIMER/REGULATOR/COMPARATOR BUILDING BLOCKS

TL432. . . . . . page 133

REGULATOR ALPHANUMERIC INDEX

INDEX TO APPLICATIONS CIRCUITS

INDEX TO APPLICATIONS CIRCUITS (Continued)

[†]The identical circuits for the TL431 appear on page 132.

LINEAR INTEGRATED CIRCUITS

TYPES LM104, LM204, LM304
NEGATIVE-VOLTAGE REGULATORS

BULLETIN NO. DL-S 12052, SEPTEMBER 1973—REVISED JUNE 1976

FORMERLY SN52104, SN72104

- Typical Load Regulation . . . 1 mV
- Typical Input Regulation . . . 0.06%
- Designed to be Interchangeable with National Semiconductor LM104, LM204, and LM304 Respectively

description

The LM104, LM204, and LM304 are monolithic integrated circuit voltage regulators that can be programmed with a single external resistor to provide any voltage between −40 volts and approximately 0 volts while operating from a single unregulated negative supply. When used with a separate floating bias supply, these devices can provide regulation with the output voltage limited only by the breakdown characteristics of the external pass transistors.

Although designed primarily for application as linear series regulators at output currents up to 25 milliamperes, the LM104, LM204, and LM304 can be used as current regulators, switching regulators, or control elements with the output current limited by the capability of the external pass transistors. The improvement factor for load regulation is approximately equal to the composite current gain of the added transistors. The devices can be used in either constant-current or fold-back current-limiting applications.

The LM104 is characterized for operation over the full military temperature range of −55°C to 125°C; the LM204 is characterized for operation from −25°C to 85°C; and the LM304 is characterized for operation from 0°C to 70°C.

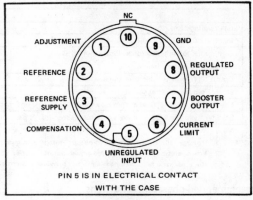

LM104, LM204 . . . L
PLUG-IN PACKAGE (TOP VIEW)

PIN 5 IS IN ELECTRICAL CONTACT WITH THE CASE

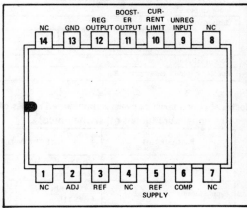

LM104 . . . J
LM204, LM304 . . . J OR N
DUAL-IN-LINE PACKAGE (TOP VIEW)

NC—No internal connection

schematic

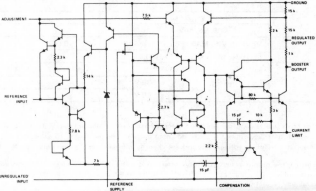

Component values shown are nominal.
Resistor values are in ohms.

77

TEXAS INSTRUMENTS
INCORPORATED
POST OFFICE BOX 5012 • DALLAS, TEXAS 75222

absolute maximum ratings over operating free-air temperature range (unless otherwise noted)

		LM104	LM204	LM304	UNIT
Input voltage (see Note 1)		−50	−50	−40	V
Input-to-output voltage differential		−50	−50	−40	V
Continuous total dissipation at (or below) 25°C	J or N package	1000	1000	1000	mW
free-air temperature (see Note 2)	L package	800	800	800	
Operating free-air temperature range		−55 to 125	−25 to 85	0 to 70	°C
Storage temperature range		−65 to 150	−65 to 150	−65 to 150	°C
Lead temperature 1/16 inch from case for 60 seconds: J or L package		300	300	300	°C
Lead temperature 1/16 inch from case for 10 seconds: N package			260	260	°C

NOTES: 1. Voltage values, except input-to-output voltage differential, are with respect to network ground terminal.
2. For operation above 25°C free-air temperature, refer to Dissipation Derating Table, Figures I, II, and III, page 90. This rating for the L package requires a heat sink that provides a thermal resistance from case to free-air, $R_{\theta CA}$, of not more than 105°C/W.

recommended operating conditions

		LM104		LM204		LM304		UNIT
		MIN	MAX	MIN	MAX	MIN	MAX	
Input voltage, V_I		−8	−50	−8	−50	−8	−40	V
Output voltage, V_O		−0.015	−40	−0.015	−40	−0.035	−30	V
Input-to-output voltage differential, $V_I - V_O$	$I_O = 20$ mA	−2	−50	−2	−50	−2	−40	V
	$I_O \leqslant 5$ mA	−0.5	−50	−0.5	−50	−0.5	−40	
Output current, I_O			20		20		20	mA
Operating free-air temperature, T_A		−55	125	−25	85	0	70	°C

electrical characteristics over recommended ranges of input and output voltage and operating free-air temperature (unless otherwise noted)

PARAMETER	TEST CONDITIONS[†]		LM104, LM204			LM304			UNIT
			MIN	TYP	MAX	MIN	TYP	MAX	
Input regulation	$V_O = -5$ V to MAX, $\Delta V_I = 0.1\,V_I$, See Notes 3 and 4			0.06	0.1		0.06	0.1	%
Ripple sensitivity	C1 = 10 μF, f = 120 Hz	$V_I = -15$ V to MAX		0.2	0.5		0.2	0.5	mV/V
		$V_I = -7$ V to −15 V		0.5	1		0.5	1	
Output regulation	$I_O = 0$ to 20 mA, $R_{SC} = 15\,\Omega$, See Note 3			1	5		1	5	mV
Output voltage scale factor	R1 = 2.4 kΩ, See Figure 2		1.8	2	2.2	1.8	2	2.2	V/kΩ
Output voltage change with temperature	T_A = MIN to T_A = 25°C				1			1	%
	T_A = 25°C to T_A = MAX				1			1	
Output noise voltage	$V_O = -5$ V to MAX, f = 10 Hz to 10 kHz	C1 = 0		0.007			0.007		%
		C1 = 10 μF		15			15		μV
Bias current	$I_O = 5$ mA	$V_O = 0$		1.7	2.5		1.7	2.5	mA
		$V_O = -30$ V					3.6	5	
		$V_O = -40$ V		3.6	5				

[†] For conditions shown as MIN or MAX, use the appropriate value specified under recommended operating conditions.

NOTES: 3. Input regulation and output regulation are measured using pulse techniques ($t_W \leqslant 10$ μs, duty cycle ≤ 5%) to limit changes in average internal dissipation. Output voltages due to large changes in internal dissipation must be taken into account separately.

4. At zero output voltage, the output variation can be determined using the ripple sensitivity. At low voltages (i.e., 0 to −5 V), the output variation determined from the ripple sensitivity must be added to the variation determined from the input regulation to determine the overall line regulation.

9

TEXAS INSTRUMENTS
INCORPORATED
POST OFFICE BOX 5012 • DALLAS, TEXAS 75222

TYPICAL APPLICATION DATA

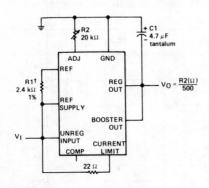

$$V_O = \frac{R2(\Omega)}{500}$$

FIGURE 1—BASIC REGULATOR CIRCUIT

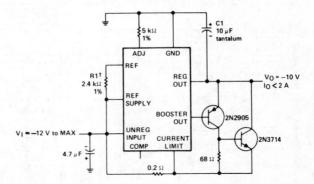

$V_O = -10$ V
$I_O < 2$ A

$V_I = -12$ V to MAX

FIGURE 2—HIGH-CURRENT REGULATOR

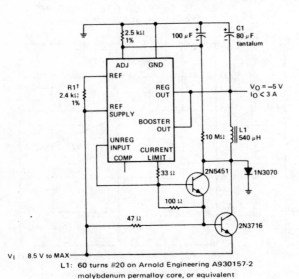

$V_O = -5$ V
$I_O < 3$ A

V_I 8.5 V to MAX

L1: 60 turns #20 on Arnold Engineering A930157-2
molybdenum permalloy core, or equivalent

FIGURE 3—SWITCHING REGULATOR

$$V_O = \frac{R2(\Omega)}{1000}$$

$V_{bias} = 10$ V

FIGURE 4—OPERATING WITH SEPARATE BIAS SUPPLY

†Trim R1 for exact scale factor.

TEXAS INSTRUMENTS
INCORPORATED
POST OFFICE BOX 5012 • DALLAS, TEXAS 75222

VOLTAGE REGULATORS

THERMAL INFORMATION

These curves are for use with the continuous dissipation ratings specified on the individual data sheets. Those ratings apply up to the temperature at which the rated level intersects the appropriate derating curve or the maximum operating free-air temperature.

J AND JG PACKAGE FREE-AIR TEMPERATURE DISSIPATION DERATING CURVES

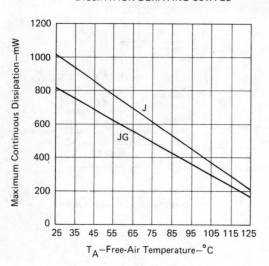

FIGURE I

L PACKAGE FREE-AIR TEMPERATURE DISSIPATION DERATING CURVES

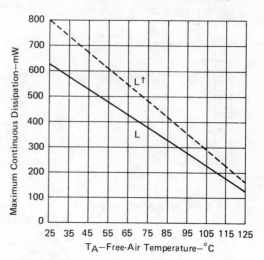

FIGURE II

N PACKAGE FREE-AIR TEMPERATURE DISSIPATION DERATING CURVES

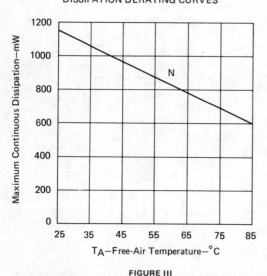

FIGURE III

P PACKAGE FREE-AIR TEMPERATURE DISSIPATION DERATING CURVES

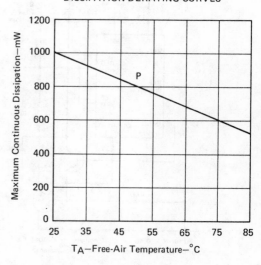

FIGURE IV

† This rating for the L package requires a heat sink that provides a thermal resistance from case to free-air, $R_{\theta CA}$, of not more than 105°C/W.

TEXAS INSTRUMENTS
INCORPORATED
POST OFFICE BOX 5012 • DALLAS, TEXAS 75222

FORMERLY SN52105, SN72305, SN72305A, SN72376

- Low Standby Current . . . 0.8 mA Typ

- Adjustable Output Voltage

- Load Regulation . . . 0.1% Max (LM105, LM205, LM305)

- Input Regulation . . . 0.06%/V Max

- Designed to be Interchangeable with National LM105, LM205, LM305, LM305A, and LM376 Respectively

description

The LM105, LM205, LM305, LM305A and LM376 are monolithic positive-voltage regulators designed for a wide range of applications from digital power supplies to precision regulators for analog systems. These devices will not oscillate under conditions of varying resistive and reactive loads and will start reliably with any load within the rating of the circuits.

The LM105 is characterized for operation over the full military temperature range of $-55°C$ to $125°C$; the LM205 is characterized for operation from $-25°C$ to $85°C$, and the LM305, LM305A, and LM376 are characterized for operation from $0°C$ to $70°C$.

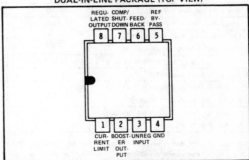

LM105 . . . JG
LM205, LM305, LM305A, LM376 . . . JG OR P
DUAL-IN-LINE PACKAGE (TOP VIEW)

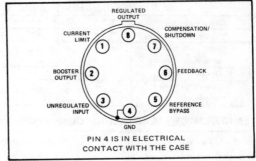

LM105, LM205, LM305, LM305A, LM376 . . . L
PLUG-IN PACKAGE (TOP VIEW)

PIN 4 IS IN ELECTRICAL CONTACT WITH THE CASE

schematic

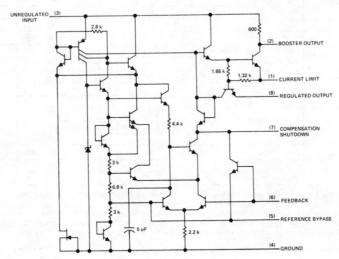

Component values shown are nominal.
Resistor values are in ohms.

TEXAS INSTRUMENTS
INCORPORATED
POST OFFICE BOX 5012 • DALLAS, TEXAS 75222

TYPES LM105, LM205, LM305, LM305A, LM376
POSITIVE-VOLTAGE REGULATORS

absolute maximum ratings over operating free-air temperature range (unless otherwise noted)

	LM105	LM205	LM305A	LM305 LM376	UNIT
Input voltage (see Note 1)	50	50	50	40	V
Input-to-output voltage differential	40	40	40	40	V
Continuous total dissipation at (or below) 25°C free-air temperature (see Note 2)	800	800	800	800	mW
Operating free-air temperature range	−55 to 125	−25 to 85	0 to 70	0 to 70	°C
Storage temperature range	−65 to 150	−65 to 150	−65 to 150	−65 to 150	°C
Lead temperature 1/16 inch from case for 60 seconds: JG or L package	300	300	300	300	°C
Lead temperature 1/16 inch from case for 10 seconds: P package		260	260	260	°C

NOTES: 1. Voltage values, except input-to-output voltage differential, are with respect to network ground terminal.

2. For operation above 25°C free-air temperature, refer to Dissipation Derating Curves, Figures I, II, and IV, page 90. This rating for the L package requires a heat sink that provides a thermal resistance from case to free-air, $R_{\theta CA}$, of not more than 105°C/W.

recommended operating conditions

	LM105		LM205		LM305A		LM305		LM376		UNIT
	MIN	MAX	MIN	MAX	MIN	MAX	MIN	MAX	MIN	MAX	
Input voltage, V_I	8.5	50	8.5	50	8.5	50	8.5	40	9	40	V
Output voltage, V_O	4.5	40	4.5	40	4.5	40	4.5	30	5	37	V
Input-to-output voltage differential, V_I-V_O	3	30	3	30	3	30	3	30	3	30	V
Output current, I_O	0	12	0	12	0	45	0	12	0	25	mA
Operating free-air temperature, T_A	−55	125	−25	85	0	70	0	70	0	70	°C

LM105, LM205, LM305 electrical characteristics[†] at 25°C free-air temperature (unless otherwise noted)

PARAMETER	TEST CONDITIONS[‡]			LM105, LM205			LM305			UNIT
				MIN	TYP	MAX	MIN	TYP	MAX	
Input regulation	$V_I-V_O \leqslant 5$ V		See Note 3		0.025	0.06		0.025	0.06	%/V
	$V_I-V_O > 5$ V				0.015	0.03		0.015	0.03	
Ripple sensitivity	C_{ref} = 10 µF,	f = 120 Hz			0.003	0.01		0.003	0.01	%/V
Output regulation (see Note 4)	I_O = 0 to I_O = 12 mA, See Note 3	R_{SC} = 10 Ω, T_A = 25°C			0.02	0.05		0.02	0.05	%
		R_{SC} = 10 Ω, T_A = MIN			0.03	0.1		0.03	0.1	
		R_{SC} = 10 Ω, T_A = MAX			0.03	0.1				
		R_{SC} = 15 Ω, T_A = MAX						0.03	0.1	
Output voltage change with temperature	T_A = MIN to T_A = 25°C					1			1	%
	T_A = 25°C to T_A = MAX					1			1	
Output noise voltage	f = 10 Hz to 10 kHz	C_{ref} = 0			0.005			0.005		%
		$C_{ref} > 0.1$ µF			0.002			0.002		
Feedback sense voltage				1.63	1.7	1.81	1.63	1.7	1.81	V
Current-limit sense voltage	R_{SC} = 10 Ω,	V_O = 0,	See Note 5	225	300	375	225	300	375	mV
Standby current	V_I = 50 V				0.8	2				mA
	V_I = 40 V							0.8	2	

[†]These specifications apply for input and output voltages within the ranges specified under recommended operating conditions and for a divider impedance of 2 kΩ presented to the feedback terminal, unless otherwise noted.

[‡]For conditions shown as MIN or MAX, use the appropriate value specified under recommended operating conditions.

NOTES: 3. Input regulation and output regulation are measured using pulse techniques ($t_w \leqslant 10$ µs, duty cycle ≤ 5%) to limit changes in average internal dissipation. Output voltage changes due to large changes in internal dissipation must be taken into account separately.

4. Load regulation and output current capacity can be improved by the addition of external transistors. The improvement factor will be approximately equal to the composite current gain of the added transistors.

5. Current-limit sense voltage is measured without an external pass transistor.

TEXAS INSTRUMENTS
INCORPORATED
POST OFFICE BOX 5012 • DALLAS, TEXAS 75222

LM305A, LM376 electrical characteristics[†] at 25°C free-air temperature (unless otherwise noted)

PARAMETER	TEST CONDITIONS[‡]			LM305A			LM376			UNIT
				MIN	TYP	MAX	MIN	TYP	MAX	
Input regulation	$V_I - V_O \leqslant 5$ V		See Note 3		0.025	0.06			0.03	%/V
	$V_I - V_O > 5$ V				0.015	0.03			0.03	
	$T_A = 0°C$ to 70°C								0.1	
Ripple sensitivity	$C_{ref} = 10$ μF,	f = 120 Hz			0.003					%/V
	f = 120 Hz								0.1	
Output regulation (see Note 4)	$I_O = 0$ to $I_O = $ MAX, See Note 3	$R_{SC} = 0$ Ω, $T_A = 25°C$			0.02	0.2			0.2	%
		$R_{SC} = 0$ Ω, $T_A = 0°C$			0.03	0.4			0.5	
		$R_{SC} = 0$ Ω, $T_A = 70°C$			0.03	0.4			0.5	
Output voltage change with temperature	$T_A = 0°C$ to $T_A = 25°C$					1			1	%
	$T_A = 25°C$ to $T_A = 70°C$					1			1	
Output noise voltage	f = 10 Hz to 10 kHz	$C_{ref} = 0$			0.005					%
		$C_{ref} > 0.1$ μF			0.002					
Feedback sense voltage				1.55	1.7	1.85				V
	$T_A = 0°C$ to $T_A = 70°C$						1.6	1.7	1.8	
Current limit sense voltage	$R_{SC} = 10$ Ω,	$V_O = 0$ V,	See Note 5	225	300	375		300		mV
Standby current	$V_I = 50$ V				0.8	2				mA
	$V_I = 30$ V								2.5	

[†]These specifications apply for input and output voltages within the ranges specified under recommended operating conditions, and for a divider impedance of 2 kΩ presented to the feedback terminal, unless otherwise noted.

[‡]For conditions shown as MIN or MAX, use the appropriate value specified under recommended operating conditions.

NOTES: 3. Input regulation and output regulation are measured using pulse techniques ($t_w \leqslant 10$ μs, duty cycle $\leqslant 5\%$) to limit changes in average internal dissipation. Output voltage changes due to large changes in internal dissipation must be taken into account separately.

4. Load regulation and output current capacity can be improved by the addition of external transistors. The improvement factor will be approximately equal to the composite current gain of the added transistors.

5. Current-limit sense voltage is measured without an external pass transistor.

TYPICAL APPLICATION DATA

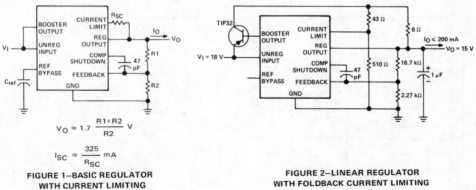

$$V_O \approx 1.7 \; \frac{R1+R2}{R2} \; V$$

$$I_{SC} \approx \frac{325}{R_{SC}} \; mA$$

FIGURE 1—BASIC REGULATOR WITH CURRENT LIMITING

FIGURE 2—LINEAR REGULATOR WITH FOLDBACK CURRENT LIMITING

TEXAS INSTRUMENTS
INCORPORATED
POST OFFICE BOX 5012 • DALLAS, TEXAS 75222

93

TYPICAL APPLICATION DATA

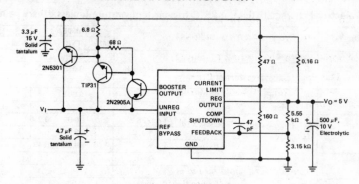

FIGURE 3—10-A REGULATOR WITH
FOLDBACK CURRENT LIMITING

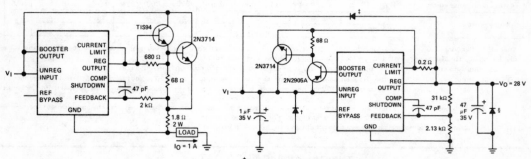

†Protects against input voltage reversal.

‡Protects against shorted input or inductive loads on unregulated supply.

§Protects against output voltage reversal.

FIGURE 4—CURRENT REGULATOR

FIGURE 5—1-A REGULATOR WITH
PROTECTIVE DIODES

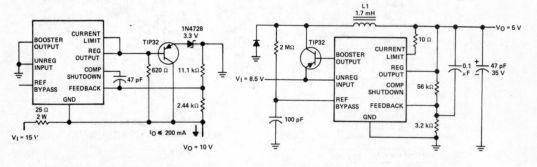

FIGURE 6—SHUNT REGULATOR

FIGURE 7—SWITCHING REGULATOR

LINEAR
INTEGRATED
CIRCUITS

TYPES LM109, LM209, LM309
5-VOLT REGULATORS

BULLETIN NO. DL-S 12056, SEPTEMBER 1973–REVISED JUNE 1976

FORMERLY SN52109, SN72309

- No External Components Required for Most Applications

- Output Current . . . 500 mA Max

- Satisfies 5-V Supply Requirements of TTL and DTL

- Virtually Blow-Out Proof Due to Internal Current Limiting, Thermal Shutdown, and Safe-Operating-Area Compensation

- Designed to be Interchangeable with National LM109, LM209, and LM309 Respectively

**LA PLUG-IN PACKAGE
(TOP VIEW)**

INPUT ①

OUTPUT ②

③ GND

PIN 3 IS IN ELECTRICAL
CONTACT WITH THE CASE

description

These monolithic 5-volt regulators are designed for use as local regulators to eliminate noise and distribution problems inherent with single-point regulation. They are specified under worst-case conditions to match the power supply requirements of TTL and DTL logic families. In other applications, these devices can be used with external components to obtain adjustable output voltages and currents or as the series-pass element in precision regulators.

schematic

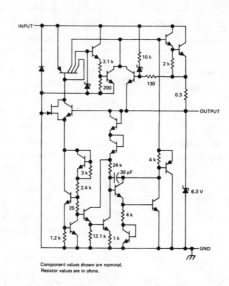

Component values shown are nominal.
Resistor values are in ohms.

absolute maximum ratings over operating temperature range (unless otherwise noted)

	LM109, LM209	LM309	UNIT
Input voltage	35	35	V
Output current	500	500	mA
Continuous total dissipation at (or below) 25°C case temperature (see Note 1)	5	4	W
Continuous total dissipation at (or below) 25°C free-air temperature (see Note 2)	600	480	mW
Operating case or virtual junction temperature range	−55 to 150	0 to 125	°C
Storage temperature range	−65 to 150	−65 to 150	°C
Lead temperature 1/16 inch from case for 60 seconds	300	300	°C

NOTES: 1. Above 25° case temperature, derate linearly at the rate of 40 mW/°C, or refer to Dissipation Derating Curve, Figure 1, next page.
2. Above 25°C free-air temperature, derate linearly at the rate of 4.8 mW/°C, or refer to Dissipation Derating Curve, Figure 2, next page.

TEXAS INSTRUMENTS
INCORPORATED
POST OFFICE BOX 5012 • DALLAS, TEXAS 75222

recommended operating conditions

	LM109 MIN	LM109 MAX	LM209 MIN	LM209 MAX	LM309 MIN	LM309 MAX	UNIT
Input voltage, V_I	7	25	7	25	7	25	V
Output current, I_O	0	500	0	500	0	500	mA
Operating virtual-junction temperature, T_J	−55	150	−25	150	0	125	°C

electrical characteristics at specified virtual junction temperature

PARAMETER	TEST CONDITIONS†		LM109, LM209 MIN	LM109, LM209 TYP	LM109, LM209 MAX	LM309 MIN	LM309 TYP	LM309 MAX	UNIT
Output voltage	V_I = 10 V, I_O = 100 mA	25°C	4.7	5.0	5.3	4.8	5.0	5.2	V
	V_I = 7 V to 25 V, I_O = 5 mA to 200 mA	Full range	4.6		5.4	4.75		5.25	
Input regulation	V_I = 7 V to V_I = 25 V	25°C		4	50		4	50	mV
Ripple rejection	f = 120 Hz	25°C		85			85		dB
Output regulation	I_O = 5 mA to I_O = 500 mA, See Note 3	25°C		20	50		20	50	mV
Output noise voltage	f = 10 Hz to 100 kHz	25°C		40			40		µV
Standby current	V_I = 7 V to 25 V	Full range		5	10		5	10	mA
Bias current change	V_I = 7 V to V_I = 25 V, I_O = 100 mA	Full range			0.5			0.5	mA
	I_O = 5 mA to I_O = 200 mA				0.8			0.8	

†Full range for LM109 is −55°C to 150°C, for LM209 is −25°C to 150°C, and for LM309 is 0°C to 125°C. All characteristics, except output noise voltage and ripple rejection, are measured using pulse techniques. t_w ⩽ 10 ms, duty cycle ⩽ 5%.

NOTE 3: Pulse techniques are used in testing to limit the average internal dissipation. Output voltage changes due to large changes in internal dissipation must be taken into account separately.

THERMAL INFORMATION

CASE TEMPERATURE DISSIPATION DERATING CURVE

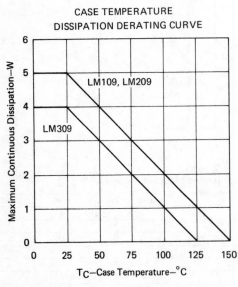

FIGURE 1

FREE-AIR TEMPERATURE DISSIPATION DERATING CURVE

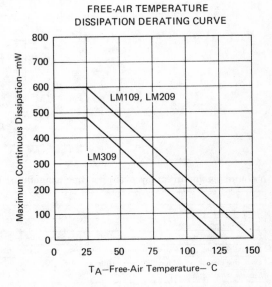

FIGURE 2

TYPICAL CHARACTERISTICS†

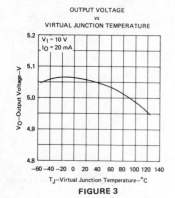

OUTPUT VOLTAGE
vs
VIRTUAL JUNCTION TEMPERATURE

FIGURE 3

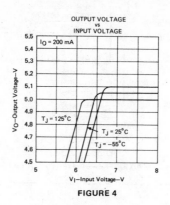

OUTPUT VOLTAGE
vs
INPUT VOLTAGE

FIGURE 4

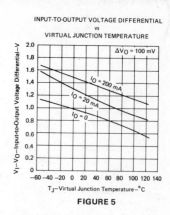

INPUT-TO-OUTPUT VOLTAGE DIFFERENTIAL
vs
VIRTUAL JUNCTION TEMPERATURE

FIGURE 5

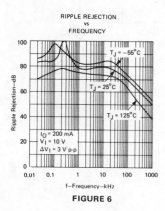

RIPPLE REJECTION
vs
FREQUENCY

FIGURE 6

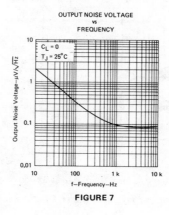

OUTPUT NOISE VOLTAGE
vs
FREQUENCY

FIGURE 7

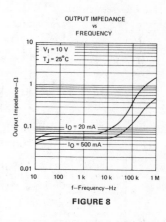

OUTPUT IMPEDANCE
vs
FREQUENCY

FIGURE 8

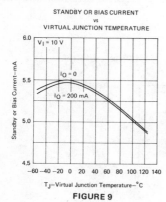

STANDBY OR BIAS CURRENT
vs
VIRTUAL JUNCTION TEMPERATURE

FIGURE 9

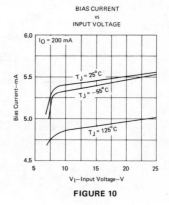

BIAS CURRENT
vs
INPUT VOLTAGE

FIGURE 10

†Data for virtual junction temperatures outside the ranges specified in the recommended operating conditions for LM209 or LM309 is not applicable for those types.

TYPICAL APPLICATION DATA

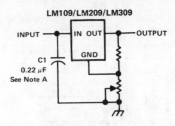

NOTE A: C1 is required if regulator is not located in close proximity to power supply filter.

FIGURE 11–ADJUSTABLE OUTPUT REGULATOR

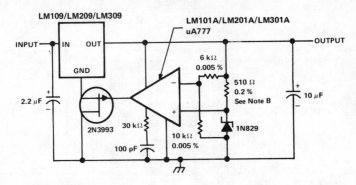

NOTES: A. All capacitors are solid tantalum.
B. This resistor determines zener current. Adjust to minimize thermal drift.

FIGURE 12–HIGH-STABILITY REGULATOR

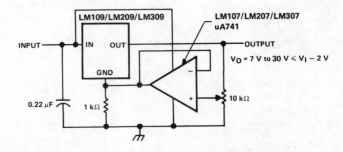

FIGURE 13–HIGH-STABILITY REGULATOR WITH ADJUSTABLE OUTPUT

TEXAS INSTRUMENTS
INCORPORATED
POST OFFICE BOX 5012 • DALLAS, TEXAS 75222

**LINEAR
INTEGRATED
CIRCUITS**

**TYPES LM117, LM217, LM317
3-TERMINAL ADJUSTABLE REGULATORS**

BULLETIN NO. DL-S 12518, SEPTEMBER 1977

- Output Voltage Range Adjustable from 1.2 V to 37 V

- Guaranteed I_O Capability of 1.5 A for TO-220 package, 500 mA for LA and TO-202 packages

- Input Regulation Typically 0.01% Per Input-Volt Change

- Output Regulation Typically 0.1%

- Peak Output Current Constant Over Temperature Range of Regulator

- Popular 3-Lead Packages

- Ripple Rejection Typically 80 dB

terminal assignments

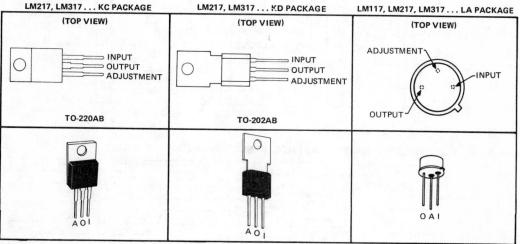

LM217, LM317 . . . KC PACKAGE (TOP VIEW) — INPUT, OUTPUT, ADJUSTMENT — TO-220AB — A O I

LM217, LM317 . . . KD PACKAGE (TOP VIEW) — INPUT, OUTPUT, ADJUSTMENT — TO-202AB — A O I

LM117, LM217, LM317 . . . LA PACKAGE (TOP VIEW) — ADJUSTMENT, INPUT, OUTPUT — O A I

description

The LM117, LM217, and LM317 are adjustable 3-terminal positive-voltage regulators capable of supplying 1.5 amperes over a differential-voltage range of 1.2 volts to 37 volts. They are exceptionally easy to use and require only two external resistors to set the output voltage. Both input and output regulation are better than standard fixed regulators. The devices are packaged in standard transistor packages that are easily mounted and handled.

In addition to higher performance than fixed regulators, these regulators offer full overload protection available only in integrated circuits. Included on the chip are current limit, thermal overload protection, and safe-area protection. All overload protection circuitry remains fully functional even if the adjustment terminal is disconnected. Normally, no capacitors are needed unless the device is situated far from the input filter capacitors in which case an input bypass is needed. An optional output capacitor can be added to improve transient response. The adjustment terminal can be bypassed to achieve very high ripple rejection, which is difficult to achieve with standard 3-terminal regulators.

Besides replacing fixed regulators, these regulators are useful in a wide variety of other applications. Since the regulator is floating and sees only the input-to-output differential voltage, supplies of several hundred volts can be regulated as long as the maximum input-to-output differential is not exceeded. Its primary application is that of a programmable output regulator, but by connecting a fixed resistor between the adjustment terminal and the output terminal, this device can be used as a precision current regulator. Supplies with electronic shutdown can be achieved by clamping the adjustment terminal to ground, which programs the output to 1.2 volts where most loads draw little current.

The LM117 is characterized for operation over the full military temperature range of $-55°C$ to $125°C$. The LM217 and LM317 are characterized for operation from $-25°C$ to $150°C$ and from $0°C$ to $125°C$ respectively.

TEXAS INSTRUMENTS
INCORPORATED
POST OFFICE BOX 5012 • DALLAS, TEXAS 75222

schematic

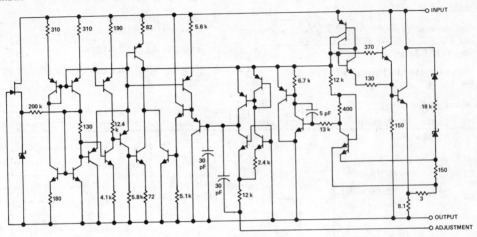

All resistors values shown are nominal and in ohms.

absolute maximum ratings over operation temperature range (unless otherwise noted)

		LM117	LM217	LM317	UNIT
Input-to-output differential voltage, $V_I - V_O$		40	40	40	V
Continuous total dissipation at 25°C free-air temperature (see Note 1)	KC (TO-220AB) package		2000	2000	mW
	KD (TO-202AB) package		1575	1575	
	LA package	600	600	600	
Continuous total dissipation at (or below) 25°C case temperature (see Note 1)	KC package		20	20	W
	KD package		2	2	
	LA package	2	2	2	
Operating free-air, case, or virtual junction temperature range		−55 to 150	−25 to 150	0 to 150	°C
Storage temperature range		−65 to 150	−65 to 150	−65 to 150	°C
Lead temperature 1/16 inch from case for 10 seconds	KC or KD packages		260	260	°C
Lead temperature 1/16 inch from case for 60 seconds	LA package	300	300	300	°C

NOTE 1: For operation above 25°C free-air or case temperature, refer to Dissipation Derating Curves, Figures 15 through 18, page 104.

recommended operating conditions

		LM117		LM217		LM317		UNIT
		MIN	MAX	MIN	MAX	MIN	MAX	
Output current, I_O	All packages	5		5		10		mA
	KC package				1500		1500	
	KD package				500		500	
	LA package		500		500		500	
Operating virtual junction temperature, T_J		−55	150	−25	150	0	125	°C

TEXAS INSTRUMENTS
INCORPORATED
POST OFFICE BOX 5012 • DALLAS, TEXAS 75222

electrical characteristics over recommended ranges of operation virtual junction temperature (unless otherwise noted)

PARAMETER	TEST CONDITIONS†		LM117,LM217 MIN	TYP	MAX	LM317 MIN	TYP	MAX	UNIT
Input regulation‡	$V_I - V_O$ = 3 V to 40 V, See Note 2	T_J = 25°C		0.01	0.02		0.01	0.04	%/V
		I_O = 10 mA to MAX		0.02	0.05		0.02	0.07	
Ripple rejection	V_O = 10 V, f = 120 Hz			65			65		dB
	V_O = 10 V, f = 120 Hz 10-µF capacitor between ADJ and ground		66	80		66	80		
Output regulation	I_O = 10 mA to MAX, T_J = 25°C, See Note 2	$V_O \leqslant 5$ V LA package			*			*	mV
		KC and KD packages		5	15		5	25	mV
		$V_O \geqslant 5$ V LA package			*			*	%
		KC and KD packages		0.1	0.3		0.1	0.5	%
	I_O = 10 mA to MAX, See Note 2	$V_O \leqslant 5$ V LA package			*			*	mV
		KC and KD packages		20	50		20	70	mV
		$V_O \geqslant 5$ V LA package			*			*	%
		KC and KD packages		0.3	1		0.3	1.5	%
Output voltage change with temperature	T_J = MIN to MAX			1			1		%
Output voltage long-term drift (see Note 3)	After 1000 h at T_J = MAX and $V_I - V_O$ = 40 V			0.3	1		0.3	1	%
Output noise voltage	f = 10 Hz to 10 kHz, T_J = 25°C			0.003			0.003		%
Minimum output current to maintain regulation	$V_I - V_O$ = 40 V			3.5	5		3.5	10	mA
Peak output current	$V_I - V_O \leqslant 15$ V	KC package	1.5	2.2		1.5	2.2		A
		KD and LA packages	0.5	0.8		0.5	0.8		
	$V_I - V_O \leqslant 40$ V	KC package	0.4			0.4			
		KD and LA packages	0.07			0.07			
Adjustment-terminal current				50	100		50	100	µA
Change in adjustment-terminal current	$V_I - V_O$ = 2.5 V to 40 V, I_O = 10 mA to MAX			0.2	5		0.2	5	µA
Reference voltage (output to ADJ)	$V_I - V_O$ = 3 V to 40 V, I_O = 10 mA to MAX, P ≤ rated dissipation		1.2	1.25	1.3	1.2	1.25	1.3	V

†Unless otherwise noted, these specifications apply for the following test conditions: $V_I - V_O$ = 5 V and I_O = 5 A for the KC (TO-220AB) package and I_O = 0.1 A for the LA and KD (TO-202AB) packages. For conditions shown as MIN or MAX, use the appropriate value specified under recommended operating conditions.

‡Input regulation is expressed here as the percentage change in output voltage per 1-volt change at the input.

NOTES: 2. Input regulation and output regulation are measured using pulse techniques ($t_w \leqslant 10$ µs, duty cycle ≤ 5%) to limit changes in average internal dissipation. Output voltage changes due to large changes in internal dissipation must be taken into account separately.

3. Since long-term drift cannot be measured on the individual devices prior to shipment, this specification is not intended to be a guarantee or warranty. It is an engineering estimate of the average drift to be expected from lot to lot.

*These specifications for this product in the LA package have not been determined. It is planned to specify values where asterisks appear above.

TEXAS INSTRUMENTS
INCORPORATED
POST OFFICE BOX 5012 • DALLAS, TEXAS 75222

TYPICAL APPLICATION DATA

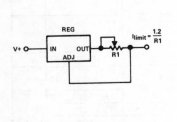

**FIGURE 1—ADJUSTABLE
VOLTAGE REGULATOR**

**FIGURE 2—0-V to 30-V REGULATOR
CIRCUIT**

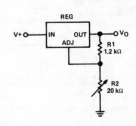

†D1 discharges C2
if output is shorted to ground.

**FIGURE 3—ADJUSTABLE REGULATOR
CIRCUIT WITH IMPROVED
RIPPLE REJECTION**

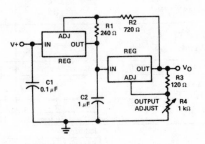

**FIGURE 4—PRECISION CURRENT
LIMITER CIRCUIT**

**FIGURE 5—TRACKING PREREGULATOR
CIRCUIT**

**FIGURE 6—1.2 to 20-V REGULATOR
CIRCUIT WITH MINIMUM
PROGRAM CURRENT**

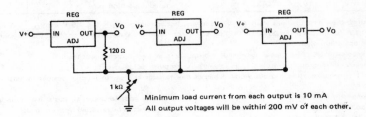

Minimum load current from each output is 10 mA
All output voltages will be within 200 mV of each other.

FIGURE 7—ADJUSTING MULTIPLE ON-CARD REGULATORS WITH A SINGLE CONTROL

NOTES: A. Use of an input bypass capacitor is recommended if regulator is far from filter capacitors.

B. Use of an output capacitor improves transient response but is optional.

C. V_{ref} equals the difference between the output and adjustment terminal voltages.

D. Output voltage is calculated from the equation: $V_O = V_{ref}\left(1 + \dfrac{R2}{R1}\right)$

TYPICAL APPLICATIONS

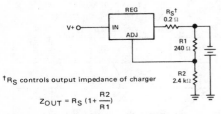

$\dagger R_S$ controls output impedance of charger

$$Z_{OUT} = R_S \left(1 + \frac{R2}{R1}\right)$$

The use of R_S allows low charging rates with a fully-charged battery.

FIGURE 8—BATTERY CHARGER CIRCUIT

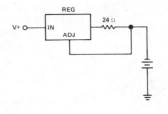

FIGURE 9—50-mA CONSTANT-CURRENT
BATTERY CHARGER CIRCUIT

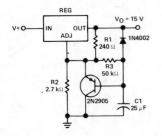

FIGURE 10—SLOW-TURN-ON 15-V
REGULATOR CIRCUIT

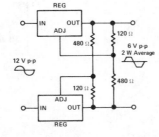

FIGURE 11—A-C VOLTAGE REGULATOR
CIRCUIT

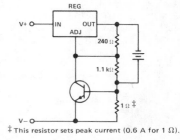

$\ddagger$ This resistor sets peak current (0.6 A for 1 Ω).

FIGURE 12—CURRENT-LIMITED
6-V CHARGER

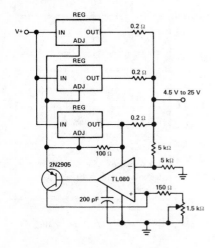

FIGURE 13—ADJUSTABLE 4-A REGULATOR

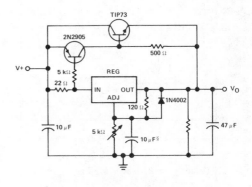

$\P$ Minimum load current is 30 mA.
$\S$ Optional capacitor improves ripple rejection

FIGURE 14—HIGH-CURRENT ADJUSTABLE REGULATOR

THERMAL INFORMATION

KC AND KD PACKAGES
FREE-AIR TEMPERATURE
DISSIPATION DERATING CURVES

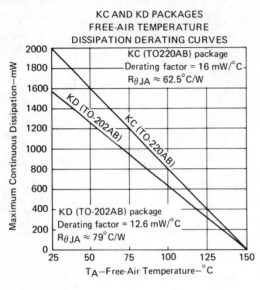

FIGURE 15

LA PACKAGE
FREE-AIR TEMPERATURE
DISSIPATION DERATING CURVE

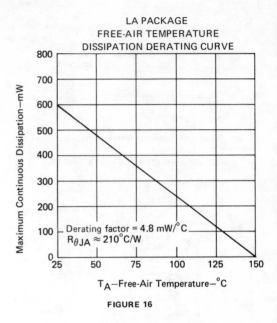

FIGURE 16

KC PACKAGE CASE TEMPERATURE
DISSIPATION DERATING CURVES

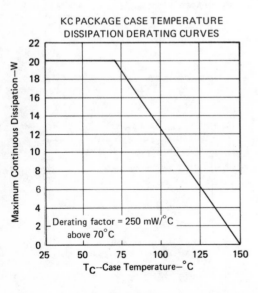

FIGURE 17

KD AND LA PACKAGES
CASE TEMPERATURE
DISSIPATION DERATING CURVES

FIGURE 18

LINEAR INTEGRATED CIRCUITS

SERIES LM340
POSITIVE-VOLTAGE REGULATORS

BULLETIN NO. DL-S 12503, SEPTEMBER 1977

- 3-Terminal Regulators
- Output Current up to 1.5 A
- No External Components
- Internal Thermal Overload Protection
- Direct Replacements for National LM340 Series
- High Power Dissipation Capability
- Internal Short-Circuit Current Limiting
- Output Transistor Safe-Area Compensation

NOMINAL OUTPUT VOLTAGE	TOLERANCE ≈10%	TOLERANCE ≈5%
5 V	LM340KC-5	LM340KC-5R
6 V	LM340KC-6	LM340KC-6R
8 V	LM340KC-8	LM340KC-8R
10 V	LM340KC-10	LM340KC-10R
12 V	LM340KC-12	LM340KC-12R
15 V	LM340KC-15	LM340KC-15R
18 V	LM340KC-18	LM340KC-18R
24 V	LM340KC-24	LM340KC-24R

KC PACKAGE
(TOP VIEW)

OUTPUT
COMMON
INPUT

TO - 220AB

INPUT   OUTPUT
COMMON

description

This series of fixed-voltage monolithic integrated-circuit voltage regulators is designed for a wide range of applications. These applications include on-card regulation for elimination of noise and distribution problems associated with single-point regulation. One of these regulators can deliver up to 1.5 amperes of output current. The internal current limiting and thermal shutdown features of these regulators make them essentially immune to overload. In addition to use as fixed-voltage regulators, these devices can be used with external components to obtain adjustable output voltages and currents and also as the power-pass element in precision regulators.

schematic

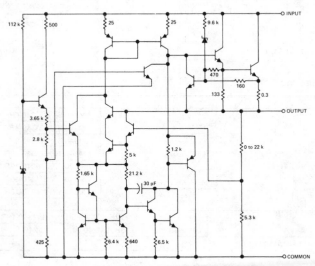

Resistor values shown are nominal and in ohms.

TEXAS INSTRUMENTS
INCORPORATED
POST OFFICE BOX 5012 • DALLAS, TEXAS 75222

SERIES LM340
POSITIVE-VOLTAGE REGULATORS

absolute maximum ratings over operating temperature range (unless otherwise noted)

Input voltage: LM340-24, LM340-24R . . . . 40 V

All others . . . . 35 V

Continuous total dissipation at 25°C free-air temperature (see Note 1) . . . . 2 W

Continuous total dissipation at (or below) 25°C case temperature (see Note 1) . . . . 15 V

Operating free-air, case, or virtual junction temperature range . . . . 0°C to 150°C

Storage temperature range . . . . −65°C to 150°C

Lead temperature 1/16 inch from case for 10 seconds . . . . 260°C

NOTE 1: For operation above 25°C free-air or case temperature, refer to Dissipation Derating Curves, Figure 1 and 2.

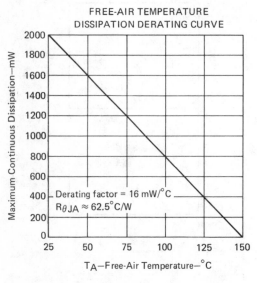

FREE-AIR TEMPERATURE
DISSIPATION DERATING CURVE

Derating factor = 16 mW/°C

$R_{\theta}JA \approx 62.5°C/W$

T_A—Free-Air Temperature—°C

FIGURE 1

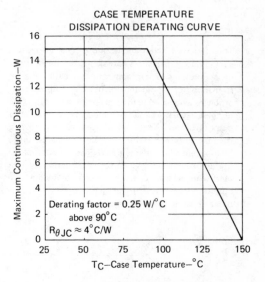

CASE TEMPERATURE
DISSIPATION DERATING CURVE

Derating factor = 0.25 W/°C above 90°C

$R_{\theta}JC \approx 4°C/W$

T_C—Case Temperature—°C

FIGURE 2

recommended operating conditions

		MIN	MAX	UNIT
Input voltage, V_I	LM340-5, LM340-5R	7	25	V
	LM340-6, LM340-6R	8	25	
	LM340-8, LM340-8R	10.5	25	
	LM340-10, LM340-10R	12.5	25	
	LM340-12, LM340-12R	14.5	30	
	LM340-15, LM340-15R	17.5	30	
	LM340-18, LM340-18R	21	33	
	LM340-24, LM340-24R	27	38	
Output current, I_O	LM340-5 thru LM340-15, LM340-5R thru LM340-15R		1.5	A
	LM340-18, LM340-18R, LM340-24, LM340-24R		1	
Operating virtual junction temperature, T_J		0	150	°C

TEXAS INSTRUMENTS
INCORPORATED
POST OFFICE BOX 5012 • DALLAS, TEXAS 75222

LM340-5, LM340-5R electrical characteristics at 25°C virtual junction temperature, V_I = 10 V, I_O = 500 mA (unless otherwise noted)

PARAMETER	TEST CONDITIONS†		LM340-5			LM340-5R			UNIT
			MIN	TYP	MAX	MIN	TYP	MAX	
			4.8	5	5.2	4.6	5	5.4	
Output voltage	I_O = 5 mA to 1 A, P ⩽ 15 W, T_A = 0°C to 70°C	V_I = 7 V to 20 V	4.75		5.25				V
		V_I = 7.7 V to 20 V				4.5		5.5	
Input regulation	V_I = 7 V to 25 V	I_O = 100 mA			50				mV
		I_O = 500 mA			100				
	V_I = 7.4 V to 25 V	I_O = 100 mA						75	
		I_O = 500 mA						150	
Ripple rejection	f = 120 Hz,	T_A = 0°C to 70°C		60			58		dB
Output regulation	I_O = 5 mA to 1.5 A				100			140	mV
Output voltage long-term drift (see Note 2)	After 1000 h at T_J and $V_I - V_O$ both at maximum rated values			20			15		mV
Output noise voltage	f = 10 Hz to 100 kHz			40			50		µV
Bias current				7	10		8	12	mA
Bias current change	T_A = 0°C to 70°C	I_O = 5 mA to 1.5 A			0.5		0.4		mA
		V_I = 7 V to 25 V			1.3				
		V_I = 7.7 V to 25 V					1		

LM340-6, LM340-6R electrical characteristics at 25°C virtual junction temperature, V_I = 11 V, I_O = 500 mA (unless otherwise noted)

PARAMETER	TEST CONDITIONS†		LM340-6			LM340-6R			UNIT
			MIN	TYP	MAX	MIN	TYP	MAX	
			5.75	6	6.25	5.5	6	6.5	
Output voltage	I_O = 5 mA to 1 A, P ⩽ 15 W, T_A = 0°C to 70°C	V_I = 8 V to 21 V	5.7		6.3				V
		V_I = 8.8 V to 21 V				5.4		6.6	
Input regulation	V_I = 8 V to 25 V	I_O = 100 mA			60				mV
		I_O = 500 mA			120				
	V_I = 8.5 V to 25 V	I_O = 100 mA						80	
		I_O = 500 mA						160	
Ripple rejection	f = 120 Hz,	T_A = 0°C to 70°C		57			55		dB
Output regulation	I_O = 5 mA to 1.5 A				120			160	mV
Output voltage long-term drift (see Note 2)	After 1000 h at T_J and $V_I - V_O$ both at maximum rated values			24			18		mV
Output noise voltage	f = 10 Hz to 100 kHz			45			55		µV
Bias current				7	10		8	12	mA
Bias current change	T_A = 0°C to 70°C	I_O = 5 mA to 1.5 A			0.5		0.4		mA
		V_I = 8 V to 25 V			1.3				
		V_I = 8.8 V to 25 V					1		

†All characteristics are measured with a capacitor across the input of 0.33 µF and a capacitor across the output of 0.1 µF. All characteristics except noise voltage and ripple rejection ratio are measured using pulse techniques (t_w ⩽ 10 ms, duty cycles ⩽ 5%). Output voltage changes due to changes in internal temperature must be taken into account separately.

NOTE 2: Since long-term drift cannot be measured on the individual devices prior to shipment, this specification is not intended to be a guarantee or warranty. It is an engineering estimate of the average drift to be expected from lot to lot.

LM340-8, LM340-8R electrical characteristics at 25°C virtual junction temperature,
V_I = 14 V, I_O = 500 mA (unless otherwise noted)

PARAMETER	TEST CONDITIONS†		LM340-8			LM340-8R			UNIT
			MIN	TYP	MAX	MIN	TYP	MAX	
Output voltage	I_O = 5 mA to 1 A, P ≤ 15 W, T_A = 0°C to 70°C		7.7	8	8.3	7.36	8	8.64	V
		V_I = 10.5 V to 23 V	7.6		8.4				
		V_I = 11 V to 23 V				7.2		8.8	
Input regulation	V_I = 10.5 V to 25 V	I_O = 100 mA			80				mV
		I_O = 500 mA			160				
	V_I = 10.7 V to 25 V	I_O = 100 mA						110	
		I_O = 500 mA						210	
Ripple rejection	f = 120 Hz,	T_A = 0°C to 70°C		55			53		dB
Output regulation	I_O = 5 mA to 1.5 A				160			210	mV
Output voltage long-term drift (see Note 2)	After 1000 h at T_J and $V_I - V_O$ both at maximum rated values			32			24		mV
Output noise voltage	f = 10 hz to 100 kHz			52			62		µV
Bias current				7	10		8	12	mA
Bias current change	T_A = 0°C to 70°C	I_O = 5 mA to 1.5 A			0.5		0.4		mA
		V_I = 10.5 V to 25 V			1.3				
		V_I = 11 V to 25 V						1	

LM340-10, LM340-10R electrical characteristics at 25°C virtual junction temperature,
V_I = 17 V, I_O = 500 mA (unless otherwise noted)

PARAMETER	TEST CONDITIONS†		LM340-10			LM340-10R			UNIT
			MIN	TYP	MAX	MIN	TYP	MAX	
Output voltage	I_O = 5 mA to 1 A, P ≤ 15 W, T_A = 0°C to 70°C		9.6	10	10.4	9.2	10	10.8	V
		V_I = 12.5 V to 25 V	9.5		10.5				
		V_I = 13.2 V to 25 V				9		11	
Input regulation	V_I = 12.5 V to 25 V	I_O = 100 mA			100				mV
		I_O = 500 mA			200				
	V_I = 13 V to 25 V	I_O = 100 mA						140	
		I_O = 500 mA						270	
Ripple rejection	f = 120 Hz,	T_A = 0°C to 70°C		54			51		dB
Output regulation	I_O = 5 mA to 1.5 A				200			270	mV
Output voltage long-term drift (see Note 2)	After 1000 h at T_J and $V_I - V_O$ both at maximum rated values			40			30		mV
Output noise voltage	f = 10 hz to 100 kHz			70			80		µV
Bias current				7	10		8	12	mA
Bias current change	T_A = 0°C to 70°C	I_O = 5 mA to 1.5 A			0.5		0.4		mA
		V_I = 12.5 V to 25 V			1.3				
		V_I = 13.2 V to 25 V						1	

†All characteristics are measured with a capacitor across the input of 0.33 µF and a capacitor across the output of 0.1 µF. All characteristics except noise voltage and ripple rejection ratio are measured using pulse techniques (t_w ≤ 10 ms, duty cycles ≤5%). Output voltage changes due to changes in internal temperature must be taken into account separately.

NOTE 2: Since long-term drift cannot be measured on the individual devices prior to shipment, this specification is not intended to be a guarantee or warranty. It is an engineering estimate of the average drift to be expected from lot to lot.

TEXAS INSTRUMENTS
INCORPORATED
POST OFFICE BOX 5012 • DALLAS, TEXAS 75222

LM340-12, LM340-12R electrical characteristics at 25°C virtual junction temperature,
V_I = 19 V, I_O = 500 mA (unless otherwise noted)

PARAMETER	TEST CONDITIONS[†]		LM340-12			LM340-12R			UNIT
			MIN	TYP	MAX	MIN	TYP	MAX	
			11.5	12	12.5	11	12	13	
Output voltage	I_O = 5 mA to 1 A, P ⩽ 15 W, T_A = 0°C to 70°C	V_I = 14.5 V to 27 V	11.4		12.6				V
		V_I = 15.3 V to 27 V				10.8		13.2	
Input regulation	V_I = 14.5 V to 30 V	I_O = 100 mA			120				mV
		I_O = 500 mA			240				
	V_I = 15 V to 30 V	I_O = 100 mA						160	
		I_O = 500 mA						320	
Ripple rejection	f = 120 Hz,	T_A = 0°C to 70°C		52			50		dB
Output regulation	I_O = 5 mA to 1.5 A				240			320	mV
Output voltage long-term drift (see Note 2)	After 1000 h at T_J and $V_I - V_O$ both at maximum rated values				48		36		mV
Output noise voltage	f = 10 Hz to 100 kHz			75			85		µV
Bias current				7	10		8	12	mA
Bias current change	T_A = 0°C to 70°C	I_O = 5 mA to 1.5 A			0.5		0.4		mA
		V_I = 14.5 V to 30 V			1.3				
		V_I = 15.3 V to 30 V					1		

LM340-15, LM340-15R electrical characteristics at 25°C virtual junction temperature,
V_I = 23 V, I_O = 500 mA (unless otherwise noted)

PARAMETER	TEST CONDITIONS[†]		LM340-15			LM340-15R			UNIT
			MIN	TYP	MAX	MIN	TYP	MAX	
			14.4	15	15.6	13.8	15	16.2	
Output voltage	I_O = 5 mA to 1 A, P ⩽ 15 W, T_A = 0°C to 70°C	V_I = 17.5 V to 30 V	14.25		15.75				V
		V_I = 18.6 V to 30 V				13.5		16.5	
Input regulation	V_I = 17.5 V to 30 V	I_O = 100 mA			150				mV
		I_O = 500 mA			300				
	V_I = 18.2 V to 30 V	I_O = 100 mA						200	
		I_O = 500 mA						400	
Ripple rejection	f = 120 Hz,	T_A = 0°C to 70°C		50			48		dB
Output regulation	I_O = 5 mA to 1.5 A				300			400	mV
Output voltage long-term drift (see Note 2)	After 1000 h at T_J and $V_I - V_O$ both at maximum rated values				60		45		mV
Output noise voltage	f = 10 Hz to 100 kHz			90			100		µV
Bias current				7	10		8	12	mA
Bias current change	T_A = 0°C to 70°C	I_O = 5 mA to 1.5 A			0.5		0.4		mA
		V_I = 17.5 V to 30 V			1.3				
		V_I = 18.6 V to 30 V					1		

[†]All characteristics are measured with a capacitor across the input of 0.33 µF and a capacitor across the output of 0.1 µF. All characteristics except noise voltage and ripple rejection ratio are measured using pulse techniques (t_w ⩽ 10 ms, duty cycles ⩽ 5%). Output voltage changes due to changes in internal temperature must be taken into account separately.

NOTE 2: Since long-term drift cannot be measured on the individual devices prior to shipment, this specification is not intended to be a guarantee or warranty. It is an engineering estimate of the average drift to be expected from lot to lot.

LM340-18, LM340-18R electrical characteristics at 25°C virtual junction temperature, V_I = 27 V, I_O = 500 mA (unless otherwise noted)

PARAMETER	TEST CONDITIONS[†]		LM340-18 MIN	TYP	MAX	LM340-18R MIN	TYP	MAX	UNIT
			17.3	18	18.7	16.6	18	19.4	
Output voltage	I_O = 5 mA to 1 A, P ≤ 15 W, T_A = 0°C to 70°C	V_I = 21 V to 33 V	17.1		18.9				V
		V_I = 22 V to 33 V				16.2		19.8	
Input regulation	V_I = 21 V to 33 V	I_O = 100 mA			180				mV
		I_O = 500 mA			360				
	V_I = 21.4 V to 33 V	I_O = 100 mA						240	
		I_O = 500 mA						480	
Ripple rejection	f = 120 Hz,	T_A = 0°C to 70°C		48			46		dB
Output regulation	I_O = 5 mA to 1 A				360			480	mV
Output voltage long-term drift (see Note 2)	After 1000 h at T_J and V_I − V_O both at maximum rated values			72			54		mV
Output noise voltage	f = 10 Hz to 100 kHz			110			120		µV
Bias current				7	10		8	12	mA
Bias current change	T_A = 0°C to 70°C	I_O = 5 mA to 1 A			0.5		0.4		mA
		V_I = 21 V to 33 V			1.3				
		V_I = 22 V to 33 V					1		

LM340-24, LM340-24R electrical characteristics at 25°C virtual junction temperature, V_I = 33 V, I_O = 500 mA (unless otherwise noted)

PARAMETER	TEST CONDITIONS[†]		LM340-24 MIN	TYP	MAX	LM340-24R MIN	TYP	MAX	UNIT
			23	24	25	22	24	26	
Output voltage	I_O = 5 mA to 1 A, P ≤ 15 W, T_A = 0°C to 70°C	V_I = 27 V to 38 V	22.8		25.2				V
		V_I = 28.5 V to 38 V				21.6		26.4	
Input regulation	V_I = 27 V to 38 V	I_O = 100 mA			240				mV
		I_O = 500 mA			480				
	V_I = 28 V to 38 V	I_O = 100 mA						320	
		I_O = 500 mA						640	
Ripple rejection	f = 120 Hz,	T_A = 0°C to 70°C		44			42		dB
Output regulation	I_O = 5 mA to 1 A				480			640	mV
Output voltage long-term drift (see Note 2)	After 1000 h at T_J and V_I − V_O both at maximum rated values			96			72		mV
Output noise voltage	f = 10 Hz to 100 kHz			170			180		µV
Bias current				7	10		8	12	mA
Bias current change	T_A = 0°C to 70°C	I_O = 5 mA to 1 A			0.5		0.4		mA
		V_I = 27 V to 38 V			1.3				
		V_I = 28.5 V to 38 V					1		

[†]All characteristics are measured with a capacitor across the input of 0.33 µF and a capacitor across the output of 0.1 µF. All characteristics except noise voltage and ripple rejection ratio are measured using pulse techniques (t_w ≤ 10 ms, duty cycles ≤ 5%). Output voltage changes due to changes in internal temperature must be taken into account separately.

NOTE 2: Since long-term drift cannot be measured on the individual devices prior to shipment, this specification is not intended to be a guarantee or warranty. It is an engineering estimate of the average drift to be expected from lot to lot.

TEXAS INSTRUMENTS
INCORPORATED
POST OFFICE BOX 5012 • DALLAS, TEXAS 75222

TYPICAL CHARACTERISTICS

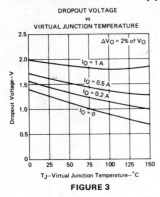

DROPOUT VOLTAGE
vs
VIRTUAL JUNCTION TEMPERATURE

FIGURE 3

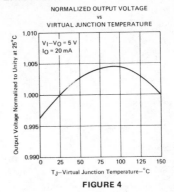

NORMALIZED OUTPUT VOLTAGE
vs
VIRTUAL JUNCTION TEMPERATURE

FIGURE 4

TL340-5
BIAS CURRENT
vs
VIRTUAL JUNCTION TEMPERATURE

FIGURE 5

TYPICAL APPLICATION DATA

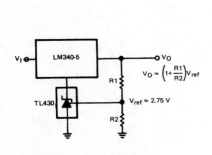

$$V_O \approx \left(1 + \frac{R1}{R2}\right) V_{ref}$$

$V_{ref} \approx 2.75$ V

FIGURE 6—ADJUSTABLE SUPPLY WITH STABLE OUTPUT FROM 8 VOLTS TO 35 VOLTS

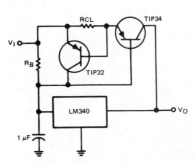

The boost circuit takes over at a level determined by R_B.

$$R_B \approx \frac{0.6 \text{ V}}{I_B}$$

where I_B is the LM340 operating level.

Maximum current limit I_{CL} is determined by R_{CL}.

$$R_{CL} \approx \frac{0.6 \text{ V}}{I_{CL}}$$

Example: If I_B is selected to be 0.5 A, then
$R_B = 1.2\ \Omega$.
If I_{CL} is 3 A, then
$R_{CL} = 0.2\ \Omega$.

FIGURE 7—OUTPUT CURRENT BOOST CIRCUIT

TEXAS INSTRUMENTS
INCORPORATED
POST OFFICE BOX 5012 • DALLAS, TEXAS 75222

- **Complete PWM Power Control Circuitry**
- **Uncommitted Outputs for Single-Ended or Push-Pull Applications**
- **Low Standby Current . . . 8 mA Typ**
- **Interchangeable With Silicon General SG1524, SG2524, and SG3524, Respectively**

description

The SG1524, SG2524, and SG3524 incorporate on single monolithic chips all the functions required in the construction of a regulating power supply, inverter, or switching regulator. They can also be used as the control element for high-power-output applications. The SG1524 family was designed for switching regulators of either polarity, transformer-coupled dc-to-dc converters, transformerless voltage doublers, and polarity converter applications employing fixed-frequency, pulse-width-modulation techniques. The complementary output allows either single-ended or push-pull application. Each device includes an on-chip regulator, error amplifier, programmable oscillator, pulse-steering flip-flop, two uncommitted pass transistors, a high-gain comparator, and current-limiting and shut-down circuitry.

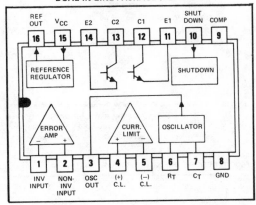

SG1524 . . . J
SG2524, SG3524 . . . J OR N
DUAL-IN-LINE PACKAGE (TOP VIEW)

The SG1524 is characterized for operation over the full military temperature range of −55°C to 125°C. The SG2524 and SG3524 are characterized for operation from 0°C to 70°C.

functional block diagram

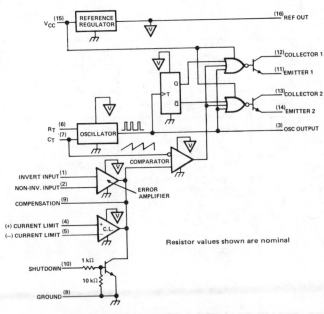

Resistor values shown are nominal

TEXAS INSTRUMENTS
INCORPORATED
POST OFFICE BOX 5012 • DALLAS, TEXAS 75222

absolute maximum ratings over operating free-air temperature range (unless otherwise noted)

Supply Voltage, V_{CC} (See Notes 1 and 2) . . . . 40 V
Collector Output Current . . . . 100 mA
Reference Output Current . . . . 50 mA
Current Through C_T Terminal . . . . −5 mA
Continuous Total Dissipation at (or below) 25°C Free-Air Temperature (See Note 3) . . . . 1000 mW
Operating Free-Air Temperature Range: SG1524 . . . . −55°C to 125°C
      SG2524, SG3524 . . . . 0°C to 70°C
Storage Temperature Range . . . . −65°C to 150°C

NOTES: 1. All voltage values are with respect to network ground terminal.
   2. The reference regulator may be bypassed for operation from a fixed 5-volt supply by connecting the V_{CC} and reference output
      pins both to the supply voltage. In this configuration the maximum supply voltage is 6 volts.
   3. For operation above 25°C free-air temperature, see Dissipation Derating Curves, page 124.

recommended operating conditions

	SG1524		SG2524, SG3524		UNIT
	MIN	MAX	MIN	MAX	
Supply voltage, V_{CC}	8	40	8	40	V
Reference output current	0	50	0	50	mA
Current thru C_T terminal	−0.03	−2	−0.03	−2	mA
Timing resistor, R_T	1.8	100	1.8	100	kΩ
Timing capacitor, C_T	0.001	0.1	0.001	0.1	μF
Operating free-air temperature	−55	125	0	70	°C

electrical characteristics over recommended operating free-air temperature range, V_{CC} = 20 V, f = 20 kHz (unless otherwise noted)

reference section

PARAMETER	TEST CONDITIONS†	SG1524			SG2524			SG3524			UNIT
		MIN	TYP‡	MAX	MIN	TYP‡	MAX	MIN	TYP‡	MAX	
Output voltage		4.8	5	5.2	4.8	5	5.2	4.6	5	5.4	V
Input regulation	V_{CC} = 8 to 40 V		10	20		10	20		10	30	mV
Ripple rejection	f = 120 Hz		66			66			66		dB
Output regulation	I_O = 0 to 20 mA		20	50		20	50		20	50	mV
Output voltage change with temperature	T_A = MIN to MAX		0.6	2		0.3	1		0.3	1	%
Short-circuit output current §	V_{ref} = 0		100			100			100		mA

†For conditions shown as MIN or MAX, use the appropriate value specified under recommended operating conditions.
‡All typical values except output voltage change with temperature are at T_A = 25°C.
§Duration of the short-circuit should not exceed one second.

electrical characteristics over recommended operating free-air temperature range, V_{CC} = 20 V, f = 20 kHz (unless otherwise noted)

error amplifier section

PARAMETER	TEST CONDITIONS	SG1524, SG2524			SG3524			UNIT
		MIN	TYP‡	MAX	MIN	TYP‡	MAX	
Input offset voltage	V_{IC} = 2.5 V		0.5	5		2	10	mV
Input bias current	V_{IC} = 2.5 V		2	10		2	10	μA
Open-loop voltage amplification		72	80		60	80		dB
Common-mode input voltage range	T_A = 25°C	1.8 to 3.4			1.8 to 3.4			V
Common-mode rejection ratio			70			70		dB
Unity-gain bandwidth			3			3		MHz
Output swing	T_A = 25°C	0.5		3.8	0.5		3.8	V

oscillator section

PARAMETER	TEST CONDITIONS†	MIN	TYP‡	MAX	UNIT
Frequency	C_T = 0.001 μF, R_T = 2 kΩ		450		kHz
Standard deviation of frequency §	All values of voltage, temperature, resistance, and capacitance constant		5		%
Frequency change with voltage	V_{CC} = 8 to 40 V, T_A = 25°C			1	%
Frequency change with temperature	T_A = MIN to MAX			2	%
Output amplitude at pin 3			3.5		V
Output pulse width at pin 3	C_T = 0.01 μF		0.5		μs

comparator section

PARAMETER	TEST CONDITIONS		MIN	TYP‡	MAX	UNIT
Maximum duty cycle, each output				45		%
Input threshold voltage at pin 9	Zero duty cycle			1		V
	Maximum duty cycle			3.5		
Input bias current				−1		μA

current limiting section

PARAMETER	TEST CONDITIONS	SG1524, SG2524			SG3524			UNIT
		MIN	TYP‡	MAX	MIN	TYP‡	MAX	
Input voltage range (either input)		−0.7 to +1			−0.7 to +1			V
Sense voltage for 2-V output at pin 9	$V_{(pin\,2)} - V_{(pin\,1)} \geqslant 50$ mV, T_A = 25°C	190	200	210	180	200	220	mV
Sense voltage	T_A = MIN to MAX		0.2			0.2		mV/°C

†For conditions shown as MIN or MAX, use the appropriate value specified under recommended operating conditions.

‡All typical values except for temperature coefficients are at T_A = 25°C.

§Standard deviation is a measure of the statistical distribution about the mean as derived from the formula $\sigma = \sqrt{\dfrac{\sum\limits_{n=1}^{N} (X_n - \overline{X})^2}{N-1}}$

TEXAS INSTRUMENTS
INCORPORATED

POST OFFICE BOX 5012 • DALLAS, TEXAS 75222

electrical characteristics over recommended operating free-air temperature range, V_{CC} = 20 V, f = 20 kHz
(unless otherwise noted)

output section

PARAMETER	TEST CONDITIONS		MIN	TYP‡	MAX	UNIT
Collector-emitter breakdown voltage			40			V
Collector off-state current	V_{CE} = 40 V			0.01	50	μA
Collector-emitter saturation voltage	I_C = 50 mA			1	2	V
Emitter output voltage	V_C = 20 V,	I_E = −250 μA	17	18		V
Turn-off voltage rise time	R_C = 2 kΩ			0.2		μs
Turn-on voltage fall time	R_C = 2 kΩ			0.1		μs

total device

PARAMETER	TEST CONDITIONS		MIN	TYP‡	MAX	UNIT
Standby current	V_{CC} = 40 V, Pin 2 at 2 V,	Pins 1,4,7,8,9,11,14 grounded, All other inputs and outputs open		8	10	mA

‡All typical values except for temperature coefficients are at T_A = 25°C.

PARAMETER MEASUREMENT INFORMATION

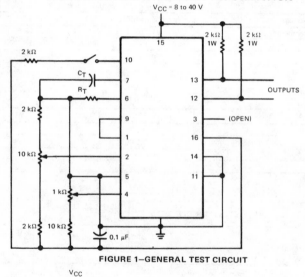

FIGURE 1—GENERAL TEST CIRCUIT

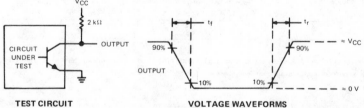

TEST CIRCUIT   VOLTAGE WAVEFORMS

FIGURE 2—SWITCHING TIMES

TEXAS INSTRUMENTS
INCORPORATED
POST OFFICE BOX 5012 • DALLAS, TEXAS 75222

TYPICAL CHARACTERISTICS

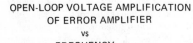

OPEN-LOOP VOLTAGE AMPLIFICATION
OF ERROR AMPLIFIER
vs
FREQUENCY

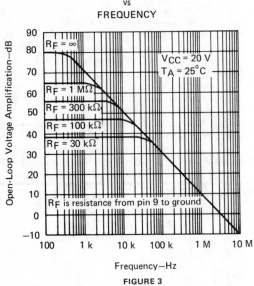

FIGURE 3

OSCILLATOR FREQUENCY
vs
TIMING RESISTANCE

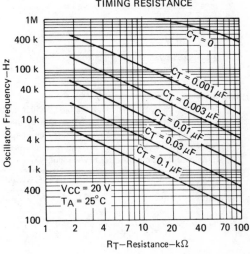

FIGURE 4

OUTPUT DEAD TIME
vs
TIMING CAPACITANCE VALUE

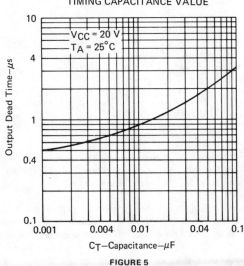

FIGURE 5

TEXAS INSTRUMENTS
INCORPORATED
POST OFFICE BOX 5012 • DALLAS, TEXAS 75222

PRINCIPLES OF OPERATION

The SG1524[†] is a fixed-frequency pulse-width-modulation voltage-regulator control circuit. The regulator operates at a fixed frequency that is programmed by one timing resistor R_T and one timing capacitor C_T. R_T establishes a constant charging current for C_T. This results in a linear voltage ramp at C_T, which is fed to the comparator providing linear control of the output pulse width by the error amplifier. The SG1524 contains an on-board 5-volt regulator that serves as a reference as well as supplying the SG1524's internal regulator control circuitry. The internal reference voltage is divided externally by a resistor ladder network to provide a reference within the common-mode range of the error amplifier as shown in Figure 6, or an external reference may be used. The output is sensed by a second resistor divider network and the error signal is amplified. This voltage is then compared to the linear voltage ramp at C_T. The resulting modulated pulse out of the high-gain comparator is then steered to the appropriate output pass transistor (Q1 or Q2) by the pulse-steering flip-flop, which is synchronously toggled by the oscillator output. The oscillator output pulse also serves as a blanking pulse to assure both outputs are never on simultaneously during the transition times. The width of the blanking pulse is controlled by the value of C_T. The outputs may be applied in a push-pull configuration in which their frequency is half that of the base oscillator, or paralleled for single-ended applications in which the frequency is equal to that of the oscillator. The output of the error amplifier shares a common input to the comparator with the current-limiting and shut-down circuitry and can be overridden by signals from either of these inputs. This common point is also available externally and may be employed to control the gain of, or to compensate, the error amplifier, or to provide additional control to the regulator.

TYPICAL APPLICATION DATA

oscillator

The oscillator controls the frequency of the SG1524 and is programmed by R_T and C_T as shown in Figure 4.

$$f \approx \frac{1.15}{R_T\,C_T}$$

where R_T is in kilohms
C_T is in microfarads
f is in kilohertz

Practical values of C_T fall between 0.001 and 0.1 microfarad. Practical values of R_T fall between 1.8 and 100 kilohms. This results in a frequency range typically from 140 hertz to 500 kilohertz.

blanking

The output pulse of the oscillator is used as a blanking pulse at the output. This pulse width is controlled by the value of C_T as shown in Figure 5. If small values of C_T are required, the oscillator output pulse width may still be maintained by applying a shunt capacitance from pin 3 to ground.

synchronous operation

When an external clock is desired, a clock pulse of approximately 3 volts can be applied directly to the oscillator output terminal. The impedance to ground at this point is approximately 2 kilohms. In this configuration R_T C_T must be selected for a clock period slightly greater than that of the external clock.

If two or more SG1524 regulators are to be operated synchronously, all oscillator output terminals should be tied together. The oscillator programmed for the minimum clock period will be the master from which all the other SG1524's operate. In this application, the C_T R_T values of the slaved regulators must be set for a period approximately 10% longer than that of the master regulator. In addition, C_T (master) = 2 C_T (slave) to ensure that the master output pulse, which occurs first, has a wider pulse width and will subsequently reset the slave regulators.

[†]Throughout these discussions, references to SG1524 apply also to SG2524 and SG3524.

TYPICAL APPLICATION DATA

voltage reference

The 5-volt internal reference may be employed by use of an external resistor divider network to establish a reference within the error amplifiers common-mode voltage range (1.8 to 3.4 volts) as shown in Figure 6, or an external reference may be applied directly to the error amplifier. For operation from a fixed 5-volt supply, the internal reference may be bypassed by applying the input voltage to both the V_{CC} and V_{REF} terminals. In this configuration, however, the input voltage is limited to a maximum of 6 volts.

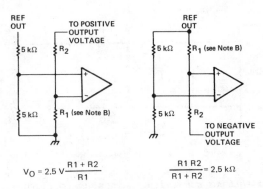

$$V_O = 2.5\ V \frac{R1 + R2}{R1} \qquad \frac{R1\ R2}{R1 + R2} = 2.5\ k\Omega$$

FIGURE 6—ERROR AMPLIFIER BIAS CIRCUITS

error amplifier

The error amplifier is a differential-input transconductance amplifier. The output is available for dc gain control or ac phase compensation. The compensation node (pin 9) is a high-impedance node (R_L = 5 megohms). The gain of the amplifier is $A_V = (0.002\ \Omega^{-1})\ R_L$ and can easily be reduced from a nominal 10,000 by an external shunt resistance from pin 9 to ground. Refer to Figure 3 for data.

compensation

Pin 9, as discussed above, is made available for compensation. Since most output filters will introduce one or more additional poles at frequencies below 200 hertz, which is the pole of the uncompensated amplifier, introduction of a zero to cancel one of the output filter poles is desirable. This can best be accomplished with a series RC circuit from pin 9 to ground in the range of 50 kilohms and 0.001 microfarads. Other frequencies can be canceled by use of the formula $f \approx 1/RC$.

shut down circuitry

Pin 9 can also be employed to introduce external control of the SG1524. Any circuit that can sink 200 microamperes can pull the compensation terminal to ground and thus disable the SG1524.

In addition to constant-current limiting, pins 4 and 5 may also be used in transformer-coupled circuits to sense primary current and shorten an output pulse should transformer saturation occur. Pin 5 may also be grounded to convert pin 4 into an additional shutdown terminal.

TEXAS INSTRUMENTS
INCORPORATED
POST OFFICE BOX 5012 • DALLAS, TEXAS 75222

119

TYPES SG1524, SG2524, SG3524
REGULATING PULSE WIDTH MODULATORS

TYPICAL APPLICATION DATA

current limiting

A current-limiting sense amplifier is provided in the SG1524. The current-limiting sense amplifier exhibits a threshold of 200 millivolts and must be applied in the ground line since the voltage range of the inputs is limited to +1 volt to −0.7 volt. Caution should be taken to ensure the −0.7-volt limit is not exceeded by either input, otherwise damage to the device may result.

Fold-back current limiting can be provided with the network shown in Figure 7. The current-limit schematic is shown in Figure 8.

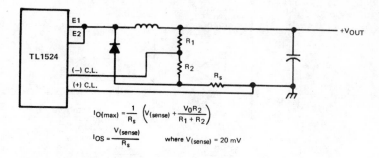

$$I_{O(max)} = \frac{1}{R_s} \left(V_{(sense)} + \frac{V_O R_2}{R_1 + R_2} \right)$$

$$I_{OS} = \frac{V_{(sense)}}{R_s} \qquad \text{where } V_{(sense)} = 20 \text{ mV}$$

FIGURE 7—FOLDBACK CURRENT LIMITING FOR SHORTED OUTPUT CONDITIONS

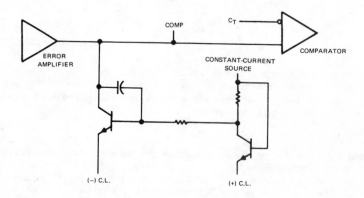

FIGURE 8—CURRENT-LIMIT SCHEMATIC

output circuitry

The SG1524 contains two identical n-p-n transistors the collectors and emitters of which are uncommitted. Each transistor has antisaturation circuitry that limits the current through that transistor to a maximum of 100 milliamperes for fast response.

477

TYPICAL APPLICATION DATA

general

There are a wide variety of output configurations possible when considering the application of the SG1524 as a voltage regulator control circuit. They can be segregated into three basic categories:

1. Capacitor-diode-coupled voltage multipliers

2. Inductor-capacitor-implemented single-ended circuits

3. Transformer-coupled circuits

Examples of these categories are shown in Figures 9, 10 and 11, respectively. Detailed diagrams of specific applications are shown in Figures 12 through 15.

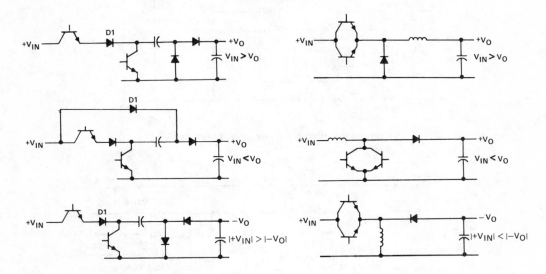

FIGURE 9—CAPACITOR-DIODE-COUPLED VOLTAGE-
MULTIPLIER OUTPUT STAGES

FIGURE 10—SINGLE-ENDED INDUCTOR CIRCUIT

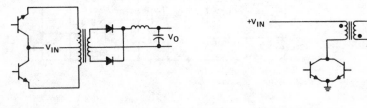

PUSH PULL

FLYBACK

FIGURE 11—TRANSFORMER-COUPLED OUTPUTS

477

TEXAS INSTRUMENTS
INCORPORATED
POST OFFICE BOX 5012 • DALLAS, TEXAS 75222

TYPICAL APPLICATION DATA

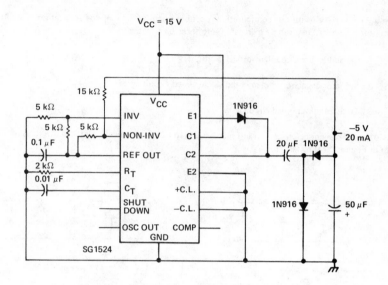

FIGURE 12—CAPACITOR-DIODE OUTPUT CIRCUIT

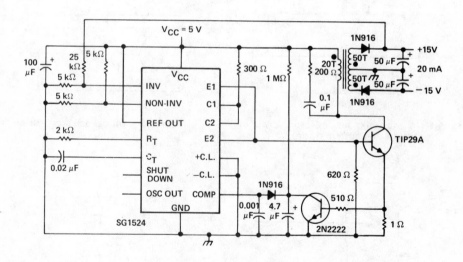

FIGURE 13 – FLYBACK CONVERTER CIRCUIT

TYPICAL APPLICATION DATA

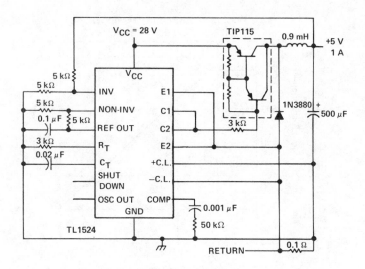

FIGURE 14—SINGLE-ENDED LC CIRCUIT

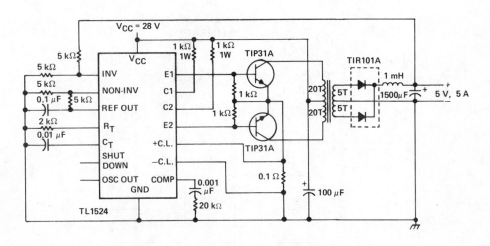

FIGURE 15—PUSH-PULL TRANSFORMER-COUPLED CIRCUIT

TEXAS INSTRUMENTS
INCORPORATED
POST OFFICE BOX 5012 • DALLAS, TEXAS 75222

477

THERMAL INFORMATION

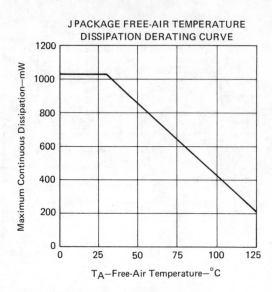

J PACKAGE FREE-AIR TEMPERATURE
DISSIPATION DERATING CURVE

FIGURE 16

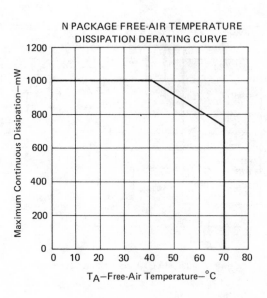

N PACKAGE FREE-AIR TEMPERATURE
DISSIPATION DERATING CURVE

FIGURE 17

- **Temperature Compensated**
- **Programmable Output Voltage**
- **Low Output Resistance**
- **Low Output Noise**
- **Sink Capability to 100 mA**

description

The TL430 is a three-terminal adjustable shunt regulator featuring excellent temperature stability, wide operating current range, and low output noise. The output voltage may be set by two external resistors to any desired value between 3 volts and 30 volts. The TL430 can replace zener diodes in many applications providing improved performance.

The TL430I is characterized for operation from $-25°C$ to $85°C$, and the TL430C is characterized for operation from $0°C$ to $70°C$.

functional block diagram

ANODE — (A) ... CATHODE (K) ... REF

JG
DUAL-IN-LINE PACKAGE
(TOP VIEW)

REF NC A NC

K NC NC NC

LP
SILECT† PACKAGE
(TOP VIEW)

CATHODE
ANODE
REF

RAK

NC—No internal connection

absolute maximum ratings over operating free-air temperature range (unless otherwise noted)

Regulator voltage (see Note 1) . . . . 30 V
Continuous regulator current . . . . 150 mA
Continuous dissipation at (or below) 25°C free-air temperature (see Note 2): JG Package . . . . 825 mW
LP package . . . . . 775 mW
Operating free-air temperature range: TL430I . . . . −40°C to 85°C
TL430C . . . . 0°C to 70°C
Storage temperature range . . . . −65°C to 150°C
Lead temperature 1/16 inch from case for 60 seconds: JG package . . . . 300°C
Lead temperature 1/16 inch from case for 10 seconds: LP package . . . . 260°C

recommended operating conditions

	MIN	MAX	UNIT
Regulator voltage, V_Z	V_{ref}	30	V
Regulator current, I_Z	2	100	mA

NOTES: 1. All voltage values are with respect to the anode terminal.
2. For operation above 25°C free-air temperature, refer to Dissipation Derating Curves, Figures 5 and 6, page 127.

† Trademark Registered U.S. Patent Office

TEXAS INSTRUMENTS
INCORPORATED
POST OFFICE BOX 5012 • DALLAS, TEXAS 75222

electrical characteristics at 25°C free-air temperature (unless otherwise noted)

PARAMETER		TEST FIGURE	TEST CONDITIONS		TL430I MIN	TL430I TYP	TL430I MAX	TL430C MIN	TL430C TYP	TL430C MAX	UNIT
V_{ref}	Reference input voltage	1	$V_Z = V_{ref}$,	$I_Z = 10$ mA	2.6	2.75	2.9	2.5	2.75	3	V
αV_{ref}	Temperature coefficient of reference input voltage	1	$V_Z = V_{ref}$, $T_A = 0°C$ to $70°C$	$I_Z = 10$ mA,		+120	+200		+120		ppm/°C
I_{ref}	Reference input current	2	$I_Z = 10$ mA, $R2 = \infty$	$R1 = 10$ kΩ,		3	10		3	10	μA
I_{ZK}	Regulator current near lower knee of regulation range	1	$V_Z = V_{ref}$			0.5	2		0.5	2	mA
I_{ZM}	Regulator current at maximum limit of regulation range	1	$V_Z = V_{ref}$		50			50			mA
		2	$V_Z = 5$ V to 30 V,	See Note 3	100			100			
r_z	Differential regulator resistance (see Note 4)	1	$V_Z = V_{ref}$, $\Delta I_Z = (52-2)$ mA			1.5	3		1.5	3	Ω
V_{nz}	Noise voltage	2	f = 0.1 Hz to 10 Hz	$V_Z = 3$ V		50			50		μV
				$V_Z = 12$ V		200			200		
				$V_Z = 30$ V		650			650		

NOTES 3. The average power dissipation, $V_Z \cdot I_Z \cdot$ duty cycle, must not exceed the maximum continuous rating in any 10-ms interval.

4. The regulator resistance for $V_Z > V_{ref}$, $r_z{}'$, is given by:

$$r_z{}' = r_z\left(1 + \frac{R1}{R2}\right)$$

PARAMETER MEASUREMENT INFORMATION

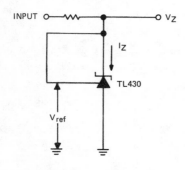

FIGURE 1—TEST CIRCUIT FOR $V_Z = V_{ref}$

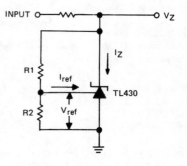

$$V_Z = V_{ref}\left(1 + \frac{R1}{R2}\right) + I_{ref} \bullet R1$$

FIGURE 2—TEST CIRCUIT FOR $V_Z > V_{ref}$

TEXAS INSTRUMENTS
INCORPORATED
POST OFFICE BOX 5012 • DALLAS, TEXAS 75222

TYPICAL CHARACTERISTICS

SMALL-SIGNAL REGULATOR IMPEDANCE
vs
FREQUENCY

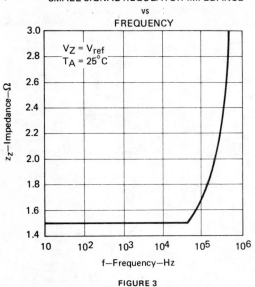

$V_Z = V_{ref}$
$T_A = 25°C$

FIGURE 3

CURRENT
vs
VOLTAGE

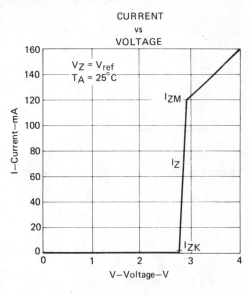

$V_Z = V_{ref}$
$T_A = 25°C$

I_{ZM}

I_Z

I_{ZK}

FIGURE 4

THERMAL INFORMATION

JG PACKAGE
DISSIPATION DERATING CURVE

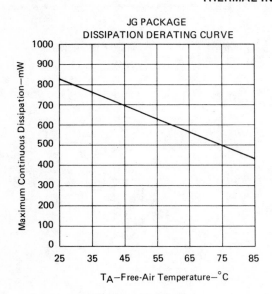

FIGURE 5

LP PACKAGE
DISSIPATION DERATING CURVE

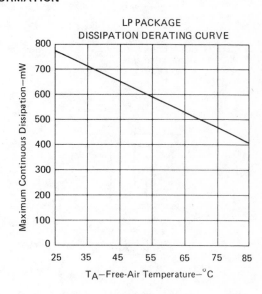

FIGURE 6

7

TYPICAL APPLICATION DATA

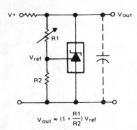

$$V_{out} \approx (1 + \frac{R1}{R2}) V_{ref}$$

FIGURE 8—SHUNT REGULATOR

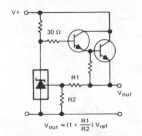

$$V_{out} \approx (1 + \frac{R1}{R2}) V_{ref}$$

FIGURE 9—SERIES REGULATOR

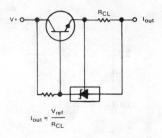

$$I_{out} = \frac{V_{ref}}{R_{CL}}$$

FIGURE 10—CURRENT LIMITER

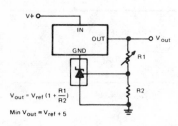

$$V_{out} = V_{ref} (1 + \frac{R1}{R2})$$

Min $V_{out} = V_{ref} + 5$

FIGURE 11—OUTPUT CONTROL OF A
THREE-THERMINAL
FIXED REGULATOR

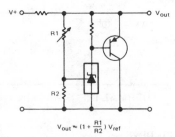

$$V_{out} \approx (1 + \frac{R1}{R2}) V_{ref}$$

FIGURE 12—HIGHER-CURRENT
APPLICATIONS

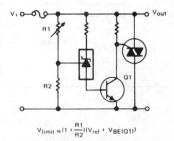

$$V_{limit} \approx (1 + \frac{R1}{R2})(V_{ref} + V_{BE(Q1)})$$

FIGURE 13—CROW BAR

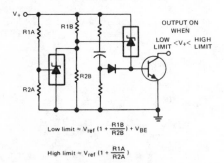

OUTPUT ON
WHEN

LOW LIMIT $< V_+ <$ HIGH LIMIT

$$\text{Low limit} \approx V_{ref} (1 + \frac{R1B}{R2B}) + V_{BE}$$

$$\text{High limit} \approx V_{ref} (1 + \frac{R1A}{R2A})$$

FIGURE 14—OVER-VOLTAGE/UNDER-VOLTAGE
PROTECTION CIRCUIT

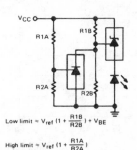

$$\text{Low limit} \approx V_{ref} (1 + \frac{R1B}{R2B}) + V_{BE}$$

$$\text{High limit} \approx V_{ref} (1 + \frac{R1A}{R2A})$$

FIGURE 15—V_{CC} MONITOR

TEXAS INSTRUMENTS
INCORPORATED
POST OFFICE BOX 5012 • DALLAS, TEXAS 75222

FUTURE PRODUCT TO BE ANNOUNCED

TYPES TL431M, TL431I, TL431C
ADJUSTABLE PRECISION SHUNT REGULATORS

SEPTEMBER 1977

- Temperature-Compensated for Operation Over the Full Rated Operating Temperature Range
- Programmable Output Voltage
- Low Output Resistance
- Low Output Noise
- Sink Current Capability to 100 mA

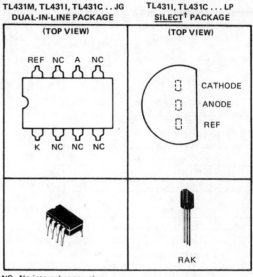

TL431M, TL431I, TL431C . . JG
DUAL-IN-LINE PACKAGE
(TOP VIEW)

TL431I, TL431C . . . LP
SILECT† PACKAGE
(TOP VIEW)

RAK

NC—No internal connection

description

The TL431 is a three-terminal adjustable regulator with guaranteed thermal stability over applicable temperature ranges. The output voltage may be set to any value between 3 V and 30 V by two resistors. Active output circuitry provides a very sharp turn-on characteristic even at low voltages, making these devices excellent replacements for zener diodes in many applications.

The TL431M is characterized for operation from -55°C to 125°C, the TL431I from -40°C to 85°C, and the TL431C from 0°C to 70°C.

functional block diagram

ANODE
(A)

REF

CATHODE
(K)

absolute maximum ratings over operating free-air temperature range (unless otherwise noted)

Regulator voltage (see Note 1) . . . . 40 V
Continuous regulator current . . . . 100 mA
Continuous dissipation at (or below) 25°C free-air temperature (see Note 2): JG package . . . . 825 mW
  LP package . . . . 775 mW
Operating free-air temperature range: TL431C . . . . 0°C to 70°C
  TL431I . . . . -40°C to 85°C
  TL431M . . . . -55°C to 125°C
Storage temperature range . . . . -65°C to 150°C
Lead temperature 1/16-inch from case for 60 seconds: JG package . . . . 300°C
Lead temperature 1/16-inch from case for 10 seconds: LP package . . . . 260°C

recommended operating conditions

	MIN	MAX	UNIT
Regulator voltage, V_Z	V_{ref}	35	V
Regulator current, I_Z	2	100	mA

NOTES: 1. All voltage values are with respect to the anode terminal.
  2. For operation above 25°C free-air temperature, refer to Dissipation Derating Curves, Figure 6 and Figure 7, page 131.

†Trademark Registered U.S. Patent Office

TEXAS INSTRUMENTS
INCORPORATED
POST OFFICE BOX 5012 • DALLAS, TEXAS 75222

TYPES TL431M, TL431I, TL431C
ADJUSTABLE PRECISION SHUNT REGULATORS

electrical characteristics at 25°C free-air temperature (unless otherwise noted)

PARAMETER		TEST FIGURE	TEST CONDITIONS		TL431M, TL431I			TL431C			UNIT
					MIN	TYP	MAX	MIN	TYP	MAX	
V_{ref}	Reference input voltage	1	$V_Z = V_{ref}$,	$I_Z = 10$ mA	2.6	2.75	2.9	2.7	2.75	2.8	V
αV_{ref}	Temperature coefficient of reference input voltage	1	$V_Z = V_{ref}$, $T_A =$ full range†	$I_Z = 10$ mA,		+30	+100		+10	+50	ppm/°C
I_{ref}	Reference input current	2	$I_Z = 10$ mA, $R2 = \infty$	$R1 = 10$ kΩ, $T_A =$ full range†		10	50		3	10	µA
I_{ZK}	Regulator current near lower knee of regulation range	1	$V_Z = V_{ref}$			0.5	2		0.5	2	mA
I_{ZM}	Regulator current at maximum limit of regulator range	1	$V_Z = V_{ref}$,	See Note 3	100			100			mA
r_z	Differential regulator resistance (see Note 4)	1	$V_Z = V_{ref}$, $\Delta I_Z = 52$ mA to 2 mA			1.5	3		1.5	3	Ω
$\dfrac{V_{nz}}{V_Z}$	Ratio of noise voltage to operating voltage		$V_Z = 3$ to 30 V, $f = 0.1$ Hz to 10 Hz	$I_Z = 10$ mA,		−95			−95		dB
t_{on}		3				100			100		µs
t_{off}		3				100			100		

†Full range is −55°C to 125°C for the TL431M, −40°C to 85°C for the TL431I, and 0°C to 70°C for the TL431C.

NOTES: 3. The average power dissipation, $V_Z \cdot I_Z \cdot$ duty cycle, must not exceed the maximum continuous rating for any 10-ms interval.

4. The regulator resistance for $V_Z > V_{ref}$, r_z', is given by:

$$r_z' = r_z \left(1 + \frac{R1}{R2}\right)$$

PARAMETER MEASUREMENT INFORMATION

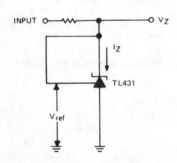

FIGURE 1—TEST CIRCUIT FOR $V_Z = V_{ref}$

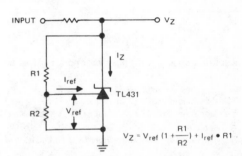

$$V_Z = V_{ref} \left(1 + \frac{R1}{R2}\right) + I_{ref} \bullet R1$$

FIGURE 2—TEST CIRCUIT FOR $V_Z > V_{ref}$

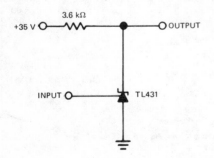

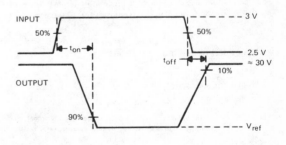

FIGURE 3—TEST CIRCUIT FOR t_{on} AND t_{off}

TEXAS INSTRUMENTS
INCORPORATED
POST OFFICE BOX 5012 • DALLAS, TEXAS 75222

TYPICAL CHARACTERISTICS

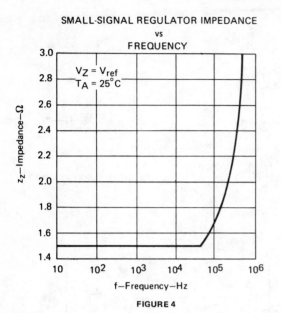

SMALL-SIGNAL REGULATOR IMPEDANCE
vs
FREQUENCY

$V_Z = V_{ref}$
$T_A = 25°C$

z_z—Impedance—Ω

f—Frequency—Hz

FIGURE 4

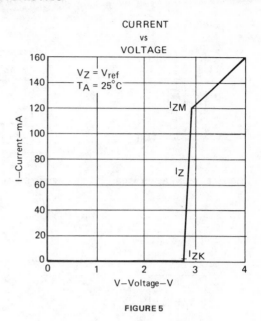

CURRENT
vs
VOLTAGE

$V_Z = V_{ref}$
$T_A = 25°C$

I_{ZM}

I_Z

I_{ZK}

I—Current—mA

V—Voltage—V

FIGURE 5

THERMAL INFORMATION

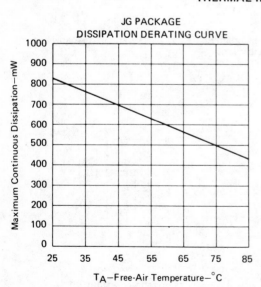

JG PACKAGE
DISSIPATION DERATING CURVE

Maximum Continuous Dissipation—mW

T_A—Free-Air Temperature—°C

FIGURE 6

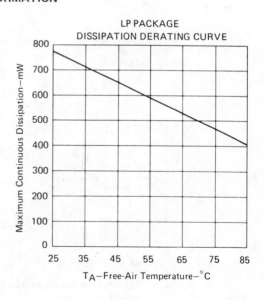

LP PACKAGE
DISSIPATION DERATING CURVE

Maximum Continuous Dissipation—mW

T_A—Free-Air Temperature—°C

FIGURE 7

TEXAS INSTRUMENTS
INCORPORATED
POST OFFICE BOX 5012 • DALLAS, TEXAS 75222

TYPICAL APPLICATION DATA

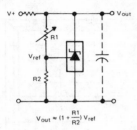

$$V_{out} \approx \left(1 + \frac{R1}{R2}\right) V_{ref}$$

FIGURE 8—SHUNT REGULATOR

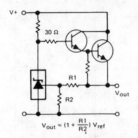

$$V_{out} \approx \left(1 + \frac{R1}{R2}\right) V_{ref}$$

FIGURE 9—SERIES REGULATOR

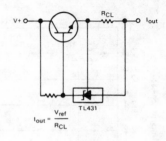

$$I_{out} = \frac{V_{ref}}{R_{CL}}$$

FIGURE 10—CURRENT LIMITER

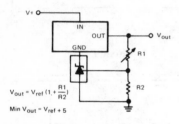

$$V_{out} = V_{ref}\left(1 + \frac{R1}{R2}\right)$$

$$\text{Min } V_{out} = V_{ref} + 5$$

FIGURE 11—OUTPUT CONTROL OF A THREE-THERMINAL FIXED REGULATOR

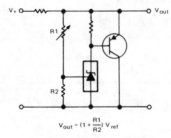

$$V_{out} = \left(1 + \frac{R1}{R2}\right) V_{ref}$$

FIGURE 12—HIGHER-CURRENT APPLICATIONS

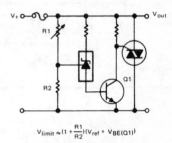

$$V_{limit} \approx \left(1 + \frac{R1}{R2}\right)(V_{ref} + V_{BE(Q1)})$$

FIGURE 13—CROW BAR

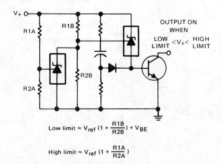

OUTPUT ON WHEN

$$\text{LOW LIMIT} < V_+ < \text{HIGH LIMIT}$$

$$\text{Low limit} \approx V_{ref}\left(1 + \frac{R1B}{R2B}\right) + V_{BE}$$

$$\text{High limit} \approx V_{ref}\left(1 + \frac{R1A}{R2A}\right)$$

FIGURE 14—OVER-VOLTAGE/UNDER-VOLTAGE PROTECTION CIRCUIT

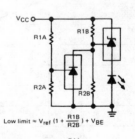

$$\text{Low limit} \approx V_{ref}\left(1 + \frac{R1B}{R2B}\right) + V_{BE}$$

$$\text{High limit} \approx V_{ref}\left(1 + \frac{R1A}{R2A}\right)$$

FIGURE 15—V_{CC} MONITOR

TEXAS INSTRUMENTS
INCORPORATED
POST OFFICE BOX 5012 • DALLAS, TEXAS 75222

- Temperature-Compensated 2.75-V Reference
- Uncommitted Output Transistor
- 100-mA Drive Capability
- High Comparator Input Impedance
- Wide Operating Voltage Range

description

The TL432 is a versatile group of building blocks developed for a broad range of comparator functions. It contains a high-gain comparator, a temperature-compensated 2.75-volt reference, and a booster transistor capable of sinking or sourcing 100 milliamperes. The uncommitted inputs and outputs of the comparator and booster transistor provide design flexibility to include series regulators, shunt regulators, detectors, timers, and current regulators. This monolithic integrated circuit can be used over a wide range of operating voltage.

TL432M . . . . . J
TL432I, TL432C . . . J OR N
DUAL-IN-LINE PACKAGE (TOP VIEW)

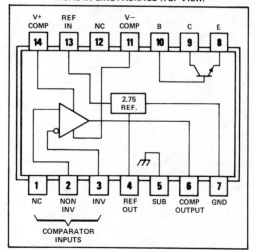

The TL432M will be characterized for operation over the full military temperature range of −55°C to 125°C. The TL432I will be characterized for operation from −40°C to 85°C, and the TL432C from 0°C to 70°C.

typical applications

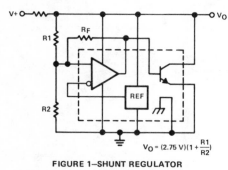

$$V_O = (2.75\text{ V})(1 + \frac{R1}{R2})$$

FIGURE 1—SHUNT REGULATOR

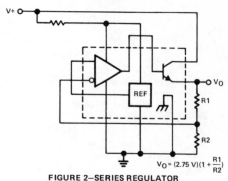

$$V_O = (2.75\text{ V})(1 + \frac{R1}{R2})$$

FIGURE 2—SERIES REGULATOR

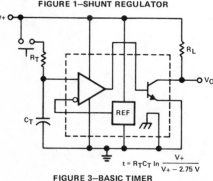

$$t = R_T C_T \ln \frac{V+}{V+ - 2.75\text{ V}}$$

FIGURE 3—BASIC TIMER

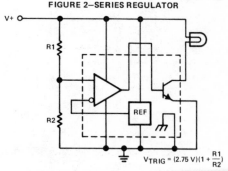

$$V_{TRIG} = (2.75\text{ V})(1 + \frac{R1}{R2})$$

FIGURE 4—OVER-VOLTAGE DETECTOR

DESIGN GOAL

This document provides tentative information on a product in the developmental stage. Texas Instruments reserves the right to change or discontinue this product without notice.

TEXAS INSTRUMENTS
INCORPORATED
POST OFFICE BOX 5012 • DALLAS, TEXAS 75222

133

- **Complete PWM Power Control Circuitry**
- **Uncommitted Outputs for Single-Ended or Push-Pull Operation**
- **Internal Circuitry Prohibits Double Pulse at Either Output**
- **Variable Dead-Time Control . . . 45% to 0% at Each Output**
- **Oscillator Capable of Stand-Alone or Driven Operation**

TL494M . . . J
TL494I, TL494C . . . J OR N
DUAL-IN-LINE PACKAGE
(TOP VIEW)

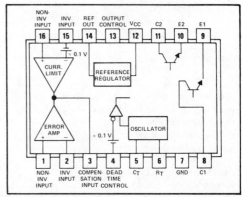

description

The TL494 incorporates on a monolithic chip all the functions required for pulse-width-modulation control circuits. Designed primarily for power supply control, the TL494 has an on-chip 5-volt regulator, error amplifier, current-limit amplifier, adjustable oscillator, dead time control comparator, pulse-steering flip-flop, and output control circuitry. The uncommitted output transistors may be operated common-collector or common-emitter. Internal circuitry provides output control for either complementary or tandem operation. The trigger for the pulse-steering flip-flop is derived from the pulse-width-modulation circuit to prevent double-pulsing of either output. Both the error amplifier and the current-limit amplifier have a common-mode input voltage range from -0.2 volt to $V_{CC} - 1.5$ volts. Fixed internal offsets provide a current-limit sense threshold of 0.1 volt for the current-limit amplifier and a 45% maximum duty cycle for the dead time control comparator. The oscillator can be programmed by passive components or driven by a master oscillator. The versatility of the TL494 makes it suitable for a variety of PWM applications including switching regulators (of either polarity) and dc-to-dc converters (with or without transformer-coupled outputs).

The TL494M will be characterized for operation over the full military temperature range of -55°C to 125°C. The TL494I will be characterized for operation from -25°C to 85°C, and the TL494C will be characterized for operation from 0°C to 70°C.

functional block diagram

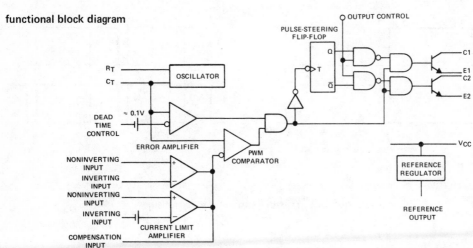

DESIGN GOAL

This document provides tentative information on a product in the developmental stage. Texas Instruments reserves the right to change or discontinue this product without notice.

TEXAS INSTRUMENTS
INCORPORATED
POST OFFICE BOX 5012 • DALLAS, TEXAS 75222

TYPES TL494M, TL494I, TL494C
PULSE-WIDTH-MODULATION CONTROL CIRCUIT

recommended operating conditions

	MIN	MAX	UNIT
Supply voltage, V_{CC}	7	40	V
Collector output voltage		40	V
Collector output current (each transistor)		200	mA

electrical characteristics

	MIN	TYP	MAX	UNIT
Amplifier common-mode input voltage range	−0.2 to V_{CC} − 2			V
Input bias current (each amplifier)			500	nA
Current-limit sense threshold		0.1		V
Collector-emitter saturation voltage (at I_C = 200 mA)		1.2		V
Range of adjustment of maximum duty cycle (each output)	0 to 45			%
Frequency range	0.001 to 200			kHz
Standard deviation of frequency		2		%
Reference output voltage	4.75		5.25	V

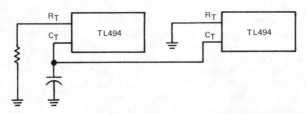

FIGURE 1—MASTER-SLAVE OSCILLATOR CONNECTION

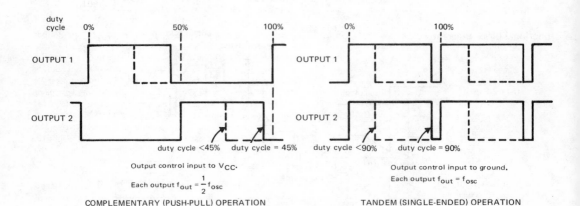

COMPLEMENTARY (PUSH-PULL) OPERATION

TANDEM (SINGLE-ENDED) OPERATION

FIGURE 2—OUTPUT DUTY CYCLE AND PHASE RELATIONSHIPS

LINEAR INTEGRATED CIRCUITS

TYPES TL497AM, TL497AI, TL497AC
SWITCHING VOLTAGE REGULATORS

BULLETIN NO. DL-S 12422, JUNE 1976–REVISED SEPTEMBER 1977

- **All Monolithic**
- **High Efficiency . . . 60% or Greater**
- **Output Current . . . 500 mA**
- **Input Current Limit Protection**
- **TTL Compatible Inhibit**
- **Adjustable Output Voltage**
- **Input Regulation . . . 0.2% Typ**
- **Output Regulation . . . 0.4% Typ**
- **Soft Start-up Capability**

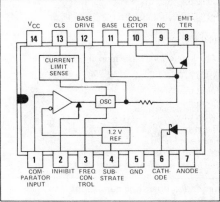

TL497AM . . . . J
TL497AI, TL497AC . . . . J OR N
DUAL-IN-LINE PACKAGE (TOP VIEW)

NC—No internal connection

description

The TL497A incorporates on a single monolithic chip all the active functions required in the construction of a switching voltage regulator. It can also be used as the control element to drive external components for high-power-output applications. The TL497A was designed for ease of use in step-up, step-down, or voltage inversion applications requiring high efficiency.

A block diagram of the TL497A is shown in the above pinout. The TL497A is a fixed-on-time variable-frequency switching voltage regulator control circuit. The on time is programmed by a single external capacitor connected between the frequency control pin and ground. This capacitor, C_T, is charged by an internal constant-current generator to a predetermined threshold. The charging current and the threshold vary proportionally with V_{CC}, thus the on time remains constant over the specified range of input voltage (5 to 12 volts). Typical on times for various values of C_T are as follows.

TIMING CAPACITOR, C_T (pF)	100	150	200	250	350	400	500	750	1000	1500	2000
ON-TIME (μs)	11	15	19	22	26	32	44	56	80	120	180

The output voltage is programmed by an external resistor ladder network (R1 and R2 in Figures 1, 2, and 3) that attenuates the desired output voltage to 1.2 volts. This feedback voltage is compared to the 1.2-volt reference by the high-gain comparator. When the output voltage decays below the programmed voltage, the comparator enables the oscillator circuit, which charges and discharges C_T as described above. The internal pass transistor is driven on during the charging of C_T. The internal transistor may be used directly for switching currents up to 500 milliampers. Its collector and emitter are uncommitted and it is current driven to allow operation from the positive supply voltage or ground. An internal Schottky diode matched to the current characteristics of the internal transistor is also available for blocking or commutating purposes. The TL479A also has on-chip current-limit circuitry that senses the peak currents in the switching regulator and protects the inductor against saturation and the pass transistor against overstress. The current limit is adjustable and is programmed by a single sense resistor, R_{CL}, connected between pin 14 and pin 13. The current-limit circuitry is activated when 0.7 volt is developed across R_{CL}. External gating is provided by the inhibit input. When the inhibit input is high, the output is turned off.

Simplicity of design is a primary feature of the TL497A. With only six external components (three resistors, two capacitors, and one inductor), the TL497A will operate in numerous voltage conversion applications (step-up, step-down, invert) with as much as 85% of the source power delivered to the load. The TL497A replaces the TL497 in all applications.

The TL497AM is characterized for operation over the full military temperature range of -55°C to 125°C, the TL497AI is characterized for operation from -25°C to 85°C, and the TL497AC from 0°C to 70°C.

TEXAS INSTRUMENTS
INCORPORATED
POST OFFICE BOX 5012 • DALLAS, TEXAS 75222

TYPES TL497AM, TL497AI, TL497AC
SWITCHING VOLTAGE REGULATORS

absolute maximum ratings over operating free-air temperature range (unless otherwise noted)

Input voltage, V_{CC} (see Note 1)	15 V
Output voltage	35 V
Comparator input voltage	5 V
Inhibit input voltage	5 V
Diode reverse voltage	35 V
Power switch current	750 mA
Diode forward current	750 mA
Continuous total dissipation at (or below) 25°C free-air temperature (see Note 2)	1000 mW
Operating free-air temperature range: TL497AM	−55°C to 125°C
TL497AI	−25°C to 85°C
TL497AC	0°C to 70°C
Storage temperature range	−65°C to 150°C
Lead temperature 1/16 inch from case for 60 seconds: J package	300°C
Lead temperature 1/16 inch from case for 10 seconds: N package	260°C

NOTES: 1. All voltage values except diode voltages are with respect to network ground terminal.
2. For operation above 25°C free-air temperature, refer to Dissipation Derating Curves, Figure I and Figure III, page 90.

recommended operating conditions

	MIN	MAX	UNIT
Input voltage, V_I	4.5	12	V
Output voltage: step-up configuration (see Figure 2)	V_I + 2	30	V
step-down configuration (see Figure 3)	V_{ref}	V_I − 1	V
negative regulator (see Figure 4)	$-V_{ref}$	−25	V
Power switch current		500	mA
Diode forward current		500	mA

electrical characteristics at specified free-air temperature, V_I = 6 V (unless otherwise noted)

PARAMETER	TEST CONDITIONS[†]		TL497AM, TL497AI			TL497AC			UNIT
			MIN	TYP[‡]	MAX	MIN	TYP[‡]	MAX	
High-level inhibit input voltage		25°C	3			2.5			V
Low-level inhibit input voltage		25°C			0.6			0.8	V
High-level inhibit input current	$V_{I(I)}$ = 5 V	Full range		0.8	1.5		0.8	1.5	mA
Low-level inhibit input current	$V_{I(I)}$ = 0 V	Full range		5	20		5	10	µA
Comparator reference voltage	V_I = 4.5 V to 6 V	Full range	1.14	1.20	1.26	1.08	1.20	1.32	V
Comparator input bias current	V_I = 6 V	Full range		40	100		40	100	µA
Switch on-state voltage	V_I = 4.5 V	I_O = 100 mA, 25°C		0.13	0.2		0.13	0.2	V
		I_O = 500 mA, Full range			1			0.85	
Switch off-state current	V_I = 4.5 V, V_O = 30 V	25°C		10	50		10	50	µA
		Full range			500			200	
Current-limit sense voltage	V_{CC} = 6 V	25°C	0.45		1	0.45		1	V
Diode forward voltage	I_O = 10 mA	Full range		0.75	0.95		0.75	0.85	V
	I_O = 100 mA	Full range		0.9	1.1		0.9	1	
	I_O = 500 mA	Full range		1.33	1.75		1.33	1.55	
Diode reverse voltage	I_O = 500 µA	Full range	30						V
	I_O = 200 µA	Full range				30			
On-state supply current		25°C		11	14		11	14	mA
		Full range			16			15	
Off-state supply current		25°C		6	9		6	9	mA
		Full range			11			10	

[†]Full range for TL497AM is −55°C to 125°C, for TL497AI is −25°C to 85°C, and for TL497AC is 0°C to 70°C.
[‡] All typical values are at T_A = 25°C.

TEXAS INSTRUMENTS
INCORPORATED
POST OFFICE BOX 5012 • DALLAS, TEXAS 75222

TYPICAL APPLICATION DATA

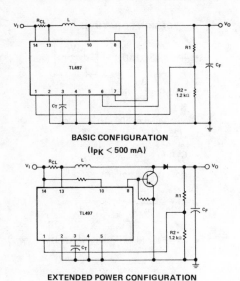

BASIC CONFIGURATION
($I_{PK} <$ 500 mA)

EXTENDED POWER CONFIGURATION
(USING EXTERNAL TRANSISTOR)

DESIGN EQUATIONS

- $I_{PK} = 2\, I_{LOAD}$ max $\left[\dfrac{V_I - V_O}{V_I} + 1 \right]$

- $L\,(\mu H) = \dfrac{V_I}{I_{PK}}\, t_{on}(\mu s)$

Choose L (50 to 500 μH), calculate
t_{on} (25 to 150 μs)

- $C_T(pF) \approx 12\, t_{on}(\mu s)$

- $R1 = (V_O - 1.2)\,k\Omega$

- $R_{CL} = \dfrac{0.5\,V}{I_{PK}}$

- $C_F(\mu F) \approx t_{on} \dfrac{\left[\dfrac{V_I}{V_O}\, I_{PK} + I_{LOAD} \right]}{V_{RIPPLE\,(PK)}}$

FIGURE 1—POSITIVE REGULATOR, STEP-UP CONFIGURATIONS

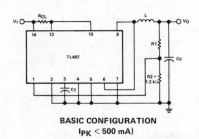

BASIC CONFIGURATION
$I_{PK} <$ 500 mA

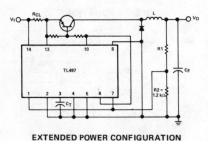

EXTENDED POWER CONFIGURATION
(USING EXTERNAL TRANSISTOR)

DESIGN EQUATIONS

- $I_{PK} = 2\, I_{LOAD}$ max

- $L\,(\mu H) = \dfrac{V_I - V_O}{I_{PK}}\, t_{on}(\mu s)$

Choose L (50 to 500 μH), calculate
t_{on} (10 to 150 μs)

- $C_T(pF) \approx 12\, t_{on}(\mu s)$

- $R1 = (V_O - 1.2)\,k\Omega$

- $R_{CL} = \dfrac{0.5\,V}{I_{PK}}$

- $C_F(\mu F) \approx t_{on} \dfrac{\left[\dfrac{V_I - V_O}{V_O}\, I_{PK} + I_{LOAD} \right]}{V_{RIPPLE(PK)}}$

FIGURE 2—POSITIVE REGULATOR, STEP-DOWN CONFIGURATIONS

TYPICAL APPLICATION DATA

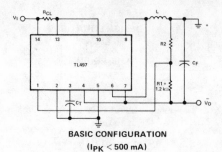

BASIC CONFIGURATION

(I$_{PK}$ < 500 mA)

EXTENDED POWER CONFIGURATION

(USING EXTERNAL TRANSISTOR)

FIGURE 3—INVERTING APPLICATIONS

DESIGN EQUATIONS

- $I_{PK} = 2\,I_{LOAD}\ max\left[1 + \dfrac{|V_O|}{V_I}\right]$

- $L\,(\mu H) = \dfrac{V_I}{I_{PK}}\,t_{on}(\mu s)$

Choose L (50 to 500 μH), calculate t_{on} (25 to 150 μs)

- $C_T(pF) \approx 12\,t_{on}(\mu s)$

- $R2 = (V_O - 1.2)\ k\Omega$

- $R_{CL} = \dfrac{0.5\ V}{I_{PK}}$

- $C_F(\mu F) \approx t_{on}\dfrac{\left[\dfrac{V_I}{|V_O|}\,I_{PK} + I_{LOAD}\right]}{V_{RIPPLE(PK)}}$

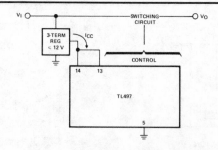

EXTENDED INPUT CONFIGURATION WITHOUT CURRENT LIMIT

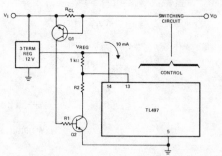

CURRENT LIMIT FOR EXTENDED INPUT CONFIGURATION

FIGURE 4—EXTENDED INPUT VOLTAGE RANGE (V$_I$ > 15 V)

DESIGN EQUATIONS

$$R_{CL} = \frac{V_{BE(Q1)}}{I_{LIMIT(PK)}}$$

$$R1 = \frac{V_I}{I_{B(Q2)}}$$

$$R2 = (V_{REG} - 1)\ 10\ k\Omega$$

TEXAS INSTRUMENTS
INCORPORATED
POST OFFICE BOX 5012 • DALLAS, TEXAS 75222

- 3-Terminal Regulator
- Output Current up to 1.5 A
- No External Components
- Internal Thermal Overload Protection
- Improved Replacement for uA7805 and LM340-05 5-Percent Regulators
- High Power Dissipation Capability
- Internal Short-Circuit Current Limiting
- Output Transistor Safe-Area Compensation

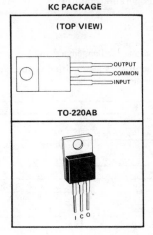

KC PACKAGE

(TOP VIEW)

OUTPUT
COMMON
INPUT

TO-220AB

I C O

description

The TL7805AC 3-percent 5-volt regulator offers improved accuracy over the uA7805 and LM340-05 regulators. This monolithic integrated circuit boasts an overall accuracy of better than 3-percent deviation over full line, load, and temperature variations and can deliver up to 1.5 amperes of output current. The internal current limiting and thermal shutdown features make it essentially immune to overload. In addition to use as a fixed-voltage regulator, the TL7805AC can be used with external components to obtain adjustable output voltages and currents and also can be used as the power pass element in precision regulators.

schematic

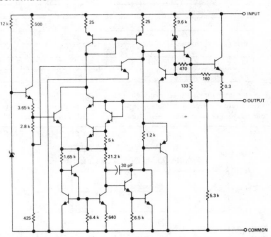

Resistor values shown are nominal and in ohms.

absolute maximum ratings over operating temperature range (unless otherwise noted)

Input voltage . . . . 35 V
Continuous total dissipation at 25°C free-air temperature (see Note 1) . . . . 2 W
Continuous total dissipation at (or below) 25° case temperature (see Note 1) . . . . 15 W
Operating free-air, case, or virtual junction temperature range . . . . 0°C to 150°C
Storage temperature range . . . . −65°C to 150°C
Lead temperature 1/16 inch from case for 10 seconds . . . . 260°C

NOTE 1: For operation above 25°C free-air or case temperature, refer to Dissipation Derating Curves, Figure 1 and Figure 2, next page.

TEXAS INSTRUMENTS
INCORPORATED
POST OFFICE BOX 5012 • DALLAS, TEXAS 75222

141

TYPE TL7805AC
3-PERCENT 5-VOLT REGULATOR

recommended operating conditions

	MIN	MAX	UNIT
Input voltage, V_I	7	25	V
Output current, I_O		1.5	A
Operating virtual junction temperature, T_J	0	125	°C

electrical characteristics at specified virtual junction temperature, V_I = 10 V, I_O = 500 mA (unless otherwise noted)

PARAMETER	TEST CONDITIONS†			MIN	TYP	MAX	UNIT
Output voltage	I_O = 5 mA to 1A,	V_I = 7 V to 20 V,	25°C	4.9	5	5.1	V
	P ≤ 15 W		0°C to 125°C	4.85		5.15	
Input regulation	V_I = 7 V to 25 V		25°C		3	50	mV
	V_I = 8 V to 12 V				1	25	
Ripple rejection	V_I = 8 V to 18 V,	f = 120 Hz	0°C to 125°C	62	78		dB
Output regulation	I_O = 5 mA to 1.5 A		25°C		15	100	mV
	I_O = 250 mA to 750 mA				5	50	
Output resistance	f = 1 kHz		0°C to 125°C		0.017		Ω
Temperature coefficient of output voltage	I_O = 5 mA		0°C to 125°C		−1.1		mV/°C
Output noise voltage	f = 10 Hz to 100 kHz		25°C		40		µV
Dropout voltage	I_O = 1 A		25°C		2.0		V
Bias current			25°C		4.2	8	mA
Bias current change	V_I = 7 V to 25 V		0°C to 125°C			1.3	mA
	I_O = 5 mA to 1 A					0.5	
Short-circuit output current			25°C		750		mA
Peak output current			25°C		2.2		A

†All characteristics are measured with a capacitor across the input of 0.33 µF and a capacitor across the output of 0.1 µF. All characteristics except noise voltage and ripple rejection ratio are measured using pulse techniques (t_W ≤ 10 ms, duty cycles ≤ 5%). Output voltage changes due to changes in internal temperature must be taken into account separately.

THERMAL INFORMATION

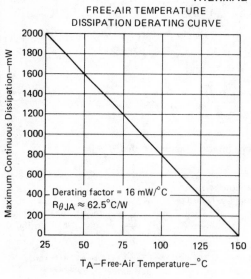

FREE-AIR TEMPERATURE
DISSIPATION DERATING CURVE

Derating factor = 16 mW/°C
$R_{\theta JA}$ ≈ 62.5°C/W

T_A—Free-Air Temperature—°C

FIGURE 1

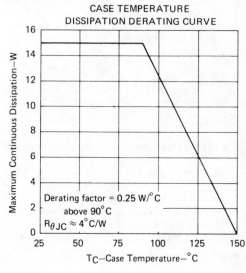

CASE TEMPERATURE
DISSIPATION DERATING CURVE

Derating factor = 0.25 W/°C above 90°C
$R_{\theta JC}$ ≈ 4°C/W

T_C—Case Temperature—°C

FIGURE 2

TEXAS INSTRUMENTS
INCORPORATED
POST OFFICE BOX 5012 • DALLAS, TEXAS 75222

FORMERLY SN52723, SN72723

- **150-mA Load Current without External Power Transistor**
- **Typically 0.02% Input Regulation and 0.03% Load Regulation (uA723M)**
- **Adjustable Current Limiting Capability**
- **Input Voltages to 40 Volts**
- **Output Adjustable from 2 to 37 Volts**
- **Designed to be Interchangeable with Fairchild μA723 and μA723C Respectively**

description

The uA723M and uA723C are monolithic integrated circuit voltage regulators featuring high ripple rejection, excellent input and load regulation, excellent temperature stability, and low standby current. The circuit consists of a temperature-compensated reference voltage amplifier, an error amplifier, a 150-milliampere output transistor, and an adjustable output current limiter.

The uA723M and uA723C are designed for use in positive or negative power supplies as a series, shunt, switching, or floating regulator. For output currents exceeding 150 mA, additional pass elements may be connected as shown in Figures 4 and 5.

The uA723M is characterized for operation over the full military temperature range of -55°C to 125°C; the uA723C is characterized for operation from 0°C to 70°C.

terminal assignments

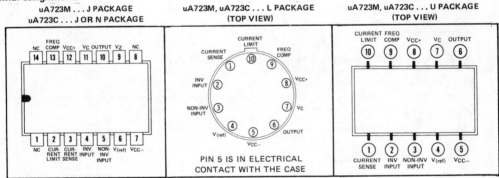

uA723M . . . J PACKAGE
uA723C . . . J OR N PACKAGE

uA723M, uA723C . . . L PACKAGE (TOP VIEW)

PIN 5 IS IN ELECTRICAL CONTACT WITH THE CASE

uA723M, uA723C . . . U PACKAGE (TOP VIEW)

NC—No internal connection

functional block diagram

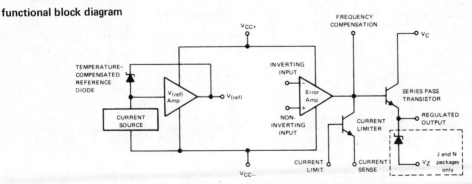

TEXAS INSTRUMENTS
INCORPORATED
POST OFFICE BOX 5012 • DALLAS, TEXAS 75222

TYPES uA723M, uA723C
PRECISION VOLTAGE REGULATORS

absolute maximum ratings over operating free-air temperature range (unless otherwise noted)

Peak voltage from V_{CC+} to V_{CC-} ($t_w \leqslant 50$ ms) . . . . 50 V
Continuous voltage from V_{CC+} to V_{CC-} . . . . 40 V
Input-to-output voltage differential . . . . 40 V
Differential input voltage to error amplifier . . . . ±5 V
Voltage between noninverting input and V_{CC-} . . . . 8 V
Current from V_Z . . . . 25 mA
Current from $V_{(ref)}$ . . . . 15 mA
Continuous total dissipation at (or below) 25°C free-air temperature (see Note 1):
    J or N package . . . . 1000 mW
    L package (see Note 2) . . . . 800 mW
    U package . . . . 675 mW
Operating free-air temperature range: uA723M Circuits . . . . −55°C to 125°C
                      uA723C Circuits . . . . 0°C to 70°C
Storage temperature range . . . . −65°C to 150°C
Lead temperature 1/16 inch from case for 60 seconds, J, L, or U package . . . . . . 300°C
Lead temperature 1/16 inch from case for 10 seconds, N package . . . . 260°C

NOTES: 1. Power dissipation = $[I_{(standby)} + I_{(ref)}]\, V_{CC} + [V_C - V_O]\, I_O$. For operation at elevated temperature, refer to Dissipation Derating Table.
      2. This rating for the L package requires a heat sink that provides a thermal resistance from case to free-air, $R_{\theta CA}$, of not more than 105°C/W.

recommended operating conditions

	MIN	MAX	UNIT
Input voltage, V_I	9.5	40	V
Output voltage, V_O	2	37	V
Input-to-output voltage differential, $V_C - V_O$	3	38	V
Output current, I_O		150	mA

electrical characteristics at specified free-air temperature (see note 3)

PARAMETER	TEST CONDITIONS†		uA723M			uA723C			UNIT
			MIN	TYP	MAX	MIN	TYP	MAX	
Input regulation	V_I = 12 V to V_I = 15 V	25°C		0.01%	0.1%		0.01%	0.1%	
	V_I = 12 V to V_I = 40 V	25°C		0.02%	0.2%		0.1%	0.5%	
	V_I = 12 V to V_I = 15 V	Full range			0.3%			0.3%	
Ripple rejection	f = 50 Hz to 10 kHz, $C_{(ref)}$ = 0	25°C		74			74		dB
	f = 50 Hz to 10 kHz, $C_{(ref)}$ = 5 μF	25°C		86			86		
Output regulation	I_O = 1 mA to I_O = 50 mA	25°C		−0.03%	−0.15%		−0.03%	−0.2%	
		Full range			−0.6%			−0.6%	
Reference voltage, $V_{(ref)}$		25°C	6.95	7.15	7.35	6.8	7.15	7.5	V
Standby current	V_I = 30 V, I_O = 0	25°C		2.3	3.5		2.3	4	mA
Temperature coefficient of output voltage		Full range		0.002	0.015		0.003	0.015	%/°C
Short-circuit output current	R_{SC} = 10 Ω, V_O = 0	25°C		65			65		mA
Output noise voltage	BW = 100 Hz to 10 kHz, $C_{(ref)}$ = 0	25°C		20			20		μV
	BW = 100 Hz to 10 kHz, $C_{(ref)}$ = 5 μF	25°C		2.5			2.5		

†Full range for uA723M is −55°C to 125°C and for uA723C is 0°C to 70°C.

NOTE 3: For all values in this table the device is connected as shown in Figure 1 with the divider resistance as seen by the error amplifier $\leqslant 10$ kΩ. Unless otherwise specified, $V_I = V_{CC+} = V_C = 12$ V, $V_{CC-} = 0$, $V_O = 5$ V, $I_O = 1$ mA, $R_{SC} = 0$, and $C_{(ref)} = 0$.

schematic

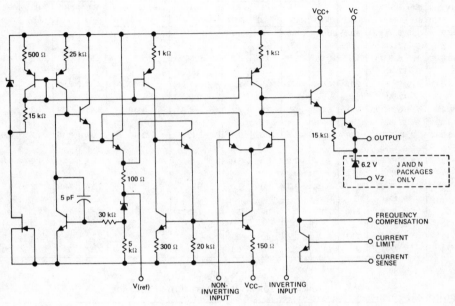

DISSIPATION DERATING TABLE

PACKAGE	POWER RATING	DERATING FACTOR	ABOVE T$_A$
J	1000 mW	8.2 mW/°C	28°C
L + heat sink†	800 mW	6.4 mW/°C	25°C
N	1000 mW	9.2 mW/°C	41°C
U	675 mW	5.4 mW/°C	25°C

†This rating for the L package requires a heat sink that provides a thermal resistance from case to free-air, R$_{\theta}$CA, of not more than 105°C/W.

TEXAS INSTRUMENTS
INCORPORATED
POST OFFICE BOX 5012 • DALLAS, TEXAS 75222

145

TABLE I

RESISTOR VALUES (kΩ) FOR STANDARD OUTPUT VOLTAGES

OUTPUT VOLTAGE (V)	APPLICABLE FIGURES (SEE NOTE 4)	FIXED OUTPUT ± 5%		OUTPUT ADJUSTABLE ± 10% (SEE NOTE 5)			OUTPUT VOLTAGE (V)	APPLICABLE FIGURES (SEE NOTE 4)	FIXED OUTPUT ± 5%		OUTPUT ADJUSTABLE ± 10% (SEE NOTE 5)		
		R1 (kΩ)	R2 (kΩ)	R1 (kΩ)	P1 (kΩ)	R2 (kΩ)			R1 (kΩ)	R2 (kΩ)	R1 (kΩ)	P1 (kΩ)	R2 (kΩ)
+3.0	1, 5, 6, 9, 11, 12 (4)	4.12	3.01	1.8	0.5	1.2	+100	7	3.57	105	2.2	10	91
+3.6	1, 5, 6, 9, 11, 12 (4)	3.57	3.65	1.5	0.5	1.5	+250	7	3.57	255	2.2	10	240
+5.0	1, 5, 6, 9, 11, 12 (4)	2.15	4.99	0.75	0.5	2.2	−6 (Note 6)	3, (10)	3.57	2.43	1.2	0.5	0.75
+6.0	1, 5, 6, 9, 11, 12 (4)	1.15	6.04	0.5	0.5	2.7	−9	3, 10	3.48	5.36	1.2	0.5	2.0
+9.0	2, 4, (5, 6, 9, 12)	1.87	7.15	0.75	1.0	2.7	−12	3, 10	3.57	8.45	1.2	0.5	3.3
+12	2, 4, (5, 6, 9, 12)	4.87	7.15	2.0	1.0	3.0	−15	3, 10	3.57	11.5	1.2	0.5	4.3
+15	2, 4, (5, 6, 9, 12)	7.87	7.15	3.3	1.0	3.0	−28	3, 10	3.57	24.3	1.2	0.5	10
+28	2, 4, (5, 6, 9, 12)	21.0	7.15	5.6	1.0	2.0	−45	8	3.57	41.2	2.2	10	33
+45	7	3.57	48.7	2.2	10	39	−100	8	3.57	95.3	2.2	10	91
+75	7	3.57	78.7	2.2	10	68	−250	8	3.57	249	2.2	10	240

TABLE II

FORMULAS FOR INTERMEDIATE OUTPUT VOLTAGES

Outputs from +2 to +7 volts [Figures 1, 5, 6, 9, 11, 12, (4)] $$V_O = V_{(ref)} \times \frac{R2}{R1 + R2}$$	Outputs from +4 to +250 volts [Figure 7] $$V_O = \frac{V_{(ref)}}{2} \times \frac{R2 - R1}{R1};$$ $$R3 = R4$$	Current Limiting $$I_{(limit)} \approx \frac{0.65\ V}{R_{sc}}$$
Outputs from +7 to +37 volts [Figures 2, 4, (5, 6, 9, 11, 12)] $$V_O = V_{(ref)} \times \frac{R1 + R2}{R2}$$	Outputs from −6 to −250 volts [Figures 3, 8, 10] $$V_O = -\frac{V_{(ref)}}{2} \times \frac{R1 + R2}{R1};$$ $$R3 = R4$$	Foldback Current Limiting [Figure 6] $$I_{(knee)} \approx \frac{V_O R3 + (R3 + R4)\,0.65\ V}{R_{sc} R4};$$ $$I_{OS} \approx \frac{0.65\ V}{R_{sc}} \times \frac{R3 + R4}{R4}$$

NOTES:
4. Figures 1 through 12 show the R1/R2 divider across either V_O or $V_{(ref)}$. Figure numbers in parentheses may be used if the R1/R2 divider is placed across the other voltage ($V_{(ref)}$ or V_O) that it was not placed across in the figures without parentheses.
5. To make the voltage adjustable, the R1/R2 divider shown in the figures must be replaced by the divider shown at the right.
6. For negative output voltages less than 9 V, V_{CC+} and V_C must be connected to a positive supply such that the voltage between V_{CC+} and V_{CC-} is greater than 9 V.
7. When 10-lead uA723 devices are used in applications requiring V_Z, an external 6.2-V regulator diode must be connected in series with the V_O terminal.

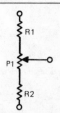

ADJUSTABLE OUTPUT CIRCUITS

TEXAS INSTRUMENTS
INCORPORATED
POST OFFICE BOX 5012 • DALLAS, TEXAS 75222

TYPICAL APPLICATION DATA

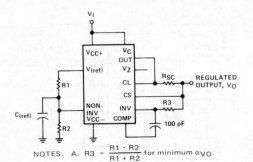

NOTES: A. $R3 = \dfrac{R1 \cdot R2}{R1 + R2}$ for minimum α_{VO}.

B. R3 may be eliminated for minimum component count. Use direct connection (i.e., $R_3 = 0$).

FIGURE 1–BASIC LOW-VOLTAGE REGULATOR (V_O = 2 TO 7 VOLTS)

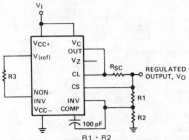

NOTES: A. $R3 = \dfrac{R1 \cdot R2}{R1 + R2}$ for minimum α_{VO}.

B. R3 may be eliminated for minimum component count. Use direct connection (i.e., $R_3 = 0$).

FIGURE 2–BASIC HIGH-VOLTAGE REGULATOR (V_O = 7 TO 37 VOLTS)

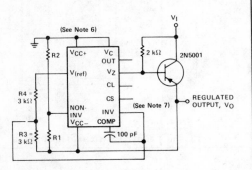

FIGURE 3–NEGATIVE-VOLTAGE REGULATOR

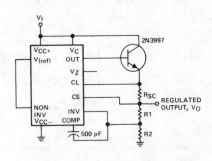

FIGURE 4–POSITIVE-VOLTAGE REGULATOR (EXTERNAL N-P-N- PASS TRANSISTOR)

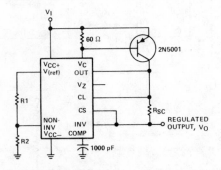

FIGURE 5–POSITIVE-VOLTAGE REGULATOR (EXTERNAL P-N-P PASS TRANSISTOR)

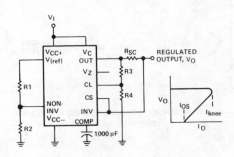

FIGURE 6–FOLDBACK CURRENT LIMITING

TYPICAL APPLICATION DATA

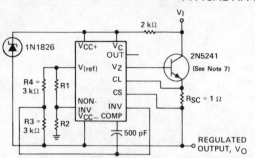

FIGURE 7—POSITIVE FLOATING REGULATOR

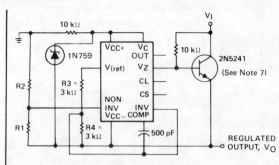

FIGURE 8—NEGATIVE FLOATING REGULATOR

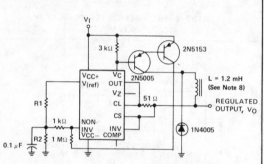

FIGURE 9—POSITIVE SWITCHING REGULATOR

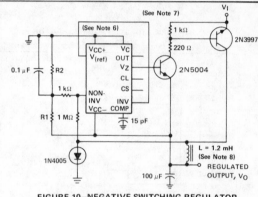

FIGURE 10—NEGATIVE SWITCHING REGULATOR

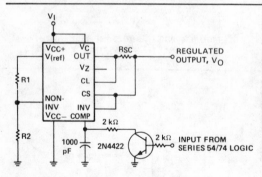

NOTE A: Current limit transistor may be used for shutdown if current limiting is not required.

FIGURE 11—REMOTE SHUTDOWN REGULATOR WITH CURRENT LIMITING

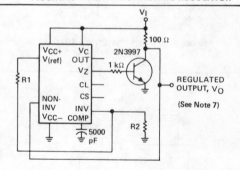

FIGURE 12—SHUNT REGULATOR

NOTES: 6. For negative output voltages less than 9 V, V_{CC+} and V_C must be connected to a positive supply such that the voltage between V_{CC+} and V_{CC-} is greater than 9 V.

7. When 10-lead uA723 devices are used in applications requiring V_Z, an external 6.2-V regulator diode must be connected in series with the V_O terminal.

8. L is 40 turns of No. 20 enameled copper wire wound on Ferroxcube P36/22-3B7 potted core, or equivalent, with 0.009-inch air gap.

TEXAS INSTRUMENTS
INCORPORATED
POST OFFICE BOX 5012 • DALLAS, TEXAS 75222

LINEAR INTEGRATED CIRCUITS

SERIES uA7800
POSITIVE-VOLTAGE REGULATORS

BULLETIN NO. DL-S 12386, MAY 1976–REVISED SEPTEMBER 1977

- 3-Terminal Regulators
- Output Current up to 1.5 A
- No External Components
- Internal Thermal Overload Protection
- Direct Replacements for Fairchild μA7800 Series
- High Power Dissipation Capability
- Internal Short-Circuit Current Limiting
- Output Transistor Safe-Area Compensation

NOMINAL OUTPUT VOLTAGE	REGULATOR
5 V	uA7805C
6 V	uA7806C
8 V	uA7808C
8.5 V	uA7885C
10 V	uA7810C
12 V	uA7812C
15 V	uA7815C
18 V	uA7818C
22 V	uA7822C
24 V	uA7824C

description

This series of fixed-voltage monolithic integrated-circuit voltage regulators is designed for a wide range of applications. These applications include on-card regulation for elimination of noise and distribution problems associated with single-point regulation. One of these regulators can deliver up to 1.5 amperes of output current. The internal current limiting and thermal shutdown features of these regulators make them essentially immune to overload. In addition to use as fixed-voltage regulators, these devices can be used with external components to obtain adjustable output voltages and currents and also as the power-pass element in precision regulators.

KC PACKAGE

(TOP VIEW)

OUTPUT
COMMON
INPUT

TO-220AB

I C O

schematic

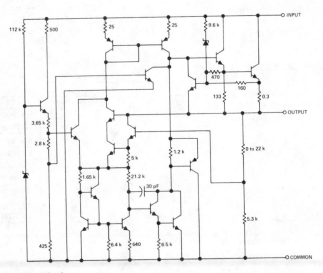

Resistor values shown are nominal and in ohms.

TEXAS INSTRUMENTS
INCORPORATED

POST OFFICE BOX 5012 • DALLAS, TEXAS 75222

SERIES uA7800
POSITIVE-VOLTAGE REGULATORS

absolute maximum ratings over operating temperature range (unless otherwise noted)

		uA78__C	UNIT
Input voltage	uA7822C, uA7824C	40	V
	All others	35	
Continuous total dissipation at 25°C free-air temperature (see Note 1)		2	W
Continuous total dissipation at (or below) 25°C case temperature (see Note 1)		15	W
Operating free-air, case, or virtual junction temperature range		0 to 150	°C
Storage temperature range		−65 to 150	°C
Lead temperature 1/16 inch from case for 10 seconds		260	°C

Note 1: For operation above 25°C free-air or case temperature, refer to Dissipation Derating Curves, Figure 1 and Figure 2.

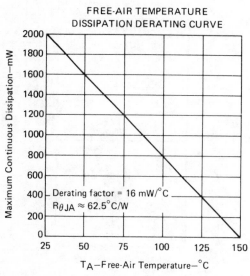

FREE-AIR TEMPERATURE
DISSIPATION DERATING CURVE

Derating factor = 16 mW/°C
$R_{\theta JA} \approx 62.5°C/W$

T_A—Free-Air Temperature—°C

FIGURE 1

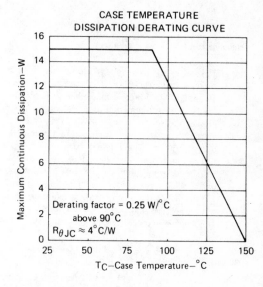

CASE TEMPERATURE
DISSIPATION DERATING CURVE

Derating factor = 0.25 W/°C
above 90°C
$R_{\theta JC} \approx 4°C/W$

T_C—Case Temperature—°C

FIGURE 2

recommended operating conditions

		MIN	MAX	UNIT
Input voltage, V_I	uA7805C	7	25	V
	uA7806C	8	25	
	uA7808C	10.5	25	
	uA7885C	10.5	25	
	uA7810C	12.5	28	
	uA7812C	14.5	30	
	uA7815C	17.5	30	
	uA7818C	21	33	
	uA7822C	25	36	
	uA7824C	27	38	
Output current, I_O			1.5	A
Operating virtual junction temperature, T_J		0	125	°C

TEXAS INSTRUMENTS
INCORPORATED
POST OFFICE BOX 5012 • DALLAS, TEXAS 75222

uA7805C electrical characteristics at specified virtual junction temperature, V_I = 10 V, I_O = 500 mA (unless otherwise noted)

PARAMETER	TEST CONDITIONS†		uA7805C			UNIT
			MIN	TYP	MAX	
Output voltage	I_O = 5 mA to 1 A, V_I = 7 V to 20 V, P ≤ 15 W	25°C	4.8	5	5.2	V
		0°C to 125°C	4.75		5.25	
Input regulation	V_I = 7 V to 25 V	25°C		3	100	mV
	V_I = 8 V to 12 V			1	50	
Ripple rejection	V_I = 8 V to 18 V, f = 120 Hz	0°C to 125°C	62	78		dB
Output regulation	I_O = 5 mA to 1.5 A	25°C		15	100	mV
	I_O = 250 mA to 750 mA			5	50	
Output resistance	f = 1 kHz	0°C to 125°C		0.017		Ω
Temperature coefficient of output voltage	I_O = 5 mA	0°C to 125°C		−1.1		mV/°C
Output noise voltage	f = 10 Hz to 100 kHz	25°C		40		μV
Dropout voltage	I_O = 1 A	25°C		2.0		V
Bias current		25°C		4.2	8	mA
Bias current change	V_I = 7 V to 25 V	0°C to 125°C			1.3	mA
	I_O = 5 mA to 1 A				0.5	
Short-circuit output current		25°C		750		mA
Peak output current		25°C		2.2		A

uA7806C electrical characteristics at specified virtual junction temperature, V_I = 11 V, I_O = 500 mA (unless otherwise noted)

PARAMETER	TEST CONDITIONS†		uA7806C			UNIT
			MIN	TYP	MAX	
Output voltage	I_O = 5 mA to 1 A, V_I = 8 V to 21 V, P ≤ 15 W	25°C	5.75	6	6.25	V
		0°C to 125°C	5.7		6.3	
Input regulation	V_I = 8 V to 25 V	25°C		5	120	mV
	V_I = 9 V to 13 V			1.5	60	
Ripple rejection	V_I = 9 V to 19 V, f = 120 Hz	0°C to 125°C	59	75		dB
Output regulation	I_O = 5 mA to 1.5 A	25°C		14	120	mV
	I_O = 250 mA to 750 mA			4	60	
Output resistance	f = 1 kHz	0°C to 125°C		0.019		Ω
Temperature coefficient of output voltage	I_O = 5 mA	0°C to 125°C		−0.8		mV/°C
Output noise voltage	f = 10 Hz to 100 kHz	25°C		45		μV
Dropout voltage	I_O = 1 A	25°C		2.0		V
Bias current		25°C		4.3	8	mA
Bias current change	V_I = 8 V to 25 V	0°C to 125°C			1.3	mA
	I_O = 5 mA to 1 A				0.5	
Short-circuit output current		25°C		550		mA
Peak output current		25°C		2.2		A

†All characteristics are measured with a capacitor across the input of 0.33 μF and a capacitor across the output of 0.1 μF. All characteristics except noise voltage and ripple rejection ratio are measured using pulse techniques (t_W ≤ 10 ms, duty cycles ≤ 5%). Output voltage changes due to changes in internal temperature must be taken into account separately.

977

TEXAS INSTRUMENTS
INCORPORATED
POST OFFICE BOX 5012 • DALLAS, TEXAS 75222

uA7808C electrical characteristics at specified virtual junction temperature,
V_I = 14 V, I_O = 500 mA (unless otherwise noted)

PARAMETER	TEST CONDITIONS†		uA7808C			UNIT
			MIN	TYP	MAX	
Output voltage	I_O = 5 mA to 1 A, V_I = 10.5 V to 23 V, P ≤ 15 W	25°C	7.7	8	8.3	V
		0°C to 125°C	7.6		8.4	
Input regulation	V_I = 10.5 V to 25 V	25°C		6	160	mV
	V_I = 11 V to 17 V			2	80	
Ripple rejection	V_I = 11.5 V to 21.5 V, f = 120 Hz	0°C to 125°C	56	72		dB
Output regulation	I_O = 5 mA to 1.5 A	25°C		12	160	mV
	I_O = 250 mA to 750 mA			4	80	
Output resistance	f = 1 kHz	0°C to 125°C		0.016		Ω
Temperature coefficient of output voltage	I_O = 5 mA	0°C to 125°C		−0.8		mV/°C
Output noise voltage	f = 10 Hz to 100 kHz	25°C		52		μV
Dropout voltage	I_O = 1 A	25°C		2.0		V
Bias current		25°C		4.3	8	mA
Bias current change	V_I = 10.5 V to 25 V	0°C to 125°C			1	mA
	I_O = 5 mA to 1 A				0.5	
Short-circuit output current		25°C		450		mA
Peak output current		25°C		2.2		A

uA7885C electrical characteristics at specified virtual junction temperature,
V_I = 15 V, I_O = 500 mA (unless otherwise noted)

PARAMETER	TEST CONDITIONS†		uA7885C			UNIT
			MIN	TYP	MAX	
Output voltage	I_O = 5 mA to 1 A, V_I = 11 V to 23.5 V, P ≤ 15 W	25°C	8.15	8.5	8.85	V
		0°C to 125°C	8.1		8.9	
Input regulation	V_I = 10.5 V to 25 V	25°C		6	170	mV
	V_I = 11 V to 17 V			2	85	
Ripple rejection	V_I = 11.5 V to 21.5 V, f = 120 Hz	0°C to 125°C	54	70		dB
Output regulation	I_O = 5 mA to 1.5 A	25°C		12	170	mV
	I_O = 250 mA to 750 mA			4	85	
Output resistance	f = 1 kHz	0°C to 125°C		0.016		Ω
Temperature coefficient of output voltage	I_O = 5 mA	0°C to 125°C		−0.8		mV/°C
Output noise voltage	f = 10 Hz to 100 kHz	25°C		55		μV
Dropout voltage	I_O = 1 A	25°C		2.0		V
Bias current		25°C		4.3	8	mA
Bias current change	V_I = 10.5 V to 25 V	0°C to 125°C			1	mA
	I_O = 5 mA to 1 A				0.5	
Short-circuit output current		25°C		450		mA
Peak output current		25°C		2.2		A

†All characteristics are measured with a capacitor across the input of 0.33 μF and a capacitor across the output of 0.1 μF. All characteristics except noise voltage and ripple rejection ratio are measured using pulse techniques (t_W ≤ 10 ms, duty cycles ≤ 5%). Output voltage changes due to changes in internal temperature must be taken into account separately.

TEXAS INSTRUMENTS
INCORPORATED
POST OFFICE BOX 5012 • DALLAS, TEXAS 75222

uA7810C electrical characteristics at specified virtual junction temperature, V_I = 17 V, I_O = 500 mA (unless otherwise noted)

PARAMETER	TEST CONDITIONS†		uA7810C MIN	uA7810C TYP	uA7810C MAX	UNIT
Output voltage	I_O = 5 mA to 1 A, V_I = 12.5 V to 25 V, P ⩽ 15 W	25°C	9.6	10	10.4	V
		0°C to 125°C	9.5	10	10.5	
Input regulation	V_I = 12.5 V to 28 V	25°C		7	200	mV
	V_I = 14 V to 20 V			2	100	
Ripple rejection	V_I = 13 V to 23 V, f = 120 Hz	0°C to 125°C	55	71		dB
Output regulation	I_O = 5 mA to 1.5 A	25°C		12	200	mV
	I_O = 250 mA to 750 mA			4	100	
Output resistance	f = 1 kHz	0°C to 125°C		0.018		Ω
Temperature coefficient of output voltage	I_O = 5 mA	0°C to 125°C		−1.0		mV/°C
Output noise voltage	f = 10 Hz to 100 kHz	25°C		70		µV
Dropout voltage	I_O = 1 A	25°C		2.0		V
Bias current		25°C		4.3	8	mA
Bias current change	V_I = 12.5 V to 28 V	0°C to 125°C			1	mA
	I_O = 5 mA to 1 A				0.5	
Short-circuit output current		25°C		400		mA
Peak output current		25°C		2.2		A

uA7812C electrical characteristics at specified virtual junction temperature, V_I = 19 V, I_O = 500 mA (unless otherwise noted)

PARAMETER	TEST CONDITIONS†		uA7812C MIN	uA7812C TYP	uA7812C MAX	UNIT
Output voltage	I_O = 5 mA to 1 A, V_I = 14.5 V to 27 V, P ⩽ 15 W	25°C	11.5	12	12.5	V
		0°C to 125°C	11.4		12.6	
Input regulation	V_I = 14.5 V to 30 V	25°C		10	240	mV
	V_I = 16 V to 22 V			3	120	
Ripple rejection	V_I = 15 V to 25 V, f = 120 Hz	0°C to 125°C	55	71		dB
Output regulation	I_O = 5 mA to 1.5 A	25°C		12	240	mV
	I_O = 250 mA to 750 mA			4	120	
Output resistance	f = 1 kHz	0°C to 125°C		0.018		Ω
Temperature coefficient of output voltage	I_O = 5 mA	0°C to 125°C		−1.0		mV/°C
Output noise voltage	f = 10 Hz to 100 kHz	25°C		75		µV
Dropout voltage	I_O = 1 A	25°C		2.0		V
Bias current		25°C		4.3	8	mA
Bias current change	V_I = 14.5 V to 30 V	0°C to 125°C			1	mA
	I_O = 5 mA to 1 A				0.5	
Short-circuit output current		25°C		350		mA
Peak output current		25°C		2.2		A

†All characteristics are measured with a capacitor across the input of 0.33 µF and a capacitor across the output of 0.1 µF. All characteristics except noise voltage and ripple rejection ratio are measured using pulse techniques (t_w ⩽ 10 ms, duty cycles ⩽ 5%). Output voltage changes due to changes in internal temperature must be taken into account separately.

TEXAS INSTRUMENTS
INCORPORATED
POST OFFICE BOX 5012 • DALLAS, TEXAS 75222

uA7815C electrical characteristics at specified virtual junction temperature,
V_I = 23 V, I_O = 500 mA (unless otherwise noted)

PARAMETER	TEST CONDITIONS†		uA7815C			UNIT
			MIN	TYP	MAX	
Output voltage	I_O = 5 mA to 1 A, V_I = 17.5 V to 30 V, P ⩽ 15 W	25°C	14.4	15	15.6	V
		0°C to 125°C	14.25		15.75	
Input regulation	V_I = 17.5 V to 30 V	25°C		11	300	mV
	V_I = 20 V to 26 V			3	150	
Ripple rejection	V_I = 18.5 V to 28.5 V, f = 120 Hz	0°C to 125°C	54	70		dB
Output regulation	I_O = 5 mA to 1.5 A	25°C		12	300	mV
	I_O = 250 mA to 750 mA			4	150	
Output resistance	f = 1 kHz	0°C to 125°C		0.019		Ω
Temperature coefficient of output voltage	I_O = 5 mA	0°C to 125°C		−1.0		mV/°C
Output noise voltage	f = 10 Hz to 100 kHz	25°C		90		μV
Dropout voltage	I_O = 1 A	25°C		2.0		V
Bias current		25°C		4.4	8	mA
Bias current change	V_I = 17.5 V to 30 V	0°C to 125°C			1	mA
	I_O = 5 mA to 1 A				0.5	
Short-circuit output current		25°C		230		mA
Peak output current		25°C		2.1		A

uA7818C electrical characteristics at specified virtual junction temperature,
V_I = 27 V, I_O = 500 mA (unless otherwise noted)

PARAMETER	TEST CONDITIONS†		uA7818C			UNIT
			MIN	TYP	MAX	
Output voltage	I_O = 5 mA to 1 A, V_I = 21 V to 33 V, P ⩽ 15 W	25°C	17.3	18	18.7	V
		0°C to 125°C	17.1		18.9	
Input regulation	V_I = 21 V to 33 V	25°C		15	360	mV
	V_I = 24 V to 30 V			5	180	
Ripple rejection	V_I = 22 V to 32 V, f = 120 Hz	0°C to 125°C	53	69		dB
Output regulation	I_O = 5 mA to 1.5 A	25°C		12	360	mV
	I_O = 250 mA to 750 mA			4	180	
Output resistance	f = 1 kHz	0°C to 125°C		0.022		Ω
Temperature coefficient of output voltage	I_O = 5 mA	0°C to 125°C		−1.0		mV/°C
Output noise voltage	f = 10 Hz to 100 kHz	25°C		110		μV
Dropout voltage	I_O = 1 A	25°C		2.0		V
Bias current		25°C		4.5	8	mA
Bias current change	V_I = 21 V to 33 V	0°C to 125°C			1	mA
	I_O = 5 mA to 1 A				0.5	
Short-circuit output current		25°C		200		mA
Peak output current		25°C		2.1		A

†All characteristics are measured with a capacitor across the input of 0.33 μF and a capacitor across the output of 0.1 μF. All characteristics except noise voltage and ripple rejection ratio are measured using pulse techniques (t_w ⩽ 10 ms, duty cycles ⩽ 5%). Output voltage changes due to changes in internal temperature must be taken into account separately.

TEXAS INSTRUMENTS
INCORPORATED
POST OFFICE BOX 5012 • DALLAS, TEXAS 75222

uA7822C electrical characteristics at specified virtual junction temperature, V_I = 31 V, I_O = 500 mA (unless otherwise noted)

PARAMETER	TEST CONDITIONS[†]		uA7822C			UNIT
			MIN	TYP	MAX	
Output voltage	I_O = 5 mA to 1 A, V_I = 25 V to 36 V, P ≤ 15 W	25°C	21.1	22	22.9	V
		0°C to 125°C	20.9		23.1	
Input regulation	V_I = 25 V to 36 V	25°C		17	440	mV
	V_I = 26 V to 34 V			6	220	
Ripple rejection	V_I = 26 V to 36 V, f = 120 Hz	0°C to 125°C	51	67		dB
Output regulation	I_O = 5 mA to 1.5 A	25°C		12	440	mV
	I_O = 250 mA to 750 mA			4	220	
Output resistance	f = 1 kHz	0°C to 125°C		0.028		Ω
Temperature coefficient of output voltage	I_O = 5 mA	0°C to 125°C		−1.3		mV/°C
Output noise voltage	f = 10 Hz to 100 kHz	25°C		160		µV
Dropout voltage	I_O = 1 A	25°C		2.0		V
Bias current		25°C		4.6	8	mA
Bias current change	V_I = 25 V to 36 V	0°C to 125°C			1	mA
	I_O = 5 mA to 1 A				0.5	
Short-circuit output current		25°C		175		mA
Peak output current		25°C		2.1		A

uA7824C electrical characteristics at specified virtual junction temperature, V_I = 33 V, I_O = 500 mA (unless otherwise noted)

PARAMETER	TEST CONDITIONS[†]		uA7824C			UNIT
			MIN	TYP	MAX	
Output voltage	I_O = 5 mA to 1 A, V_I = 27 V to 38 V, P ≤ 15 W	25°C	23	24	25	V
		0°C to 125°C	22.8		25.2	
Input regulation	V_I = 27 V to 38 V	25°C		18	480	mV
	V_I = 30 V to 36 V			6	240	
Ripple rejection	V_I = 28 V to 38 V, f = 120 Hz	0°C to 125°C	50	66		dB
Output regulation	I_O = 5 mA to 1.5 A	25°C		12	480	mV
	I_O = 250 mA to 750 mA			4	240	
Output resistance	f = 1 kHz	0°C to 125°C		0.028		Ω
Temperature coefficient of output voltage	I_O = 5 mA	0°C to 125°C		−1.5		mV/°C
Output noise voltage	f = 10 Hz to 100 kHz	25°C		170		µV
Dropout voltage	I_O = 1 A	25°C		2.0		V
Bias current		25°C		4.6	8	mA
Bias current change	V_I = 27 V to 38 V	0°C to 125°C			1	mA
	I_O = 5 mA to 1 A				0.5	
Short-circuit output current		25°C		150		mA
Peak output current		25°C		2.1		A

[†] All characteristics are measured with a capacitor across the input of 0.33 µF and a capacitor across the output of 0.1 µF. All characteristics except noise voltage and ripple rejection ratio are measured using pulse techniques (t_W ≤ 10 ms, duty cycles ≤ 5%). Output voltage changes due to changes in internal temperature must be taken into account separately.

TEXAS INSTRUMENTS
INCORPORATED
POST OFFICE BOX 5012 • DALLAS, TEXAS 75222

LINEAR
INTEGRATED CIRCUITS

SERIES uA78L00
POSITIVE-VOLTAGE REGULATORS

BULLETIN NO. DL-S 12353, JANUARY 1976–REVISED APRIL 1977

- 3-Terminal Regulators
- Output Current up to 100 mA
- No External Components
- Internal Thermal Overload Protection
- Unusually High Power Dissipation Capability
- Direct Replacement for Fairchild μA78L00 Series
- Internal Short-Circuit Current Limiting

NOMINAL OUTPUT VOLTAGE	5% OUTPUT VOLTAGE TOLERANCE	10% OUTPUT VOLTAGE TOLERANCE
2.6 V	uA78L02AC	uA78L02C
5 V	uA78L05AC	uA78L05C
6.2 V	uA78L06AC	uA78L06C
8 V	uA78L08AC	uA78L08C
9 V	uA78L09AC	uA78L09C
10 V	uA78L10AC	uA78L10C
12 V	uA78L12AC	uA78L12C
15 V	uA78L15AC	uA78L15C

JG
DUAL-IN-LINE PACKAGE

LP
SILECT† PACKAGE

description

This series of fixed-voltage monolithic integrated-circuit voltage regulators is designed for a wide range of applications. These applications include on-card regulation for elimination of noise and distribution problems associated with single-point regulation. In addition, they can be used with power-pass elements to make high-current voltage regulators. One of these regulators can deliver up to 100 mA of output current. The internal current limiting and thermal shutdown features of these regulators make them essentially immune to overload. When used as a replacement for a Zener-diode—resistor combination, an effective improvement in output impedance of typically two orders of magnitude can be obtained together with lower bias current.

(TOP VIEW)

OUTPUT
COMMON
NC   NC

INPUT
NC NC NC

(TOP VIEW)

INPUT
COMMON
OUTPUT

TO-226AA

OCI

NC — No internal connection

schematic

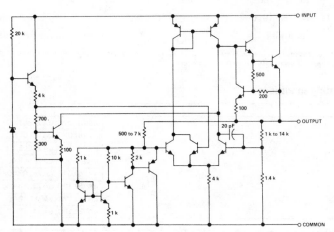

20 k
4 k
700
300
100
500 to 7 k
1 k
10 k
2 k
4 k
1 k
500
200
100
20 pF
1 k to 14 k
1.4 k
INPUT
OUTPUT
COMMON

Resistor values shown are nominal and in ohms.

† Trademark of Texas Instruments

477

TEXAS INSTRUMENTS
INCORPORATED
POST OFFICE BOX 5012 • DALLAS, TEXAS 75222

SERIES uA78L00
POSITIVE-VOLTAGE REGULATORS

absolute maximum ratings over operating temperature range (unless otherwise noted)

		uA78L02AC, uA78L02C THRU uA78L10AC, uA78L10C	uA78L12AC, uA78L12C uA78L15AC, uA78L15C	UNIT
Input voltage		30	35	V
Continuous total dissipation at 25°C free-air temperature (see Note 1)	JG package	825	825	mW
	LP package	775	775	
Continuous total dissipation at (or below) 25°C case temperature (see Note 1)		1600	1600	mW
Operating free-air, case, or virtual junction temperature range		0 to 150	0 to 150	°C
Storage temperature range		−65 to 150	−65 to 150	°C
Lead temperature 1/16 inch from case for 10 seconds		260	260	°C

NOTE 1: For operation above 25°C free-air or case temperature, refer to Dissipation Derating Curves, Figure 1 and Figure 2.

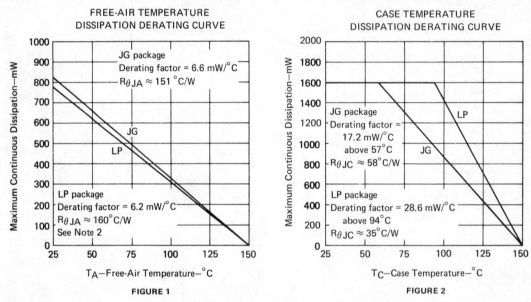

FREE-AIR TEMPERATURE DISSIPATION DERATING CURVE

JG package
Derating factor = 6.6 mW/°C
$R_{\theta JA} \approx 151\ °C/W$

JG

LP

LP package
Derating factor = 6.2 mW/°C
$R_{\theta JA} \approx 160°C/W$
See Note 2

T_A—Free-Air Temperature—°C

FIGURE 1

CASE TEMPERATURE DISSIPATION DERATING CURVE

JG package
Derating factor = 17.2 mW/°C above 57°C
$R_{\theta JC} \approx 58°C/W$

LP

JG

LP package
Derating factor = 28.6 mW/°C above 94°C
$R_{\theta JC} \approx 35°C/W$

T_C—Case Temperature—°C

FIGURE 2

NOTE 2: This curve for the LP package is based on thermal resistance, $R_{\theta JA}$, measured in still air with the device mounted in an Augat socket. The bottom of the package was 3/8 inch above the socket.

recommended operating conditions

		MIN	MAX	UNIT
Input voltage, V_I	uA78L02C, uA78L02AC	4.75	20	V
	uA78L05C, uA78L05AC	7	20	
	uA78L06C, uA78L06AC	8.5	20	
	uA78L08C, uA78L08AC	10.5	23	
	uA78L09C, uA78L09AC	11.5	24	
	uA78L10C, uA78L10AC	12.5	25	
	uA78L12C, uA78L12AC	14.5	27	
	uA78L15C, uA78L15AC	17.5	30	
Output current, I_O			100	mA
Operating virtual junction temperature, T_J		0	125	°C

47

TEXAS INSTRUMENTS
INCORPORATED
POST OFFICE BOX 5012 • DALLAS, TEXAS 75222

uA78L02AC, uA78L02C electrical characteristics at specified virtual junction temperature, V_I = 9 V, I_O = 40 mA (unless otherwise noted)

PARAMETER	TEST CONDITIONS†		uA78L02AC MIN	TYP	MAX	uA78L02C MIN	TYP	MAX	UNIT
Output voltage	V_I = 4.75 V to 20 V, I_O = 1 mA to 40 mA	25°C	2.5	2.6	2.7	2.4	2.6	2.8	V
		0°C to 125°C	2.45		2.75	2.35		2.85	
	I_O = 1 mA to 70 mA		2.45		2.75	2.35		2.85	
Input regulation	V_I = 4.75 V to 20 V	25°C		20	100		20	125	mV
	V_I = 5 V to 20 V			16	75		16	100	
Ripple rejection	V_I = 6 V to 16 V, f = 120 Hz	25°C	43	51		42	51		dB
Output regulation	I_O = 1 mA to 100 mA	25°C		12	50		12	50	mV
	I_O = 1 mA to 40 mA			6	25		6	25	
Output noise voltage	f = 10 Hz to 100 kHz	25°C		30			30		µV
Dropout voltage		25°C		1.7			1.7		V
Bias current		25°C		3.6	6		3.6	6	mA
		125°C			5.5			5.5	
Bias current change	V_I = 5 V to 20 V	0°C to 125°C			2.5			2.5	mA
	I_O = 1 mA to 40 mA				0.1			0.2	

uA78L05AC, uA78L05C electrical characteristics at specified virtual junction temperature, V_I = 10 V, I_O = 40 mA (unless otherwise noted)

PARAMETER	TEST CONDITIONS†		uA78L05AC MIN	TYP	MAX	uA78L05C MIN	TYP	MAX	UNIT
Output voltage	V_I = 7 V to 20 V, I_O = 1 mA to 40 mA	25°C	4.8	5	5.2	4.6	5	5.4	V
		0°C to 125°C	4.75		5.25	4.5		5.5	
	I_O = 1 mA to 70 mA		4.75		5.25	4.5		5.5	
Input regulation	V_I = 7 V to 20 V	25°C		32	150		32	200	mV
	V_I = 8 V to 20 V			26	100		26	150	
Ripple rejection	V_I = 8 V to 18 V, f = 120 Hz	25°C	41	49		40	49		dB
Output regulation	I_O = 1 mA to 100 mA	25°C		15	60		15	60	mV
	I_O = 1 mA to 40 mA			8	30		8	30	
Output noise voltage	f = 10 Hz to 100 kHz	25°C		42			42		µV
Dropout voltage		25°C		1.7			1.7		V
Bias current		25°C		3.8	6		3.8	6	mA
		125°C			5.5			5.5	
Bias current change	V_I = 8 V to 20 V	0°C to 125°C			1.5			1.5	mA
	I_O = 1 mA to 40 mA				0.1			0.2	

†All characteristics are measured with a capacitor across the input of 0.33 µF and a capacitor across the output of 0.1 µF. All characteristics except noise voltage and ripple rejection ratio are measured using pulse techniques (t_w ≤ 10 ms, duty cycle ≤ 5%). Output voltage changes due to changes in internal temperature must be taken into account separately.

TEXAS INSTRUMENTS
INCORPORATED
POST OFFICE BOX 5012 • DALLAS, TEXAS 75222

uA78L06AC, uA78L06C electrical characteristics at specified virtual junction temperature,
V_I = 12 V, I_O = 40 mA (unless otherwise noted)

PARAMETER	TEST CONDITIONS[†]		uA78L06AC			uA78L06C			UNIT
			MIN	TYP	MAX	MIN	TYP	MAX	
Output voltage	V_I = 8.5 V to 20 V, I_O = 1 mA to 40 mA	25°C	5.95	6.2	6.45	5.7	6.2	6.7	V
		0°C to 125°C	5.9		6.5	5.6		6.8	
	I_O = 1 mA to 70 mA		5.9		6.5	5.6		6.8	
Input regulation	V_I = 8.5 V to 20 V	25°C		35	175		35	200	mV
	V_I = 9 V to 20 V			29	125		29	150	
Ripple rejection	V_I = 10 V to 20 V, f = 120 Hz	25°C	40	48		39	48		dB
Output regulation	I_O = 1 mA to 100 mA	25°C		16	80		16	80	mV
	I_O = 1 mA to 40 mA			9	40		9	40	
Output noise voltage	f = 10 Hz to 100 kHz	25°C		46			46		µV
Dropout voltage		25°C		1.7			1.7		V
Bias current		25°C		3.9	6		3.9	6	mA
		125°C			5.5			5.5	
Bias current change	V_I = 9 V to 20 V	0°C to 125°C			1.5			1.5	mA
	I_O = 1 mA to 40 mA				0.1			0.2	

uA78L08AC, uA78L08C electrical characteristics at specified virtual junction temperature,
V_I = 14 V, I_O = 40 mA (unless otherwise noted)

PARAMETER	TEST CONDITIONS[†]		uA78L08AC			uA78L08C			UNIT
			MIN	TYP	MAX	MIN	TYP	MAX	
Output voltage	V_I = 10.5 V to 23 V, I_O = 1 mA to 40 mA	25°C	7.7	8	8.3	7.36	8	8.64	V
		0°C to 125°C	7.6		8.4	7.2		8.8	
	I_O = 1 mA to 70 mA		7.6		8.4	7.2		8.8	
Input regulation	V_I = 10.5 V to 23 V	25°C		42	175		42	200	mV
	V_I = 11 V to 23 V			36	125		36	150	
Ripple rejection	V_I = 13 V to 23 V, f = 120 Hz	25°C	37	46		36	46		dB
Output regulation	I_O = 1 mA to 100 mA	25°C		18	80		18	80	mV
	I_O = 1 mA to 40 mA			10	40		10	40	
Output noise voltage	f = 10 Hz to 100 kHz	25°C		54			54		µV
Dropout voltage		25°C		1.7			1.7		V
Bias current		25°C		4	6		4	6	mA
		125°C			5.5			5.5	
Bias current change	V_I = 11 V to 23 V	0°C to 125°C			1.5			1.5	mA
	I_O = 1 mA to 40 mA				0.1			0.2	

[†]All characteristics are measured with a capacitor across the input of 0.33 µF and a capacitor across the output of 0.1 µF. All characteristics except noise voltage and ripple rejection ratio are measured using pulse techniques (t_w ≤ 10 ms, duty cycle ≤ 5%). Output voltage changes due to changes in internal temperature must be taken into account separately.

47

TEXAS INSTRUMENTS
INCORPORATED
POST OFFICE BOX 5012 • DALLAS, TEXAS 75222

uA78L09AC, uA78L09C electrical characteristics at specified virtual junction temperature,
V_I = 16 V, I_O = 40 mA (unless otherwise noted)

PARAMETER	TEST CONDITIONS†		uA78L09AC			uA78L09C			UNIT
			MIN	TYP	MAX	MIN	TYP	MAX	
Output voltage	V_I = 12 V to 24 V, I_O = 1 mA to 40 mA	25°C	8.6	9	9.4	8.3	9	9.7	V
		0°C to 125°C	8.55		9.45	8.1		9.9	
	I_O = 1 mA to 70 mA		8.55		9.45	8.1		9.9	
Input regulation	V_I = 12 V to 24 V	25°C		45	175		45	225	mV
	V_I = 13 V to 24 V			40	125		40	175	
Ripple rejection	V_I = 13 V to 24 V, f = 120 Hz	25°C	37	45		36	45		dB
Output regulation	I_O = 1 mA to 100 mA	25°C		19	90		19	90	mV
	I_O = 1 mA to 40 mA			11	40		11	40	
Output noise voltage	f = 10 Hz to 100 kHz	25°C		58			58		µV
Dropout voltage		25°C		1.7			1.7		V
Bias current		25°C		4.1	6		4.1	6	mA
		125°C			5.5			5.5	
Bias current change	V_I = 13 V to 24 V	0°C to 125°C			1.5			1.5	mA
	I_O = 1 mA to 40 mA				0.1			0.2	

uA78L10AC, uA78L10C electrical characteristics at specified virtual junction temperature,
V_I = 17 V, I_O = 40 mA (unless otherwise noted)

PARAMETER	TEST CONDITIONS†		uA78L10AC			uA78L10C			UNIT
			MIN	TYP	MAX	MIN	TYP	MAX	
Output voltage	V_I = 13 V to 25 V, I_O = 1 mA to 40 mA	25°C	9.6	10	10.4	9.2	10	10.8	V
		0°C to 125°C	9.5		10.5	9		10	
	I_O = 1 mA to 70 mA		9.5		10.5	9		10	
Input regulation	V_I = 13 V to 25 V	25°C		51	175		51	225	mV
	V_I = 14 V to 25 V			42	125		42	175	
Ripple rejection	V_I = 14 V to 25 V, f = 120 Hz	25°C	37	44		36	44		dB
Output regulation	I_O = 1 mA to 100 mA	25°C		20	90		20	90	mV
	I_O = 1 mA to 40 mA			11	40		11	40	
Output noise voltage	f = 10 Hz to 100 kHz	25°C		62			62		µV
Dropout voltage		25°C		1.7			1.7		V
Bias current		25°C		4.2	6		4.2	6	mA
		125°C			5.5			5.5	
Bias current change	V_I = 14 V to 25 V	0°C to 125°C			1.5			1.5	mA
	I_O = 1 mA to 40 mA				0.1			0.2	

†All characteristics are measured with a capacitor across the input of 0.33 µF and a capacitor across the output of 0.1 µF. All characteristics except noise voltage and ripple rejection ratio are measured using pulse techniques (t_w ≤ 10 ms, duty cycle ≤ 5%). Output voltage changes due to changes in internal temperature must be taken into account separately.

uA78L12AC, uA78L12C electrical characteristics at specified virtual junction temperature, V_I = 19 V, I_O = 40 mA (unless otherwise noted)

PARAMETER	TEST CONDITIONS[†]		uA78L12AC			uA78L12C			UNIT
			MIN	TYP	MAX	MIN	TYP	MAX	
Output voltage	V_I = 14.5 V to 27 V, I_O = 1 mA to 40 mA	25°C	11.5	12	12.5	11.1	12	12.9	V
		0°C to 125°C	11.4		12.6	10.8		13.2	
	I_O = 1 mA to 70 mA		11.4		12.6	10.8		13.2	
Input regulation	V_I = 14.5 V to 27 V	25°C		55	250		55	250	mV
	V_I = 16 V to 27 V			49	200		49	200	
Ripple rejection	V_I = 15 V to 25 V, f = 120 Hz	25°C	37	42		36	42		dB
Output regulation	I_O = 1 mA to 100 mA	25°C		22	100		22	100	mV
	I_O = 1 mA to 40 mA			13	50		13	50	
Output noise voltage	f = 10 Hz to 100 kHz	25°C		70			70		µV
Dropout voltage		25°C		1.7			1.7		V
Bias current		25°C		4.3	6.5		4.3	6.5	mA
		125°C			6			6	
Bias current change	V_I = 16 V to 27 V	0°C to 125°C			1.5			1.5	mA
	I_O = 1 mA to 40 mA				0.1			0.2	

uA78L15AC, uA78L15C electrical characteristics at specified virtual junction temperature, V_I = 23 V, I_O = 40 mA (unless otherwise noted)

PARAMETER	TEST CONDITIONS[†]		uA78L15AC			uA78L15C			UNIT
			MIN	TYP	MAX	MIN	TYP	MAX	
Output voltage	V_I = 17.5 V to 30 V, I_O = 1 mA to 40 mA	25°C	14.4	15	15.6	13.8	15	16.2	V
		0°C to 125°C	14.25		15.75	13.5		16.5	
	I_O = 1 mA to 70 mA		14.25		15.75	13.5		16.5	
Input regulation	V_I = 17.5 V to 30 V	25°C		65	300		65	300	mV
	V_I = 20 V to 30 V			58	250		58	250	
Ripple rejection	V_I = 18.5 V to 28.5 V, f = 120 Hz	25°C	34	39		33	39		dB
Output regulation	I_O = 1 mA to 100 mA	25°C		25	150		25	150	mV
	I_O = 1 mA to 40 mA			15	75		15	75	
Output noise voltage	f = 10 Hz to 100 kHz	25°C		82			82		µV
Dropout voltage		25°C		1.7			1.7		V
Bias current		25°C		4.6	6.5		4.6	6.5	mA
		125°C			6			6	
Bias current change	V_I = 20 V to 30 V	0°C to 125°C			1.5			1.5	mA
	I_O = 1 mA to 40 mA				0.1			0.2	

[†]All characteristics are measured with a capacitor across the input of 0.33 µF and a capacitor across the output of 0.1 µF. All characteristics except noise voltage and ripple rejection ratio are measured using pulse techniques ($t_w \leq$ 10 ms, duty cycle $\leq$ 5%). Output voltage changes due to changes in internal temperature must be taken into account separately.

TEXAS INSTRUMENTS
INCORPORATED
POST OFFICE BOX 5012 • DALLAS, TEXAS 75222

LINEAR INTEGRATED CIRCUITS

- 3-Terminal Regulators
- Output Current up to 500 mA
- No external components
- Internal Thermal Overload Protection
- Direct Replacements for Fairchild μA78M00 Series and National LM341 Series
- High Power Dissipation Capability
- Internal Short-Circuit Current Limiting
- Output Transistor Safe-Area Compensation

NOMINAL OUTPUT VOLTAGE	−55°C TO 150°C OPERATING TEMPERATURE RANGE	0°C TO 125°C OPERATING TEMPERATURE RANGE
5 V	uA78M05M	uA78M05C
6 V	uA78M06M	uA78M06C
8 V	uA78M08M	uA78M08C
12 V	uA78M12M	uA78M12C
15 V	uA78M15M	uA78M15C
20 V	uA78M20M	uA78M20C
22 V	uA78M22M	uA78M22C
24 V	uA78M24M	uA78M24C
PACKAGES	LA	KC, KD, and LA

description

This series of fixed-voltage monolithic integrated-circuit voltage regulators is designed for a wide range of applications. These applications include on-card regulation for elimination of noise and distribution problems associated with single-point regulation. One of these regulators can deliver up to 500 milliamperes of output current. The internal current limiting and thermal shutdown features of these regulators make them essentially immune to overloald. In addition to use as fixed-voltage regulators, these devices can be used with external components to obtain adjustable output voltages and currents and also as the power pass element in precision regulators.

schematic

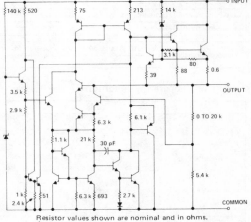

Resistor values shown are nominal and in ohms.

terminal assignments

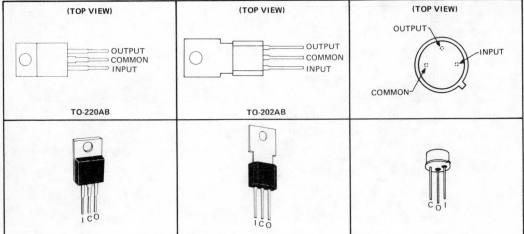

KC PACKAGE (TOP VIEW)
OUTPUT
COMMON
INPUT
TO-220AB

KD PACKAGE (TOP VIEW)
OUTPUT
COMMON
INPUT
TO-202AB

LA PACKAGE (TOP VIEW)
OUTPUT
INPUT
COMMON

TEXAS INSTRUMENTS
INCORPORATED
POST OFFICE BOX 5012 • DALLAS, TEXAS 75222

absolute maximum ratings over operating temperature range (unless otherwise noted)

		uA78M05M THRU uA78M24M	uA78M05C THRU uA78M24C	UNIT
Input voltage	uA78M20 thru uA78M24	40	40	V
	All others	35	35	
Continuous total dissipation at 25°C free-air temperature (see Note 1)	KC (TO-220AB) package	2	2	W
	KD(TO-202AB) package	1.5	1.5	
	LA package	0.6	0.6	
Continuous total dissipation at (or below)25°C case temperature (see Note 1)	KC and KD packages	7.5	7.5	W
	LA package	5	5	
Operating free-air, case, or virtual junction temperature range		−55 to 150	0 to 150	°C
Storage temperature range		−65 to 150	−65 to 150	°C
Lead temperature 1/16 inch from case for 10 seconds	KC and KD packages		260	°C
Lead temperature 1/16 inch from case for 60 seconds	LA package	300	300	°C

NOTE 1: For operation above 25°C free-air or case temperature, refer to Dissipation Derating Curves, Figures 1 through 4, page 188.

recommended operating conditions

		MIN	MAX	UNIT
Input voltage, V_I	uA78M05M, uA78M05C	7	25	V
	uA78M06M, uA78M06C	8	25	
	uA78M08M, uA78M08C	10.5	25	
	uA78M12M, uA78M12C	14.5	30	
	uA78M15M, uA78M15C	17.5	30	
	uA78M20M, uA78M20C	23	35	
	uA78M22M, uA78M22C	24	38	
	uA78M24M, uA78M24C	27	38	
Output current, I_O			500	mA
Operating virtual junction temperature, T_J	uA78M05M thru uA78M24M	−55	150	°C
	uA78M05C thru uA78M24C	0	125	

TEXAS INSTRUMENTS
INCORPORATED
POST OFFICE BOX 5012 • DALLAS, TEXAS 75222

uA78M05M, uA78M05C electrical characteristics at specified virtual junction temperature, V_I = 10 V, I_O = 350 mA (unless otherwise noted)

PARAMETER	TEST CONDITIONS†		uA78M05M MIN	TYP	MAX	uA78M05C MIN	TYP	MAX	UNIT
Output voltage	I_O = 5 mA to 350 mA	25°C	4.8	5	5.2	4.8	5	5.2	V
	V_I = 8 V to 20 V	−55°C to 150°C	4.7		5.3				
	V_I = 7 V to 20 V / 0°C to 125°C					4.75		5.25	
Input regulation	V_I = 7 V to 25 V, I_O = 200 mA	25°C		3	50		3	100	mV
	V_I = 8 V to 20 V / V_I = 8 V to 25 V	25°C		1	25		1	50	
Ripple rejection	V_I = 8 V to 18 V, I_O = 100 mA, f = 120 Hz	−55°C to 150°C / 0°C to 125°C	62			62			dB
	I_O = 300 mA	25°C	62	80		62	80		
Output regulation	I_O = 5 mA to 500 mA	25°C		20	50		20	100	mV
	I_O = 5 mA to 200 mA			10	25		10	50	
Temperature coefficient of output voltage	I_O = 5 mA	−55°C to 150°C / 0°C to 125°C		−1			−1		mV/°C
Output noise voltage	f = 10 Hz to 100 kHz	25°C		40			40		µV
Dropout voltage		25°C		2			2		V
Bias current		25°C		4.5	6		4.5	6	mA
Bias current change	I_O = 200 mA, V_I = 8 V to 25 V	0°C to 125°C			0.8			0.8	mA
	I_O = 5 mA to 350 mA	−55°C to 150°C / 0°C to 125°C			0.5			0.5	
Short-circuit output current	V_I = 35 V	25°C		300			300		mA
Peak output current		25°C		700			700		A

†All characteristics are measured with a capacitor across the input of 0.33 µF and a capacitor across the output of 0.1 µF. All characteristics except noise voltage and ripple rejection ratio are measured using pulse techniques (t_W ≤ 10 ms, duty cycle ≤ 5%). Output voltage changes due to changes in internal temperature must be taken into account separately.

TEXAS INSTRUMENTS
INCORPORATED
POST OFFICE BOX 5012 • DALLAS, TEXAS 75222

TYPES uA78M06M, uA78M06C
POSITIVE-VOLTAGE REGULATORS

uA78M06M, uA78M06C electrical characteristics at specified virtual junction temperature, V_I = 11 V, I_O = 350 mA (unless otherwise noted)

PARAMETER	TEST CONDITIONS[†]		uA78M06M			uA78M06C			UNIT
			MIN	TYP	MAX	MIN	TYP	MAX	
Output voltage	I_O = 5 mA to 350 mA	25°C	5.75	6	6.25	5.75	6	6.25	V
	V_I = 9 V to 21 V (M), V_I = 8 V to 21 V (C)	−55°C to 150°C (M), 0°C to 125°C (C)	5.7		6.3	5.7		6.3	
Input regulation	I_O = 200 mA, V_I = 8 V to 25 V	25°C		5	60		5	100	mV
	V_I = 9 V to 20 V	25°C		1.5	30		1.5	50	
Ripple rejection	V_I = 9 V to 19 V, f = 120 Hz, I_O = 100 mA	−55°C to 150°C (M), 0°C to 125°C (C)	59			59			dB
	I_O = 300 mA	25°C	59	80		59	80		
Output regulation	I_O = 5 mA to 500 mA	25°C		20	60		20	120	mV
	I_O = 5 mA to 200 mA	25°C		10	30		10	60	
Temperature coefficient of output voltage	I_O = 5 mA	−55°C to 150°C (M), 0°C to 125°C (C)		−0.5			−0.5		mV/°C
Output noise voltage	f = 10 Hz to 100 kHz	25°C		45			45		µV
Dropout voltage		25°C		2			2		V
Bias current		25°C		4.5	6		4.5	6	mA
Bias current change	I_O = 200 mA, V_I = 9 V to 25 V	−55°C to 150°C (M), 0°C to 125°C (C)			0.8			0.8	mA
	I_O = 5 mA to 350 mA	−55°C to 150°C (M), 0°C to 125°C (C)			0.5			0.5	
Short-circuit output current	V_I = 35 V	25°C		270			270		mA
Peak output current		25°C		700			700		A

†All characteristics are measured with a capacitor across the input of 0.33 µF and a capacitor across the output of 0.1 µF. All characteristics except noise voltage and ripple rejection ratio are measured using pulse techniques ($t_w \leq$ 10 ms, duty cycle $\leq$ 5%). Output voltage changes due to changes in internal temperature must be taken into account separately.

TEXAS INSTRUMENTS
INCORPORATED
POST OFFICE BOX 5012 • DALLAS, TEXAS 75222

uA78M08M, uA78M08C electrical characteristics at specified virtual junction temperature, V_I = 14 V, I_O = 350 mA (unless otherwise noted)

PARAMETER	TEST CONDITIONS†	uA78M08M MIN	TYP	MAX	uA78M08C MIN	TYP	MAX	UNIT
Output voltage	I_O = 5 mA to 350 mA, V_I = 11.5 V to 23 V, 25°C	7.7	8	8.3	7.7	8	8.3	V
	V_I = 10.5 V to 23 V, −55°C to 150°C	7.6		8.4				
	V_I = 10.5 V to 25 V, 0°C to 125°C				7.6		8.4	
Input regulation	I_O = 200 mA, V_I = 11 V to 20 V, 25°C		6	60		6	100	mV
	V_I = 11 V to 25 V, 25°C		2	30		2	50	
Ripple rejection	V_I = 11.5 V to 21.5 V, I_O = 100 mA, f = 120 Hz, −55°C to 150°C	56						dB
	0°C to 125°C				56			
	I_O = 300 mA, 25°C	56	80		56	80		
Output regulation	I_O = 5 mA to 500 mA, 25°C		25	80		25	160	mV
	I_O = 5 mA to 200 mA, 25°C		10	40		10	80	
Temperature coefficient of output voltage	I_O = 5 mA, −55°C to 150°C		−0.5					mV/°C
	I_O = 5 mA, 0°C to 125°C					−0.5		
Output noise voltage	f = 10 Hz to 100 kHz, 25°C		52			52		µV
Dropout voltage	25°C		2			2		V
Bias current	25°C		4.6	6		4.6	6	mA
Bias current change	I_O = 200 mA, V_I = 11.5 V to 25 V, −55°C to 150°C			0.8				mA
	V_I = 10.5 V to 25 V, 0°C to 125°C						0.8	
	I_O = 5 mA to 350 mA, −55°C to 150°C			0.5				
	0°C to 125°C						0.5	
Short-circuit output current	V_I = 35 V, 25°C		250			250		mA
Peak output current	25°C		700			700		A

† All characteristics are measured with a capacitor across the input of 0.33 µF and a capacitor across the output of 0.1 µF. All characteristics except noise voltage and ripple rejection ratio are measured using pulse techniques (t_w ≤ 10 ms, duty cycle ≤ 5%). Output voltage changes due to changes in internal temperature must be taken into account separately.

uA78M12M, uA78M12C electrical characteristics at specified virtual junction temperature, V_I = 19 V, I_O = 350 mA (unless otherwise noted)

PARAMETER	TEST CONDITIONS†			uA78M12M			uA78M12C			UNIT
				MIN	TYP	MAX	MIN	TYP	MAX	
Output voltage	I_O = 5 mA to 350 mA	V_I = 15.5 V to 27 V	25°C	11.5	12	12.5	11.5	12	12.5	V
		V_I = 14.5 V to 27 V	−55°C to 150°C	11.4		12.6				
		V_I = 14.5 V to 27 V	0°C to 125°C				11.4		12.6	
Input regulation	I_O = 200 mA	V_I = 16 V to 25 V	25°C		8	60		8	100	mV
		V_I = 16 V to 30 V			2	30		2	50	
Ripple rejection	V_I = 15 V to 25 V, f = 120 Hz	I_O = 100 mA	−55°C to 150°C	55						dB
			0°C to 125°C				55			
		I_O = 300 mA	25°C	55	80		55	80		
Output regulation	I_O = 5 mA to 500 mA		25°C		25	120		25	240	mV
	I_O = 5 mA to 200 mA				10	60		10	120	
Temperature coefficient of output voltage	I_O = 5 mA		−55°C to 150°C		−1					mV/°C
			0°C to 125°C					−1		
Output noise voltage	f = 10 Hz to 100 kHz		25°C		75			75		µV
Dropout voltage	I_O = 200 mA		25°C		2			2		V
Bias current			25°C		4.8	6		4.8	6	mA
Bias current change	I_O = 200 mA	V_I = 15 V to 30 V	−55°C to 150°C			0.8				mA
		V_I = 14.5 V to 30 V	0°C to 125°C						0.8	
	I_O = 5 mA to 350 mA		−55°C to 150°C			0.5				
			0°C to 125°C						0.5	
Short-circuit output current	V_I = 35 V		25°C		240			240		mA
Peak output current			25°C		700			700		A

†All characteristics are measured with a capacitor across the input of 0.33 µF and a capacitor across the output of 0.1 µF. All characteristics except noise voltage and ripple rejection ratio are measured using pulse techniques (t_w ≤ 10 ms, duty cycle ≤ 5%). Output voltage changes due to changes in internal temperature must be taken into account separately.

uA78M15M, uA78M15C electrical characteristics at specified virtual junction temperature, V_I = 23 V, I_O = 350 mA (unless otherwise noted)

PARAMETER	TEST CONDITIONS†		uA78M15M			uA78M15C			UNIT
			MIN	TYP	MAX	MIN	TYP	MAX	
Output voltage		25°C	14.4	15	15.6	14.4	15	15.6	V
	I_O = 5 mA to 350 mA	V_I = 18.5 V to 30 V (−55°C to 150°C) / V_I = 17.5 V to 30 V (0°C to 125°C)	14.25		15.75	14.25		15.75	
Input regulation	I_O = 200 mA	V_I = 17.5 V to 30 V, 25°C		10	60		10	100	mV
	I_O = 200 mA	V_I = 20 V to 30 V, 25°C		3	30		3	50	
Ripple rejection	V_I = 18.5 V to 28.5 V, I_O = 100 mA, f = 120 Hz	−55°C to 150°C / 0°C to 125°C	54			54			dB
Output regulation	I_O = 5 mA to 500 mA	25°C		25	150		25	300	mV
	I_O = 5 mA to 200 mA	25°C		10	75		10	150	
Temperature coefficient of output voltage	I_O = 5 mA	−55°C to 150°C / 0°C to 125°C		−1			−1		mV/°C
Output noise voltage	f = 10 Hz to 100 kHz	25°C		90			90		µV
Dropout voltage		25°C		2			2		V
Bias current		25°C		4.8	6		4.8	6	mA
Bias current change	I_O = 200 mA	V_I = 18.5 V to 30 V (−55°C to 150°C) / V_I = 17.5 V to 30 V (0°C to 125°C)			0.8			0.8	mA
	I_O = 5 mA to 350 mA	−55°C to 150°C / 0°C to 125°C			0.5			0.5	
Short-circuit output current	V_I = 35 V	25°C		240			240		mA
Peak output current		25°C		700			700		A

† All characteristics are measured with a capacitor across the input of 0.33 µF and a capacitor across the output of 0.1 µF. All characteristics except noise voltage and ripple rejection ratio are measured using pulse techniques ($t_w \leqslant$ 10 ms, duty cycle $\leqslant$ 5%). Output voltage changes due to changes in internal temperature must be taken into account separately.

TEXAS INSTRUMENTS
INCORPORATED
POST OFFICE BOX 5012 • DALLAS, TEXAS 75222

uA78M20M, uA78M20C electrical characteristics at specified virtual junction temperature,
$V_I = 29$ V, $I_O = 350$ mA (unless otherwise noted)

PARAMETER	TEST CONDITIONS†			uA78M20M			uA78M20C			UNIT
				MIN	TYP	MAX	MIN	TYP	MAX	
Output voltage	$I_O = 5$ mA to 350 mA		25°C	19.2	20	20.8	19.2	20	20.8	V
		$V_I = 24$ V to 35 V	–55°C to 150°C	19		21				
		$V_I = 23$ V to 35 V	0°C to 125°C				19		21	
Input regulation	$I_O = 200$ mA	$V_I = 23$ V to 35 V	25°C		10	60		10	100	mV
		$V_I = 24$ V to 35 V			5	30		5	50	
Ripple rejection	$I_O = 100$ mA, f = 120 Hz		–55°C to 150°C / 0°C to 125°C	53			53			dB
	$I_O = 300$ mA		25°C	53	70		53	70		
Output regulation	$I_O = 5$ mA to 500 mA		25°C		30	200		30	400	mV
	$I_O = 5$ mA to 200 mA				10	100		10	200	
Temperature coefficient of output voltage	$I_O = 5$ mA		–55°C to 150°C / 0°C to 125°C		–1.1			–1.1		mV/°C
Output noise voltage	f = 10 Hz to 100 kHz		25°C		110			110		µV
Dropout voltage	$I_O = 200$ mA		25°C		2			2		V
Bias current			25°C		4.9	6		4.9	6	mA
Bias current change	$I_O = 200$ mA	$V_I = 24$ V to 35 V / $V_I = 23$ V to 35 V	–55°C to 150°C / 0°C to 125°C			0.8			0.8	mA
	$I_O = 5$ mA to 350 mA		–55°C to 150°C / 0°C to 125°C			0.5			0.5	
Short-circuit output current	$V_I = 35$ V		25°C		240			240		mA
Peak output current			25°C		700			700		A

†All characteristics are measured with a capacitor across the input of 0.33 µF and a capacitor across the output of 0.1 µF. All characteristics except noise voltage and ripple rejection ratio are measured using pulse techniques ($t_w \leq 10$ ms, duty cycle $\leq 5\%$). Output voltage changes due to changes in internal temperature must be taken into account separately.

uA78M22M, uA78M22C electrical characteristics at specified virtual junction temperature, $V_I = 31$ V, $I_O = 350$ mA (unless otherwise noted)

PARAMETER	TEST CONDITIONS[†]		uA78M22M			uA78M22C			UNIT
			MIN	TYP	MAX	MIN	TYP	MAX	
Output voltage	$V_I = 26$ V to 36 V	25°C	21.1	22	22.9	21.1	22	22.9	V
	$V_I = 25$ V to 36 V	−55°C to 150°C / 0°C to 125°C	20.9		23.1	20.9		23.1	
Input regulation	$V_I = 25$ V to 36 V	25°C		10	60		10	100	mV
$I_O = 200$ mA	$V_I = 26$ V to 34 V			5	30		5	50	
Ripple rejection	$V_I = 26$ V to 36 V, f = 120 Hz, $I_O = 100$ mA	−55°C to 150°C / 0°C to 125°C	51			51			dB
	$I_O = 300$ mA	25°C	51	70		51	70		
Output regulation	$I_O = 5$ mA to 500 mA	25°C		30	220		30	440	mV
	$I_O = 5$ mA to 200 mA	25°C		10	110		10	220	
Temperature coefficient of output voltage	$I_O = 5$ mA	−55°C to 150°C / 0°C to 125°C		−1.1			−1.1		mV/°C
Output noise voltage	f = 10 Hz to 100 kHz	25°C		160			160		μV
Dropout voltage		25°C		2			2		V
Bias current		25°C		4.9	6		4.9	6	mA
Bias current change	$I_O = 200$ mA $V_I = 26$ V to 36 V	−55°C to 150°C / 0°C to 125°C			0.8			0.8	mA
	$V_I = 25$ V to 36 V									
	$I_O = 5$ mA to 350 mA	−55°C to 150°C / 0°C to 125°C			0.5			0.5	
Short-circuit output current	$V_I = 35$ V	25°C		240			240		mA
Peak output current		25°C		700			700		A

[†] All characteristics are measured with a capacitor across the input of 0.33 μF and a capacitor across the output of 0.1 μF. All characteristics except noise voltage and ripple rejection ratio are measured using pulse techniques ($t_w \leqslant 10$ ms, duty cycle $\leqslant 5\%$). Output voltage changes due to changes in internal temperature must be taken into account separately.

uA78M24M, uA78M24C electrical characteristics at specified virtual junction temperature, V_I = 33 V, I_O = 350 mA (unless otherwise noted)

PARAMETER	TEST CONDITIONS†	uA78M24M			uA78M24C			UNIT
		MIN	TYP	MAX	MIN	TYP	MAX	
Output voltage	I_O = 5 mA to 350 mA, V_I = 28 V to 38 V, 25°C	23	24	25	23	24	25	V
	V_I = 27 V to 38 V, −55°C to 150°C, 0°C to 125°C	22.8		25.2	22.8		25.2	
Input regulation	I_O = 200 mA, V_I = 27 V to 38 V, 25°C		10	60		10	100	mV
	V_I = 30 V to 36 V, 25°C		5	30		5	50	
Ripple rejection	I_O = 100 mA, V_I = 28 V to 38 V, f = 120 Hz, −55°C to 150°C, 0°C to 125°C	50			50			dB
	I_O = 300 mA, 25°C	50	70		50	70		
Output regulation	I_O = 5 mA to 500 mA, 25°C		30	240		30	480	mV
	I_O = 5 mA to 200 mA, 25°C		10	120		10	240	
Temperature coefficient of output voltage	I_O = 5 mA, −55°C to 150°C, 0°C to 125°C		−1.2			−1.2		mV/°C
Output noise voltage	f = 10 Hz to 100 kHz, 25°C		170			170		µV
Dropout voltage	25°C		2			2		V
Bias current	25°C		5	6		5	6	mA
Bias current change	I_O = 200 mA, V_I = 28 V to 38 V, V_I = 27 V to 38 V, −55°C to 150°C, 0°C to 125°C			0.8			0.8	mA
	I_O = 5 mA to 350 mA, −55°C to 150°C, 0°C to 125°C			0.5			0.5	
Short-circuit output current	V_I = 35 V, 25°C		240			240		mA
Peak output current	25°C		700			700		A

†All characteristics are measured with a capacitor across the input of 0.33 µF and a capacitor across the output of 0.1 µF. All characteristics except noise voltage and ripple rejection ratio are measured using pulse techniques ($t_w \leqslant$ 10 ms, duty cycle $\leqslant$ 5%). Output voltage changes due to changes in internal temperature must be taken into account separately.

TEXAS INSTRUMENTS
INCORPORATED
POST OFFICE BOX 5012 • DALLAS, TEXAS 75222

LINEAR
INTEGRATED CIRCUITS

SERIES uA7900
NEGATIVE-VOLTAGE REGULATORS

BULLETIN NO. DL-S 12404, JUNE 1976–REVISED SEPTEMBER 1977

- 3-Terminal Regulators
- Output Current up to 1.5 A
- No External Components
- Internal Thermal Overload Protection
- Direct Replacements for Fairchild μA7900 Series
- Essentially Equivalent to National LM320 Series
- High Power Dissipation Capability
- Internal Short-Circuit Current Limiting
- Output Transistor Safe-Area Compensation

NOMINAL OUTPUT VOLTAGE	REGULATOR
–5 V	uA7905C
–5.2 V	uA7952C
–6 V	uA7906C
–8 V	uA7908C
–12 V	uA7912C
–15 V	uA7915C
–18 V	uA7918C
–24 V	uA7924C

description

This series of fixed-negative-voltage monolithic integrated-circuit voltage regulators is designed to complement Series uA7800 in a wide range of applications. These applications include on-card regulation for elimination of noise and distribution problems associated with single-point regulation. One of these regulators can deliver up to 1.5 amperes of output current. The internal current limiting and thermal shutdown features of these regulators make them essentially immune to overload. In addition to use as fixed-voltage regulators, these devices can be used with external components to obtain adjustable output voltages and currents and also as the power pass element in precision regulators.

KC PACKAGE
(TOP VIEW)

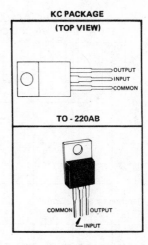

OUTPUT
INPUT
COMMON

TO - 220AB

COMMON   OUTPUT
INPUT

schematic

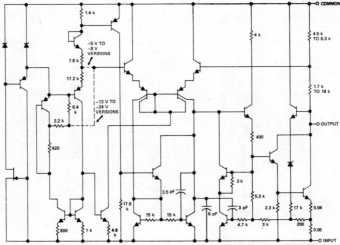

Resistor values shown are nominal and in ohms.

TEXAS INSTRUMENTS
INCORPORATED
POST OFFICE BOX 5012 • DALLAS, TEXAS 75222

absolute maximum ratings over operating temperature range (unless otherwise noted)

		uA7905C THRU uA7924C	UNIT
Input voltage	uA7924C	−40	V
	All others	−35	
Continuous total dissipation at 25°C free-air temperature (see Note 1)		2	W
Continuous total dissipation at (or below) 25°C case temperature (see Note 1)		15	W
Operating free-air, case, or virtual junction temperature range		0 to 150	°C
Storage temperature range		−65 to 150	°C
Lead temperature 1/8 inch from case for 10 seconds		260	°C

NOTE 1: For operation above 25°C free-air or case temperature, refer to Dissipation Derating Curves, Figure 1 and Figure 2.

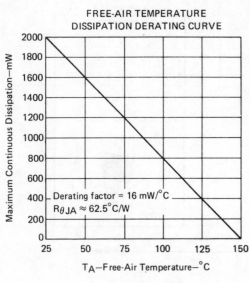

FREE-AIR TEMPERATURE
DISSIPATION DERATING CURVE

Derating factor = 16 mW/°C
$R_{\theta}JA \approx 62.5°C/W$

T_A−Free-Air Temperature−°C

FIGURE 1

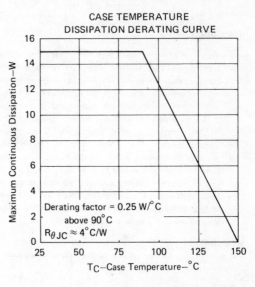

CASE TEMPERATURE
DISSIPATION DERATING CURVE

Derating factor = 0.25 W/°C
above 90°C
$R_{\theta}JC \approx 4°C/W$

T_C−Case Temperature−°C

FIGURE 2

recommended operating conditions

		MIN	MAX	UNIT
Input voltage, V_I	uA7905C	−7	−25	V
	uA7952C	−7.2	−25	
	uA7906C	−8	−25	
	uA7908C	−10.5	−25	
	uA7912C	−14.5	−30	
	uA7915C	−17.5	−30	
	uA7918C	−21	−33	
	uA7924C	−27	−38	
Output current, I_O			1.5	A
Operating virtual junction temperature, T_J		0	125	°C

uA7905C electrical characteristics at specified virtual junction temperature, $V_I = -10$ V, $I_O = 500$ mA (unless otherwise noted)

PARAMETER	TEST CONDITIONS†		uA7905C			UNIT
			MIN	TYP	MAX	
Output voltage	$I_O = 5$ mA to 1 A, $V_I = -7$ V to -20 V, P ≤ 15 W	25°C	−4.8	−5	−5.2	V
		0°C to 125°C	−4.75		−5.25	
Input regulation	$V_I = -7$ V to -25 V	25°C		3	100	mV
	$V_I = -8$ V to -12 V			1	50	
Ripple rejection	$V_I = -8$ V to -18 V, f = 120 Hz	0°C to 125°C	54	60		dB
Output regulation	$I_O = 5$ mA to 1.5 A	25°C		15	100	mV
	$I_O = 250$ mA to 750 mA			5	50	
Temperature coefficient of output voltage	$I_O = 5$ mA	0°C to 125°C		−0.4		mV/°C
Output noise voltage	f = 10 Hz to 100 kHz	25°C		125		μV
Dropout voltage	$I_O = 1$ A	25°C		1.1		V
Bias current		25°C		1	2	mA
Bias current change	$V_I = -7$ V to -25 V	0°C to 125°C			1.3	mA
	$I_O = 5$ mA to 1 A				0.5	
Peak output current		25°C		2.1		A

uA7952C electrical characteristics at specified virtual junction temperature, $V_I = -10$ V, $I_O = 500$ mA (unless otherwise noted)

PARAMETER	TEST CONDITIONS†		uA7952C			UNIT
			MIN	TYP	MAX	
Output voltage	$I_O = 5$ mA to 1 A, $V_I = -7.2$ V to -20 V, P ≤ 15 W	25°C	−5	−5.2	−5.4	V
		0°C to 125°C	−4.95		−5.45	
Input regulation	$V_I = -7.2$ V to -25 V	25°C		3	100	mV
	$V_I = -8.2$ V to -12 V			1	50	
Ripple rejection	$V_I = -8.2$ V to -18 V, f = 120 Hz	0°C to 125°C	54	60		dB
Output regulation	$I_O = 5$ mA to 1.5 A	25°C		15	100	mV
	$I_O = 250$ mA to 750 mA			5	50	
Temperature coefficient of output voltage	$I_O = 5$ mA	0°C to 125°C		−0.4		mV/°C
Output noise voltage	f = 10 Hz to 100 kHz	25°C		125		μV
Dropout voltage	$I_O = 1$ A	25°C		1.1		V
Bias current		25°C		1	2	mA
Bias current change	$V_I = -7.2$ V to -25 V	0°C to 125°C			1.3	mA
	$I_O = 5$ mA to 1 A				0.5	
Peak output current		25°C		2.1		A

†All characteristics are measured with a capacitor across the input of 0.33 μF and a capacitor across the output of 0.1 μF. All characteristics except noise voltage and ripple rejection ratio are measured using pulse techniques (t_w ≤ 10 ms, duty cycle ≤ 5%). Output voltage changes due to changes in internal temperature must be taken into account separately.

TEXAS INSTRUMENTS
INCORPORATED
POST OFFICE BOX 5012 • DALLAS, TEXAS 75222

uA7906C electrical characteristics at specified virtual junction temperature, $V_I = -11$ V, $I_O = 500$ mA (unless otherwise noted)

PARAMETER	TEST CONDITIONS[†]		uA7906C			UNIT
			MIN	TYP	MAX	
Output voltage	$I_O = 5$ mA to 1 A, $V_I = -8$ V to -21 V, P ⩽ 15 W	25°C	−5.75	−6	−6.25	V
		0°C to 125°C	−5.7		−6.3	
Input regulation	$V_I = -8$ V to -25 V	25°C		5	120	mV
	$V_I = -9$ V to -13 V			1.5	60	
Ripple rejection	$V_I = -9$ V to -19 V, f = 120 Hz	0°C to 125°C	54	60		dB
Output regulation	$I_O = 5$ mA to 1.5 A	25°C		14	120	mV
	$I_O = 250$ mA to 750 mA			4	60	
Temperature coefficient of output voltage	$I_O = 5$ mA	0°C to 125°C		−0.4		mV/°C
Output noise voltage	f = 10 Hz to 100 kHz	25°C		150		µV
Dropout voltage	$I_O = 1$ A	25°C		1.1		V
Bias current		25°C		1	2	mA
Bias current change	$V_I = -8$ V to -25 V	0°C to 125°C			1.3	mA
	$I_O = 5$ mA to 1 A				0.5	
Peak output current		25°C		2.1		A

uA7908C electrical characteristics at specified virtual junction temperature, $V_I = -14$ V, $I_O = 500$ mA (unless otherwise noted)

PARAMETER	TEST CONDITIONS[†]		uA7908C			UNIT
			MIN	TYP	MAX	
Output voltage	$I_O = 5$ mA to 1 A, $V_I = -10.5$ V to -23 V, P ⩽ 15 W	25°C	−7.7	−8	−8.3	V
		0°C to 125°C	−7.6		−8.4	
Input regulation	$V_I = -10.5$ V to -25 V	25°C		6	160	mV
	$V_I = -11$ V to -17 V			2	80	
Ripple rejection	$V_I = -11.5$ V to -21.5 V, f = 120Hz	0°C to 125°C	54	60		dB
Output regulation	$I_O = 5$ mA to 1.5 A	25°C		12	160	mV
	$I_O = 250$ mA to 750 mA			4	80	
Temperature coefficient of output voltage	$I_O = 5$ mA	0°C to 125°C		−0.6		mV/°C
Output noise voltage	f = 10 Hz to 100 kHz	25°C		200		µV
Dropout voltage	$I_O = 1$ A	25°C		1.1		V
Bias current		25°C		1	2	mA
Bias current change	$V_I = -10.5$ V to -25 V	0°C to 125°C			1	mA
	$I_O = 5$ mA to 1 A				0.5	
Peak output current		25°C		2.1		A

[†]All characteristics are measured with a capacitor across the input of 0.33 µF and a capacitor across the output of 0.1 µF. All characteristics except noise voltage and ripple rejection ratio are measured using pulse techniques (t_w ⩽ 10 ms, duty cycle ⩽ 5%). Output voltage changes due to changes in internal temperature must be taken into account separately.

uA7912C electrical characteristics at specified virtual junction temperature, $V_I = -19$ V, $I_O = 500$ mA (unless otherwise noted)

PARAMETER	TEST CONDITIONS†		uA7912C			UNIT
			MIN	TYP	MAX	
Output voltage	$I_O = 5$ mA to 1 A, $V_I = -14.5$ V to -27 V, P ⩽ 15 W	25°C	−11.5	−12	−12.5	V
		0°C to 125°C	−11.4		−12.6	
Input regulation	$V_I = -14.5$ V to -30 V	25°C		10	240	mV
	$V_I = -16$ V to -22 V			3	120	
Ripple rejection	$V_I = -15$ V to -25 V, f = 120 Hz	0°C to 125°C	54	60		dB
Output regulation	$I_O = 5$ mA to 1.5 A	25°C		12	240	mV
	$I_O = 250$ mA to 750 mA			4	120	
Temperature coefficient of output voltage	$I_O = 5$ mA	0°C to 125°C		−0.8		mV/°C
Output noise voltage	f = 10 Hz to 100 kHz	25°C		300		µV
Dropout voltage	$I_O = 1$ A	25°C		1.1		V
Bias current		25°C		1.5	3	mA
Bias current change	$V_I = -14.5$ V to -30 V	0°C to 125°C			1	mA
	$I_O = 5$ mA to 1 A				0.5	
Peak output current		25°C		2.1		A

uA7915C electrical characteristics at specified virtual junction temperature, $V_I = -23$ V, $I_O = 500$ mA (unless otherwise noted)

PARAMETER	TEST CONDITIONS†		uA7915C			UNIT
			MIN	TYP	MAX	
Output voltage	$I_O = 5$ mA to 1 A, $V_I = -17.5$ V to -30 V, P ⩽ 15 W	25°C	−14.4	−15	−15.6	V
		0°C to 125°C	−14.25		−15.75	
Input regulation	$V_I = -17.5$ V to -30 V	25°C		11	300	mV
	$V_I = -20$ V to -26 V			3	150	
Ripple rejection	$V_I = -18.5$ V to -28.5 V, f = 120 Hz	0°C to 125°C	54	60		dB
Output regulation	$I_O = 5$ mA to 1.5 A	25°C		12	300	mV
	$I_O = 250$ mA to 750 mA			4	150	
Temperature coefficient of output voltage	$I_O = 5$ mA	0°C to 125°C		−1		mV/°C
Output noise voltage	f = 10 Hz to 100 kHz	25°C		375		µV
Dropout voltage	$I_O = 1$ A	25°C		1.1		V
Bias current		25°C		1.5	3	mA
Bias current change	$V_I = -17.5$ V to -30 V	0°C to 125°C			1	mA
	$I_O = 5$ mA to 1 A				0.5	
Peak output current		25°C		2.1		A

†All characteristics are measured with a capacitor across the input of 0.33 µF and a capacitor across the output of 0.1 µF. All characteristics except noise voltage and ripple rejection ratio are measured using pulse techniques (t_W ⩽ 10 ms, duty cycle ⩽ 5%). Output voltage changes due to changes in internal temperature must be taken into account separately.

TEXAS INSTRUMENTS
INCORPORATED
POST OFFICE BOX 5012 • DALLAS, TEXAS 75222

TYPES uA7918C, uA7924C
NEGATIVE-VOLTAGE REGULATORS

uA7918C electrical characteristics at specified virtual junction temperature,
$V_I = -27$ V, $I_O = 500$ mA (unless otherwise noted)

PARAMETER	TEST CONDITIONS†		uA7918C			UNIT
			MIN	TYP	MAX	
Output voltage	$I_O = 5$ mA to 1 A, $V_I = -21$ V to -33 V, P ≤ 15 W	25°C	-17.3	-18	-18.7	V
		0°C to 125°C	-17.1		-18.9	
Input regulation	$V_I = -21$ V to -33 V	25°C		15	360	mV
	$V_I = -24$ V to -30 V			5	180	
Ripple rejection	$V_I = -22$ V to -32 V, f = 120 Hz	0°C to 125°C	54	60		dB
Output regulation	$I_O = 5$ mA to 1.5 A	25°C		12	360	mV
	$I_O = 250$ mA to 750 mA			4	180	
Temperature coefficient of output voltage	$I_O = 5$ mA	0°C to 125°C		-1		mV/°C
Output noise voltage	f = 10 Hz to 100 kHz	25°C		450		µV
Dropout voltage	$I_O = 1$ A	25°C		1.1		V
Bias current		25°C		1.5	3	mA
Bias current change	$V_I = -21$ V to -33 V	0°C to 125°C			1	mA
	$I_O = 5$ mA to 1 A				0.5	
Peak output current		25°C		2.1		A

uA7924C electrical characteristics at specified virtual junction temperature,
$V_I = -33$ V, $I_O = 500$ mA (unless otherwise noted)

PARAMETER	TEST CONDITIONS†		uA7924C			UNIT
			MIN	TYP	MAX	
Output voltage	$I_O = 5$ mA to 1 A, $V_I = -27$ V to -38 V, P ≤ 15 W	25°C	-23	-24	-25	V
		0°C to 125°C	-22.8		-25.2	
Input regulation	$V_I = -27$ V to -38 V	25°C		18	480	mV
	$V_I = -30$ V to -36 V			6	240	
Ripple rejection	$V_I = -28$ V to -38 V, f = 120 Hz	0°C to 125°C	54	60		dB
Output regulation	$I_O = 5$ mA to 1.5 A	25°C		12	480	mV
	$I_O = 250$ mA to 750 mA			4	240	
Temperature coefficient of output voltage	$I_O = 5$ mA	0°C to 125°C		-1		mV/°C
Output noise voltage	f = 10 Hz to 100 kHz	25°C		600		µV
Dropout voltage	$I_O = 1$ A	25°C		1.1		V
Bias current		25°C		1.5	3	mA
Bias current change	$V_I = -27$ V to -38 V	0°C to 125°C			1	mA
	$I_O = 5$ mA to 1 A				0.5	
Peak output current		25°C		2.1		A

†All characteristics are measured with a capacitor across the input of 0.33 µF and a capacitor across the output of 0.1 µF. All characteristics except noise voltage and ripple rejection ratio are measured using pulse techniques (t_W ≤ 10 ms, duty cycle ≤ 5%). Output voltage changes due to changes in internal temperature must be taken into account separately.

TEXAS INSTRUMENTS
INCORPORATED
POST OFFICE BOX 5012 • DALLAS, TEXAS 75222

LINEAR INTEGRATED CIRCUITS

SERIES uA79M00
NEGATIVE-VOLTAGE REGULATORS

BULLETIN NO. DL-S 12405, JUNE 1976–REVISED SEPTEMBER 1977

- 3-Terminal Regulators
- Output Current up to 500 mA
- No External Components
- Direct Replacements for Fairchild μA79M00 Series
- High Power Dissipation Capability
- Internal Short-Circuit Current Limiting
- Output Transistor Safe-Area Compensation

NOMINAL OUTPUT VOLTAGE	−55°C TO 150°C OPERATING TEMPERATURE RANGE	0°C TO 125°C OPERATING TEMPERATURE RANGE
−5 V	uA79M05M	uA79M05C
−6 V	uA79M06M	uA79M06C
−8 V	uA79M08M	uA79M08C
−12 V	uA79M12M	uA79M12C
−15 V	uA79M15M	uA79M15C
−20 V	uA79M20M	uA79M20C
−24 V	uA79M24M	uA79M24C
PACKAGES	LA	KC, KD, and LA

description

This series of fixed-negative-voltage monolithic integrated-circuit voltage regulators is designed to complement Series uA78M00 in a wide range of applications. These applications include on-card regulation for elimination of noise and distribution problems associated with single-point regulation. One of these regulators can deliver up to 500 milliamperes of output current. The internal current limiting and thermal shutdown features of these regulators make them essentially immune to overload. In addition to use as fixed-voltage regulators, these devices can be used with external components to obtain adjustable output voltages and currents and also as the power pass element in precision regulators.

schematic

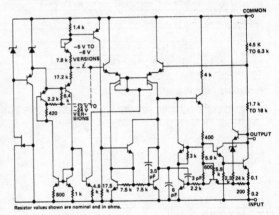

Resistor values shown are nominal and in ohms.

terminal assignments

KC PACKAGE (TOP VIEW)	KD PACKAGE (TOP VIEW)	LA PACKAGE (TOP VIEW)
OUTPUT / INPUT / COMMON TO-220AB	OUTPUT / INPUT / COMMON TO-202AB	OUTPUT / COMMON / INPUT

TEXAS INSTRUMENTS
INCORPORATED
POST OFFICE BOX 5012 • DALLAS, TEXAS 75222

absolute maximum ratings over operating temperature range (unless otherwise noted)

		uA79M05M THRU uA79M24M	uA79M05C THRU uA79M24C	UNIT
Input voltage	uA79M20, uA79M24	−40	−40	V
	All others	−35	−35	
Continuous total dissipation at 25°C free-air temperature (see Note 1)	KC (TO-220AB) package	2	2	W
	KD (TO-202AB) package	1.5	1.5	
	LA package	0.6	0.6	
Continuous total dissipation at (or below) 25°C case temperature (see Note 1)	KC and KD package	7.5	7.5	W
	LA package	5	5	
Operating free-air, case or virtual junction temperature range		−55 to 150	0 to 150	°C
Storage temperature range		−65 to 150	−65 to 150	°C
Lead temperature 1/16 inch from case for 10 seconds	KC and KD packages		260	°C
Lead temperature 1/16 inch from case for 60 seconds	LA package	300	300	°C

NOTE 1: For operation above 25°C free-air or case temperature, refer to Dissipation Derating Curves, Figures 1 through 4, page 188.

recommended operating conditions

		MIN	MAX	UNIT
Input voltage, V_I	uA79M05	−7	−25	V
	uA79M06	−8	−25	
	uA79M08	−10.5	−25	
	uA70M12	−14.5	−30	
	uA79M15	−17.5	−30	
	uA79M20	−23	−35	
	uA79M24	−27	−38	
Output current, I_O			500	mA
Operating virtual junction temperature, T_J	uA79M05M thru uA79M24M	−55	150	°C
	uA79M05C thru uA79M24C	0	125	

uA79M05M, uA79M05C electrical characteristics at specified virtual junction temperature, $V_I = -10$ V, $I_O = 350$ mA (unless otherwise noted)

PARAMETER	TEST CONDITIONS†			uA79M05M MIN	TYP	MAX	uA79M05C MIN	TYP	MAX	UNIT
Output voltage	I_O = 5 mA to 350 mA, V_I = −7 V to −25 V		25°C	−4.8	−5	−5.2	−4.8	−5	−5.2	V
			−55°C to 150°C	−4.75		−5.25				
			0°C to 125°C				−4.75		−5.25	
Input regulation	V_I = −7 V to −25 V		25°C		7	50		7	50	mV
	V_I = −8 V to −18 V		25°C		3	30		3	30	
Ripple rejection	V_I = −8 V to −18 V, f = 120 Hz	I_O = 100 mA	−55°C to 150°C	50						dB
			0°C to 125°C				50			
		I_O = 300 mA	25°C	54	60		54	60		
Output regulation	I_O = 5 mA to 500 mA		25°C		75	100		75	100	mV
	I_O = 5 mA to 350 mA				50			50		
Temperature coefficient of output voltage	I_O = 5 mA		−55°C to 150°C		−0.4					mV/°C
			0°C to 125°C					0.4		
Output noise voltage	f = 10 Hz to 100 kHz		25°C		125			125		µV
Dropout voltage			25°C		1.1			1.1		V
Bias current			25°C		1	2		1	2	mA
Bias current change	V_I = −8 V to −25 V		−55°C to 150°C			0.4				mA
			0°C to 125°C						0.4	
	I_O = 5 mA to 350 mA		−55°C to 150°C			0.4				
			0°C to 125°C						0.4	
Short circuit output current	V_I = −30 V		25°C		140			140		mA
Peak output current			25°C		650			650		A

†All characteristics are measured with a 2-µF capacitor across the input and a 1-µF capacitor across the output. All characteristics except noise voltage and ripple rejection ratio are measured using pulse techniques ($t_w \leqslant$ 10 ms, duty cycle $\leqslant$ 5%). Output voltage changes due to changes in internal temperature must be taken into account separately.

76

uA79M06M, uA79M06C electrical characteristics at specified virtual junction temperature,
  V_I = −11 V, I_O = 350 mA (unless otherwise noted)

PARAMETER	TEST CONDITIONS†			uA79M06M			uA79M06C			UNIT
				MIN	TYP	MAX	MIN	TYP	MAX	
Output voltage	I_O = 5 mA to 350 mA, V_I = −8 V to −25 V		25°C	−5.75	−6	−6.25	−5.75	−6	−6.25	V
			−55°C to 150°C	−5.7		−6.3				
			0°C to 125°C				−5.7		−6.3	
Input regulation	V_I = −8 V to −25 V		25°C		7	60		7	60	mV
	V_I = −9 V to −19 V				3	40		3	40	
Ripple rejection	V_I = −9 V to −19 V, f = 120 Hz	I_O = 100 mA	−55°C to 150°C	50						dB
			0°C to 125°C				50			
		I_O = 300 mA	25°C	54	60		54	60		
Output regulation	I_O = 5 mA to 500 mA		25°C		80	120		80	120	mV
	I_O = 5 mA to 350 mA				55			55		
Temperature coefficient of output voltage	I_O = 5 mA		−55°C to 150°C		−0.4					mV/°C
			0°C to 125°C					−0.4		
Output noise voltage	f = 10 Hz to 100 kHz		25°C		150			150		μV
Dropout voltage			25°C		1.1			1.1		V
Bias current			25°C		1	2		1	2	mA
Bias current change	V_I = −9 V to −25 V		−55°C to 150°C			0.4				mA
			0°C to 125°C						0.4	
	I_O = 5 mA to 350 mA		−55°C to 150°C			0.4				
			0°C to 125°C						0.4	
Short circuit output current	V_I = −30 V		25°C		140			140		mA
Peak output current			25°C		650			650		A

†All characteristics are measured with a 2-μF capacitor across the input and a 1-μF capacitor across the output. All characteristics except noise voltage and ripple rejection ratio are measured using pulse techniques (t_w ≤ 10 ms, duty cycle ≤ 5%). Output voltage changes due to changes in internal temperature must be taken into account separately.

TEXAS INSTRUMENTS
INCORPORATED
POST OFFICE BOX 5012 • DALLAS. TEXAS 75222

uA79M08M, uA79M08C electrical characteristics at specified virtual junction temperature,
$V_I = -19$ V, $I_O = 350$ mA (unless noted)

PARAMETER	TEST CONDITIONS†		uA79M08M MIN	TYP	MAX	uA79M08C MIN	TYP	MAX	UNIT
Output voltage	I_O = 5 mA to 350 mA, V_I = −10.5 V to −25 V	25°C	−7.7	−8	−8.3	−7.7	−8	−8.3	V
		−55°C to 150°C	−7.6		−8.4				
		0°C to 125°C				−7.6		−8.4	
Input regulation	V_I = −10.5 V to −25 V	25°C		8	80		8	80	mV
	V_I = −11 V to −21 V			4	50		4	50	
Ripple rejection	V_I = −11.5 V to −21.5 V, f = 120 Hz, I_O = 100 mA	−55°C to 150°C	50						dB
		0°C to 125°C				50			
	I_O = 300 mA	25°C	54	59		54	59		
Output regulation	I_O = 5 mA to 500 mA	25°C		90	160		90	160	mV
	I_O = 5 mA to 350 mA			60			60		
Temperature coefficient of output voltage	I_O = 5 mA	−55°C to 150°C		−0.6					mV/°C
		0°C to 125°C					−0.6		
Output noise voltage	f = 10 Hz to 100 kHz	25°C		200			200		µV
Dropout voltage		25°C		1.1			1.1		V
Bias current		25°C		1	2		1	2	mA
Bias current change	V_I = −10.5 V to −25 V	−55°C to 150°C			0.4				mA
		0°C to 125°C						0.4	
	I_O = 5 mA to 350 mA	−55°C to 150°C			0.4				
		0°C to 125°C						0.4	
Short circuit output current	V_I = −30 V	25°C		140			140		mA
Peak output current		25°C		650			650		A

† All characteristics are measured with a 2-µF capacitor across the input and a 1-µF capacitor across the output. All characteristics except noise voltage and ripple rejection ratio are measured using pulse techniques ($t_W \leqslant 10$ ms, duty cycle $\leqslant 5\%$). Output voltage changes due to changes in internal temperature must be taken into account separately.

TEXAS INSTRUMENTS
INCORPORATED
POST OFFICE BOX 5012 • DALLAS, TEXAS 75222

uA79M12M, uA79M12C electrical characteristics at specified virtual junction temperature,
V_I = −19 V, I_O = 350 mA (unless otherwise noted)

PARAMETER	TEST CONDITIONS[†]		uA79M12M			uA79M12C			UNIT
			MIN	TYP	MAX	MIN	TYP	MAX	
Output voltage		25°C	−11.5	−12	−12.5	−11.5	−12	−12.5	V
	I_O = 5 mA to 350 mA, V_I = −14.5 V to −30 V	−55°C to 150°C	−11.4		−12.6				
		0°C to 125°C				−11.4		−12.6	
Input regulation	V_I = −14.5 V to −30 V	25°C		9	80		9	80	mV
	V_I = −15 V to −25 V			5	50		5	50	
Ripple rejection	V_I = −15 V to −25 V, I_O = 100 mA f = 120 Hz	−55°C to 150°C	50						dB
		0°C to 125°C				50			
	I_O = 300 mA	25°C	54	60		54	60		
Output regulation	I_O = 5 mA to 500 mA	25°C		65	240		65	240	mV
	I_O = 5 mA to 350 mA			45			45		
Temperature coefficient of output voltage	I_O = 5 mA	−55°C to 150°C		−0.8					mV/°C
		0°C to 125°C					−0.8		
Output noise voltage	f = 10 Hz to 100 kHz	25°C		300			300		µV
Dropout voltage		25°C		1.1			1.1		V
Bias current		25°C		1.5	3		1.5	3	mA
Bias current change	V_I = −14.5 V to −30 V	−55°C to 150°C			0.4				mA
		0°C to 125°C						0.4	
	I_O = 5 mA to 350 mA	−55°C to 150°C			0.4				
		0°C to 125°C						0.4	
Short circuit output current	V_I = −30 V	25°C		140			140		mA
Peak output current		25°C		650			650		A

[†]All characteristics are measured with a 2-µF capacitor across the input and a 1-µF capacitor across the output. All characteristics except noise voltage and ripple rejection ratio are measured using pulse techniques (t_W ⩽ 10 ms, duty cycle ⩽ 5%). Output voltage changes due to changes in internal temperature must be taken into account separately.

uA79M15M, uA79M15C electrical characteristics at specified virtual junction temperature,
$V_I = -23$ V, $I_O = 350$ mA (unless otherwise noted)

PARAMETER	TEST CONDITIONS†		uA79M15M			uA79M15C			UNIT
			MIN	TYP	MAX	MIN	TYP	MAX	
Output voltage	I_O = 5 mA to 350 mA, V_I = −17.5 V to −30 V	25°C	−14.4	−15	−15.6	−14.4	−15	−15.6	V
		−55°C to 150°C	−14.25		−15.75				
		0°C to 125°C				−14.25		−15.75	
Input regulation	V_I = −17.5 V to −30 V	25°C		9	80		9	80	mV
	V_I = −18 V to −28 V			7	50		7	50	
Ripple rejection	V_I = −18.5 V to −28.5 V, I_O = 100 mA, f = 120 Hz	−55°C to 150°C	50						dB
		0°C to 125°C				50			
	I_O = 300 mA	25°C	54	59		54	59		
Output regulation	I_O = 5 mA to 500 mA	25°C		65	240		65	240	mV
	I_O = 5 mA to 350 mA			45			45		
Temperature coefficient of output voltage	I_O = 5 mA	−55°C to 150°C		−1					mV/°C
		0°C to 125°C					−1		
Output noise voltage	f = 10 Hz to 100 kHz	25°C		375			375		μV
Dropout voltage		25°C		1.1			1.1		V
Bias current		25°C		1.5	3		1.5	3	mA
Bias current change	V_I = −17.5 V to −30 V	−55°C to 150°C			0.4				mA
		0°C to 125°C						0.4	
	I_O = 5 mA to 350 mA	−55°C to 150°C			0.4				
		0°C to 125°C						0.4	
Short circuit output current	V_I = −30 V	25°C		140			140		mA
Peak output current		25°C		650			650		A

†All characteristics are measured with a 2-μF capacitor across the input and a 1-μF capacitor across the output. All characteristics except noise voltage and ripple rejection ratio are measured using pulse techniques (t_W ≤ 10 ms, duty cycle ≤ 5%). Output voltage changes due to changes in internal temperature must be taken into account separately.

676

uA79M20M, uA79M20C electrical characteristics at specified virtual junction temperature, $V_I = -29$ V, $I_O = 350$ mA (unless otherwise noted)

PARAMETER	TEST CONDITIONS†			uA79M20M			uA79M20C			UNIT
				MIN	TYP	MAX	MIN	TYP	MAX	
Output voltage	I_O = 5 mA to 350 mA, V_I = −23 V to −35 V		25°C	−19.2	−20	−20.8	−19.2	−20	−20.8	V
			−55°C to 150°C	−19		−21				
			0°C to 125°C				−19		−21	
Input regulation	V_I = −23 V to −35 V		25°C		12	80		12	80	mV
	V_I = −24 V to −34 V				10	70		10	70	
Ripple rejection	V_I = −24 V to −34 V, f = 120 Hz	I_O = 100 mA	−55°C to 150°C	50						dB
			0°C to 125°C				50			
		I_O = 300 mA	25°C	54	58		54	58		
Output regulation	I_O = 5 mA to 500 mA		25°C		75	300		75	300	mV
	I_O = 5 mA to 350 mA				50			50		
Temperature coefficient of output voltage	I_O = 5 mA		−55°C to 150°C		−1					mV/°C
			0°C to 125°C					−1		
Output noise voltage	f = 10 Hz to 100 kHz		25°C		500			500		µV
Dropout voltage			25°C		1.1			1.1		V
Bias current			25°C		1.5	3.5		1.5	3.5	mA
Bias current change	V_I = −23 V to −35 V		−55°C to 150°C			0.4				mA
			0°C to 125°C						0.4	
	I_O = 5 mA to 350 mA		−55°C to 150°C			0.4				
			0°C to 125°C						0.4	
Short circuit output current	V_I = −30 V		25°C		140			140		mA
Peak output current			25°C		650			650		A

†All characteristics are measured with a 2-µF capacitor across the input and a 1-µF capacitor across the output. All characteristics except noise voltage and ripple rejection ratio are measured using pulse techniques ($t_w \leqslant$ 10 ms, duty cycle $\leqslant$ 5%). Output voltage changes due to changes in internal temperature must be taken into account separately.

676

uA79M24M, uA79M24C electrical characteristics at specified virtual junction temperature,
V_I = −33 V, I_O = 350 mA (unless otherwise noted)

PARAMETER	TEST CONDITIONS[†]			uA79M24M MIN	TYP	MAX	uA79M24C MIN	TYP	MAX	UNIT
Output voltage	I_O = 5 mA to 350 mA, V_I = −27 V to −38 V		25°C	−23	−24	−25	−23	−24	−25	V
			−55°C to 150°C	−22.8		−25.2				
			0°C to 125°C				−22.8		−25.2	
Input regulation	V_I = −27 V to −38 V		25°C		12	80		12	80	mV
	V_I = −28 V to −38 V				12	70		12	70	
Ripple rejection	V_I = −28 V to −38 V, f = 120 Hz	I_O = 100 mA	−55°C to 150°C	50						dB
			0°C to 125°C				50			
		I_O = 300 mA	25°C	54	58		54	58		
Output regulation	I_O = 5 mA to 500 mA		25°C		75	300		75	300	mV
	I_O = 5 mA to 350 mA				50			50		
Temperature coefficient of output voltage	I_O = 5 mA		−55°C to 150°C		−1					mV/°C
			0°C to 125°C					−1		
Output noise voltage	f = 10 Hz to 100 kHz		25°C		600			600		µV
Dropout voltage			25°C		1.1			1.1		V
Bias current			25°C		1.5	3.5		1.5	3.5	mA
Bias current change	V_I = −27 V to −38 V		−55°C to 150°C			0.4				mA
			0°C to 125°C						0.4	
	I_O = 5 mA to 350 mA		−55°C to 150°C			0.4				
			0°C to 125°C						0.4	
Short circuit output current	V_I = −30 V		25°C		140			140		mA
Peak output current			25°C		650			650		A

[†]All characteristics are measured with a 2-µF capacitor across the input and a 1-µF capacitor across the output. All characteristics except noise voltage and ripple rejection ratio are measured using pulse techniques ($t_w \leqslant$ 10 ms, duty cycle $\leqslant$ 5%). Output voltage changes due to changes in internal temperature must be taken into account separately.

TEXAS INSTRUMENTS
INCORPORATED
POST OFFICE BOX 5012 • DALLAS, TEXAS 75222

SERIES uA79M00
NEGATIVE-VOLTAGE REGULATORS

THERMAL INFORMATION

KC AND KD PACKAGES FREE-AIR TEMPERATURE DISSIPATION DERATING CURVES

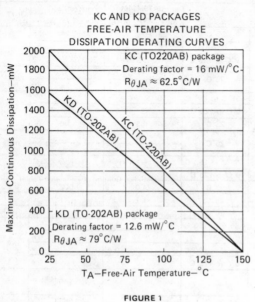

KC (TO220AB) package
Derating factor = 16 mW/°C
$R_{\theta JA} \approx 62.5°C/W$

KD (TO-202AB)

KC (TO-220AB)

KD (TO-202AB) package
Derating factor = 12.6 mW/°C
$R_{\theta JA} \approx 79°C/W$

Maximum Continuous Dissipation—mW

T_A—Free-Air Temperature—°C

FIGURE 1

KC AND KD PACKAGES CASE TEMPERATURE DISSIPATION DERATING CURVES

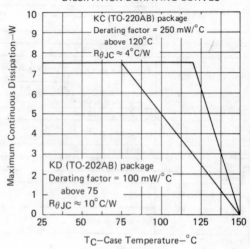

KC (TO-220AB) package
Derating factor = 250 mW/°C
above 120°C
$R_{\theta JC} \approx 4°C/W$

KD (TO-202AB) package
Derating factor = 100 mW/°C
above 75
$R_{\theta JC} \approx 10°C/W$

Maximum Continuous Dissipation—W

T_C—Case Temperature—°C

FIGURE 2

LA PACKAGE FREE-AIR TEMPERATURE DISSIPATION DERATING CURVE

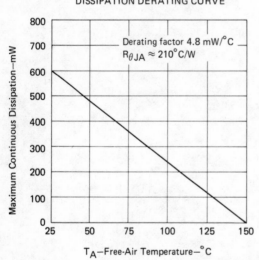

Derating factor 4.8 mW/°C
$R_{\theta JA} \approx 210°C/W$

Maximum Continuous Dissipation—mW

T_A—Free-Air Temperature—°C

FIGURE 3

LA PACKAGE CASE TEMPERATURE DISSIPATION DERATING CURVE

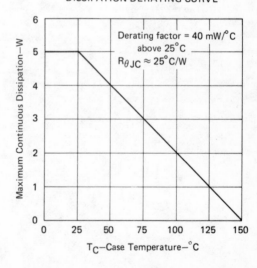

Derating factor = 40 mW/°C
above 25°C
$R_{\theta JC} \approx 25°C/W$

Maximum Continuous Dissipation—W

T_C—Case Temperature—°C

FIGURE 4

TEXAS INSTRUMENTS
INCORPORATED
POST OFFICE BOX 5012 • DALLAS, TEXAS 75222

ORDERING INSTRUCTIONS

Electrical characteristics presented in this data book, unless otherwise noted, apply for the circuit type(s) listed in the page heading regardless of package. The availability of a circuit function in a particular package is denoted by an alphabetical reference above the pin-connection diagram(s). These alphabetical references refer to mechanical outline drawing shown in this section.

Factory orders for cirucits described in this data book should include a five-part type number as explained in the following example.

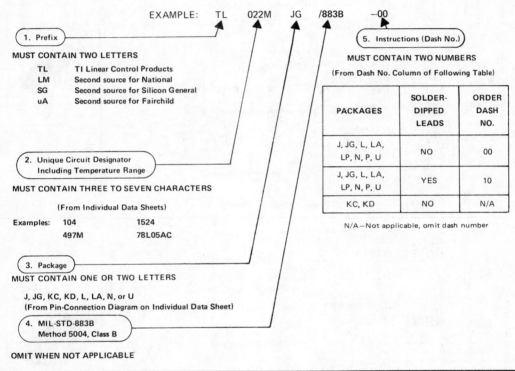

EXAMPLE: TL 022M JG /883B –00

1. Prefix

MUST CONTAIN TWO LETTERS

TL	TI Linear Control Products
LM	Second source for National
SG	Second source for Silicon General
uA	Second source for Fairchild

2. Unique Circuit Designator Including Temperature Range

MUST CONTAIN THREE TO SEVEN CHARACTERS

(From Individual Data Sheets)

Examples: 104   1524
          497M   78L05AC

3. Package

MUST CONTAIN ONE OR TWO LETTERS

J, JG, KC, KD, L, LA, N, or U
(From Pin-Connection Diagram on Individual Data Sheet)

4. MIL-STD-883B Method 5004, Class B

OMIT WHEN NOT APPLICABLE

5. Instructions (Dash No.)

MUST CONTAIN TWO NUMBERS

(From Dash No. Column of Following Table)

PACKAGES	SOLDER-DIPPED LEADS	ORDER DASH NO.
J, JG, L, LA, LP, N, P, U	NO	00
J, JG, L, LA, LP, N, P, U	YES	10
KC, KD	NO	N/A

N/A—Not applicable, omit dash number

Circuits are shipped in one of the carriers shown below. Unless a specific method of shipment is specified by the customer (with possible additional costs), circuits will be shipped in the most practical carrier.

Flat (U)	Dual-In-Line (J, JG, N, P)	Plug-In (L, LA, LP)
—Barnes Carrier	—Slide Magazines	—Barnes Carrier
—Milton Ross Carrier	—A-Channel Plastic Tubing	—Sectioned Cardboard Box
	—Barnes Carrier	—Individual Cardboard Box
	—Sectioned Cardboard Box	
	—Individual Plastic Box	

TEXAS INSTRUMENTS
INCORPORATED

POST OFFICE BOX 5012 • DALLAS, TEXAS 75222

VOLTAGE REGULATOR CIRCUITS
ORDERING INSTRUCTIONS AND MECHANICAL DATA

J ceramic dual-in-line packages

These hermetically sealed dual-in-line packages consist of a ceramic base, ceramic cap, and a 14- or 16-lead frame. Hermetic sealing is accomplished with glass. The packages are intended for insertion in mounting-hole rows on 0.300 (7,62) centers (see Note a). Once the leads are compressed and inserted, sufficient tension is provided to secure the package in the board during soldering. Tin-plated ("bright-dipped") leads (−00) require no additional cleaning or processing when used in soldered assembly.

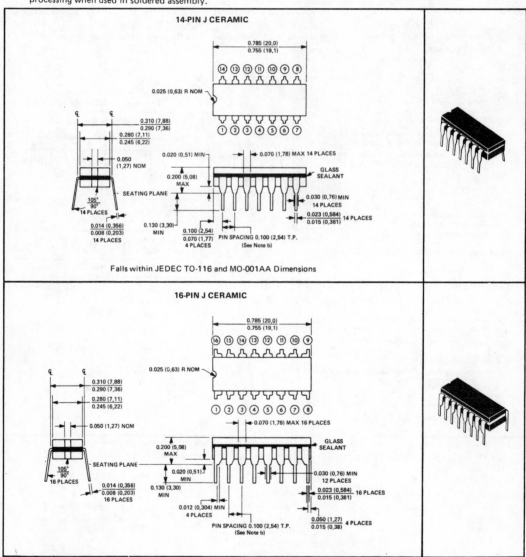

14-PIN J CERAMIC

Falls within JEDEC TO-116 and MO-001AA Dimensions

16-PIN J CERAMIC

NOTES: a. All dimensions are in inches and parenthetically in millimeters. Inch dimensions govern.

b. Each pin centerline is located within 0.010 (0,26) of its true longitudinal position.

JG ceramic dual-in-line package

This hermetically sealed dual-in-line package consists of a ceramic base, ceramic cap, and 8-lead frame. The package is intended for insertion in mounting-hole rows on 0.300 (7,62) centers (see Note a). Once the leads are compressed and inserted, sufficient tension is provided to secure the package in the board during soldering. Tin-plated ("bright-dipped") leads require no additional cleaning or processing when used in soldered assembly.

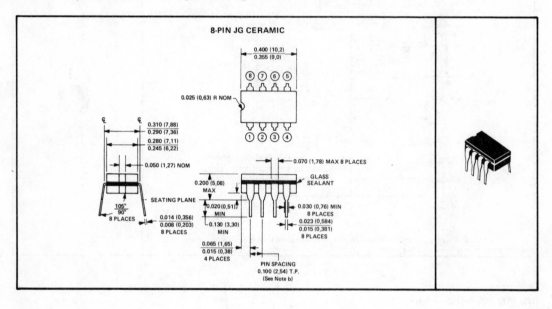

8-PIN JG CERAMIC

NOTES: a. All dimensions are in inches and parenthetically in millimeters. Inch dimensions govern.
b. Each pin centerline is located within 0.010 (0,26) of its true longitudinal position.

VOLTAGE REGULATOR CIRCUITS
ORDERING INSTRUCTIONS AND MECHANICAL DATA

KC (TO-220AB) package

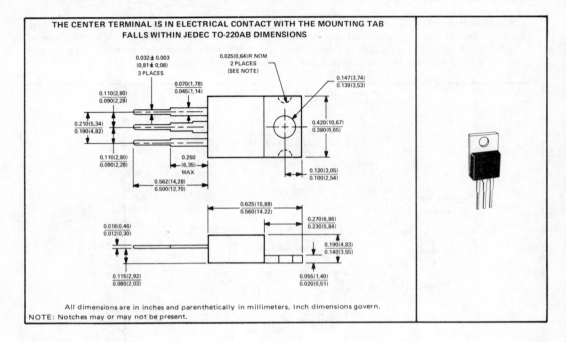

THE CENTER TERMINAL IS IN ELECTRICAL CONTACT WITH THE MOUNTING TAB
FALLS WITHIN JEDEC TO-220AB DIMENSIONS

All dimensions are in inches and parenthetically in millimeters. Inch dimensions govern.
NOTE: Notches may or may not be present.

KD (TO-202AB) package

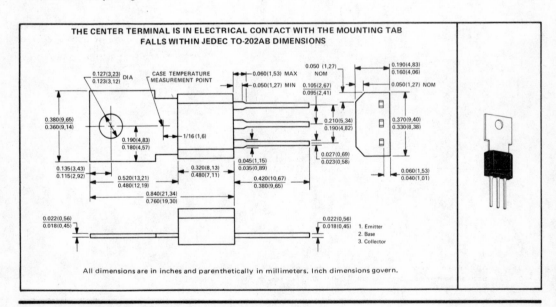

THE CENTER TERMINAL IS IN ELECTRICAL CONTACT WITH THE MOUNTING TAB
FALLS WITHIN JEDEC TO-202AB DIMENSIONS

1. Emitter
2. Base
3. Collector

All dimensions are in inches and parenthetically in millimeters. Inch dimensions govern.

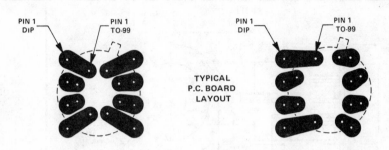

TYPICAL
P.C. BOARD
LAYOUT

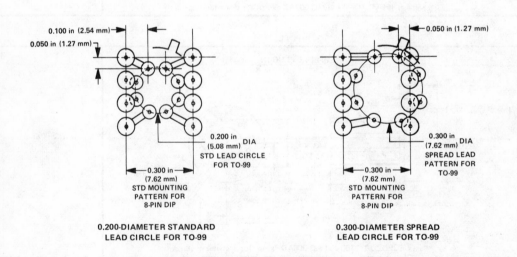

0.200-DIAMETER STANDARD
LEAD CIRCLE FOR TO-99

0.300-DIAMETER SPREAD
LEAD CIRCLE FOR TO-99

PRINTED CIRCUIT BOARD PATTERN THAT ALLOWS
INTERCHANGEABILITY OF 8-PIN DUAL-IN-LINE
PACKAGE WITH TO-99 PLUG-IN PACKAGE

VOLTAGE REGULATOR CIRCUITS
ORDERING INSTRUCTIONS AND MECHANICAL DATA

L plug-in package

These hermetically sealed plug-in packages each consist of a welded metal base and cap with individual leads secured by an insulating glass sealant. The gold-plated leads (–00) require no additional cleaning or processing when used in soldered assembly.

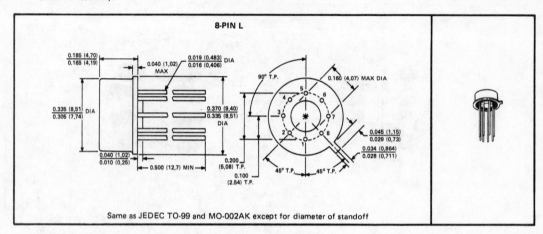

8-PIN L

Same as JEDEC TO-99 and MO-002AK except for diameter of standoff

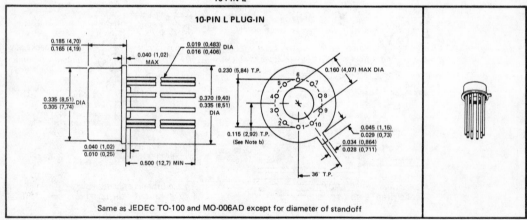

10-PIN L

10-PIN L PLUG-IN

Same as JEDEC TO-100 and MO-006AD except for diameter of standoff

NOTES: a. All linear dimensions are in inches and parenthetically in millimeters. Inch dimensions govern.
         b. Each lead is located within 0.007 (0.18) of its true position at maximum material condition.

TEXAS INSTRUMENTS
INCORPORATED
POST OFFICE BOX 5012 • DALLAS, TEXAS 75222

LA Plug-in package

These hermetically sealed plug-in packages each consist of a welded metal base and cap with individual leads secured by an insulating glass sealant. The gold-plated leads (−00) require no additional cleaning or processing when used in soldered assembly.

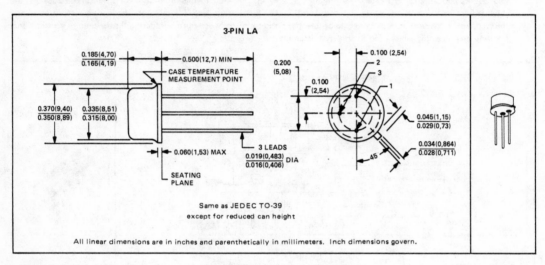

3-PIN LA

Same as JEDEC TO-39
except for reduced can height

All linear dimensions are in inches and parenthetically in millimeters. Inch dimensions govern.

LP *Silect*[†] plastic package

The silect package is an encapsulation in a plastic compound specifically designed for this purpose. The package will withstand soldering temperatures without deformation. The package exhibits stable characteristics under high-humidity conditions and is capable of meeting MIL-STD-202C, Method 106B.

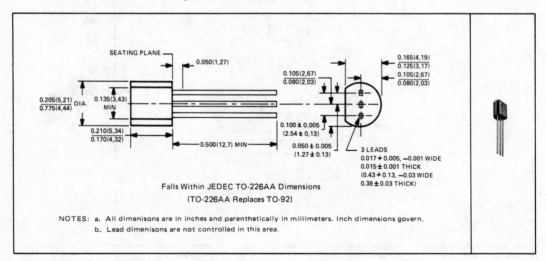

Falls Within JEDEC TO-226AA Dimensions
(TO-226AA Replaces TO-92)

NOTES: a. All dimenisons are in inches and parenthetically in millimeters. Inch dimensions govern.
   b. Lead dimenisons are not controlled in this area.

[†]Trademark Registered U.S. Patent Office.

TEXAS INSTRUMENTS
INCORPORATED
POST OFFICE BOX 5012 • DALLAS, TEXAS 75222

VOLTAGE REGULATOR CIRCUITS
ORDERING INSTRUCTIONS AND MECHANICAL DATA

N plastic dual-in-line packages

These dual-in-line packages consist of a circuit mounted on a 14- or 16-lead frame and encapsulated within an electrically nonconductive plastic compound. The compound will withstand soldering temperature with no deformation and circuit performance characteristics remain stable when operated in high-humidity conditions. The packages are intended for insertion in mounting-hole rows on 0.300 (7,62) centers (see Note a). Once the leads are compressed and inserted, sufficient tension is provided to secure the package in the board during soldering. Leads require no additional cleaning or processing when used in soldered assembly.

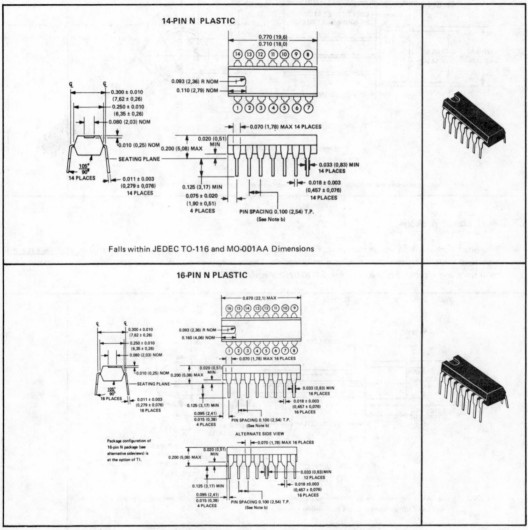

Falls within JEDEC TO-116 and MO-001AA Dimensions

NOTES: a. All dimensions are in inches and parenthetically in millimeters. Inch dimensions govern.

b. Each pin centerline is located within 0.010 (0,26) of its true longitudinal position.

TEXAS INSTRUMENTS
INCORPORATED
POST OFFICE BOX 5012 • DALLAS, TEXAS 75222

9

P dual-in-line plastic package

This dual-in-line package consists of a circuit mounted on an 8-lead frame and encapsulated in an electrically, nonconductive plastic compound. The compound will withstand soldering temperature with no deformation and circuit performance characteristics remain stable when operated under high-humidity conditions. This package is intended for insertion in mounting hole rows on 0.300 (7,62) centers (see Note a). Once the leads are compressed and inserted, sufficient tension is provided to secure the package in the board during soldering. Silver-plated leads require no additional cleaning or processing when used in soldered assembly.

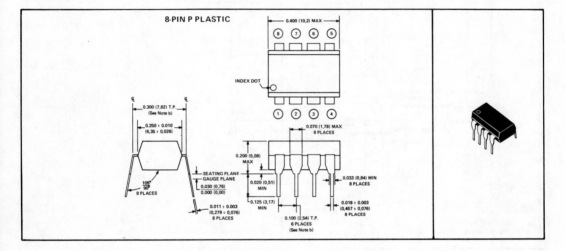

NOTES: a. All dimensions are in inches and parenthetically in millimeters. Inch dimensions govern.

          b. Each pin centerline is within 0.005 (0,127) radius of true position at the gauge plane with maximum material condition and unit installed.

TEXAS INSTRUMENTS
INCORPORATED

POST OFFICE BOX 5012 • DALLAS, TEXAS 75222

VOLTAGE REGULATOR CIRCUITS
ORDERING INSTRUCTIONS AND MECHANICAL DATA

U ceramic flat packages

These flat packages consist of a ceramic base, ceramic cap, and 10- or 14-lead frame. Circuit bars are alloy-mounted. Hermetic sealing is accomplished with glass. Tin-plated leads require no additional cleaning or processing when used in soldered assembly.

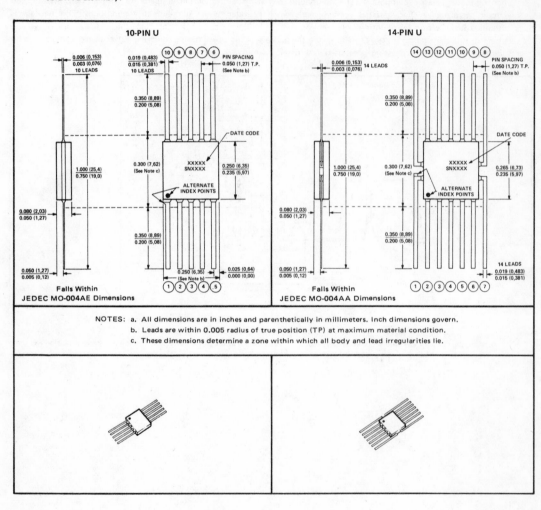

NOTES: a. All dimensions are in inches and parenthetically in millimeters. Inch dimensions govern.
b. Leads are within 0.005 radius of true position (TP) at maximum material condition.
c. These dimensions determine a zone within which all body and lead irregularities lie.

TEXAS INSTRUMENTS
INCORPORATED
POST OFFICE BOX 5012 • DALLAS, TEXAS 75222